A Deadly Portrayal

LM Milford

ISBN: 978-1-913778-14-9

Cover art by Jessica Bell

For Helen, Paul and Ozzy the dog
Just for being there for me
xxx

Prologue

Natasha Kent stared down at the screen of her smartphone. Swallowing hard, she fought the urge to throw up in the quadrangle. This was nothing like the performance anxiety and pre-show nerves she'd dealt with for years. She watched the video on the screen of her phone, hand shaking, whether from fear or anger she wasn't sure. He was the only one who'd had the recording, and she'd watched him delete it. But now someone else had a copy. Why had he shared it with them? She looked again at the email attached to the video.

If you don't go to the police and admit what you've done, I will release this video on social media. You know what that will do to your reputation. If he'd told the truth, he had a chance to save you but didn't take it. So now it's your turn. Maybe you have more of a conscience, but I doubt it. You have a week to comply. If you don't, then I'll know what to do.

Natasha read the email three times, then locked the screen of her phone. She barely noticed the students milling around in all directions, shouting to each other as they moved in and out of the high-ceilinged, glass-fronted atrium of Allensbury Dance and Drama School. Legs trembling, she sat on a stone bench near the front doors.

She didn't understand. What had she done? How could she go to the police when she didn't know what for?

Natasha got to her feet, and scooped up her sports bag. He was going to explain why someone else had that video. She would make him.

Checking her phone again, she realised there were only ten minutes to get changed and into the auditorium for rehearsal. She'd speak to him afterwards. Squaring her shoulders, Natasha marched towards the building. He was going to do what she wanted. It was only two weeks to the end-of-year showcase, and she didn't need this now. He wasn't going to ruin her life. She would make sure of that.

Chapter 1

Travers McGovern sat in the darkened theatre, his eyes glued to the stage. It was brightly lit, but with the house lights down, he knew the dancers weren't aware they had an audience. The lycra-clad men and women stood in a group, with one man issuing instructions.

'Natasha,' Dominic said, 'I want you over there.' He pointed to centre stage. There was a general titter among the group. Even the man laughed. 'Not like that,' he said mock-sternly, rolling his eyes at them.

'At least not anymore, eh, Dominic?' asked a short, blonde woman, whose hair was scraped back so tightly into a bun that Travers thought it made her look like she'd had a bad face lift. She stepped over to Dominic and ran a hand down his arm. He shook her away and turned towards centre stage.

Natasha showed no sign of having heard the woman's comment and walked flat-footed in ballet pointe shoes to her place in the middle of the stage. She ran a hand over her hair to ensure that no strands had escaped from the tight bun on the back of her head and adjusted the cropped, sleeveless, blue cardigan she was wearing over a grey-and-white leotard and leggings. Her brown skin glowed under the bright stage lights.

The other dancers stood or sat watching from the side of the stage.

The music began, easily recognisable as Swan Lake, and Natasha rose en pointe. Her arms fluttered like wings as she tiptoed across the stage, but when she came to perform a series of pirouettes, she

3

over-rotated, slipped and thudded heavily to the floor, landing on her side. Travers sat forward in his seat. Was she hurt? A fall could be serious.

There were snorts of laughter from some of the other dancers as Natasha sat rubbing her elbow and checking her skin for any scrapes.

'God, Natasha, that was elegant,' called a male dancer, seated on the floor, grinning.

'You'd better not do that during our group piece at the showcase,' said the blonde woman. 'You know there'll be agents there. It won't look good if you can't even stay on your feet.'

'Leave Nat alone,' said Dominic, striding forward and holding out a hand to help her up. She took it and he pulled her to her feet. She swayed for a moment and Travers growled quietly in his throat as the man held her slender waist to steady her. He had no right to touch her. She rubbed her forehead and then pushed his hands away. Travers sat back in his seat.

'I'm fine,' she snapped. A look of annoyance crossed the young man's face, but he said nothing. 'I'll just go again from the top, if that's OK?'

'Sorry, Nat.' Dominic glanced down at his watch. 'We've run out of time for today.'

'There's no time to run through my solo?' the blonde dancer demanded, hands on hips.

Dominic shook his head. 'No, someone else has the theatre booked out for the rest of the day, so we can't stay here.'

The female dancer took a couple of steps towards him. 'We all have to practise,' she said, jutting out her chin. 'Not just her.' She jabbed a finger towards Natasha, who was still rubbing her elbow. 'If your girlfriend wasn't dancing like Nellie the Elephant, we'd all get a chance.' She turned to Natasha, who had sat down on the stage and was unwrapping the ribbons that wound around her ankles to take off her shoes. 'I swear to God, Natasha, if you balls up my chance by taking up all the rehearsal time, I'll bloody kill you.'

'Look,' Natasha said with mock concern, 'Tara, I don't think there's enough time in the week for the practice you need, and there's nothing I can do about that.' She got to her feet and brushed the stage dirt from her leggings. Then, shoving her shoes into her bag, she turned back to Tara, who glared, hands on hips, clearly unable to think of a reply to the dig. Natasha grinned smugly, picked up her bag, and strolled away.

The dancers packed up their belongings and headed out through the wings to the backstage area. Travers waited until they had all gone before he got to his feet. He needed to speak to Natasha alone. She needed to know this wasn't his fault. He got up and walked quietly out through the back door of the auditorium.

In the shadows, a figure lurked, smiling and watching Travers as he left. They were both rattled, very rattled. But every action has a consequence, and they'd soon pay for what they'd done.

Chapter 2

Travers stamped back into his office and slammed the door. It had been row after row all day today, and he was sick of it. Everyone was against him. Teaching didn't really suit him; he'd known that all along. Too much temptation. But needs must when the acting roles dried up. He looked at the signed photo on the wall of the cast of *Our Friends*. He'd been the star of that show for so many years. Then they'd written him out, told him to leave quietly without a fuss to keep the story out of the media. Somehow, they'd bought off the little bitch and made it all go away. It didn't feel like six years had gone by. He sighed. There just weren't parts out there that were meaty enough for him, really. His moron of an agent had suggested taking on a side hustle while the risk of a scandal died down. These things always did, he was assured, but then the man had dumped him.

He'd tried to get his foot in the door of local theatre – thinking his name, his career, his history would count for something – but it hadn't. It was such a clique, such a closed scene, that he felt his skills were being wasted.

Maybe it was a sign that it was time to move on, move away from everything. He'd already put some plans in place, but he needed money for that. He could have one last try at Sarah, but he wasn't confident it would bring him what he wanted.

He scrubbed a hand over his face. A vodka, that's what he needed. Crossing the room to his wooden desk, he pulled out the bottom drawer. It squeaked slightly.

'Ah, my old friend,' he said, pulling out a bottle and a glass tumbler. There was just enough time for a cheeky one before he headed home to face the music there. He sighed, walked back across the room to the sofa – his casting couch, he liked to call it – and flopped down. He poured a generous two fingers of the spirit – OK, maybe closer to three – and slumped against the cushions, taking a swig. The vodka felt good as it hit the back of his throat and he felt his muscles relax. He placed the bottle on the floor, close at hand, and swigged back the rest of the measure. Then he felt something, a twinge in the back of his throat, an all too familiar and frightening twinge.

He tried to cough, but it didn't work. The tightening feeling was getting worse. In fact, he could feel his throat swelling. He sat forward and pulled at the neck of his shirt, trying to loosen his collar, but his fingers scrabbled uselessly at the button. He knew what this meant and reached for his expensive brown leather satchel. But when he pulled open the flap, a quick look inside showed nothing but a notebook, a Thermos mug and a couple of heavily chewed biros. Where was it? He reached inside and ran his hands around every square inch of the interior of the bag. Nothing. He gasped, upending the bag, unable to believe what was happening. He looked around the room and his eye rested on his desk. Yes, there was one in his drawer.

Staggering across the room, he was struggling to get any oxygen. He leaned heavily on the surface of the desk, gasping as he forced his arm to pull open the drawer. But inside, all he saw was stationery. His tongue had swollen to fill his mouth; his windpipe had closed entirely. A hand scrabbled at his throat, a reflex action as he knew it would do nothing. He fell to the floor with a heavy thump. Within seconds, his eyes were wide and sightless.

A face looked through the glass plate in the wooden office door and smiled. Then it disappeared from view.

Chapter 3

When Emma Fletcher arrived at the *Allensbury Post*'s office on Tuesday morning, she already had a tension headache building behind her eyes. As the newspaper's crime reporter, she'd been called out the previous evening by the fire brigade to an incident where a gas leak had caused an explosion at a house in the north of the town. The occupant had escaped with only minor injuries after three neighbours had rushed to the rescue and dragged him out of the building. Just moments later, a wall of the house had crashed down, covering nearby properties with dust and damaging the pub next door. The landlord and his wife were uninjured but shocked, having been in bed upstairs asleep when the incident occurred. She'd been at the scene for nearly two hours and had spent an hour writing up her story for that morning's edition.

Getting to bed after midnight, she'd slept badly, partly the adrenaline of the call-out and partly because she'd received a worrying text from her boyfriend Dan. She'd cancelled a cosy evening in to attend the job, and it wasn't the first time it had happened in the last fortnight. She thought that, as a news reporter on the same paper, Dan understood it went with the territory. But his message said *We need to talk*, and Emma knew that the resulting conversation never ended well.

The man himself was already at his desk next to hers when she thumped her bag into her chair and began taking off her coat. He greeted her, barely taking his eyes away from his screen as his fingers tapped rapidly on the keyboard. His short brown hair was sticking up all over the place due to his habit of ruffling it when he was concentrating, and she wanted to smooth it.

'I got you that,' Dan said, nodding towards the takeaway coffee on her desk. 'It might be a bit cold by now.'

She smiled and took a grateful sip. 'Just right. What did you want to talk about?' she asked, putting her bag onto the floor and sitting down.

Dan waved a hand. 'Not now, I'm on deadline. Later.'

Emma had to be content with that. She knew the score when the early-morning edition was on deadline: all hands on deck to make sure there were no empty spaces on the pages.

Her eyes were struggling to focus on her computer screen until the caffeine began to ease the headache. She jumped when the phone on her desk rang. Out of the corner of her eye, she could see Dan smirking, and glared at him as she picked up the receiver.

When the voice spoke in her ear, she sat up straight and grabbed a notebook and pen. She saw Dan out of the corner of her eye stand up and point to the news editor, indicating that the story she was waiting for was flying electronically towards her. Then he stretched his arms above his head, yawned widely and looked over her shoulder, trying to read her notes.

'And where's that?' Emma asked the caller, pointing to the words she'd written. Suspicious death. Then she froze. 'It's where?' she repeated. 'Allensbury Dance and Drama School? And he's been there overnight?' When the caller finished speaking, Emma hung up the phone and jumped to her feet, throwing the notebook and pen into her handbag. Dan took a step back in surprise at the sudden movement.

'Gotta go,' she said, turning away to head back to the car park.

'Take care,' Dan called.

She turned to look back at him. His face showed no indication of what he wanted to talk about. That would have to wait. Duty called.

Chapter 4

Detective Inspector Jude Burton stood several feet inside the door of Travers McGovern's domain, surveying it with her hands on her hips.

Photographs of McGovern with various celebrities covered three walls, along with a signed poster of the cast of a TV soap opera, and framed reviews of plays he'd starred in. The fourth wall had a large bookcase, which didn't feature many books.

'He's obviously very proud of his work,' she remarked, gesturing to the walls.

Detective Sergeant Mark Shepherd pointed to a three-dimensional rectangular glass trophy on a bookcase. 'If I was "Sexiest Man in a Soap Opera", I'd be showing it off as well.'

Burton, immaculately dressed from her blonde ponytail down to her four-inch heels, covered in crime scene booties, stood on the only bit of floor the CSI team would allow. Shepherd lounged in the doorway, not even allowed into the room by the forensic team. His rugby player's physique and size-eleven feet took up a lot of floor space. She looked up from the body to the tall, lanky uniformed officer who was sharing the doorway.

'He was obviously attractive, if you go in for floppy blond hair in a man. Take me through it again,' she said.

The man rustled the pages of his notebook and began. 'Travers McGovern, forty-two. The cleaner came round at about six thirty this morning. She was vacuuming in the corridor when she noticed the door was ajar. She opened it and there he was, lying on the floor.'

'Did she touch anything?'

The officer nodded. 'She went to him and checked for a pulse, thinking he's just fainted or something. He was already cold, so she ran to her boss and they called us.'

'Does she know him?'

'Nah, she only works mornings, and he's not one for early starts, so I've been told.'

Shepherd smiled. 'When was he last seen?'

The officer looked at his notebook again. 'He was last seen coming up the stairs towards his office at about five thirty yesterday evening.'

Burton frowned and then turned to the pathologist, Doctor Eleanor Brody. 'Got anything for me?' she asked.

Brody turned and glared at her. 'I've barely had a chance to start,' she snapped.

Burton raised her hands in surrender.

Brody leaned back towards the body, sniffing at his face.

'That's attractive,' Shepherd commented, wrinkling his nose.

Ignoring him, Brody sat back on her heels. 'There's a scent I can't place,' she said, looking around as if the answer might suddenly present itself. She looked up at Burton. 'On first look, I'd say he was asphyxiated.'

'Smothered?' Burton asked, looking around the room. 'Rather than strangled?'

Brody nodded as her eyes followed Burton's. 'There are some scratches on his neck as if someone pulled a chain from around it, but his skin is flushed as if he was deprived of oxygen.'

'There aren't any loose cushions around or anything like that,' Shepherd remarked, gesturing around the room.

'The killer took it away?' Burton suggested.

Brody exhaled heavily and shook her head. 'No idea. I should be able to tell you more after the post-mortem.'

Burton pointed to a bottle of spirits and glass, which were being carefully bagged and labelled by two CSIs. 'He was drinking?' she asked.

'Vodka,' said Shepherd, reading the label. He looked down at Travers. 'And it's a habit, judging by the dry skin on his face. Alcoholics gets dry skin from dehydration,' he explained. Then he frowned. 'They usually choose vodka because it doesn't smell as much as other spirits,' he remarked. Burton and Brody both looked at him quizzically.

He gestured towards Brody. 'You said you could smell something? Is it vodka?'

Brody looked up at him, her brow furrowing so much that Burton was concerned that it may stay that way permanently. 'That's a good point. There is definitely something. I can't put my finger on what it is, but Mark's right, there shouldn't be a smell at all.'

'And only one glass,' Shepherd said. 'He was drinking alone.'

'Why not go home if you wanted a drink?' Burton asked.

'There were rehearsals for the end-of-year showcase going on 'til after seven o'clock last night,' Shepherd said, looking over the uniformed officer's shoulder at his scribbled notes. 'Maybe he was supposed to be going to one of those and stopped off for a snifter on the way?' He looked at the man, but the officer shook his head.

'As far as I can make out, he wasn't down to attend any of the rehearsals.'

'So why was he still here?' Burton asked, looking around the room again. 'Why not go home for his vodka?'

'Waiting for someone?' the officer suggested.

'Or did he come in here and someone was waiting for him?' Shepherd asked.

'And they poured him a drink before they smothered him? But with what?' Burton asked, gesturing around the room.

A fully suited CSI appeared beside her, holding out an evidence bag containing a fluffy scarf. Burton took it and held it up to the light.

'A woman's scarf,' she said. 'Lovely colour. Can you open it for me?' The CSI looked like he was going to argue, but Brody gave him the nod. He slit open the bag, carefully noting on the plastic that he had done so, and then held it out. Burton took it and sniffed.

'Nice perfume,' she said, holding out the bag to Shepherd. He sniffed and nodded. Burton held it out to Brody. 'Is that what you can smell on him?'

The pathologist shook her head. 'No, it's not that. I don't know what it is.'

Burton handed back the bag, and the CSI carefully resealed and annotated it. 'So what's he doing with a woman's scarf in his office?'

Shepherd raised his eyebrows. 'There are a lot of female students. Maybe one of them left it here by accident after a tutorial or something.'

Burton frowned. 'But it's July; why would they be wearing a scarf?'

'Could be part of a costume?' Shepherd suggested.

Burton nodded and puffed out her cheeks. 'So we can't rule out a female assailant,' she said.

Shepherd scribbled in his notebook.

Burton frowned again and then turned to Shepherd. 'Did anyone report him missing?' she asked.

Shepherd shook his head.

'Is there no one at home?' Burton asked.

'There's a wife. Uniforms are with her now.'

Burton looked surprised. 'She didn't report him missing?'

'No, but maybe she thought he was going to be away for the night.'

'Good point. We'll go there once we've finished here.' She stopped and looked around. 'Where's the principal gone?'

Shepherd pointed over his shoulder. 'She wanted to speak to the students about what's happened, and then she said she'd come back.'

Burton nodded. 'Let's save her the trouble and find her.' She stepped carefully into the doorway and then turned, opening her mouth to speak.

'Post-mortem as soon as I can,' Brody said, without looking up from the notes she was making on a clipboard. 'I'll call you.'

Burton nodded as she took off her crime scene suit and then turned to follow Shepherd along the corridor.

Chapter 5

They found the college principal, Sally-Anne Faber, standing on the bottom step of the spiral staircase leading down into the atrium, watching as students milled around and headed for the exit. She turned and climbed the stairs to meet them.

'Thank you for giving me time to explain things to the students,' she said with a weak smile. 'Those who were here late yesterday are speaking to your officers.' She gestured to a queue of students waiting patiently to speak to one of the four uniformed constables lined up in the corridor. 'The rest of them, as you can see, I've sent home. No sense in keeping them here when they are so upset. Plus, it keeps them out from under your feet,' she said.

Burton nodded. 'They're very obedient,' she said.

Sally-Anne smiled. 'Discipline is something talented dancers and actors excel at,' she said. She glanced towards the front doors of the college. 'They know when to follow instructions.'

Shepherd followed her gaze. 'A sudden death can be a lot to take in,' he said, 'particularly when it's someone you see around every day.'

Sally-Anne nodded.

'Can we buy you a coffee?' Burton asked, gesturing to the café on the ground floor.

Sally-Anne shook her head. 'Let's go to my office. We can speak privately there.' She turned and led the way along a nearby corridor. The walls were painted a bland white, but the red-and-green patterned carpet livened it up a bit. Or resulted in a severe headache. Burton and Shepherd followed her. She led them down a series of corridors and then unlocked a wooden door with her name on it.

'Sorry we've had to take a circuitous route,' she said. 'The other staircase is quicker, but it's – well – you can see.' She gestured towards the blue-and-white police tape crossing the corridor leading to Travers McGovern's office.

The office was extremely tidy. There were no papers out on the wooden knee-hole desk, which sat at one end of the room. Framed posters of school showcases, pantomimes and plays were displayed proudly on the walls. A tall bookcase held some A4 folders and stacks of what looked like glossy programmes from theatre performances. On a small table to the left of the desk sat a plant, which Burton recognised.

Seeing her looking, Sally-Anne stroked a leaf as she passed.

'A peace lily,' she said, smiling at it. 'The school is usually such a whirlwind of activity and, while I enjoy it, sometimes it's nice to have some tranquillity.'

Burton smiled. 'Maybe I need one of those for my office,' she said.

Sally-Anne directed them to chairs at the round table in the corner of her office and sat down opposite them. 'I can't believe Travers is dead,' she said, shaking her head. 'Do you have any idea how it happened?'

'Not yet,' Burton said. 'Our pathologist will carry out a post-mortem later. All we can say for certain is that he was drinking vodka in his office and was last seen at about half past five yesterday evening.'

Sally-Anne sighed. 'I'd warned him about the drinking.'

Burton raised her eyebrows. 'You knew about it? Was it a regular thing?'

Sally-Anne paused and glanced towards the door to check it was fully closed. Then she nodded. 'I caught him a few times smelling of whiskey and I warned him to stop it. Something like that could put my students at risk. He stopped smelling of drink and I thought he'd taken the warning seriously.'

'But he'd just turned to another type of drink,' Shepherd said, looking up from his notebook.

15

Sally-Anne nodded. 'Clearly,' she said.

'What did you think of Travers McGovern?' Burton asked. 'Did you like him?'

Sally-Anne sighed. 'He is – was – just good enough as an actor for us to hire him. He trained here and when he left, he thought he was destined for great things.'

Shepherd smiled. 'You didn't agree with his assessment?' he asked.

Sally-Anne shrugged. 'He was before my time, but he wasn't as good as he thought he was from what I've heard. I think he expected the roles and agent representation to just come rolling in,' she said. 'In reality, it's much harder than that.'

Burton frowned. 'I thought he was a success,' she said.

Sally-Anne nodded. 'Eventually, after playing a lot of small parts, which he usually glosses over, he got the part in the soap opera, *Our Friends*, and he stayed for about five years in total, if memory serves. He won an award for "Sexiest Man in a Soap".' She smiled. 'He was a good-looking man, better looking than he was an actor, but it completely went to his head.'

Shepherd smiled. 'Thought a lot of himself, did he?'

Sally-Anne nodded. 'When they wrote him out of the soap opera, I think that hit him hard. He never really got another television part of the same level. He tried the theatre because he thought that was just what out-of-work actors do to fill in time between television roles, but then found there's actually a lot more to it. It's a completely different kettle of fish to working with cameras and having to do entire scenes without being able to do more than one take.'

'Why did he leave the soap opera?' Burton asked.

'It's a bit of a mystery,' Sally-Anne said. 'He never really went into it. Just said it was time for a change.' She rolled her eyes.

'And that's code for...?' Burton asked.

'His departure from the show was very sudden, so I suspected he'd fallen out with someone and they'd given him the chop. Like I said, he thought he was more important than he actually was.'

'Why did you hire him if you didn't really rate him?' Burton asked.

Sally-Anne gave a small shrug. 'In all honesty, I felt sorry for him, how his career had stagnated. He was really desperate for work. Plus, he was a bit of a draw for the students.'

Shepherd raised his eyebrows. 'He impressed them?'

'Some of them,' she said. 'There was usually a small number who would hang on his every word, those who wanted to do the quick leap.' She smiled. 'Those who believed that was what he'd actually done.'

'That wasn't all of them?' Burton asked.

Sally-Anne shook her head. 'Most of the kids who come here have been around dancing classes and theatre companies for most of their lives. They know how hard it is to make it "for real", as someone once put it to me.'

'For real?' Shepherd repeated.

Sally-Anne smiled. 'We get all types of students here, Detective,' she said. 'Some want to be "serious actors" and go on stage with the Royal Shakespeare Company. Others want the quick stardom that they think comes with getting into a long-running soap.' She smiled affectionately. 'They think that's a steady job. They don't know how quickly a director or writer changes their mind about the storyline they're working on. If you don't fit that story, then you're out.'

Burton frowned. 'They're idealistic?' she asked.

Sally-Anne nodded. 'Some are, some aren't.'

Shepherd looked up. 'Were you afraid that Travers McGovern would give them false hope?'

Sally-Anne pursed her lips. 'I hoped they'd hear his story about the trials and tribulations of getting into a soap opera, but he gave them a very sanitised version. It almost sounded as if he'd gone straight from college to *Our Friends*, which was far from the truth. It must have taken about ten years for him to get that gig.' Then she smiled. 'But we have umpteen other teachers and visiting experts who could tell them otherwise.'

Burton smiled. 'They make the point that it's not a secure job, then?'

Sally-Anne shrugged. 'No acting or dancing job ever is. It's harder for dancers because all it takes is one injury and there's your career gone. I've seen it happen to talented dancers. It's very sad.' She clasped her hands on top of the table. 'Anyway,' she continued, 'is there anything else you want to know about Travers?'

'Was he particularly close to anyone? Staff or students?' Burton asked.

Sally-Anne's face clouded. 'Not really among the staff,' she said. 'He was a bit too full of himself for their liking.'

Shepherd paused in his scribbling. 'What about students?' he asked.

Sally-Anne paused for a moment. 'No one that I'd noticed,' she said, looking down at her clasped hands.

'Can you think of anyone who might have wanted to hurt Mr McGovern?' Shepherd asked, looking up from his notebook.

Sally-Anne's eyes widened. 'You think someone killed him?'

Burton took a deep breath. 'It's early in the investigation, but it's something we need to consider. Can you think of anyone who didn't get on with him? Any issues?'

Sally-Anne puffed out her cheeks. 'He might not have been the most popular person, but I can't imagine anyone wanting him dead,' she said.

Shepherd stopped scribbling and looked at Burton. She got to her feet.

'I think that's all we need for now. We will also need to speak to the staff as well.'

Sally-Anne stood up, nodding. 'I've given the same instructions to them as I've given to the students. Those who were here late are waiting in the staff room and we can arrange a time for you to speak to the others later.'

Burton and Shepherd thanked her and left the office.

'OK, let's get the uniforms to interview the staff, as well as students,' Burton said. 'We need to get over and speak to the wife. See if she can think of anyone who would want to hurt her husband.'

Chapter 6

Students were streaming out of the doors of the school as Emma arrived. As she headed towards the entrance, she felt like a salmon desperately trying to swim upstream. She was almost knocked off her feet by a burly male student carrying a sports bag. He gripped her arm to prevent her falling, apologising, leaving Emma just enough time to detain him and ask if he knew what was happening.

'One of the drama teachers is dead,' he told her, shifting his bag to his other shoulder and bashing into a woman passing on his other side. 'Someone found him on the floor in his office.'

'Who is it?' Emma asked.

'Travers McGovern,' came the answer. 'The cleaner found him. She's in a right state apparently and—' But before he could say anymore, there was a surge in the crowd and he was buffeted away.

Emma scribbled the details in her notebook and looked around. Then she spotted a familiar tear-stained face, sitting on a bench to the side of the building entrance.

A woman in tracksuit bottoms and a denim jacket sat alone, apparently unaware of the people standing in groups around her, heads together in full-on gossip mode. A large canvas tote bag lay at her feet and her head drooped.

Emma approached. 'Natasha?' she asked. 'What's wrong?' This was not the usual smiley, graceful woman who taught the adult ballet classes she was secretly taking.

The woman looked up, wiping the back of her hand across her face and smearing her eye make-up. She stared for a moment and then said, 'Emma? What are you doing here?'

When Emma explained about the call to the office and mentioned the dead teacher, Natasha's face crumpled and tears started sliding down her face. Standing there awkwardly, not really knowing what to do, Emma dug a hand into her shoulder bag for a small packet of tissues. But before she could hand them over, Natasha wiped a sleeve across her face.

'Oh,' she said, looking down at the sleeve as if surprised to find it covered in warm caramel-shaded make-up.

'How about using these?' Emma offered the packet.

Natasha gave a weak smile and took the tissues, pulling one out of the pack and offering it back. Emma shook her head to show that she could keep them.

'My mum will kill me,' Natasha said, holding up the sleeve. 'She only just got the face paint out of it from the dance class I taught last weekend. The Tumble Tots can be a bit boisterous.'

Emma smiled. 'You enjoy teaching?' she asked.

Natasha nodded. 'It's such fun watching people develop. You're one of my best,' she said with a watery smile.

Emma blushed. 'I don't think so. I was there, remember? It's the wine we drank at the summer party that's fuddling your brain.'

Natasha smiled and then stared sadly down at the ground.

'Was Travers McGovern a friend of yours?' Emma asked, sitting down beside her on the bench.

The dancer opened her mouth to reply, but before she could, a voice called, 'Natasha? Are you OK?'

Emma turned to see a short man with glasses and a round, balding head. He reminded her of a mole.

'Oh, hi, Mr Dickens,' Natasha said, wiping her eyes and face with another tissue.

'Who are you?' he demanded, looking Emma up and down suspiciously.

'This is Emma; she's a student in my adult improvers' ballet class,' Natasha said, gesturing to her unnecessarily.

Emma smiled, but the mole man continued to look at her as if she were in the way.

'Natasha, I thought Sally-Ann told everyone to go home? Why are you still on campus? Do you need to speak to the police?'

Emma stayed silent, wondering if that was true.

Natasha shook her head and got to her feet. 'No, I wasn't on campus after five thirty, so they said they didn't need me.' She glanced at her watch. 'I think I'll just head home. I'm getting a bit of a headache,' she said.

'I think that's for the best,' the mole said, moving behind Natasha as if to shepherd her away.

Turning to Emma, Natasha said, 'Call me and we'll get a coffee or something. You've got my number from class, yeah?'

Emma nodded. 'I'll definitely call,' she said.

Natasha turned and began walking away, but then she turned back and stared at Emma, as if trying to send a message without speaking. She disappeared through a side gate and up the street outside. Emma turned and found the mole staring at her. She stared back.

'Who are you?' he asked, hands on hips.

Emma introduced herself and then frowned. 'Have we met before?' she asked, feeling a bell ringing in the back of her brain.

But the man was backing away, muttering something about assignments to mark.

'I'm here to find out more about what happened to Travers McGovern. Did you know him? Any chance of a comment?'

'Very sad,' Mr Dickens said, taking off his glasses and polishing the lenses on his jumper.

'Did you know him well?' she asked, pen poised against her notebook.

Mr Dickens opened his mouth to speak, seemed to think better of it and closed it again. Then he glanced at his watch.

'Sorry, I'd better go and ... There'll be stuff I need to...' Without finishing either sentence, he thanked Emma and went back into the school.

She frowned as he retreated. Mr Dickens looked really familiar, but she couldn't put her finger on where she'd seen him before. Then she

21

took a deep breath. Time for a word from the principal.

***

But instead of Sally-Anne Faber, Emma's next prey turned out to be Burton and Shepherd, who were just leaving the building as she arrived. She grinned at them, and Burton sighed.

'I wondered when we'd be seeing you,' she said.

Emma stood with her pen poised. 'What can you tell me?'

'The same as we can usually tell you at this stage,' Burton said. 'Nothing.'

Emma gave a mock frown. 'There must be something you can tell me? I know who he was,' she said, holding up her notebook to show them the name written there. 'Has his family been told?'

Burton sighed. 'Yes, they have, but I don't want you round there until we give you permission. I know you have ways of finding them before we tell you where they are,' she said, holding up a hand to stop Emma from speaking, 'but give them a break, eh?'

Emma looked like she wanted to disagree, but nodded with bad grace. 'You'll ask them to speak to me though, won't you?' she asked.

Burton nodded. 'Yes, but if they say no, you stick to it,' she said sternly.

Emma nodded back reluctantly.

'Have you found anything out?' Shepherd asked, nodding to Emma's notebook.

She shrugged. 'Not really. Only one student spoke to me and all he knew was that a teacher was dead. They all look really shocked. I suppose that's understandable when someone murdered their teacher.' She looked hopefully at Burton, but the detective inspector was too smart to fall for that one.

'Nice try, but we've no cause of death yet, so you'll just have to wait on that one.'

'When will the post-mortem be done?' Emma asked.

'I can't give you anything now. Any updates will come through the press office, so call them later,' Burton said, glancing at her watch, the signal Emma recognised as showing she was outstaying her welcome.

'In the meantime,' Shepherd said, 'if you hear anything on the grapevine, let us know.'

'Only if you do the same,' Emma called after them as they walked away towards the car park.

Chapter 7

When Sarah McGovern opened the front door, she looked composed, but the tell-tale signs – a reddening of the eyes and a sniff that sounded like she had a heavy cold – told their own story. She stood back to let them into the house and directed them down a long corridor, which led to an enormous kitchen. As well as the usual kitchen appliances and acres of work surfaces and cupboards set around the walls, there was room for a large dining table for eight. Skylights and floor-to-ceiling sliding doors out to the garden made the room so light it felt like they were outside.

Sarah followed them into the room, sniffing loudly. She pulled at the cuff of her jumper sleeve and wiped it across her eyes.

A police officer in plain clothes was busying herself at the kettle with mugs and tea bags. She looked up and smiled at Burton and Shepherd. 'Can we get you anything?' she asked, waving a hand towards the tea-making area.

'Tea would be lovely,' Shepherd said, but Burton declined.

'Is there somewhere we can talk?' she asked.

Sarah led the way into a corner of the kitchen where two low, wicker sofas with red cushion pads stood around a low glass-and-wicker table. She sat on one and directed them to sit on the other. They did so with some difficulty, given Shepherd's size.

'We're very sorry for your loss,' Burton began.

Sarah sniffed. 'What happened to him?' she asked. 'The other officers just said someone found him dead.'

Burton nodded. 'We don't know what happened yet, but we believe he was alone. Did he have any medical conditions we need to know about?'

Sarah nodded and sniffed. 'He's really allergic to peanuts. But he wouldn't have eaten anything with them in it, and he carries those EpiPens everywhere with him.'

Shepherd pulled out his notebook and pen and started taking notes. 'How long had you known about his allergy?'

Sarah frowned. 'We found out about the allergy a couple of years ago. Someone gave him a biscuit that had peanuts in it. Fortunately, another person there had an EpiPen, otherwise he'd have died.'

Shepherd sat back to allow the family liaison officer to put his tea on the table and smiled his thanks. The woman placed a cup in front of Sarah McGovern as well and then retired to the kitchen area. Shepherd could see she was watching Sarah closely.

'Your husband wasn't wearing any allergy alert jewellery when the cleaner found him. Did he usually have something?'

Sarah looked up sharply. 'Yes, he wore a necklace. Usually the first thing people do when they think you're choking or something is open your collar so they would see it quickly.' She looked from Burton to Shepherd and back again. 'You said he wasn't wearing it? Why would he have taken it off?'

'That's something we can look into,' Burton said, as Shepherd took a micro-sip of his tea and decided it was too hot.

'But I don't understand why he wouldn't just grab one of his EpiPens?' Sarah asked, scrubbing at her leaking eyes again. 'He would have known what was happening.'

Shepherd looked at Burton. She fixed her eyes on Sarah.

'How many EpiPens would he have had?' she asked.

Sarah frowned and puffed out her cheeks. 'Probably about five or six. That first attack frightened him and he was really paranoid about having one to hand.'

Burton was frowning off into the distance, so Shepherd stepped in.

'Our pathologist will carry out a post-mortem and then we should know more about what happened.'

'Do you have to cut him up?' Sarah whimpered.

Shepherd nodded. 'Unfortunately, we need to do that to find out what happened to him. It's standard procedure in a sudden death.' He paused. 'When did you last see your husband?' he asked.

Sarah sniffed and tugged at her sleeve again. 'Yesterday morning,' she said. 'I was getting ready for work and having breakfast. I was up and fully dressed and he was lounging about in his pyjamas.' She frowned. 'In fact, now that I think of it, that was weird. I'm normally in the office by eight thirty, so I was up at around seven o'clock. He had a later start than me because his first lesson wasn't until ten o'clock. Sorry, they're not lessons; they're "workshops".' She sketched the quote marks in the air. When she saw Shepherd smile, she smiled back. 'It always sounded pretentious to me, but Travers preferred that to "lesson".'

'It was unusual for your husband to be up and about very early?' Burton asked.

Sarah nodded.

'Did he say anything about what he was going to be doing yesterday, apart from the workshop?' Burton asked.

Sarah looked at her and sighed. 'He said he had a full day, mostly preparing for this bloody showcase.' When Burton and Shepherd raised their eyebrows, she continued, 'It's an end-of-year thing the students do. It's quite a big deal. They sell tickets to the public like a real theatre. There's also sometimes talent scouts and agents looking for the best performers.'

'Does your husband enjoy that sort of thing?' Shepherd asked.

Sarah nodded. 'He was in his element,' she said. 'I'll be glad when it's over because it's even making me anxious. Or at least, it was.' Then she frowned.

'What is it?' Shepherd asked.

'Well,' Sarah began, 'Travers was more on edge than usual. He's been at the school for a few years now, so he's done shows before, but he was really working the students hard this year. Kept saying he wanted it to be the "best ever".'

'As if he had a personal stake in it?' Shepherd asked.

Sarah frowned and then nodded. 'You could look at it that way,' she said.

'You said that you last saw him that morning. Did you speak to him or hear from him during the day?' Shepherd asked.

Sarah rubbed her nose and sniffed. 'I got a text from him at about four thirty to say that he was staying late at school.' Her voice sounded strained.

'Was that because he had rehearsals?' Shepherd asked, looking up from his scribbled notes.

Sarah shrugged. 'I don't know.'

'You didn't report him missing when he didn't come home?' Shepherd asked.

Sarah looked a little uncomfortable. 'I went to bed early and assumed he'd be home at some point. I didn't realise he wasn't here 'til this morning. Then I got the knock from your officers and...' She trailed off, bottom lip wobbling.

Burton nodded. 'Thanks, Mrs McGovern,' she said. 'I think that's everything we need for now. You've been really helpful.' She got to her feet and Shepherd followed. Sarah began to follow, but Shepherd waved a hand for her to stay where she was.

'We'll see ourselves out,' he said.

They walked back up the corridor to the front door. The plain-clothes officer appeared.

'Keep a close eye on her,' Shepherd said.

The woman nodded. 'That's what I'm here for,' she said with a smile.

When the door had shut behind them, Burton looked at Shepherd.

'I don't recall anyone at the scene mentioning EpiPens,' she said. 'Do you remember seeing any?'

Shepherd shook his head. 'You think someone took them away?'

As they walked down the drive and got into the car, Burton said, 'She said he always has five or six pens on him.' She pointed back towards the house with a thumb.

'At least we can give Brody an idea of what she's looking for,' Shepherd said.

Burton pulled out her phone as she settled in the passenger seat. 'I'll call her and then it's back to the station to see how the uniforms are getting along with taking statements. I want to know who saw him last and who knew about the peanut allergy.'

Chapter 8

Back at the *Allensbury Post*'s office, Emma was hammering out the story on her computer keyboard. She stopped and peered down at the lines and loops of shorthand in her notebook. There wasn't much to write, as yet. She only had a bland statement from the drama school's press officer because the principal 'wasn't available' and nothing from the police. She'd not got any of the students to go on record either. They'd all wanted to know how much she'd pay them for the story. As if a local paper had any cash for that, she thought; they'd been watching too much telly. She'd tried calling the police press office but had met a stone wall.

'Didn't you speak to Burton at the scene?' Suzy, the police press officer, had asked.

'I tried, but she said to call you.'

Suzy had laughed. 'Knowing full well that she's not given me anything yet either,' she said.

'The students are saying he was murdered,' Emma had lied, knowing full well that she was on a fishing trip.

But Suzy was too experienced to fall for that one. 'Nice try. You know better than to try that one on me,' the press officer had said.

Emma said, 'Humph,' making Suzy laugh. With a goodbye, she hung up the phone.

Dan glanced across at her. 'What's up?' he asked.

Emma rubbed her face with both hands. 'This story is so frustrat-

29

ing. They found a teacher dead at the school and the students won't comment unless they're paid for it. I was sure there'd be some idle speculation for me to pick up.'

Dan swung his chair to face her, eyebrows raised. 'What are the police saying?' he asked.

'They're not saying anything.'

Dan shrugged. 'They'll be waiting on forensics and the post-mortem before they say anything. That's standard stuff. Is anyone using the "M" word yet?'

Emma sighed and jabbed a finger towards her computer screen. 'Sadly not, but would Burton and Shepherd not say if it wasn't suspicious?'

Dan gave her a patient look. 'How long have you been doing this job? You know they need the post-mortem before they can say for sure.' He scooted over on his chair's wheels and dug her in the ribs. Then he read over her shoulder and shrugged.

'That's all you can say, isn't it?' He glanced over at Daisy, the news editor, and lowered his voice. 'She knows that there's nothing more you can write, so she'll be OK with it.' He rolled his chair back to his own desk.

Emma sighed, saved her story and sent it to Daisy. Then she stared at the blank white page of a new document and the blinking cursor on her screen. She could feel Dan staring at her.

'What is it?' he asked.

'I bumped into this woman I know, Natasha. She's a student at the school, an amazing ballet dancer.'

Dan raised an eyebrow. 'How do you know a ballet dancer?' he asked, but Emma flapped a hand to quieten him.

'That's not important. It was strange because she was in floods of tears about this guy who's died. Actually sobbing. I had to give her all my tissues.'

Dan frowned. 'Drama school students can be hysterical,' he said, putting the back of his hand to his forehead and pretending to swoon. 'It's all that emotion on stage; they don't know how to turn it off.'

Emma glared at him. 'No, it was different. She seemed almost too upset.'

'What are you getting at?' he asked. 'You think there might be more to the relationship than teacher and student?'

Emma nodded. 'She's a very pretty girl.'

Dan shrugged. 'What did she say when you asked her?'

'Why would you think I'd asked her?' Emma asked, sharply.

Dan laughed. 'Oh, come on, Em, you know you would have asked her straight out what was going on.'

She pouted. 'Well, I didn't,' she said, trying to sound dignified. Then she wrinkled. 'I didn't get a chance,' she admitted, making Dan laugh. 'A teacher came over and Natasha made her excuses. She said we should meet up though.'

'There you go. You'll get a second chance,' Dan said, grinning. 'See what secrets you can interrogate out of her.'

Chapter 9

'Why can't she tell us by phone?' Shepherd asked as he drove the car out onto the main road the next morning.

'Apparently we have to see it,' Burton replied, checking that her seatbelt was fastened.

Eleanor Brody had called so early that Burton hadn't even taken off her coat.

'That was quick,' Burton had said into her mobile.

'I found out something interesting, and I thought you'd want to see it as soon as possible. Meet me at the morgue.' The pathologist had hung up before Burton could say another word.

Burton had immediately waved at Shepherd to follow her to the car.

When they got to the morgue, a smiling Eleanor Brody led them through to the main room where Travers McGovern's body lay on a trolley, covered by a sheet.

'You're smiling,' Shepherd said, eyeing Brody. 'That's a good sign, right?'

Brody nodded. 'Oh yes, I think you'll like this one.' She picked up her clipboard. 'Mr Travers' wife has been in to identify the body,' she said, examining the contents of the clipboard.

'How was she?' Shepherd asked.

'Much as you'd expect. She managed a stiff upper lip until she saw the body and was then inconsolable,' Brody said.

Shepherd nodded. 'She was a bit like that yesterday. Contained but on the edge of breaking down.'

'So, what is this thing we need to see?' Burton asked, breaking into the conversation.

Brody nodded. 'After you called yesterday, I made sure I checked the stomach contents carefully and there were no signs he'd eaten anything with peanuts in, but—'

Burton interrupted. 'Are you sure?'

Brody glared at her. 'Let me finish,' she said sternly. 'I said he hadn't eaten anything with peanuts in, but what I did find was vodka with a little something added to it.' Burton and Shepherd waited. 'Peanut oil,' Brody said, slightly smugly.

'Peanut oil?' Shepherd asked, head tilting to one side.

Brody nodded. 'Concentrated peanut oil. That's what I could smell on him yesterday. The vodka delivered the peanut oil. It would have hit him before he even realised.'

'Did CSI find any EpiPens at the scene?' Burton asked.

Brody shook her head. 'I checked that as well. No pens in his desk, bag or coat pocket.'

Shepherd exhaled heavily. 'He didn't stand a chance,' he said. Brody nodded. 'Was he drinking alone?' Shepherd continued.

Brody consulted her clipboard. 'CSI reports finding no other glasses in the room, but someone else could have taken them. What was interesting, they said, was that the door handle was wiped clean, apart from Travers' fingerprints from when he entered the room.'

'Someone had been in there,' Shepherd said, looking at Burton.

Burton took a deep breath and puffed out her cheeks. 'Someone put the peanut oil in his drink, knowing the effect it would have,' she said, 'and they took away the one thing that would save him.' She looked at Shepherd, who looked slightly sick. 'They could have been with him when it happened and tidied up after themselves.'

'Someone just set him up to die,' he said, rubbing the neatly clipped dark hair on the back of his head with a beefy hand. 'Without the adrenaline, he didn't stand a chance.'

Burton nodded. 'We're looking for someone who not only knew about the peanut allergy, but also knew that he liked a cheeky vodka tipple in the afternoon,' she said.

Brody was looking from one detective to the other, following the conversation. 'Someone from the school?' she asked.

'Could be,' Shepherd said, 'or it could be someone from outside the school who wanted him to die on campus. They would need to get past security, though.'

Burton stared up at the ceiling for a moment. Then she said, 'We'd better speak to his wife again and see if she knew about the vodka or whether there's anyone who would want to kill him.'

'Don't you want to know the time of death?' Brody asked as Burton turned to go.

Burton turned back. 'Always,' she said.

'I'm placing it roughly between six thirty and maybe ten thirty,' Brody said.

'You can't be more accurate?'

Brody glared. 'You're lucky to have that tight a time window,' she said.

Burton raised a hand in apology.

'Hang on,' Shepherd said, 'he was last seen going to his office at five thirty. Based on your time of death window, he didn't start drinking the vodka for at least another hour, maybe more. What was he doing in that time period?'

Burton frowned. 'He was called away somewhere?' she asked.

'If he left his office after five thirty, someone must have seen him,' Shepherd said. 'It sounds like there were plenty of people around.'

Burton nodded. 'Let's go back to the drama school.'

'I'll email you a copy of the rest of the report,' Brody said as they turned to go.

When they got outside the morgue, Burton caught sight of the expression on Shepherd's face.

'What are you thinking?' she asked.

'I'm wondering whether Sarah McGovern had a reason to kill her husband,' he said.

'Why would you say that?'

Shepherd swung the car keys around his finger. 'She knew he was very allergic to peanuts, so she'd have known how to do it and make it look like an accident.'

'Motive?'

'He messaged her to say he was going to be late, but he didn't say why. And she didn't ask.'

'You think she would have asked why? When she knew he was working on the showcase?' Burton asked.

Shepherd paused at the driver's door, looking at Burton across the roof of the car. 'But surely rehearsals wouldn't go on 'til ten o'clock.'

'You think he was seeing someone else?'

Shepherd wrinkled his nose. 'I don't know. The rehearsals seem like a convenient reason to go missing a lot. Would you not get the teeniest bit suspicious?'

Burton pulled open her door and settled herself in the passenger seat. 'It's a bit of a stretch, but let's see what her reaction is when we tell her it wasn't an accident. See if she knew anything before we told her.'

Chapter 10

When several phone calls to Natasha went unanswered the next morning, Emma began to scan her social media accounts and found that she was a voracious user of several platforms. Emma found endless pictures of ballerinas, videos of ballet performances and daily videos about her preparations for the end-of-year showcase.

'Wow, she's a fan of herself, isn't she?' Dan asked, looking over Emma's shoulder.

'She's a performer,' Emma said, laughing. 'She's used to being centre of the stage and screen.'

'Hmmm, I wonder how many times she took that one before she was happy with it,' Dan replied, pointing at a picture of Natasha and another pretty dark-skinned woman with the same springy curly hair pouting at the camera. 'Who's that with her?'

Emma leaned forward to look at the screen more closely. 'I think it's her sister. I've met her briefly once or twice.'

She scanned the page again, deliberately not looking at Dan who seemed poised, waiting for an explanation as to how she knew Natasha and her sister. She sat back in surprise when the page auto-refreshed and a message popped up.

'Natasha Kent wants to be your friend,' Dan read over her shoulder. 'There you go, accept it.'

Emma clicked the button and immediately a chat box opened.

'Emma, I need to speak to you. It's urgent.'

Emma typed back, 'Sure. Where do you want to meet?'

The response came almost immediately. 'I've got to go to school for a rehearsal. Can you meet me there in about an hour?'

'Of course. How are you feeling today?'

But Natasha's icon had gone grey, meaning that she'd logged off.

Emma sat back and looked at Dan. 'Wonder what she's got to say,' she said.

Dan frowned. 'At least you've only got an hour to wait,' he replied.

***

It might have been only one day since Travers McGovern died, but the campus had returned to full capacity in terms of numbers and the volume of conversations. It was a warm July day and the students milled around in the quadrangle outside the building, plumes of cigarette smoke rising above most groups. Emma wrinkled her nose and tried not to breathe too deeply.

After a quick circuit of the area, she couldn't see Natasha among the many faces. She pulled out her phone to check for any other messages from her when a nearby voice used Natasha's name.

'Hopefully she's in the studio already practising, for once,' said a short blonde, taking a deep drag of her cigarette. She was deepening her voice, clearly trying to sound like a modern-day Marlene Dietrich. Emma raised an eyebrow. In some places, such pretention might work; in Allensbury, it just sounded daft.

'Come on, Tara,' said one of the men in the group, 'she hasn't missed that many rehearsals.'

Over her shoulder, Emma saw Tara throw him a filthy look. 'She's been way off the mark for weeks. Turning up late, falling over and getting on at Dominic for no reason.'

The man opened his mouth to speak, but Tara continued her tirade. 'When she *is* here, she's distracted, missing cues, falling over.' She sniggered. 'Little miss perfect ballet dancer sprawled on the floor like a sack of spuds.' That was definitely not in the vocabulary of a sultry

1930s actress, Emma thought.

'Give her a break,' said another woman. She was also smoking a cigarette as if her life depended on it. 'Everyone's a bit edgy at the moment. She seemed much better the day before yesterday. Maybe she's got herself sorted.'

'She'd better have,' Tara snapped. 'I've told Dominic that I'm not having her in the group number if she's just going to fall over and ruin it.' She moved out of the group momentarily to stub out her cigarette on top of a nearby bin and then returned. She seemed much less self-assured without it; her hands seemed unsure what to do. She pulled a mobile phone from the pocket of her tracksuit bottoms and looked at the screen. 'Come on,' she said, bending to scoop up a large shoulder bag. The top was open and Emma could see a pair of ballroom dancing shoes. 'Time for rehearsals.'

En masse, the group obediently picked up their bags and followed her towards the building.

Emma watched them go and then followed at a safe distance. If Natasha was going to be part of this group, then it would be a good chance to see just how much her dancing was suffering. Clearly, it wasn't just Travers McGovern's death that was upsetting her.

Chapter 11

When Emma snuck into the back row of the auditorium, she found the stage was brightly lit and the dancers stretching themselves into impossible positions. Emma winced as one girl, seated on the floor, stretched a leg so far it was almost behind her head. Emma scanned the group and finally recognised the slender body in the pink leotard and leggings. She also recognised Tara as part of the group as well, glaring at Natasha across the stage as they both stretched. Then a dark-haired man stepped into the middle of the stage and clapped his hands.

'OK,' he said, 'we're only a couple of weeks from the showcase, so we need to make this practice count. No slip ups,' he added, with a look towards Natasha, who nodded.

Tara made a quiet snorting noise and then got to her feet. She struck an exaggerated pose, hands on hips.

'Did you hear that, Nat? Maybe if you can't stay on your feet, someone else should take the lead on the tango scene,' she sneered.

Natasha took a step towards Tara and snapped, 'What did you say?'

The other woman retreated a few steps and the man stepped forward to block Natasha's path. He murmured into her ear, but Natasha continued to push, intent on shoving him aside. He used a shoulder to nudge her away to centre stage, holding her there.

'We don't have time to change the routine, so we're going as we are,' he said, glaring at Tara.

Tara was smirking, clearly enjoying winding Natasha up, but she also looked wary, as if she was worried about what would happen if Natasha escaped from behind him.

The man stood, holding Natasha's hand, whispering to her while she stared at her feet. He shook her arm and she nodded up at him.

'Right,' he said, letting go of her hand and turning back to the group, 'let's get started.'

The rehearsal began with a group number, with the women performing an energetic can-can. Emma loved seeing normal people transformed into characters. Swept away by the music, she admired the choreography. It looked very complicated to her untrained eye. She saw Natasha wobble a few times, but the number finished without incident, as did the performance of Tara and the man who had started the rehearsal to an Elton John classic.

When they arrived at an extremely dramatic Argentinian tango, a scene designed to show off the drama with dancing that bordered on the erotic, Natasha, already in character, sashayed forward. Three of the male dancers took up places on the stage, all looking very menacing. When a gravelly voice started singing, Emma felt the hairs go up on her arms. Things started well with Natasha dancing with each of the men in turn, but then a particularly swinging leg from Natasha saw her slip on her high heels and fall to the floor, almost pulling the male dancer with her.

'Cut!' the man yelled, and the music halted. 'For fuck's sake, Nat,' he said, hauling her back to her feet, 'what is wrong with you?'

'Sorry, Dominic,' she said, stretching to touch her toes and shaking out her legs.

'Let's try again,' Dominic said, glancing at his watch. 'We've not got time to go from the top, so we'll just pick it up where we were.'

The music restarted and everything proceeded well until the group section of the number. Now there were eight couples on the stage performing the intricate tango steps in a small space. As Natasha spun away from Dominic and back to a close hold, a swinging leg again threw her off balance and she fell, almost knocking over the neighbouring couple. This time she didn't leap back to her feet. Instead she sat there, head hanging, panting.

'Natasha, I swear to God,' Dominic said, holding out a hand to her, 'if you mess up this number on the night, I'll bloody kill you.'

Natasha slapped away his hand and quickly got to her feet, brushing herself down. 'Maybe I should just quit, eh?' she said, her temper flaring suddenly. She stepped forward and jabbed a finger into his chest. Dominic took a pace back, looking shocked. 'You'd like that, wouldn't you?'

'No, I—' he began, but Natasha carried on as if he hadn't spoken.

'Maybe I should just quit dancing altogether? Would that make you happy?' she demanded.

'Nat, no, look—' Dominic began, but he stepped back when her finger jabbed into his chest.

'I thought you had my back, but you're as bad as the rest of them, nit-picking everything,' she snapped.

'Nat—' Dominic tried again, but Natasha wasn't listening.

'I'm trying my best. You know about—' Natasha stopped speaking and Dominic opened his mouth to respond, but she waved a hand to silence him.

The group of dancers stared silently at the scene unfolding in front of them.

'I told you she wasn't good enough,' Tara called, strutting towards Dominic and Natasha. Emma saw Dominic take a deep breath as if steeling himself for what was to come.

Natasha rounded on Tara, but the latter hadn't finished.

'I thought black people were supposed to have rhythm.'

There was a collective gasp from the dancers. A moment of silence ensued before Natasha leapt towards Tara. Fortunately, Dominic's reflexes were ready and waiting. He grabbed Natasha, scooped her off her feet, and carried her away to the wings. She was snarling and kicking, fighting him every step of the way. He pinned her into the corner of the stage, whispering and trying to calm her down. Whatever he said seemed to work because Natasha turned her back on Tara, shouldered her bag and stormed off the stage, down the short flight of stairs to the floor of the auditorium and towards the side door. The door slammed behind her, the sound echoing around the theatre.

Not waiting to see the fallout of Tara's comment, Emma got to her feet and hurried out of the auditorium. She caught sight of Natasha heading towards the changing rooms and doubled her pace. Tara's comment was horrific, but why had Natasha flared up before that? She needed to know what was going on.

Chapter 12

Emma heard a slam as she pushed open the changing-room door. She put her head into the washroom section and found just one cubicle occupied. She could hear a woman sobbing.

'Nat?' she called. 'Nat, is that you?'

A couple of loud sniffs quelled the sobbing. 'Who's that?'

'It's me, Emma.'

After a few more sniffs, the door unlocked and Natasha appeared, tears running down her face. She walked to the sink and grabbed a few paper towels. When she blotted her face, streaks appeared in her carefully applied make-up.

'Oh bollocks,' she said, looking at herself in the mirror. Leaning over the sink, she splashed cold water onto her cheeks, rubbed at them and groaned again. 'Better get this sorted now. I don't want anyone seeing me like this.'

'I'm sure people would understand you being upset when Tara says things like that,' Emma said, pointing back towards the door with her thumb.

Natasha groaned. 'It's disgusting, but I've dealt with a lot of that crap over the years. It's just her. She always knows what buttons to press. Dominic should have let me—'

'I think it was best that he didn't,' Emma said, 'or you'd have ended up in court.'

Natasha put her face in her hands. 'You're right, I shouldn't have let

43

her get to me. There's enough gossip to go around already. Guard the door, will you?'

Surprised by the order, Emma crossed to the door and leaned back against it.

'What gossip?' she asked, watching Natasha pull a make-up bag out of her sports bag. The latter walked across to the sink and started unpacking the contents. 'That you're sleeping with Travers McGovern?'

Natasha met her eyes in the mirror. 'How did you know?' she asked, her mouth pulling down at the corners.

Emma nodded. 'An educated guess, based on how upset you were yesterday. How long has it been going on?'

'Six months or so,' Natasha said, spreading liquid foundation across her cheeks and forehead with a sponge. She saw the expression on Emma's face and turned. 'He said he loved me,' she said, her bottom lip beginning to wobble. She took a deep breath and turned back to the mirror.

'Is that why you're messing up rehearsals?' Emma asked, moving to lean against the wall opposite the door so she could see Natasha in the mirror.

The latter raised her head to meet Emma's eye. 'Who told you that?'

Emma gestured to the changing-room door. 'I just watched that one,' she said, 'and from what I overheard earlier, it's not a one-off.'

Natasha's bottom lip wobbled again and tears started running down her face. Emma took her arm and led her away from the mirror to sit on the wooden bench that ran around the room. Natasha dug her hand into her sports bag and pulled out the packet of tissues Emma had given her the previous day. She wiped her eyes and blew her nose in a very non-ballerina way. Her hands fell into her lap.

'What's going on, Nat?' Emma asked, patting one of Natasha's hands.

'Oh, so much. I'm not sure how much more I can take.' Tears threatened again, but Natasha held them back by tilting her face to the ceiling. 'There's a video,' she said, 'of me and Travers having sex.'

Emma's eyes widened. 'You let him video you?' she asked.

Natasha shook her head. She dug a hand into her sports bag and pulled out her mobile phone. A couple of taps of the screen and she

44

held it out to Emma. 'Read this email,' she said.

Emma's eyes scanned the screen and her eyes widened. 'Who sent that?' she asked, looking up at Natasha.

Natasha shrugged. 'That's the problem. I don't know. I know who made the video. It was Travers. He did it without telling me, so I went mental at him and made him delete it.'

'But obviously he didn't.'

Natasha nodded.

'But this isn't from him, is it?' Emma held up the phone. 'He wouldn't threaten to ruin your life, your reputation? Surely he'd be ruined as well.'

Natasha nodded. 'He'd have lost his job and probably his marriage, but men can ride that kind of thing out, can't they? He'd be a "naughty boy", a stud for shagging a younger woman. I would be a slag. It would destroy my career before it's even begun.'

'And you don't know who this is from?' Emma asked, handing back the phone.

Natasha shook her head, eyes filling with tears again. 'No. I thought with Travers dead that it would be over, but yesterday I got another email saying that nothing had changed. I'm still going to pay for what I've done.'

'What have you done?'

Natasha shook her head. 'That's just it, I don't know. Maybe it's the affair with Travers and the emails are from his wife. Maybe she found the video on his phone or something. But would she really want to do this straight after he's died? Would she not be grieving?'

Emma took a breath and puffed out her cheeks. 'Grief affects people in different ways,' she said. 'She might be angry with him, but taking it out on you instead. I'm trying to get an interview with her so I'll see what I can find out.'

Natasha stared at her. 'Really? You would do that?' she asked, almost in a whisper.

'Of course. If she *is* blackmailing you, maybe I can get her to stop.' She paused. 'Maybe she went further and killed Travers when she found out about the affair.'

Natasha gasped. 'You think she killed him?'

Emma shrugged. 'It's a possibility. For now, concentrate on your dancing,' she said, 'and leave the investigating to me. I'll be in touch as soon as I've got something.'

Chapter 13

When Emma returned to the office, she found Dan about to head up to the office kitchen to make a round of tea.

'Do you want—?' he began.

'Yes. I'll give you a hand,' Emma interrupted, grabbing the mug from her desk.

Dan gave her a funny look. 'You're never usually this keen to help with tea making,' he said, but the look on Emma's face told him that tea was not really on her mind. 'What is it?' he asked as they walked out of the office.

'Not here,' Emma hissed.

They climbed the stairs to the office kitchen, but Emma waited until they were inside with the door closed before she told Dan what she'd found out.

'A sex tape?' he asked, eyes widening. 'Why the hell did she agree to that?'

'She didn't have a choice because he made it without telling her.'

Dan picked up the kettle. 'And she thought he'd deleted it, but then it turns out someone else has a copy?'

Emma nodded. 'At first she thought it was Travers who was black-mailing her, but I think it's his wife.'

Dan paused while filling the kettle. 'His wife? Typical that he's married.'

Emma wrinkled her nose. 'I know what you mean. But what if she

47

found out about the affair? She might have found the video on his phone.'

Dan finished filling the kettle, plugged it in and switched it on. He leaned back against the work surface and looked at her. 'OK, the wife is a plausible story. But – and you won't like this – what about Natasha herself? She was angry with him for taking the video in the first place, but then she found out he'd shared it with someone else...'

Emma frowned. 'But she said they were in love and...'

She trailed away and Dan raised his eyebrows.

'What?' he asked.

Emma frowned, head tilted to one side. 'No, that's not right. She said, "He said he loved me." That he loved her.'

Dan had opened the cupboard to find tea bags and was throwing them into mugs. 'And she wasn't feeling the same way?'

Emma shrugged. 'I don't know. I mean, she seems genuinely gutted that he's dead but you think that could be a smokescreen?'

Dan turned his back to the kettle and leaned against the work surface, arms folded. 'They've been having a thing for six months. Maybe she got bored with him, told him it was over and that's why he threatened to release the tape?'

Emma nodded, staring at the kettle as steam plumed from the spout.

'But it's the tone of the blackmail message. It says he had a chance to make it go away and didn't take it. Now she has to admit what she's done. Why would Travers send her that?'

'OK, so maybe she was angry that he let someone else get hold of the video. She might have told him to deal with the blackmailer and when he didn't, she got angry and killed him.'

'Thinking the blackmailer would stop if Travers was dead?' Emma asked.

Dan shrugged. 'Maybe they got into a fight about him sharing the video or letting her get blackmailed. She lost her temper and whacked him with something.'

'She's certainly proved she has a temper,' Emma said. She recounted the incident at the rehearsal.

Dan's eyes widened. 'It's a good job that Dominic bloke is strong.

She could have taken Tara's head off.'

Emma nodded. 'To be honest, though, Nat was already kicking off at Dominic for the comments about her dancing. I think she was so worried about the sex tape getting out that she's been off her game.'

'What if she'd told Travers she was ending it because she had to concentrate on dancing?' Dan asked. 'So he gave the recording to someone else as revenge?'

Emma scratched her head and pushed back a stray strand of red hair. 'His ego was so dented he threatened to ruin her life?'

Dan shrugged. 'I'd be pretty miffed if someone dumped me for that reason.'

Emma nodded. 'A lot of athletes need to focus on their career above everything else. She's a talented dancer and she could go on to whatever she wants. Maybe you're right and she felt she'd outgrown him, wanted to move on—'

'And he wasn't ready to let her?' Dan turned to the kettle, which had boiled and switched itself off. He picked it up and began pouring hot water into mugs.

Emma folded her arms and stared off into the distance. 'Maybe he liked to be the one doing the dumping, and being dumped was too much for his ego,' she said.

'His revenge has backfired on him because he's ended up dead,' Dan said, 'but what could Natasha have done that was so bad that someone wants to ruin her life?'

'Having an affair?' Emma asked.

'Wife kills husband and threatens to ruin the woman he was sleeping with?'

Emma took a deep breath and puffed out her cheeks. 'I've no idea.'

'Have the police said anything about the cause of death?' Dan asked, bending down to get milk out of the fridge. 'Can you pass me a teaspoon?'

Emma pulled open the nearest drawer and took one out. She handed it to him and he started scooping tea bags out of mugs. 'Nothing yet,' she said. 'No sign of what's happened or even whether it's suspicious.'

'Burton's playing cards close to her chest?' Dan asked.

Emma nodded. 'Either that or she doesn't actually know anything yet herself,' she admitted. 'They seem to have kept the spread of information to a minimum and no one actually seems to know what happened apart from that he died in his office.'

Dan finished putting milk into mugs and put the bottle back in the fridge. 'How did you leave it with Natasha?'

'I said I'd try to find out who's blackmailing her. Yes, I know, it's going to be tough,' she said as Dan raised his eyebrows, 'and, to be honest, I'm not even sure where to start.'

Dan picked up the tray of mugs. 'Let's have a cuppa, I'll finish the article I'm writing and then we can brainstorm some ideas.'

'Sounds like a plan,' Emma said, holding the door open for him. 'I'm open to any suggestions at this point.'

Chapter 14

They arrived at Sarah McGovern's house and Burton's phone beeped as the car stopped. She looked down at the screen.

'Aha, the report from Brody.'

'Wow, she types fast. She can do my paperwork if she gets it done that quickly,' Shepherd said, disentangling himself from his seatbelt.

Burton opened the email attachment and her eyes scanned down the page. She stopped and held up her phone. Shepherd peered at the screen and his eyes widened.

'Exactly,' Burton said, as if he'd spoken aloud. 'Let's see what she's got to say about that.'

It was the police liaison officer who opened the door.

'Sarah's having a lie down,' she told them. 'I think going to the morgue hit her harder than she was expecting. She's realised he's really gone.'

'Can we speak to her? We've got post-mortem results,' Burton said.

The liaison officer nodded. 'When we were at the morgue, I heard the doctor on the phone to you.' She turned and started climbing the stairs. 'Go through to the kitchen,' she said over her shoulder. 'I'll bring her down.'

Burton led the way down the hallway into the kitchen.

'Would you want a place like this?' she asked, looking around the shiny, clean surfaces. The garden outside the French windows included an immaculately manicured lawn and well-maintained flowerbeds.

She looked back at Shepherd and he shook his head.

'A bit too big for just little old me,' he said, 'but Stacey would have loved it.'

Burton mentally kicked herself for asking, because his wife died in a hit-and-run collision several years previously. But Sarah McGovern's appearance in the kitchen spared her from saying anything else.

She looked worse than the previous day, washed out and red-eyed. She smiled wanly and showed them to the wooden dining table. When they declined her offer of coffee, she sat down opposite and looked at them expectantly.

'We now know,' Burton began, 'that your husband's death wasn't an accident.'

'What?' Sarah gasped. 'Someone killed him? I thought it was anaphylactic shock.'

Burton nodded. 'It was, but we believe someone deliberately added peanut oil to a bottle of vodka your husband kept in his desk drawer in the office.'

Sarah sighed heavily and Burton raised an eyebrow.

'You knew about the vodka?' she asked.

Sarah nodded. 'He's always had a weakness for spirits, so I don't keep them in the house. They were too much of a temptation.' She sighed. 'I had a feeling that he was getting it elsewhere.'

Burton paused as Shepherd pulled out his notebook and pen. When he was ready, she continued.

'Our crime scene investigators didn't find any EpiPens in his office, so we have to consider the fact that someone took them away.'

Sarah stared at her, mouth falling slightly open. 'Someone took away...' she began before trailing off, as if imagining her husband's panic when he realised he couldn't treat himself.

'Can you think of anyone who might have wanted to hurt your husband?' Burton asked.

Sarah McGovern considered for a moment and then shook her head.

'He did sometimes rub people up the wrong way. He could be a bit full of himself, but when you've been a soap opera star and won awards, you can understand it, can't you?'

'There wasn't anyone who he'd had an argument with ... fallen out with?'

'Not that I'm aware of,' Sarah said.

Burton paused. Then she said, 'Our CSI team also tested the sofa in your husband's office and we found DNA from four different women.'

Sarah stared at her. 'So he had different women sitting on his sofa, so what? They were probably there to talk about performances.'

Burton cleared her throat awkwardly. 'It was more intimate DNA.'

Sarah put her face into her hands and gave a shuddering sigh.

'You knew he was seeing someone else? Seeing other women?' Shepherd asked, looking up from his notebook.

Sarah wiped the kitchen towel under each of her eyes, which were full of tears. 'When a non-smoker comes home reeking of cigarettes, booze, cheap perfume, or all three, you know he's up to something, don't you?' She addressed the last remark to Burton and then sniffed hard. 'Do you think one of them could have killed him?'

Burton leaned forward on the table, resting her forearms on it. 'Where were you on the night your husband died?' she asked.

Sarah recoiled and leapt up from the table. 'You're asking me for an alibi?' she demanded.

Burton stared at her stonily, head cocked to one side.

Shepherd got up from his seat and gestured for Sarah to sit down again, which she did.

'Where were you?' he asked her, gently, sitting down in the chair next to her.

Sarah's face was expressionless as she looked at him. 'I was at work. I stayed late because I knew there was nothing to come home to.'

'Until what time?' Shepherd asked.

Sarah shrugged. 'I think I got back here about six thirty or maybe a little later,' she said.

Burton frowned. 'Did anyone see you leave the office or return home?' she asked.

Sarah shrugged again. 'I was the last one to leave the office, so there was no one else there,' she said. 'Maybe a neighbour saw me when I got home.'

'When did your colleagues leave the office?' Shepherd asked.

Sarah shrugged. 'I don't know. It's not the sort of job where you clock in and out.'

'You didn't notice when people said goodbye to you?' Burton asked.

'Well, I wasn't making notes on it, if that's what you mean,' Sarah snapped.

There was an uncomfortable silence. Then Shepherd spoke.

'The last sighting of your husband was at five thirty that evening,' he said. 'He was last seen going upstairs to his office and, so far, no one has come forward to say they saw him or spoke to him after that.' He paused and Sarah stared at him.

'You think that because I can't prove when I left the office or when I returned home that I went via the school and killed him?' she demanded.

Shepherd said nothing, but looked back at her steadily.

'Oh my God, I've just lost my husband and you're accusing me of murdering him?' she asked, banging her palms against the table.

Before Burton or Shepherd could answer, there was the sound of a key in the front door and a man's voice calling, 'Hello? Sarah, where are you?'

Sarah called, 'In the kitchen.' She got to her feet.

A tall, balding, well-built man in his late-forties appeared in the kitchen doorway, clutching two bulging Tesco carrier bags. He halted and stared at Burton and Shepherd.

'Who's this?' he demanded, walking into the room and dumping the carrier bags on the worktop.

'It's the police,' Sarah told him, introducing Burton and Shepherd. 'My brother, Tony Standing.' They both stood and Shepherd held out a hand, but the man made no move to shake it. He glared at them, hands on hips.

'What have they said now?' he asked Sarah.

'Someone murdered Travers,' Sarah said, her eyes filling with tears again. 'Someone put peanut oil in his vodka.'

Tony stared at her. 'How do you know that?' he asked, turning on Burton and Shepherd.

'Our pathologist found it during the post-mortem,' Burton told him.

Tony snorted. 'Serves him right for drinking in the office,' he said. Burton raised her eyebrows. 'I had very little time for my brother-in-law,' he continued. 'He made life very difficult for Sarah and now she's free of him.' He put an arm around Sarah and squeezed her.

She wiped her eyes with the tissue she'd pulled from her sleeve. 'They think I did it,' she whispered.

Tony Standing swelled indignantly. 'What? Why would Sarah do that? How could you think that—?'

But Burton raised a hand and he fell silent.

'Mr Standing, we have to consider all options. Your sister doesn't have an alibi for that evening and so we have to ask these questions.'

She turned to Sarah. 'I think that's all for now, Mrs McGovern. We'll keep you posted on how the case is progressing.' Sarah shook hands with them both and turned towards the kitchen door. In the doorway, Burton paused.

'Mr Standing, where were you yesterday evening?' As she hoped, the man's jaw dropped slightly.

'Me? You're asking me for an alibi?' he demanded.

'Yes. Where were you?'

Tony Standing's jaw worked several times. 'I was at home,' he said.

'Anyone corroborate that?' Burton asked, in a tone designed to provoke.

When Tony said nothing, Burton turned and went through the doorway. 'Don't worry, we'll see ourselves out,' she called over her shoulder.

As they left the kitchen, they heard the rustling of the shopping bag and Sarah saying, 'You shouldn't have said that.'

Tony made a scoffing noise. 'There's no point in hiding how I feel.'

Once the door was closed behind them, Burton said, 'He likes to tell it how it is. We'll have to come back another time when he's not here. We'll get nothing from her with him in attendance.'

Shepherd paused by the dark-blue Mercedes that had now joined Sarah's mint-green Fiat 500 on the drive. He took out his notebook and wrote the registration number on a clean page.

Answering Burton's questioning look, he said, 'There's clearly no

love lost. I'd like to check exactly where Mr Standing was on the
evening his brother-in-law died.'

Chapter 15

Burton arrived in the CID office, fresh from an update to her boss on the case's lack of significant progress. She found Shepherd staring at his computer screen, leaning forward in concentration.

'You'll damage your eyes doing that,' she said, putting a takeaway coffee cup down on the desk beside his mouse.

He laughed. 'I've not been doing it that long, so I think I'll be OK.'

'What have you got?' Burton asked, sitting on the chair behind him and blowing into the hole in the plastic lid of the cup clutched in her hand. She peered over his shoulder at the video frozen on his screen.

'It's the college CCTV footage from the day when Travers McGovern was murdered.' Shepherd pointed to the screen. 'This is from the afternoon. They've also emailed over the footage from the evening.'

Burton straightened up. 'Anything come up yet?'

Shepherd shook his head. He reached for his coffee without looking around and almost knocked it onto the floor. 'Whoops,' he said, grabbing it.

'That'll teach you to look at what you're doing,' said Burton with a smile.

Shepherd laughed and turned back to the screen. He raised the coffee to his lips, but stopped with the cup halfway. He transferred it to his left hand and reached for the mouse.

'What?' Burton asked.

Shepherd was rewinding the footage slightly. He set it to play and peered more closely at the screen. Then he paused it and sat back with a slightly smug grin.

'What?' Burton asked again.

'Recognise this?' Shepherd asked, pointing to a dark-blue Mercedes with a meaty finger.

Burton leaned forward and peered at the screen. 'Is that—?'

Shepherd flicked through his notebook, found the page and held it up to show Burton the registration number he'd scribbled earlier in the day.

'It belongs to Tony Standing,' he said, 'and what was he doing parked outside the college at three o'clock in the afternoon?'

As they watched, the car pulled out of the parking space on the street and drove away.

Burton raised an eyebrow. 'It looks like he was just sitting in the car,' she said.

'Watching the college,' Shepherd said.

Burton frowned. 'He could have parked up to go somewhere nearby on foot.'

Shepherd shook his head. 'I've viewed the last thirty minutes of footage and he's not moved from the car,' he said. He turned back to his computer and opened the second file, which contained evening footage.

'What are you looking for?' Burton asked.

'I want to see—' Shepherd stopped talking as he opened up the footage from the camera that recorded the comings and goings at the front gates of the school. He was fast-forwarding the footage when he spotted what he was looking for and stopped it. Then he scrolled back a few seconds and pointed to a figure who was striding through the gates.

'He looks like a man on a mission,' Burton said.

'Now we need to ask Mr Standing why he was on the college campus on the night his brother-in-law died.'

***

Tony Standing looked unimpressed when he opened his front door to find Burton and Shepherd on the other side of it.

'What do you want?' he demanded.

Burton smiled, but it didn't reach her eyes. 'We need to talk about your brother-in-law,' she said.

Standing sighed heavily and stood back to allow them inside. His house was approximately half the size of his sister's, meaning that Shepherd took up a lot of the space in the hallway.

The other man looked him up and down and said, 'You'd better come through to the kitchen.'

As they passed what must have been the living room door, a woman's voice called over the sound of a loud comedy programme, 'Who is it?'

'Just the police,' Standing replied. 'Got questions about Travers.' The volume of the canned laughter rose and Standing led the way into the kitchen, closing the door firmly behind them. When seated at the kitchen table, without an offer of tea or coffee, Burton opened the conversation.

'Why were you sitting in your car outside Allensbury Dance and Drama School on the afternoon that Travers was killed?' she asked.

Standing scowled. 'Is it a crime to park your car when there are no restrictions on that street?' he demanded.

Shepherd looked up from his notebook. 'No, it's not a crime to be parked there, but what confused me was that you didn't get out of the car. You just parked up and were watching the college.'

'I wasn't watching it,' Standing said, glaring at Shepherd. 'I stopped to take a phone call.'

'It must have been a long call,' Shepherd said. 'You were there for a good half an hour.'

Standing said nothing.

Burton leaned down to pull a folded sheet of paper from her hand-bag and flattened it onto the table surface. She pushed it across to Standing and he peered down at it. 'What's this?' he asked.

'It's a still image from the dance school's CCTV camera later that day,' she said. 'From the night that Travers was killed.' She pointed a finger at the figure, frozen in time as it walked through the gates.

'That's you, isn't it?'

Standing leaned over and peered at the photograph. Then he sat back in his chair and shrugged.

Shepherd leaned forward and tapped a finger on the image. 'You see, the time code on this is about quarter past five, just fifteen minutes before your brother-in-law was last seen alive.' He paused. 'Did you go to his office?'

Standing said nothing, but leaned his folded arms on the table.

Burton leaned in too. 'I think you did. I think you followed him and you killed him.'

'I wouldn't have used bloody peanut oil,' Standing said loudly. He stood up suddenly, and the wooden chair he was sitting on scraped across the floor and fell over with a loud crash. 'I'd have strangled him with my bare hands.'

Shepherd stood up, too. 'Sit down, Mr Standing,' he said calmly.

Standing glared at him for a minute, and then sat down and pulled his chair back to the table.

'You wanted to kill your brother-in-law?' Burton asked.

'It's a figure of speech,' Standing said, trying for an insouciant shrug.

Burton and Shepherd stared at him in silence. After a couple of uncomfortable minutes, Standing sighed. 'OK, I was on campus,' he said. 'I went to have it out with him.'

'Have what out?' Burton asked.

'He's cheating on my sister,' Standing said.

Burton looked at Shepherd, eyebrows raised. 'You thought he was having an affair?'

Standing snorted. 'I didn't think it, I knew it. That's if shagging a student makes it an affair.'

'A student?' Burton asked. 'How do you know that?'

'I saw them together.'

'Having sex?' Shepherd asked.

Standing shook his head. 'No, but they were very lovey dovey.'

Burton raised an eyebrow. 'And that made you angry?'

'Yes, of course it did. Poor Sarah is working hard to keep a roof over their heads and what's he doing? Prancing about as if he was an ac-tor'

– he put the emphasis on the second syllable of the word – 'spending every penny he had and giving Sarah nothing. Always in debt and even asked me for money. She should never have married him.'

'Why did she marry him?' Shepherd asked.

Standing waved a hand in front of his face. 'He was a pretty boy, always has been. He swept her off her feet and having someone like him interested in her was flattering, I suppose. At least, someone like he was ten years ago, all money and celebrity. Losing his looks now, getting a bit wrinkly and pulling young girls to prove he's still got it.' He scowled.

'Girls? Plural?' Shepherd asked.

Standing shrugged. 'Only one that I know of for sure, but there's bound to have been others.' He made another snorting noise. 'She was kinda pretty, if you go for a face caked in make-up. Skinny body, Afro hair.'

'A dancer, do you think?' Burton asked.

'Probably. Clearly not a lot of brains if she falls for Travers' old crap.' Standing's face darkened with anger.

'Did you see them together the night he died?' Burton asked.

Standing shook his head. 'I only went to the college to talk to him, to ask him to stop the affairs or I would tell Sarah.' He paused, glaring down at the table, his hands clenched so hard that his knuckles had gone white.

'You found him in his office?' Shepherd asked.

Standing shook his head. 'No, he was standing in the atrium texting someone when I saw him. I demanded to see him in private and we went to one of the dance studios.'

Burton raised her eyebrows. 'Hardly private,' she said. 'Why not go to his office?'

Standing shrugged. 'It was nearer and there was no one in there.'

'You argued?' Burton asked.

Standing nodded. 'Yes, I shouted at him, told him I'd seen him and that he had to stop the affair. It would break Sarah's heart if she found out. After everything she's done for him.' His face became almost a snarl.

'What did he say?' Burton asked.

'He laughed in my face. He said he wouldn't give up this girl. Said they loved each other and they wanted to be together.'

Shepherd looked up from scribbling in his notebook. 'And what did you say?'

'I reminded him of his marriage vows, but he just laughed more and said they were going to be together. "I'm not giving up Natasha for anything," he said.'

Burton and Shepherd looked at each other. 'Natasha? Did he say a surname?' Burton asked.

'No.' Standing sat back in his chair and folded his arms. 'And I'm saying no more unless you arrest me.'

Chapter 16

Emma's routine call to the police press office the next morning was more fruitful than it had been the previous two days.

'We've got a cause of death,' Suzy told her.

'Excellent,' Emma said and then stopped. 'Sorry, I meant—'

Suzy laughed. 'Don't worry, I know what you meant.'

'What is it?' Emma asked.

'Travers McGovern died from anaphylactic shock.'

'He was allergic to something?' Emma asked.

There was a short silence and Emma knew Suzy was reading her notes. 'Yup, seems to have been peanuts.'

'So it was an accident?' Emma was scribbling in her notebook as she spoke.

'The forensics suggest otherwise,' Suzy said, 'because there was peanut oil in a drink he had.'

Emma stiffened in her seat. 'He drank something with peanuts in?' she repeated.

'That's what I've been told.'

Emma frowned. 'Why would he drink something with peanuts in it if he was allergic?'

'We don't know yet how the peanut oil got into the drink, so at the moment it's being treated as suspicious and inquiries are ongoing,' Suzy said.

'But surely when he felt an attack coming on, he'd have just treated himself with an EpiPen,' Emma said. 'People with allergies usually have loads, don't they?'

'Off the record, there weren't any at the scene,' Suzy said.

Emma raised her eyebrows. 'He didn't have any? That's weird.'

'That's why we're still treating it as suspicious,' Suzy replied.

'They think someone took them away?' Emma asked in a hushed voice.

'I can't comment on that,' came the flat party-line reply.

'Do they know what the drink was?' Emma asked.

'I've not been told, so you'll just have to wait on that.'

When Emma hung up the phone, she sat for a moment in silence, staring at her notebook. Dan and Ed, who stood talking across their computers, fell silent and looked at her.

'What is it?' Dan asked.

Emma repeated her conversation with Suzy.

'He wouldn't have drunk something knowing it had peanuts in though, would he?' Ed asked.

Emma shook her head. 'So someone else must have given it to him.'

Dan looked queasy. 'Knowing that it could kill him? That's cold.' He fiddled with the rolled-up sleeve of his shirt. 'Do you think the same person also took the EpiPens away?'

They looked at each other, contemplating the idea that someone would take away the life-saving medicine.

Emma shrugged. 'I don't know. But it would have to be someone that he trusted if he'd take a drink from them without checking what was in it.'

'Or the person lied to him and said it didn't have peanuts in,' Ed said, shoving his hands into his trouser pockets.

Emma rubbed her nose, frowning.

'What are you thinking?' Ed asked.

'He died in his office, so either the drink was already in there, he brought it in himself or someone else gave it to him?' she said.

'Would he not have checked what he was drinking? If he's allergic, you'd think he was careful about it,' Dan said.

'But,' Ed pointed at Dan, 'why would he check something that he'd brought to the office himself or that was already in his office?'

'Someone could have snuck in and spiked it, whatever it was,' Emma suggested.

Dan ruffled his already dishevelled hair. 'The killer must have known he would go back to the office that day and drink it without thinking,' he said. 'Otherwise he might have checked for the EpiPens and replaced them if he realised they were missing.'

Emma sat silently for a moment while Dan and Ed watched her. Then she stood up.

'Someone at the college must know about his allergy,' she said. 'Maybe they also know what drink he liked or what he kept in the office.'

Dan nodded. 'Your mate, Natasha, for one,' he said. 'She was seeing him. I bet she'd know.'

Emma rubbed her forehead and winced. 'I thought of that too, but I don't think Natasha would hurt him. She—' Then she stopped. She was about to say that Natasha loved Travers, but then she wondered if that was true. Travers had videoed them having sex without her permission and shared it with someone else. Now Natasha's reputation was on the line. She was under a lot of pressure and had thought Travers was a threat to her. Having seen her flare up in the dance rehearsal, she knew Natasha had a temper. But could she have done something so cold as to feed him peanuts and take away the medicine that would save his life?

'I need to talk to her,' she said.

Chapter 17

Natasha insisted on meeting away from the college campus and instead chose the park next to Allensbury Castle.

'You sounded serious,' she said as Emma sat down next to her on the wooden bench. 'I didn't want anyone else to overhear. Plus, I needed to get away from college for a while. The place feels about ready to explode.'

Emma smiled. 'A death on campus will do that,' she said.

Natasha nodded. 'I think everyone is a bit blindsided, and there are so many rumours circulating about what happened to him. I doubt any of it is true.' She sighed. 'In all honesty, it's been like a pressure cooker for weeks. Harsh as it may sound, I think most people are more worried about the showcase than Travers.'

Emma stared at her. 'That's still going ahead?'

Natasha nodded. 'They're going with the theory that Travers would have said the show must go on.' She smiled. 'Which is exactly what he would have said. We've still got two weeks to go before "the night",' she said, sketching air quote marks.

'How are you feeling about it?' Emma asked.

Natasha sighed. 'I feel sick. I'm not sure whether that's anxiety about the blackmail or worry that I might screw up the showcase.' She looked at Emma. 'Have you had any luck finding out who the blackmailer is?'

Emma shook her head. 'Not yet.' Then she took a deep breath. 'The police have done Travers' post-mortem.'

Natasha turned to face her, looking like she was braced for bad news. 'Did they find something?'

Emma took a deep breath. 'Yes. He died from anaphylactic shock.'

Natasha's eyes opened wide and her jaw dropped. 'What? He'd eaten peanuts? He can't have done; he was always really careful.'

Emma sighed and closed her eyes. 'You knew about the peanut allergy,' she said.

Natasha nodded. 'Anyone who spent any time with him, or ate with him, would know that,' she said.

'I was really hoping you'd say you didn't know,' Emma replied.

'Why? Did he eat something with peanuts in?'

Emma shook her head. 'They found peanut oil in his system, and they reckon it was in a drink he had.'

'He'd never have knowingly drunk something with peanuts in it,' Natasha said, shaking her head. 'It must have been an accident.'

Emma shook her head. 'The police are considering whether someone deliberately gave it to him.'

The shock showed on Natasha's face. 'But how could they have done that? He was really careful about what he ate and drank.'

'Is there anything he used to drink without checking it for peanuts?' Emma asked.

Natasha's hand flew to her mouth. 'The vodka,' she said in a whisper.

Emma stared at her. 'What vodka?'

'He always had a bottle of vodka in his desk drawer,' Natasha said. 'I'd told him off about it. He was always having what he called "a cheeky tipple" before he went home.'

'He'd never have thought that there'd be peanuts in something in his own desk,' Emma said. There was a brief silence as they both contemplated Travers McGovern's last moments of life.

'What will the police do next?' Natasha added, shifting to get comfortable on the wooden bench.

Emma puffed out her cheeks. 'Talk to everyone who knew him and try to work out who added the peanut oil and when.'

Natasha nodded. 'That's easy enough. I was in his office with him the day before he died and he had some vodka then. He was fine, so there can't have been anything in it then.'

'You need to tell the police that,' Emma said.

'What? Why?'

'It'll narrow down the window for the vodka being tampered with and help them work out who could have done it.'

'I can't tell them anything.'

Emma frowned at her. 'But Nat, you said that there were already rumours about you and Travers circulating. Surely people already know?'

Natasha was silent.

Emma sighed, exasperated. 'Well, it doesn't matter now if people find out. Tell the police that you saw him drink the vodka the previous day straight away. Believe me, it's much better that they find out everything from you rather than from someone else. You want to get as much credit with the investigating officer as you can. She's tough, but she'll be fair if you're honest with her.'

Natasha said nothing, looking down at her feet. 'Why do I need credit with her?'

Emma stared at her. 'Nat, you had motive ... the sex tape. You had means ... you knew about his vodka. And opportunity too ... you've been in and out of his office all the time.'

Natasha continued to examine her trainers.

Emma plucked at a loose thread on her trousers. 'Did he lock his office?'

Natasha frowned. 'Usually he did, but he sometimes forgot.' Then she stared at Emma, eyes wide. 'You think someone sneaked into his office on the day he died and spiked the vodka?'

Emma nodded. 'And took away all the EpiPens. Someone wanted him to go into shock and not be able to treat himself.' She shuddered, suddenly feeling sick.

Tears had filled Natasha's eyes again. 'Who would do something so horrible?' she asked.

Emma braced herself. 'You have a pretty big motive, as well as the means and opportunity.'

There was a silence. As it dragged on, Emma looked up to find

Natasha staring at her.

'You think I killed him?'

Emma frowned. 'No, not really, but if I'm going down that road, believe me, Burton and Shepherd will do the same. They will find out about you and Travers, and it's much better that you tell them what you know before someone else tells them.'

'Where would I get peanut oil?' Natasha snapped.

Emma looked at her steadily, then shrugged. 'I'm sure you can find it easily on the internet or a health food shop or something.'

Natasha took a deep breath and sighed. 'I was angry and I wanted to hurt him, but I'd never have killed him.' She clasped Emma's hand. 'Please, you have to believe me.'

Emma looked at her. 'Where were you the day he died?' she asked.

Natasha pushed herself off the bench and began pacing in front of Emma, counting each point on her fingers. 'I went to college at nine o'clock. I had dance classes all morning and then in the afternoon I went to the library to finish an essay for English lit.' She ran a hand through her hair. 'I went to see Mr Dickens to hand it in and that must have been about three thirty because I had to wait for him to come out of a lesson.' She stopped walking and frowned.

'What?' Emma asked.

'Actually, I thought he'd be in class, but he came along the corridor and saw me waiting. He said he'd had to pop out and leave the class, but he took my essay and said he'd get it back to me soon.'

Emma nodded. 'And then?'

Natasha began pacing again. 'Then from four o'clock until about five thirty, I had rehearsals. Jules came to pick me up after that.'

'What time did she pick you up?'

'She came straight from work.' Natasha frowned. 'I didn't even see Travers that day. Plus, I wasn't the only person on campus with an axe to grind.'

'What do you mean?'

'Tara Wallis, you saw her yesterday in my dancing group.' Emma winced and nodded. 'I was going up to Travers' office to see him last week and I heard raised voices. There wasn't anyone around, but I hid round the corner from his office. The door flew open so hard it hit the wall and I peeped to see who it was. She was standing in the doorway and she yelled at him: "I'll make you sorry for what you've done. You'll regret this."'

'What do you think she was talking about? Was he sleeping with her as well?'

Natasha shook her head. 'No, he would never do that. When I asked Travers about it, he said it was nothing, said they'd been working on a scene, but he was having a larger vodka than usual and his hands were shaking.'

'Drinking vodka in the middle of the day?' Emma asked, raising an eyebrow. 'When anyone could have seen him?'

Natasha nodded. 'I was about to lay into him about it,' she said, 'but his expression stopped me. He looked...' she paused '...worried.'

'Worried?' Emma asked.

Natasha shook her head. 'No, I'm wrong. It wasn't worried; it was more scared.' She paused. 'Do you think Tara had something to do with his murder?'

Emma smiled grimly. 'I'm sure I can find out.'

Chapter 18

An hour later, Emma was knocking on Sarah McGovern's front door. The woman had given permission for Emma's tribute piece and seemed pleased to see her.

'I hope you don't mind doing this,' Emma said. 'We like to celebrate someone's achievements and the police said you were happy to speak to me.'

Sarah nodded. 'It's so nice to have someone who wants to talk about him as a person,' she said, leading the way into an immaculately tidy front room. The sofa was so hard that the cushion barely moved when Emma sat on it. Not a room designed for slumping comfortably. Emma politely declined coffee and Sarah perched on a chair opposite her.

'So, what do you want to know?' she asked, clasping her hands.

'I know it's hard to talk about your loved one at a time like this,' Emma said, bringing in her caring and concerned act, 'but as your husband was well-known locally, we wanted to do a feature about him and his career. The drama school has given me some comments, but I wanted to find out more about his career, y'know, and his latest acting work, as well as his time as a teacher.'

Sarah stared into space for a moment, as if thinking of the best description. 'He's difficult to put into words,' she said, which Emma thought was an odd turn of phrase. 'He was all about work, really. All he wanted to do was act.'

'Addicted to the footlights?' Emma asked with a smile.

'More the cameras. TV was his first love.'

'He looks like he's spent more time on the stage than anything else,' Emma said. She pointed to a photograph hanging near a large mirror, showing Travers mid-scene on a theatre stage. There was also a very dated cast photograph from *Our Friends*. 'What was he working on most recently?'

Sarah sighed. 'He's been in a few local plays in the last couple of years, just small parts. There just weren't the TV opportunities that there used to be for him. He'd been spending so much time teaching and rehearsing that he hadn't had time to take on anything major.'

Presumably that translated as 'couldn't get a part', Emma thought to herself.

'He was in *Our Friends* for so long it must have been difficult not to get typecast as the loveable rogue,' she said.

'That can be a real risk,' Sarah said seriously, 'particularly when you're so good at portraying that role.'

Emma nodded as she scribbled in her notebook. 'Did he have a favourite play or programme he was in?'

Sarah frowned for a moment, then said, '*Our Friends* was close to the top of the list, but I think his part in *Hamlet* was his favourite.'

Emma tried not to smile at the reference. 'He was an actor in the "play within a play", wasn't he?' she asked. It was one of the most minor parts of the play, if her memory served her correctly.

Sarah nodded earnestly. 'He was also understudy to one of the main parts, but the actor was always available so he didn't get to step up. It was a shame because he spent ages learning all his lines. He'd have been playing opposite a really famous actor from the telly, but he never really saw him.' She fell silent, as if she was remembering her husband's disappointment.

'What was he in most recently?' Emma asked.

Sarah smiled. 'He was in a production of *An Inspector Calls* for a local theatre company. It wasn't a big part, but I think his name added a bit of kudos to the posters.' She spoke the words proudly, but Emma had a feeling she was quoting Travers. She'd met a few of the local actors before and they wouldn't have been happy having someone in the cast with a head as big as his.

Sarah fell silent and looked at Emma expectantly. Emma scrabbled around her brain for another question.

'Did he enjoy working at the drama school?' she asked.

'Oh yes,' said Sarah, nodding emphatically. 'He loved being able to give something back to his old school, sharing his knowledge and experience with the youngsters. "Paying it forward," he always used to say. He said that it was good for the kids to see that even though acting was a tough gig to get into, someone from Allensbury could do it if they were prepared to work hard.'

'Did he have any favourite students? Anyone he thought could really make it?' Emma asked, internally rolling her eyes at Travers' clearly high opinion of himself. She looked up from her notebook just in time to see a shadow pass over Sarah's face. Then it cleared and she smiled.

'No one in particular. He didn't think it was right to play favourites with the students. I think he saw a lot of talent but he said they needed a lot of improvement. He was just the person to draw it out of them.'

Emma smiled. 'Some teachers just have the knack of inspiring students, don't they?' she said. Sarah nodded proudly, and Emma took a punt.

'It was such a shame how he died,' she said. 'The police told me it was anaphylactic shock. Was he allergic to something?'

Sarah nodded. 'Peanuts,' she said. Her eyes filled with tears. 'I don't know how it could have happened because he always carried EpiPens everywhere with him.'

'And he didn't have any with him?' Emma asked, feigning shock. 'Could someone have taken them from him?'

But she realised she'd pushed it too far when Sarah's face closed down.

'I don't want to talk about it,' she said. 'I want people to remember my husband for who he was and what he did; to remember him as a talented actor and a man who did a lot for the community, rather than for the way he died.' She got to her feet and started ushering Emma out. 'I'm sorry, but we'll have to leave it there. I have things to get on with.'

As the front door closed behind Emma, she looked down at her notebook. It was no surprise that Sarah knew about her husband's peanut allergy, but why had she clammed up when Emma asked about the pens being removed? Did that mean that Sarah was involved? Did she know about the affair with Natasha and decide to get even?

Whatever it was, she was going to need some help to put it together.

***

Dan answered his phone on the second ring.

'Em?' he asked. 'Where are you? You've been ages. Are you still with Natasha?'

'Sorry,' Emma said, wriggling in her car seat, trying to get comfortable. She'd parked her car around the corner from the McGoverns' house and hoped Sarah wouldn't leave and see her. 'Suzy from the police press office called to say that Sarah McGovern was happy to talk, so I came straight here.' She heard Dan take a deep breath.

'How was she?' he asked.

Emma shrugged. 'As you'd expect. Visibly upset but happy to talk about his career and contribution to the community.'

Dan snorted. 'I'm not sure that sleeping with your students is considered a contribution to the community,' he said.

Emma ignored him. 'What was interesting though,' she said, 'is that when I asked if someone had taken his EpiPens away, she clammed up and said she had nothing more to say.'

Dan was silent for a moment. 'What are you reading into that?' he asked.

Emma rubbed her nose. 'Who is better placed to raid his coat and bag and take the pens away?'

'You think she made sure he couldn't treat himself?' Dan asked, sounding sceptical. 'She also put the peanut oil in the vodka? She'd need to have been able to get into his office on campus.'

'She could have had a spare key cut or—'

'Just happened to find the door unlocked?'

'Natasha said he sometimes forgot to lock it.'

'It sounds like you're grasping at straws a bit,' Dan said. He was silent for a moment and then asked, 'How did you get on with Natasha?'

Emma gave him a precis of the discussion.

There was another silence on the other end of the line. 'Dan? Are you still there?' Emma demanded.

When Dan spoke, he sounded hesitant. 'So, by her own admission, she was on campus at the time that he died?'

'I don't know an exact time of death, but he was last seen at about five thirty,' Emma said.

'And she didn't say exactly what time she left?' Dan asked.

Emma frowned. 'No, she just said her sister picked her up after she finished work. You think she killed him?' she asked.

'I'm not saying that, as such,' Dan said, his voice fading slightly. 'Hang on,' he said. 'I'm going outside so I can talk to you properly.' She heard footsteps clumping downstairs. A door opened and closed. 'That's better,' Dan said. 'Can you hear me?'

'Yes,' Emma said. 'Why do you think she did it?'

Dan sighed. 'I'm sure you've worked out that she had a powerful motive, given that he'd made that sex tape, claimed to have deleted it and then let someone else get hold of it.'

'That's what I said to her,' Emma said. 'I told her she has to tell Burton about the tape and the vodka before anyone else does.' She paused. 'But what about this Tara woman?'

Dan snorted. 'That's another thing,' he said. 'She's also diverted you away from herself by suggesting an alternative, who may well have nothing to do with it.'

'You think I shouldn't follow up with Tara?' Emma asked. She could hear a rustle as if Dan was shaking his head.

'I don't think it's sensible to go in yet,' Dan said. 'You've already said you don't know that she's involved in this at all, apart from what Natasha has told you. From where I'm standing, she has more motive than anyone else and a reason to lie about it.' He paused. 'Come back to the office. We can work out our next steps.' When Emma said nothing, Dan said, 'Why would Tara answer your questions, anyway? She doesn't know you from Adam.'

Grudgingly, Emma agreed to return to the office, said goodbye and hung up the phone. Putting the key into the ignition, she fired up the engine. She hated it when Dan was right.

Chapter 19

When Emma returned to the office, Dan looked up as she dumped her bag on the floor beside her chair. He raised his eyebrows and she frowned.

'What?'

He grinned. 'I'm surprised you've come straight back. I was sure you'd go off and try to find Tara.'

Emma glared at him. 'I said I was coming back, didn't I?'

Dan pulled a disbelieving face. 'Since when have you ever listened to my advice?'

Emma knew he was deliberately goading her, but couldn't help firing up. 'I always listen to what you say, even if I don't agree with you and—'

Dan laughed and prodded her in the ribs. 'I'm only teasing.'

Emma tried to glare at him but he fluttered his eye lashes and she started to laugh.

'What did you want to talk to me about?' she asked.

Dan frowned. 'What?'

'You texted me the other day and said you wanted to talk.'

'Oh, yeah that. Well,' he glanced around, 'this isn't the best place, but what I was going to ask was—'

'Hey, you're back,' Ed called as he walked back to his desk near Emma and Dan's. He grinned at Dan. 'You owe me a fiver.'

Emma looked from one to the other. 'You were taking bets on me?'

Dan nodded. 'I was so sure you'd ignore me. I'll have to give you it later, mate,' he said to Ed, who rolled his eyes.

'Story of my life,' he said, grinning.

Emma glared at him. 'Well, you can use it to buy me a drink.' Ed pulled a shocked face and then winked at her with a cheeky grin.

'What did you find out from Travers' wife?' he asked, still standing looking at Emma across the bank of desks.

Emma recounted her conversation with Sarah McGovern.

'*An Inspector Calls*?' Dan asked, frowning. 'Was that the one we saw in Tildon a couple of months ago?'

Emma nodded. 'Well, I saw the play; you fell asleep.'

Ed laughed.

Dan looked shamefaced. 'It was really warm in there and those seats are too comfy.'

Emma shook her head. 'I'm surprised I didn't remember Travers' name from the cast list. It's quite distinctive, isn't it?'

'Is he a regular member of the cast?' Ed asked, reaching for his tea mug and looking disappointed when he found it empty.

'I don't know, but I know who will.' Emma turned and looked over towards the corner of the office. 'Oh damn it, Malcolm's not here.'

'Did someone call?'

Emma started as Malcolm Treadwell, the newspaper's arts correspondent, appeared behind her. 'At your service,' he said, his deep, smooth voice sounding fresh out of a play at the Royal Shakespeare Theatre. He made a mock courtly bow to Emma and she laughed.

'Speak of the devil and he appears,' Dan said.

'Now be careful, Ed; I could take offence at that,' Malcolm said.

Dan and Ed looked at each other and sniggered. Malcolm was eccentric and never seemed able to tell them apart, despite them bearing no resemblance to one another.

'It's like those two chaps on TV,' he'd once told Dan while halfway through his third sherry at a work Christmas party. 'They always appear as a pair and I never know who is who.'

But now Malcolm was staring at Emma.

'What can I do for you?' he asked.

Emma turned and sat on the edge of her desk, facing Malcolm.

'What do you know about Travers McGovern?' she asked.

Malcolm frowned and stroked his beard. 'He's dead,' he pointed out.

Emma sighed. 'Before that, Malcolm. He was involved in local theatre, wasn't he?'

Malcolm rolled his eyes. 'He had a few bit parts, sweetie, nothing major.'

'He was working down at The Regency in Tildon recently, wasn't he?'

Malcolm frowned, then held up a forefinger. 'Wait here,' he said and walked away across the office.

'Is he coming back?' Ed asked, watching the arts reporter.

'I hope so,' Emma said, standing up and turning around to watch Malcolm go. She was right. The arts reporter ran a finger through the pile of theatre programmes on the shelf above his desk. He found the one he wanted and returned across the office, waving it in the air.

'Here you go, *An Inspector Calls*. I knew I'd seen him recently.' He beamed as he handed Emma the programme.

She flipped through the pages and found the cast list. Her eye had to run a long way down it before she found Travers' name.

'The butler,' she said, holding up the page for Dan to see.

He laughed. 'I'm not surprised he wasn't boasting about that one. A bit of a comedown for him, wouldn't you think?'

Malcolm was shaking his head. 'I suspect he'd have been more vocal if he'd got the part he'd auditioned for,' he said with a smug grin.

'What did he go for?' Emma asked.

'Inspector Goole,' came the reply.

'The lead role?' Emma asked. 'And he didn't get it?'

Malcolm shook his head. 'No, it went to Neville Shuster. He's a stalwart of the company, leads on everything. A very talented actor.' He grinned smugly, as if he was barely containing a secret.

Emma eyed him. 'I'm guessing there's something more you have to tell us,' she said, making a rolling motion with her hand to tell Malcolm to speed up.

'Well,' Malcolm leaned in and lowered his voice, 'the word is that Travers and Neville did not get on. Neville considered him a bit of a

Johnny-come-lately, who thought he could just waltz into the company and take the best roles.'

'But he didn't?' Dan asked.

Malcolm shook his head. 'I've heard they butted heads a lot during rehearsal because Travers was determined to get the top job. But, when push came to shove, the director preferred Neville. Of course, there was a reason it was more competitive this time.'

'Why?' Dan asked.

'For the first time, the Tildon Players are taking a show on the road, so to speak. They're off on tour around some theatres in Kent. It might not sound much to you, but it's a big deal for them,' Malcolm said, looking round at Emma, Dan and Ed, who were all hanging on his every word. 'Bigger audiences and better theatres. You never know who might be watching or what opportunities could come your way.'

'Clearly Travers didn't go off on tour,' Ed said.

'Neither did Neville Shuster,' Malcolm said, another sly grin sliding across his face.

Emma stared at him. 'But Neville was in the lead role. Why didn't he go?'

'Travers got him dropped,' Malcolm said.

'Why? What had he done?' Emma demanded.

'Inappropriate behaviour with a younger female actor.' He grinned salaciously as Emma's eyes widened. 'They've suspended him while they investigate, but you know what happens to actors who have that allegation hanging over them.'

'What did the woman say?' Dan asked.

Malcolm shook his head. 'Apparently she denies everything, says nothing happened. She seemed quite affronted that anyone would suggest it.'

'And no one believes her?' Ed asked.

'They think he's frightened her into keeping quiet. Neville swears it's all nonsense, but people say there's no smoke without fire.'

Emma frowned. 'What made Neville think that the allegation came from Travers?'

Malcolm shrugged. 'I think it was the timing. They'd just found out who was going to be going on the tour and next thing Neville is suspended. Travers denied any knowledge of the allegations, but Neville blamed him.'

'What did he do?' Dan said.

'He punched Travers in the face right in the middle of rehearsal,' Malcolm said, clearly relishing the scandal. 'Neville yelled Travers had ruined his life and his future career, and swore he'd get his revenge. Very theatrical, don't you think?' He grinned.

Dan turned to look at Emma. She was staring off into the distance, head tilted to one side.

'What is it?' he asked.

'He said he was going to get revenge. What if he knew about Travers and Natasha and was going to tell everyone about their relationship?'

Dan nodded. 'The irony can't have escaped him that Travers was doing exactly the same as he'd accused Neville of.'

Emma picked up a pen from her desk and spun it in her fingers. 'We need to ask him,' she said.

'Do you think he could be the blackmailer?' Dan asked.

Emma shook her head. 'How would he have got the video? It's not like Travers would give it to him. But he might know something.' She looked at Malcolm. 'Mal, would you be able to put me in touch with Neville?'

Malcolm grinned. 'Allow me to make some calls and I'll get back to you.'

Chapter 20

Burton was contemplating the bulky pile of witness statements on her desk. A cheerful uniformed sergeant had plonked them down in front of her, proclaiming that his team had now finished, but if she needed anything else to 'just holler'. There was a light cough and she looked up to see Shepherd leaning in her doorway, notebook in hand.

'That should keep you busy,' he remarked with a grin, nodding towards the statements.

Burton snorted.

'They've done a thorough job,' Shepherd said. He laughed as Burton turned pleading eyes on him. 'OK, I'll take half and you take half,' he said, attempting to create two equal-sized piles of paper. Burton accepted hers and picked up the first one. She glanced up, saw a detective constable passing, pulling on a jacket, and shouted to him. He stuck his head round the door.

'Where are you going?' she asked.

The man looked surprised. The boss didn't normally keep such a close eye. 'I was going next door for a coffee,' he said.

'I was hoping you were going to say that,' Burton said. 'Can you grab one for us as well?'

The man grinned. Burton with a coffee was much nicer than Burton without, so he took the orders and disappeared.

'I thought you were going to cheat and delegate some of your statements,' Shepherd said with a grin.

Burton laughed. 'As if I would shirk my duties,' she said. 'The rest of the team is up to their eyes.'

Silence descended on the room as they both delved into the stacks of paper in front of them. The coffees arrived and thanks issued, but with eyes barely raised from the statements.

Then Burton gave a sharp intake of breath and Shepherd looked up. 'Got something?' he asked.

She nodded. 'I think I might have.' She paused, eyes scanning down the page.

Shepherd sat patiently for a minute or two and then asked, 'Well?'

Burton looked up at him. 'David Dickens, teacher of English Literature—'

'They have something as bland as that at a dance school?' Shepherd interrupted.

Burton shrugged. 'Maybe it helps them interpret the plays and stuff they do. Anyway,' she continued, 'he said that when he was coming into work one morning last week, he can't remember exactly but thinks it might have been Friday—'

'So three days before Travers' murder,' Shepherd interrupted.

Burton nodded. 'Mr Dickens says he saw Travers McGovern having a stand-up row with a student. Apparently, it started in the car park behind the college and then continued right the way through the building and up to Travers' office.'

'Did no one else notice?' Shepherd asked, eyebrows raised.

Burton shook her head. 'Apparently it was early in the day, about eight o'clock in the morning. Mr Dickens said he was in early to mark some essays.'

'He didn't fancy doing that at home?'

Burton scanned the statement again and then laughed. 'He says breakfast time at home with three small children is an incentive to head into work early.'

'Someone else shirking their duties?' Shepherd asked with a laugh.

Burton smiled. 'No, he says he does school pickup and bath-time.' She paused. 'I don't know which one is worst.'

Shepherd laughed. 'I thought your two girls were really well-behaved when I met them.'

'Yes, and it took a lot of threats and bribery to get them to behave for Uncle Mark,' Burton said. 'Actually, I'm being unfair. They're usually very good, but when they're not, it's a nightmare.'

'So, Mr Dickens escapes the breakfast melee and heads into work early,' Shepherd said.

Burton's eyes scanned down the statement. 'He hears shouting in the car park, but thinks nothing of it initially. Then from the mezzanine overlooking the atrium, as he's heading for the staff room, the shouting gets louder. He hangs around and looks over the railings. Travers McGovern marches across the atrium, heading for the stairs, pursued by a man who he recognises as a student.'

'Could he hear what they were saying?'

'He wasn't a hundred percent sure, but he thought he heard the student say, "You need to effing leave her alone—"'

'Effing?' Shepherd asked, a smile pulling at the corners of his mouth.

Burton held up the statement, which was clearly taken down verbatim, and pointed to the word. 'Exactly what Mr Dickens says: "You need to effing leave her alone and let her get on with it". Travers McGovern replied, "You don't know what you're talking about," and then the student said, "If you mess her up, and mess our show up, then I'll finish you."'

Shepherd raised an eyebrow. 'And?'

'He heard no more because Travers went into his office and tried to close the door, but the student followed him. The door slammed and he could hear them shouting but didn't think it was right to eavesdrop.'

Shepherd sighed. 'Typical. Did he see Travers again that day?'

'Yes, they had an all-staff meeting later in the morning and when he asked Travers if he was OK, he was told everything was fine. Clearly Travers hadn't known that anyone had overheard the argument.'

Shepherd leaned back in his chair and crossed his legs, one ankle resting on the opposite knee. 'That argument suggests that someone else knew about Travers and Natasha's relationship.'

Burton scratched her chin. 'And we need to find out who that was.' She stood up. 'Mr Dickens doesn't name the student in the statement, but maybe he'll be more forthcoming in person.'

Picking up her handbag, she carefully tucked the statement inside. 'Let's head back to the dance school and see if we can find out.'

***

David Dickens looked surprised when he found Burton and Shepherd being shown into the silent staff room, where he sat enjoying a coffee and reading a book.

'But I gave your uniformed officers my statement the other day,' he blustered, attempting to rise from the low wooden-framed armchair he was sitting in. 'I don't know anything else.'

But Burton waved for him to stay where he was, as she and Shepherd took seats opposite him.

'We just have a few follow-up questions,' she said. 'You told the officers that you overheard a row between Travers McGovern and a student on Friday last week.'

Dickens nodded. 'Yes, I did. I was a bit surprised actually, because I've not seen Travers in college that early before. He usually swans in at ten o'clock, just in time for his first workshop.'

'Remind me where you overheard the argument,' Shepherd said.

'I was walking in from the car park at the back of the college and I could hear voices outside behind me,' Mr Dickens said.

'What were they saying?' Burton asked.

'I couldn't hear at first because they were too far away, but as I went upstairs, they came into the atrium.'

'And the student's name was?' Shepherd asked, pulling out a notebook and pen.

Mr Dickens pursed his lips. 'I'm not a gossip,' he said, folding his arms.

'It's not gossip when you're involved in a murder inquiry,' Burton snapped.

Mr Dickens held out for another couple of seconds but could not withstand Burton's glare.

'Dominic Randall,' he said. 'I was a bit surprised to see them together because I didn't think Dominic took any of Travers' classes.'

'And they were shouting about a woman?' Shepherd asked.

Mr Dickens sighed. 'This is all in the statement I gave to your other officer.'

'Indulge me,' Shepherd said, with a smile that didn't reach his eyes. 'Dominic was telling Travers to leave someone alone, a woman.'

'But Travers was refusing?' Shepherd asked, flicking to a new page in his notebook.

Mr Dickens shrugged. 'Like I told your officers, I only caught snippets as they came up the stairs, but once they were in Travers' office, I didn't listen at the keyhole,' he added primly.

Burton stared at him thoughtfully, making Dickens squirm in his seat.

'Do you know who they were talking about?' she asked.

Dickens shook his head.

'Thank you, Mr Dickens. You've been really helpful,' Burton said, getting to her feet.

The man's shoulders visibly relaxed. 'Well, I'm always happy to help.'

'We'd like to have a word with Dominic Randall,' Burton said. 'Where might we find him?'

'The office will give you his timetable,' Mr Dickens said.

As they left the room, Burton paused at the door. 'If you overhear anything else, you will let us know, won't you?'

Mr Dickens nodded, but she was pleased to see him squirm again as she turned away.

Chapter 21

Burton and Shepherd tracked down Dominic Randall in a dance studio on the first floor, where he was performing some complicated stretches.

'We don't do those after rugby,' Shepherd remarked.

Dominic gave him a slightly disdainful look. 'Dance training is a bit more sophisticated than that,' he said, in a voice that had clearly had elocution lessons. But a slight Allensbury twang remained.

'We need to talk,' Burton said. She was pleased to see that the request discomforted the dancer.

'Why? I don't know anything about Travers McGovern,' Dominic said, pulling at the hem of his T-shirt and shifting his weight from one foot to the other several times.

'You had an argument with him,' Burton said. 'A witness overheard you threaten him and now he's dead.'

Dominic folded his arms across his muscled torso. 'Who told you that?' he demanded. 'I've never argued with him.' But there was false bravado in his voice.

'We have a witness, a reliable witness,' Burton said. 'Why did you threaten him?'

When Dominic said nothing, Shepherd asked, 'You didn't like Travers McGovern, did you?'

'No.' Dominic almost spat the word. 'He was always bragging about what he'd done and sleazing over the girls.'

'Did it go any further than sleazing?' Burton asked, frowning.

Dominic shrugged, but couldn't quite meet Burton's eye.

'Who did you mean when you told him not to "mess her up" or you'd finish him?' Burton asked.

'Nobody,' Dominic said, too quickly.

'Was it Natasha?' Burton asked, tilting her head to one side, remembering the name Tony Standing had told them. Her reward came when the student looked surprised, but quickly recovered and gave a shrug only a sulky teenager could manage.

'Why would it be?' he asked, looking down at his feet.

Burton and Shepherd stayed silent, both staring at Dominic.

'Oh ... okay ... I went out with Nat for a while. It wasn't serious.' But the look in his eyes suggested otherwise.

'Has she been seeing Travers as well?' Shepherd asked. He caught Burton's eye and she frowned.

Dominic sighed heavily. 'I don't know for certain, but I suspected. Nat was screwing up the routines we were doing; something was distracting her. It's dangerous dancing when one person isn't concentrating. That's how you get hurt.' His arms flopped to his side. 'Nat wouldn't talk to me about it, so I tried Travers.' He shrugged again. 'It was obvious pretty soon that there was something going on because he was really worried when I started asking questions.'

'Did he admit they were in a relationship?' Shepherd asked.

Dominic snorted. 'I was sure it wasn't a relationship for him. You know he's married?' Burton and Shepherd nodded. 'I was worried about Nat, so I went and asked him. He tried to deny it, but I could tell he was lying. Eventually, he admitted it. Said he wouldn't give her up, even though I told him he was going to ruin her career.'

'Why didn't you tell anyone?' Burton asked. 'A student-teacher relationship is inappropriate.'

Dominic shook his head. 'There was no point. It would have been his word against mine.'

'Natasha wouldn't have spoken up?' Burton asked.

Dominic gave her a scornful look. 'She's hardly going to admit it, is she?'

'Where were you at five thirty on the night Travers McGovern died?'

Shepherd asked.

'I was here.' Dominic gestured around the room they were standing in.

Shepherd looked around at the mirrored walls. 'Anyone else with you?'

Dominic shook his head, eyes cast down to the floor. 'No, just me. I'd had an awful rehearsal during the day and I wanted to be sure of my steps, so I came here to practise.'

'Did anyone see you leave?' Burton asked.

Dominic shrugged. 'I don't know. I didn't talk to anyone, but they might have seen me. There were still people around. Rehearsals were still going on.'

'What time did you leave?' Shepherd asked.

Dominic thought for a moment. 'It was just after six o'clock, I think. My mum sent a text asking what I was making for dinner. I'd forgotten it was my turn, so I packed up and hopped to it. She's been working long hours recently, so I wanted to have it on the table when she got home.'

Burton frowned. 'Very commendable. Did you see anyone else around?

Dominic looked at the floor, reluctant to say anything, but then mumbled 'Natasha.'

'What's Natasha's surname?' Burton demanded, trying to control her irritation.

Dominic looked like he was going to refuse to speak, but then said, 'Kent.'

Burton raised an eyebrow. 'Where was she?' she asked.

Dominic shifted his weight from one foot to the other. 'She was standing on the mezzanine above the atrium. She looked like she was texting or something.'

'Near Travers McGovern's office?' Shepherd asked with a sideways glance at Burton, taking in Dominic's fidgeting.

'It's near a lot of teachers' offices,' Dominic said quickly, clearly realising that he'd dropped Natasha into trouble. 'She could have been on her way to see any of them.'

Shepherd continued to scribble in his notebook. 'Did you see which way she went after texting?' he asked.

Dominic shook his head. 'No, I left college straight after that, so I didn't see what she did next.'

Shepherd nodded and looked at Burton, who was staring silently at Dominic. The dancer fidgeted and looked down at the studio floor, refusing to meet her eye.

Then, after a few moments, he looked up. 'Is there anything else?' he asked.

Before Burton could respond, the studio doors clattered open and a group of women in ballet clothes arrived. They halted at the sight of Dominic and the detectives, collided with each other, and giggled. One stepped forward.

'We've got this room booked now,' she said, almost apologetically.

Dominic packed his bag, glad that his ordeal seemed to be over.

'We may need to speak to you again,' Burton warned him. 'Be somewhere that we can find you.'

Chapter 22

Malcolm worked at double speed and on Saturday morning Emma and Dan were heading to Neville Shuster's house. Weekend traffic around Tildon was a nightmare as ever, and it was almost four o'clock by the time they parked outside Neville's house in a leafy suburb.

'Acting must be quite lucrative,' Dan said as he got out of the car.

Emma nodded. 'It's massive,' she said, looking up at the detached four-bedroomed house with a garden all around it and a brand-new BMW in the driveway.

'I'm really surprised he agreed to meet us at home,' Dan said as they walked towards the house.

'I doubt he'd want to discuss this out in the open,' Emma replied, reaching up to press the doorbell. It surprised her to hear a standard doorbell chime. She'd been expecting something a little more theatrical. The door opened and Neville Shuster stood looking at them. When Emma introduced Dan and herself, Neville stepped back to allow them inside.

He led the way into a sumptuous living room. The actor was an imposing figure, over six feet tall and broad shouldered. He ruffled a hand through blond curly hair as he perched on an armchair and gestured for Dan and Emma to sit on a sofa.

'Malcolm said you wanted to talk to me about Travers McGovern,' he said, his jaw clenching as he said the name.

'You know he's dead?' Emma asked.

Neville nodded. 'I saw it in the paper. Couldn't happen to a nicer bloke,' he added.

Emma winced. No one deserved to die the way Travers had. 'Malcolm told us you and Travers didn't get on.'

Neville snorted. 'That's an understatement.'

'How well did you know him?'

Neville shrugged. 'Enough to know that he wasn't as good an actor as he thought he was.'

Dan leaned forward. 'Travers wasn't a usual member of the cast, was he? Do you often get guest actors when you're doing plays?' he asked.

Neville puffed out his cheeks. 'It only happens when an arrogant bastard lies and flatters his way in,' he said. 'He thought he could just barge into the company and take over.'

'Malcolm said he tried to take the lead part, but that you got it.' Dan paused. 'But then you got dropped when the play went on tour.'

Neville took a deep breath and groaned. 'Gossip spreads easily, doesn't it? You obviously already know why I got dropped.'

'Is it true?' Emma asked.

'No, it bloody well isn't. Camilla and I have never even been alone together. She's tried to tell everyone that, but no one will listen to her. They think I've threatened her into denying it. She's utterly humiliated and ruined.'

Emma held Neville's gaze. 'You think it was Travers who made up the story?'

'Of course it was,' Neville snapped. 'Who else? He was out to get me from the start, sulking when he didn't get the lead role. He thought that if he discredited me, he'd get to go on tour.'

'But he didn't?'

Neville shook his head. 'The director decided we didn't need the butler character anymore. Travers didn't get his way, so he's ruined my life and my future career at the same time.'

'How do you mean?' Dan asked. 'If you did nothing wrong, an investigation will clear you, won't it?'

Neville gave a short laugh. 'No matter what any investigation finds, my career is over. It's all over social media. The usual "no smoke without fire" brigade is out in force,' he mimicked in a whiney voice.

'What's worse is that I can't do anything about it. If you search for my name now, all you get is allegations of sexual misconduct and not the years I've put into acting. Any director will look at that first and won't take me on.' He sighed heavily. 'He got his revenge beautifully, don't you think? I'll never work in acting again and probably not anywhere else either.'

Emma watched as Neville hung his head and wiped at his eyes. She felt awful, but knew she had to go ahead.

'Where were you on Monday night?' Emma asked.

Neville said nothing.

'Did you go to the school?' she pressed.

Neville looked up and saw the expression on Emma's face. 'Hey, wait a minute. You think I killed him?' he asked, looking startled. 'No, no, I didn't.'

'You've admitted you hated him,' Emma said. 'You had a motive to do it.'

'Did you know about his peanut allergy?' Dan put in. Neville looked at him, bewildered.

'What? Of course I did. Everyone in the cast and the whole bloody theatre knew; he made such a song and dance about it. I thought he was being a drama queen, but maybe...' Neville's voice trailed away as he realised how serious the situation had been.

'So you were at the college on Monday?' Emma asked. When Neville said nothing, she continued, 'Do you know Natasha Kent?'

That got a reaction. 'Why do you ask that?'

'Do you know her?' Emma insisted.

Neville nodded. 'I met her through a variety performance we did at the Regency last year. I taught a couple of classes at the college too. She wasn't in class, but I saw her around.' He stopped, clenching his jaw as if trying to stop words getting out.

Dan leaned forward, his elbows on his knees. 'You were trying to get your revenge on Travers, weren't you?' he asked.

'What do you mean?' Neville asked, shifting in his seat.

'You were going to ruin his career, weren't you? You knew about Natasha and him being in a relationship.'

Neville growled. 'I went to have it out with him last week and I saw them together. It made me so angry I just wanted to—' He broke off.

'Kill him?' Dan put in.

'It's so fucking ironic,' Neville spat. 'He was the one abusing younger women, risking someone else's career. I had to stop him.'

'You were protecting Natasha?' Emma asked, giving him a dubious look.

'I tried,' Neville said. 'She's an excellent dancer, I mean superb, and could have been a prima ballerina in any company she wanted. When I saw her at the school, I tried to talk to her about Travers.'

'What did she say?'

Neville shook his head. 'She brushed me off, said I didn't know what I was talking about. When I pushed her and said I'd seen them together, she just sighed and said, "Neville, it's all in hand, don't worry." Then she smiled, patted me on the arm and walked away.'

'It's all in hand?' Emma repeated. 'What did she mean by that?'

Neville shrugged. 'No idea, but next thing he's dead and...' He trailed away.

Emma sat back in her chair and looked at Dan.

'But you went to the school on Monday night, didn't you?' Dan asked, picking up the conversational baton.

'Yes. I went to have it out with him once and for all; threatened to out him, get photos and tell everyone what he was doing.'

'What did he say?' Emma asked, leaning forward.

'He freaked out, started yelling at me, saying he wouldn't let me ruin his life or hers. Like he hadn't already humiliated Camilla.' Neville widened his eyes and shrugged. 'He was demanding to know how I'd got the video, but I said I knew nothing about a video. I genuinely had no idea what he was talking about. Then he got a text message and literally tried to throw me out of his office.' Neville gestured his own body. 'He didn't get very far.'

Emma stifled a grin. 'Did he say who the text was from?'

Neville shook his head. 'No, but it freaked him out, even more than he already was. He said I had to leave, so I did.'

'Did you see anyone else near his office?' Dan asked.

'As I was coming down the stairs, I bumped into a guy hurrying up. He was a big lad, dark hair.'

'Did he go into Travers' office?'

Neville shrugged. 'I looked back when I got to the bottom of the stairs and he'd disappeared, so I don't know.' He took a deep breath. 'But whoever sent him that text clearly frightened him a lot more than I did.'

Chapter 23

Unable to get an appointment with Sally-Anne the previous day, Burton and Shepherd returned to the dance school on Saturday. The campus was as busy as a weekday with school-age children and their parents arriving in a flood, along with older students. The principal stood in the middle of the atrium, greeting parents and children, some by name, and waving them towards their various activities.

'Busy today,' Shepherd said when the atrium finally cleared and Sally-Anne was walking towards them, pushing her hair back from her face.

She smiled. 'It's never quiet,' she said. 'We have the children's acting and dance classes as usual, but also extra rehearsals for the older students ahead of the showcase.' She looked down the corridor to where a group of giggling ten-year-old ballet dancers were heading into a studio. 'It's lovely to see such enthusiasm.' She looked at Burton and Shepherd. 'I'm guessing this isn't a social call. Shall we go up to my office?' she asked.

When they were all seated, she clasped her hands and leaned forward on the desk.

'How can I help?'

'We need to speak to one of your students,' Burton began. 'Natasha Kent.'

Sally-Anne raised her eyebrows. 'Natasha? Why would you want to speak to her?'

'We believe she was in a relationship with Travers McGovern,' Burton said bluntly.

'What?' Sally-Anne demanded. 'Who told you that?'

'Another student,' Burton said.

Sally-Anne ran a hand through her hair. 'I was hoping no one else knew,' she said.

Burton's eyebrows shot up. 'You knew about it?' she demanded.

Sally-Anne nodded, her cheeks reddening. 'I had my suspicions. I'd seen them together a few times on campus, not doing anything,' she said, 'just hanging out together.'

'What did you do?' Burton asked.

'I spoke to Travers. He denied it all, of course. I asked around a few other staff, but no one else knew anything, so I let it go.'

'Surely a relationship between a teacher and a student is a serious breach of your safeguarding. Did the board of governors not insist on an investigation?' Burton asked, surprised.

Sally-Anne said nothing.

'You didn't tell them,' Burton concluded, glowering.

'The reputation of the school is very important to me.'

'More important than the safety of your students?' Burton asked.

Sally-Anne sighed. 'No, of course not.'

'Where were you on Monday night? What time did you leave campus?' Burton asked, glaring at the principal.

Sally-Anne looked shocked. 'You think I—'

'He was threatening your school,' Shepherd interrupted. 'Your reputation was at stake.'

'But I would never have...' Sally-Anne trailed off under Shepherd's gaze.

'What time did you leave campus?' he asked.

Running a hand through her hair, the principal frowned. 'I didn't leave until about seven thirty when the last rehearsal finished. I was supervising.' She saw the glance between Burton and Shepherd. 'I was on the ground floor and nowhere near Travers' office. I left through the back door into the car park.'

'We'll be checking that,' Shepherd said, scribbling in his notebook.

'We need to speak to Natasha now and get her side of this story,'

Burton said.

Burton looked at Shepherd as Sally-Anne tapped away at the keys on her computer.

She looked from the computer screen to the wall clock. 'She's actually on campus, teaching a Tumble Tots class right now. Shall I take you down?'

As the detectives followed her into the corridor, Shepherd said, 'Tumble Tots sounds like it should be fun.'

Sally-Anne grimaced. 'They're very cute, but they can be a bunch of little terrors when they get going.'

As they followed Sally-Anne down the corridor, Shepherd whispered to Burton, 'She knew he was having an affair with a student.'

Burton eyed Sally-Anne as she walked away. 'And she didn't launch an investigation. Travers McGovern wasn't exactly superb teacher material if he was drinking during the day and sleeping with a student.'

Shepherd nodded. 'And what would a principal concerned with the reputation of the college do if that reputation was at risk?' He paused. 'She was on campus during our time-of-death window and could easily have taken a break from rehearsal to go to see Travers.'

'Get one of the DCs to check the CCTV footage for when she left. We need footage from inside the school as well,' Burton said.

Sally-Anne had reached the end of the corridor and was looking at them expectantly. They caught her up and she led the way down the stairs.

As they headed for the door of the dance studio, Burton said quietly to Shepherd, 'We know Natasha was around college on the night Travers died. Maybe she thought he was going to leave his wife and then found out that he had no intention of doing it.'

'Woman scorned?' Shepherd asked and Burton nodded. 'If they're seeing each other, she'd know about the peanut allergy as well.'

Burton nodded grimly. 'Let's see what Natasha has to say for herself.'

***

A wall of noise hit Burton and Shepherd as they stepped into the dance studio. About thirty two- and three-year-old children were laughing, chattering and falling over as they attempted dance moves.

Among the children stood a slender woman in ballet clothes and leg warmers, giggling as much as they were. Then she clapped her hands and the children fell silent.

'OK, we're going to try some new steps today,' she said, and all the children cheered. They watched as Natasha turned to face the mirrored wall and raised her arms out to her sides to the level of her shoulders. The children all did the same, one accidentally poking the eye of the little girl standing beside him. Burton glared at Shepherd, who was fighting to hold back a smile.

'That's exactly what I would have done,' he said. 'I've always been clumsy.'

Burton snorted.

The mother of the crying girl descended to comfort her and soon order was restored. Natasha demonstrated stepping three times to the left, then performing a plié before stepping back to the starting point.

'Let's all try that together,' she said. The class performed the movement. 'And now this way,' she said, performing the movement to the right. The children mostly managed to follow and no one fell over. 'Well done,' Natasha said, turning to the class and clapping her hands, a big smile on her face. Then she spotted Sally-Anne, Burton and Shepherd and her face fell. Sally-Anne clutched Shepherd's arm as she slipped off her shoes.

'We have to protect the floor,' she said, seeing his puzzled look. Then she wove her way through the dancing toddlers to the front of the room, patting a few heads as she passed by. She whispered in Natasha's ear and the dancer's eyes widened. She whispered back and then nodded at Burton and Shepherd.

Sally-Anne returned to the detectives and slipped her feet back into her shoes.

'Natasha will finish in about ten minutes and she'll meet you at the café.'

Burton opened her mouth, but Shepherd accepted. Sally-Anne returned to her office and he led the way to the café.

'Why didn't you insist she came straight away?' Burton asked. 'What if she does a flit?'

Shepherd gave her a patient look. 'Did you see her face when she saw us? She wants to know what we know.'

Chapter 24

Shepherd's instinct proved correct. Ten minutes later, Natasha appeared, dressed in tracksuit bottoms and trainers. She had freed her tightly curled hair from its ballerina-style bun. A bulging canvas tote bag was hanging from the crook of her arm and she set it on the floor as she sat down, smiling nervously.

'Can I get you a coffee?' he asked.

Natasha shook her head and wrinkled her nose. 'No thanks, I can't stand the smell of it.' She glanced at the clock on the wall. 'I don't really have long before I have to go.' She looked from Burton to Shepherd. 'Why did you want to talk to me?'

Burton smiled. 'We need to ask you some questions about Travers McGovern,' she said.

Natasha shifted in her seat, her hands in her lap. 'Why? He was only a teacher,' she said, trying to give an unconcerned shrug, but her eyes filled with tears. She kept them from falling by looking up at the ceiling.

Shepherd pulled out his notebook and found a clean page. 'We've heard that he was more than that,' he said, clicking out the nib of his pen.

Natasha looked at him. 'Who told you that?' she asked.

'Is it true?' Shepherd asked, ignoring her question.

Natasha sighed and looked down at the table, pulling the sleeves of her jumper down over her hands. 'Do you have to write all this down?'

she asked, looking at him with pleading eyes.

'Unfortunately, yes,' Shepherd said, adding her name and the date to the top of the page.

'How long had you been seeing each other?' Burton asked.

'About six months,' Natasha said, wiping a hand across her face. 'It started when I took one of his masterclasses. I don't really do drama, but one of my friends did, so I went along with her. He said I was really talented,' she said. Seeing the look on Burton's face, she nodded. 'I know, they all say that, don't they? Sleazy casting directors, theatre managers, whoever? But he wasn't like that. When he realised I wasn't falling for it, he just laughed it off. It became our little private joke.' She sighed. 'Something like that bonds you, doesn't it?'

'Once you'd started *bonding*,' Shepherd asked, looking disapproving, 'what happened next?'

'There was a movie night on campus,' Natasha said. '*Black Swan*. It's about a dance company putting on the ballet *Swan Lake*, but it's more of a psychological thriller. Not my usual type of film, because it's quite dark and scary, but it intrigued me, because I love *Swan Lake*.'

'And Travers offered to take you?' Burton asked.

Natasha laughed. 'No, he wasn't that obvious. He just turned up, as if he was there to see the film. He asked if he could sit by me.'

'And tried to schmooze you by pretending to love the film?' Shepherd asked.

'I think he started off like that, but I shushed him when it started. The next thing he's snoring in the chair next to me.' She laughed again. 'I never let him live that down.' She sighed. 'By this point I was starting to fancy him because he wasn't acting how I'd expected. He was good-looking, but I knew he'd had a lot of women when he was in the soaps. I didn't want to be a notch on his bedpost, but he was really kind and interested in the same things as me. Once we started seeing each other, I realised I was in love with him.'

'Enough to sleep with him?' Shepherd asked.

Natasha nodded, her eyes filling with tears again.

'And you knew he was married?' Burton asked.

Natasha nodded, looking slightly embarrassed. 'I've even met his wife. She came to college once to pick him up,' she said. 'She didn't know about us; at least I'm sure she didn't.' She looked at Burton and Shepherd, suddenly anxious. 'She doesn't know, does she? That's not who told you?'

Burton shook her head. 'And the fact you met her didn't stop you from having an affair?' she asked.

Natasha looked down at her hands, still covered by her jumper. 'No. I couldn't. I was totally into him and he felt the same.'

Burton and Shepherd exchanged a look. Where had they heard that one before?

'Did he say he was going to leave his wife?' Burton asked.

Natasha nodded. 'Yes, he was just waiting for the right time to tell her and then we were going to be together.' She halted and looked down at her hands.

'You didn't think he was being honest?' Burton asked.

Natasha sighed. 'I'm not sure whether I wanted him to be, I...' She trailed off. 'I'm not sure how serious I was anymore. My dancing needs to be my priority now.'

The detectives looked at each other and then back at Natasha.

'Did you see him on the day he died?' Shepherd asked.

Natasha blinked at the sudden change of direction. 'No, I didn't,' she said, awkwardly.

'Would you usually see him?' Burton asked.

'Sometimes; I mean, not every day,' Natasha said.

Burton looked at Shepherd and saw that he looked as confused as she was.

'You didn't see him at all on the day he died? You weren't in his office at any point or didn't bump into him on campus?' she asked, gesturing around. 'It's not a big place.'

Natasha shook her head. 'No, I didn't. I had rehearsals and ballet lessons most of the day.' But she shifted awkwardly in her seat.

Burton leaned forward, resting her forearms on the table. 'What time did you leave college on that night?'

Natasha shifted in her seat. 'I left at about five thirty,' she said, but she didn't meet Burton's eye.

'What if I told you that someone said they saw you at about six o'clock, standing on the mezzanine, near Travers' office, texting?'

Natasha sniffed. 'I didn't go to Travers' office, I didn't see him and I left campus at five thirty. My sister came to pick me up. Whoever said they saw me was lying.'

Burton frowned and sat back in her seat. 'Did you know he was allergic to peanuts?' she asked.

Natasha nodded. 'I can't believe that's how he died,' she said. 'He was always so careful.'

'How did you know that's what killed him?' Burton asked.

Natasha avoided her gaze. 'I ... I must have heard someone say it,' she said, but her cheeks had flushed slightly.

'Who else knew about the allergy?' Shepherd asked.

Natasha shrugged. 'Anyone who hung out with him would know,' she said. 'He was really obsessed with it, quite rightly.' She looked down at her sleeve and rubbed at the stain. 'His wife would know,' she pointed out significantly. When neither Burton nor Shepherd replied, she said, 'What happened? Had he eaten something with peanuts in?'

There was a watchful air about Natasha that puzzled Burton. She shook her head.

'No,' she said. 'Someone added peanut oil to a bottle of vodka he kept in his desk drawer.'

Natasha's feigned look of surprise suggested that any acting classes weren't working much, Burton thought.

Shepherd narrowed his eyes as he looked up from his notebook. 'You knew he had the vodka in his desk drawer?' he asked.

Natasha nodded, looking down at her hands. 'I saw him drink it the day before he died and he was fine,' she said.

Shepherd paused, pen hovering above his notebook. 'You saw him drink the vodka the day before he died?'

The corners of Natasha's mouth pulled down. 'I'd warned him about drinking in his office,' she mumbled. 'Maybe if I'd tried harder to stop him or confiscated the bottle, this wouldn't have happened.' Tears threatened again, but she held it together.

Shepherd shook his head. 'Whoever did this would have just found another way,' he said.

Natasha took a shuddering breath and exhaled heavily. Then she checked her watch. 'Did you need anything else? I have to go. My sister is picking me up just now.'

'One more thing,' Burton asked. 'Can you think of anyone who would want to harm Travers?'

Natasha frowned. 'No, I don't think—' she began, but a voice cut across her loudly.

'Natasha? What are you doing? I've been waiting for you outside for ten minutes.' A short, dark-haired woman who resembled Natasha was marching in their direction, a set of car keys dangling from her left hand.

'Sorry, Jules. These guys are from the police; they wanted to speak to me about Travers.'

Jules waved a hand as if to sweep away the comment. 'I've called you, like, four times,' she said pointedly.

Natasha saw the look that passed between Burton and Shepherd and quickly made the introductions.

Jules stood over Natasha, a protective hand on her shoulder. 'We need to go now,' she said. 'I need to get Nat home.'

Shepherd raised his eyebrows and Burton got to her feet. Natasha followed.

'That's all we need for now,' Burton said to Natasha, handing her a business card, 'but if you think of anything else, just call us.'

Natasha nodded and Jules grabbed her bag from the floor.

'We need to go,' she said again, grabbing Natasha by the elbow and leading her away. Natasha waved goodbye to Burton and Shepherd, allowed herself to be led away. As they left, Jules asked, 'How did your rehearsal go?' They didn't hear Natasha's response, but she was nodding.

Burton sat down beside Shepherd, watching the sisters walking away. 'She already knew about the peanut oil and that the allergy killed him,' she said.

Shepherd nodded, looking down at his notebook. 'They were having an affair and he says he's going to leave his wife. Then doesn't.'

Burton rubbed her chin. 'But what's interesting is that she doesn't seem to have wanted him to. Could he have been insisting and she killed him to get him out of the way?'

Shepherd frowned. 'There's also the time discrepancy. She says she left at five thirty, but Dominic Randall says he saw her there at six o'clock. Who's telling the truth?'

'She also lied to her sister about what she was doing today,' Shepherd commented.

Burton nodded. 'I noticed that.' She exhaled heavily. 'Right, let's get back to the station. I need to have a think about what to do next.'

Chapter 25

'So, someone texted Travers and he ran straight off to see them,' Dan said as Emma drove past the sign, welcoming them back to Allensbury. 'Neville said he looked scared, but scared of what? Scared of who it was or what they might say or do? Who could that be?'

Emma shook her head. 'No idea. Also, we only have Neville Shuster's word that it happened.'

'Could it have been Natasha?' Dan asked, looking at Emma's profile.

She sighed without taking her eyes off the road. 'I suppose it could, but why would she scare him?'

'She'd scare me if she'd just found out I'd let someone else get hold of that sex tape. He must know she has a temper and that she'd be livid with him.'

'But poisoning the vodka, knowing it would kill him, just doesn't feel like a flash of anger,' Emma said. 'It's premeditated. And taking away the EpiPens is just...' She trailed away, not wanting to think of Travers McGovern's last moments.

'Cruel?' Dan asked. 'It doesn't sound like something a teenager with a history of flying off the handle would do.'

Emma frowned as she slowed down, flicked on the indicator and turned into the car park outside Dan and Ed's flat. 'Natasha also said she hadn't seen him that day.'

'She wouldn't be the first person to lie to give themselves an alibi,'

Dan pointed out, looking up at the building. 'Look, I can cancel on Ed if you want and we can spend some more time on the case,' he said, turning back to look at her.

But Emma shook her head as she pulled into a parking space. 'Ed was going on and on about the Boys' Night Out all day yesterday. I don't think he'd forgive me if I stole you away from him.'

Dan frowned. 'He has been a bit down recently.'

'He needs the cheering up only you can bring.'

'Flatterer,' Dan said with a wink.

'Go on, get out before Ed sees us and thinks I'm using my womanly wiles to tempt you away.'

Dan leaned across to give her a kiss. 'Any time you want to show me those wiles, I'm up for it.'

Emma laughed and kissed him back. He opened the car door and stepped out. Then he leaned back into the car.

'Are you going to mention Neville to Burton?'

Emma stared out of the windscreen, thinking. 'I'll call her. She needs to know to check Travers' phone for that text message that freaked him out.'

'OK, let me know how you get on, but don't you dare solve the case without me.'

Emma laughed. 'I won't.'

Dan slammed the car door and waved. As she drove away, Emma watched him in the rear-view mirror as he unlocked the door to the building and disappeared inside.

When she got home, she went straight to the kitchen and put on the kettle. She needed to think over what Neville Shuster had told them, but first she had to call Burton. She looked at her watch and saw that it was ten past six. Burton might be off duty, but she could just leave a message on her voicemail.

She went back into the living room and rifled through her handbag for her mobile.

When she looked at the screen, she saw there were four missed calls from Natasha and a voicemail. Damn it, her phone had been on silent and the messages were all sent about fifteen minutes previously.

She dialled her voicemail service and a scared voice spoke in her ear.

'Emma? It's Natasha. I've ... I've found some evidence. I know who the killer is. Call me ASAP.'

Emma dialled Natasha's number with shaking hands, but it went straight to voicemail.

Where are you? she texted.

Her message tone sounded almost immediately. *I can't talk here, but can you meet me at the benches in the park near the castle? I'm frightened.*

I'm on my way.

Emma was already halfway out the door before the message had finished sending.

***

It was quicker to get to Castle Park on foot than by car, so Emma ran through the back streets. But she had to take a longer route after finding her usual path blocked by cars queuing to get round some temporary traffic lights on one of the narrowest streets.

Panting heavily, she arrived at the top of the hill and saw the benches in front of her. There was no sign of Natasha. She slowed down as she walked across the flat area towards the meeting place, trying to get her breath back.

'Nat?' she called. 'Nat, are you here?'

She dug a hand in her bag and pulled out her phone. She dialled Natasha's number, but it rang and then went to voicemail.

'Nat? Where are you? I'm at the benches now. Are you coming?'

Still trying to catch her breath, she looked around. A rustle in the trees behind her made her jump. She squinted into the bushes and saw a canvas tote bag, lying on its side, contents dumped onto fallen leaves. She stepped forward, ducking under a low-hanging tree branch to get a better look. Then she screamed and screamed.

On the ground lay the spread-eagled body of Natasha, blood from a stomach wound soaking through her cream cotton T-shirt.

Emma staggered backwards, catching her foot on a tree root and crashing to the ground. Pain shot up her spine and made her gasp. With shaking hands, she dialled nine-nine-nine.

Chapter 26

Wrapped in a silver foil blanket, Emma sat shivering on a bench near to the white tent that hid Natasha's body. She couldn't take her eyes off it, imagining the body sprawled on the dirt and leaves. Tears were running down her face, and she wiped them away with a shaking hand.

A voice shouted, 'Emma? Emma? What's going on?'

She looked up to see Dan waving at her from the entrance to the park, where he was being held at bay by the police officer at the cordon.

'That's my girlfriend,' he told the woman, jabbing a finger towards Emma. 'I need to be there.'

The woman looked about to argue when Shepherd appeared and spoke to her. She nodded and raised the tape so Dan could get through. Shepherd tried to keep pace as Dan almost ran along the path towards Emma. As he arrived, she tried to stand up, but her legs just couldn't do it. Dan dropped onto the bench and wrapped his arms around her.

'What's happened?' he asked, peering into her face. 'Why are you in the park?'

Emma gulped in air, trying to steady herself. 'It's Natasha,' she said. 'Someone's murdered her.'

Dan stared at her. 'What?' he gasped. He looked up at Shepherd, who nodded. 'How?'

'There's loads of blood ... her stomach ... I think she's been—' Emma tried to speak, but a fresh wave of tears overwhelmed her. Dan squeezed her tighter. Emma saw another officer signal, and Shepherd excused himself.

'Just breathe,' Dan whispered. Emma hiccupped and took a deep breath. 'Why were you here?' he asked.

Emma explained about the missed call and the voicemail. 'If only my phone hadn't been on silent, I'd have got here sooner and I could have saved her.'

'You don't know that. You could have been lying there next to her,' Dan said soberly. Emma looked at him and a fresh wave of tears began. He hugged her more tightly.

'What evidence did she have?' he asked when Emma could breathe and speak again. 'She told you before that she wasn't at college when Travers died, so she can't have witnessed the murder.'

Emma nodded. 'If she'd seen that, she would have told the police.'

'What could she have found out? The police cordoned off his office after the murder, so she can't have been in there.'

'Why didn't she just go to the police?' Emma asked, tears starting afresh. Dan picked up her handbag and dug inside, producing a small packet of tissues. He pulled one out and handed it to her. He put her bag back on the ground, keeping the packet in hand.

'She trusted you,' he said. 'Maybe she wasn't sure what she had and wanted your advice before she went to the police. She knows you know Burton and Shepherd; maybe she was hoping you'd come with her.'

'Here you go,' said a voice, making them jump. Standing over them was a uniformed constable holding a takeaway cup from a local café. 'I caught them just before they closed.' She squatted down in front of them and tried to put the cup into Emma's hands, but they were shaking so badly that Dan grabbed it before it ended up on the pavement.

'Thanks,' he said.

The constable smiled. 'Hot tea with lots of sugar,' she said. 'Just what the doctor orders for shock.' She stood up. 'I'll just be over here if you need anything.' She pointed towards the tape.

'Can't we go home?' Dan asked. 'Emma needs to get somewhere warm.'

'DI Burton will want to speak to her. Shouldn't be long.'

As she turned away, Dan suddenly winced and removed his arm from around Emma.

'Ouch, they're not wrong about the contents being hot,' he said, quickly switching the cup to his other hand.

Emma reached for the cup and Dan put it into her hands. 'Careful,' he said, watching the cup shake, ready to grab it if necessary. Emma didn't take a drink – just held it.

'Someone must have overheard her when she called me,' she said, 'and followed her here.'

She tried to take a sip but decided the tea was still too hot. The heat in her hands was certainly calming the shakes.

Emma was staring down at the ground when a pair of large, very shiny leather shoes appeared in front of her. She looked up into the sympathetic face of DS Shepherd. She and Dan shuffled along the bench to make room for him. He sat down, angling his body towards Emma.

'How are you doing?' he asked.

Emma held out the tea, hands trembling less than before. 'Good for shock, apparently,' she said.

Shepherd smiled. 'First rule in police training college,' he said. 'Make tea.'

Emma tried to smile back, but failed.

'Sorry to have to go through this now—' Shepherd started to say, but Emma shook her head.

'You need me to do it, so let's get on.'

Shepherd nodded and pulled out his notebook. 'OK, tell me from the start, as much as you can remember.'

Emma explained about the phone message, coming to the park and finding Natasha.

'Have you still got the message?' Shepherd asked.

Emma nodded. She handed her cup to Dan and pulled her phone out of her handbag. She dialled her voicemail and put the phone on speaker so Shepherd and Dan could both hear it. They listened in silence. When the message finished, Shepherd pointed at the phone with his pen.

'I'll need a copy of that,' he said, and Emma nodded.

Shepherd frowned. 'Natasha said she knew who had killed Travers McGovern?'

113

'Yes. Last time I saw her we were talking about the peanut oil in the vodka and—'

'She knew about that already?' Shepherd asked, cocking his head on one side.

Emma shook her head. 'No, I told her about the peanut oil. She already knew there was a bottle of vodka in his desk drawer and she assumed someone had spiked it.'

'She told us he often drank in the office,' Shepherd said, scribbling in his notebook.

Emma nodded. 'She said he usually did it in the evening, but she'd previously caught him during the day as well and had told him off about it.'

Shepherd nodded. 'You know they were having an affair?' he asked.

'Yes,' Emma said. 'She told me about it. Well, I'd seen her on the day he died. She was in floods of tears and I thought that was weird.'

'So you asked her about it?' Shepherd asked.

Emma nodded. 'Not right away.'

Shepherd finished scribbling and looked up. 'It seems like quite a personal admission on her part.'

Emma shook her head. 'I've known her for a while. I've been taking an adult ballet class.'

'And Natasha was in the class?' Shepherd asked.

'No, she was teaching it,' Emma said. 'She's an excellent teacher. Everyone in the class loved her.'

'Did you hear or see anything when you got here?' Shepherd asked.

'I heard a rustling in the bushes,' Emma said, pointing towards the tent. 'Natasha was supposed to be by the benches, but I couldn't see her. The noise startled me and I looked towards it and that's when I—' She broke off as tears overwhelmed her.

'That could have been the killer,' Dan said to Shepherd over Emma's head as he hugged her tightly.

Shepherd nodded, making a note of Emma's comment and referring to the time she'd arrived at the scene.

Then Burton appeared. 'How are you doing?' she asked, looking down at Emma.

Tears rolled down Emma's face again. 'Why would anyone want to hurt Natasha?' she asked between sobs.

'Look,' Burton said kindly, squatting down as best she could in a skirt and high heels, 'you've had a terrible shock. Why don't you go home and rest up? We've got everything we need from you for now.' She looked at Shepherd for confirmation and he nodded. 'We'll come and see you again tomorrow. I'm sure we'll have more questions.'

She got to her feet and Shepherd stood, too. 'Look after her,' Burton said to Dan.

He nodded and got to his feet, pulling Emma with him. They returned the foil blanket to the paramedics and set off for home. Emma was still wondering what evidence Natasha had discovered and how the killer knew she had it.

Shepherd held his notebook up to show Burton.

'The killer might have still been here?' she asked sharply.

He nodded. 'We need to search the area, but I'm guessing they're long gone. See if you can get a dog unit down here because they'll be our only chance when it's this dark. I'll get CSI to widen their cordon to include the whole wooded area as best they can. We can get uniforms up to the shops around here now. See if they saw anyone.'

Burton turned and waved at the nearest uniformed officer. She approached and Burton issued an order.

The officer nodded. 'Some are closed already,' she said, 'but we'll pick those up in the morning.'

'We need to know if they saw anyone running away at the relevant time.' The officer left and Burton turned to Shepherd. 'It's a long shot. If it was me, I'd have taken off across the park where it's darkest.'

As he turned away, radio in hand to marshal the troops, Burton was looking up and down the path and then at the lamp posts. 'Let's see what CCTV they've got around here. The cameras might have picked something up. We need to find a trail and fast.'

Chapter 27

The following morning, Burton stood back and allowed Shepherd to knock on the door of the Kents' three-storey Victorian house.

A woman, who could only be Natasha's mother, with the same smooth coffee-coloured skin and bushy hair, peered at them around the door she'd opened a crack. Burton and Shepherd held up warrant cards and introduced themselves. The woman stepped back to let them in.

'We're through there,' she said, wiping at bloodshot eyes with a tissue and pointing them into a beautifully decorated sitting room. Two sofas and an armchair faced each other, previously pointed at a TV hanging above the fireplace. Mrs Kent followed them into the room and gestured for them to sit down. A man came in from the direction of the kitchen and Burton recognised him as one of the family liaison officers, obviously dispatched to support the Kents. She didn't know him by name, but nodded a greeting.

'Can I get you a cuppa?' he asked.

'No, we're fine, thanks,' Burton said, keen to get started.

He looked expectantly at Mrs Kent, who asked for a coffee.

'Thanks, love,' she said as the man exited. 'He's been such a help,' she said as Burton and Shepherd settled into seats. 'It's very kind of you to send someone to us.'

A younger woman perched on one sofa, huddled into herself, elbows resting on her knees. Mrs Kent sat down next to her and pulled another tissue from a box.

'My older daughter, Julietta,' she said, 'or Jules, as everyone calls her.'

Burton nodded. 'We've met before,' she said, giving Julietta a smile.

The latter stared blankly at Burton. 'We have?'

Puzzled, Burton nodded. 'Yes, we were at the dance school yesterday talking to your sister. In the café.'

But Julietta showed no sign of remembering them. Burton eyed her, not sure whether she was lying. Surely no one could be that unobservant.

Shepherd began. 'We're very sorry for your loss,' he said, looking from one woman to the other. They both nodded, accepting his words. That's why he leads these situations, Burton thought to herself. His personal experience of grief and the knock on the door from a police officer made him more sensitive to the feelings of relatives. She'd been the one to deliver the news that his wife had been killed, and the image of his face in that moment would never leave her. Now he had the unenviable task of delivering the dreaded message.

'There's no easy way to say this,' he said, sitting forward in his chair. 'Natasha's injuries suggest she was murdered.'

The silence in the room was so total that Burton could hear the clock in the kitchen ticking through the open door at the end of the room. Then Mrs Kent started crying, noisy body-wracking sobs that seemed to shake the whole sofa.

Julietta had gone completely still. 'What?' she asked, quietly, staring at Shepherd as if he was crazy. 'She can't have been...? Why would anyone...?'

'We're waiting for confirmation from the post-mortem, but the nature of her wounds suggests someone killed her,' Shepherd said.

Mrs Kent was rocking back and forth, and Julietta put an arm around her, seemingly without knowing what she was doing.

'I'm so sorry,' Shepherd said. Mrs Kent gave several loud gulps and blew her nose loudly. It took several more tissues before she could speak.

'Someone killed her? But why?' Her devastation was painful to see.

Burton leaned forward. 'That's exactly what we're going to find out,' she said. 'Can you think of anyone who might want to hurt Natasha?'

Mrs Kent shook her head. 'She was such a lovely girl. She didn't have an enemy in the world,' she said, tears running down her cheeks and dripping off her chin, unnoticed.

Burton looked at Julietta. 'Miss Kent, can you think of anyone?'

Julietta paused and then said, 'Dominic Randall.'

Mrs Kent turned and stared at her daughter. 'Dominic? You think Dominic would kill her? They've known each other for years; why would you say that?'

'He was pretty hacked off when she dumped him.'

'Jules, there's a big difference between being upset at being dumped and killing someone,' her mother said, shocked. 'Besides, she said that they'd both got over it recently and were "sort of friends again", whatever that means.'

Julietta was staring at her mother. 'When did she tell you that?' she demanded.

Mrs Kent shrugged. 'About a month ago.' She looked at Burton and Shepherd. 'She and Dominic dance together, but then got involved. Not uncommon, but not always the best idea.'

'It would make things awkward if you break up,' Burton said.

Mrs Kent nodded. 'And that's exactly what happened. Natasha would never tell me exactly what went on, but they barely spoke for the next couple of months, apart from when they were dancing.' She looked at Julietta. 'Did she ever say anything to you about what happened between them?'

Julietta shook her head but kept her eyes on the floor.

'Do you think they'd started seeing each other again?' Burton asked.

Mrs Kent rubbed at her eyes with an already sodden tissue. 'She was texting someone and was really secretive about it. Then I overheard her talking on the phone and, I don't know why, but I thought it was him. It was how she used to talk to him before.'

Shepherd scribbled in his notebook.

'Can you tell us when you last saw Natasha?' he asked, looking at the two women.

Mrs Kent frowned and looked at Julietta. 'Yesterday morning. We always have breakfast together, to make sure she eats something,' she said.

'Did she have a problem with food?' Shepherd asked.

Mrs Kent shook her head. 'She had a few issues in the past, but we nipped it in the bud. She knew she had to eat with us in the morning to get a good start to the day and she's been known to put away a rather large sausage butty from time to time,' she said, smiling sadly at the memory.

Shepherd looked at Julietta. 'And you?' he asked.

She frowned. 'I was going to work, so I asked if she was going anywhere and needed a lift. She said she wasn't going out,' she said, with an odd note in her voice that Burton couldn't place. 'I always took her when she wanted to go somewhere.'

'Like picking her up from rehearsals?' Shepherd asked, remembering the conversation the previous day.

Julietta nodded. 'I took her to college every day. She needed to get there on time and the bus is really unreliable,' she said. 'Then I brought her home after school.'

Burton raised her eyebrows. 'You were obviously very close,' she said.

Julietta nodded. 'I would do anything for her,' she said. 'Anything she needed, she came straight to me.' There was a note of pride in Julietta's voice, but Shepherd noticed an expression flit across Mrs Kent's face. It was gone too quickly for him to put his finger on what it was.

'What time did Natasha go out yesterday?' Burton asked, looking at Natasha's mother.

Mrs Kent puffed out her cheeks, making her fringe rise and fall on her forehead. 'It must have been about nine thirty. She said she'd had a text to say she needed to be in college for a rehearsal and that she was getting the bus.'

'How was she when she left?' Burton asked.

Mrs Kent frowned. 'She was a bit quiet. It's been a tough week, with that teacher being found dead on Tuesday. She said she hadn't slept very well, but she seemed happy to be going.'

'Did either of you speak to her during the day?' he asked.

Mrs Kent shook her head. 'Not until about six o'clock when she texted me to tell me she had to see someone so she wouldn't be home for dinner. I said I'd keep something back for her.' The corners of her mouth pulled down as she remembered the food, and why it hadn't been eaten.

Shepherd gestured towards Julietta. 'You saw her at college at lunchtime,' he said.

Julietta nodded, but she was staring off into the distance with an odd look on her face.

'Had you arranged to pick her up?'

Julietta shook herself and looked at him. 'What?' she asked.

'You came to college to pick her up. Was that pre-arranged? You said she'd told you she wasn't going out.'

Julietta shook her head. 'She'd said she wasn't going out, but then a friend came into the bank where I work and said she'd seen Natasha going to school.' She frowned. 'I don't know why she hadn't told me that.'

'And she would normally tell you?' Shepherd asked.

Julietta nodded. 'When I got a break, I called Nat and left her a message saying I'd pick her up when she had finished. She texted back to say she'd get the bus home, but she couldn't do that.'

Burton raised an eyebrow. 'Couldn't? She'd already got the bus in.'

Julietta shook her head. 'I always pick her up,' she said, as if that was obvious.

'Natasha told you when to come?' Burton asked.

'Yes,' Julietta said. 'I took an early lunch. I was on time, but she was late.'

Shepherd nodded with a smile. 'Sorry, that was our fault,' he said. He looked at Mrs Kent. 'We were speaking to Natasha about Travers McGovern's death,' he explained.

Mrs Kent stared at him. 'Why would you have been speaking to her about that?' she asked, looking from Burton to Shepherd and back again.

Shepherd looked up from his notebook. 'We've been speaking to everyone who was on campus when he died,' he said, giving her his most comforting smile. 'We wanted to find out if she'd seen anything.'

Mrs Kent nodded and wiped at her eyes with a tissue. 'And had she?'

Burton shook her head. 'We don't think so,' she said. She braced herself. 'We have to ask this, it's standard procedure, but where were you both yesterday evening, when Natasha was killed?'

'You're asking us for an alibi?' Julietta demanded. 'Why would you do that?'

'Jules...' Mrs Kent put a calming hand on her daughter's arm '...she just said it's standard procedure.' She took a deep breath and said, 'What time was it when ... you know when...' She seemed unable to speak the words as if it would confirm that her daughter was really dead.

'Again, we need to get confirmation from the post-mortem, but we believe it was about six twenty in the evening,' Shepherd said.

'You know so exactly?'

Shepherd leaned forward. 'The person who found Natasha arrived at around that time, but there was nothing she could do to help, unfortunately. She called the police and an ambulance, but it was too late.'

Mrs Kent took a shuddering breath. 'I was here, making dinner for Jules and myself.'

'Can anyone confirm that?' Shepherd asked.

She nodded. 'Sheila, from two doors down, popped in to return a book she'd borrowed.' Her face crumpled and the tears started again. 'I can't believe I was doing something so mundane when ... when...' The sobs overcame her and Julietta squeezed her tightly.

'And you, Julietta,' Shepherd asked, 'where were you?'

'Do you have to do this now? Can't you see Mum's upset?' Julietta snapped.

'It gets it out of the way,' Shepherd said gently.

She sniffed. 'I was here with Mum. I went out to meet a friend briefly, but then I came home.'

'What time was that?'

Julietta eyed Shepherd and looked as if she was going to refuse to answer. 'I don't know. I was back here with Mum for dinner. We were at home all night. Is that good enough for you?'

Shepherd nodded. 'Like we said, it's standard procedure to check on everyone.'

Burton spoke. 'Can we see Natasha's bedroom, please?'

Mrs Kent nodded. 'Of course,' she said, beginning to stand up, but Julietta was already on her feet.

'I'll take you,' she said.

Burton and Shepherd got to their feet and followed her out of the room.

Chapter 28

Burton and Shepherd followed Julietta up a narrow, somewhat-creaky staircase.

'That's Mum's room,' she said, pointing at one door that stood ajar. 'My room.' She pointed at another. Then she led the way to the top floor. A step a third of the way up creaked loudly under Julietta's foot. 'This is Natasha's.'

She threw open the door, and the first impression was that of an old-fashioned ice cream parlour. Everything was pink, even the duvet cover on the single bed. Posters of ballerinas were stuck on two of the walls, and stickers on the sides of the white-and-gold wardrobe were also ballerinas. On the wall of the room, there was a poster for an exercise regime that Shepherd thought would have finished him off.

'Natasha told us that was her favourite,' he said, pointing to another poster advertising *Swan Lake*. The ballerina was on pointe, arms stretched behind her like wings, muscles rippling.

Julietta nodded enthusiastically. 'Oh yes, she always loved it, right from when we were little.' She pointed towards the picture that Shepherd was looking at. 'That's Darcey Bussell,' she said. 'She was Natasha's hero.'

Burton was looking at the exercise poster and wincing. 'Did she do that every day?' she asked.

Julietta nodded again. 'That's why she has the bigger room,' she said.

'I'm surprised,' Burton said. 'Usually the older person nabs the bigger room.' She smiled at Julietta, but the latter shook her head earnestly.

'She needed the space more than I do,' she said.

'I painted my little girl's room much like this,' Burton said. 'She's just turned six. I'm surprised Natasha hasn't re-decorated recently.'

Julietta shook her head. 'I repainted it as a surprise for her last year while she was away on a residential course. Her room's always been like this.'

Burton raised her eyebrows. 'You painted without asking her? What did she say?'

'She was a bit surprised, but she loved it,' Julietta said, pointedly, glaring at Burton. 'She appreciated that I'd done something nice for her.' But Burton had the feeling that Natasha had probably felt quite the opposite. The room felt strangely oppressive. It was immaculate and somewhat lacking in personality. She got no proper sense of Natasha apart from pink and ballet. It was not like the woman she'd interviewed just a day or so earlier. She'd had passions outside of dancing and a good deal of personality.

'It's very tidy,' she said, walking across to the bookcase, glancing at Julietta over her shoulder.

Julietta nodded. 'That was Nat all over. Very disciplined.'

Shepherd was at the desk. He pulled at the desk drawer. It resisted slightly, but a sharp tug slid it open. Inside, pens and pencils were neatly lined up, with a pack of sticky notes sitting on top of a couple of pristine notebooks. Then he spotted one that was particularly dog-eared hidden at the back of the drawer. He slid it out and turned his back to Julietta as he opened it. It wasn't a notebook, but a week-to-view diary for the year. Flicking back through the previous three months, something caught his eye. He slipped the diary to Burton as he crossed to the wardrobe. He pulled open the doors and flipped through the clothes hanging inside. There was the usual attire of the teenage girl. Jeans, tops and sportswear neatly hung alongside leggings and wrap-around cardigans, all in colour order.

Right in the corner was a bag of what looked like dry cleaning. He pulled it out and opened the zip. He blinked when the light caught the beaded front of a ballroom-style dress.

'One of Natasha's costumes?' he asked.

Julietta grinned. 'Not something you'd wear to go down Allensbury high street on a Saturday afternoon,' she said, stepping forward to finger the fabric. 'It's for the showcase, or rather it was for the showcase.' She stepped away, wiping at a tear that had suddenly welled up. 'Sorry,' she said.

'Don't be sorry,' Shepherd said. 'It's perfectly normal.' He closed the doors of the wardrobe and turned to look around the room. He spotted a door in the corner. 'Another wardrobe?' he asked Julietta.

She frowned. 'No, I don't think it's in use. I think Mum had it painted over.'

Shepherd stepped across and examined the door. 'The hinges were oiled recently.' He turned the handle and tugged the door, but it stayed shut. Then something flagged in his head and he returned to the desk. Pulling the drawer open slightly, he felt inside. His fingers felt something sticky taped to the inside of the desk. With a bit of fiddling, he detached it and pulled out a key. He looked at Julietta and her mouth had fallen open slightly. He stripped the tape away and returned to the door. The key slid into the lock and a quick turn opened the door. He reached inside and flicked a light switch. It was more like a small room than a wardrobe. He blinked as the bulb lit, showing an Aladdin's cave of sparkly costumes. He pulled out a bright pink dress and held it up.

'The Sugar Plum Fairy,' said Burton quickly. When Shepherd looked puzzled, she added, '*The Nutcracker*.'

'Fair enough.' Shepherd grinned and turned to Julietta.

She was staring at him wide-eyed. 'I've never seen that before in my life,' she said, slowly.

'Never?' Shepherd asked, surprised.

Julietta crossed the room and examined the dress carefully. 'She danced the part a couple of years ago, but that dress was totally different.'

A heavy silence fell on the room.

'Mind if I take a photo?' Shepherd asked, pulling out his phone. He hung it on the wardrobe door while he snapped a picture, and then

125

Julietta took it and held it up against herself. 'I doubt it would fit me now,' she said.

Burton looked around from where she was examining a bookcase. 'You dance as well?' she asked.

Julietta nodded. 'I used to. I started first. Then one day my mum was early picking me up from class and had Natasha with her. The teacher let Nat join the class.' She laughed softly. 'Nat was so young she could barely stand and kept falling over, but she still got back up and carried on.'

'And she got bitten by the bug?' Shepherd asked.

'Yes.' Julietta's abrupt tone made Shepherd turn round from the wardrobe he was still rifling through. The rest of the clothes were standard for young women, as far as he could tell.

'You weren't competitive?' Burton asked, looking over her shoulder.

Julietta gave a little laugh. 'Why would we be?'

'My girls always seem to do everything at the same time. Then it's all about who's better than who.' When Julietta didn't speak, Burton turned fully to face her. 'But then there's more of an age gap between you, isn't there?' she asked.

Julietta nodded. 'Five years.' She gave a short laugh. 'Mum always says that Natasha came as a bit of a surprise.'

Shepherd smiled at her. 'A shock to your system as well, I imagine,' he said.

Julietta shrugged. 'When she was little, I didn't really do much with her because I was so much older. When she started dancing—'

'She became more interesting?' Burton asked.

Julietta was looking down at the floor, fighting her wobbling bottom lip.

'Do you still dance now?' Shepherd asked. He was almost inside the cupboard, looking through the contents, and Burton could see a few flashes as he took photos.

Julietta shook her head. 'No, I did for a long time, but I stopped five years ago.'

'Why? If you don't mind me asking,' he asked, sticking his head back into the room.

126

'I injured my knee,' Julietta said, bringing his attention back to her. 'I was practising a routine for the end-of-year showcase.' She shrugged. 'It's a big deal, so I went overboard, practising for hours. I fell during one routine but I got up and carried on, regardless.'

'Been there and done that on the rugby field,' Shepherd said, turning back to the cupboard. 'Then always paid for it the next day.' When Julietta said nothing, he reappeared. Tears had filled her eyes. 'Here,' he said, digging into his pocket. She took the tissue he offered her and dabbed at her face.

Seeing his questioning look, she said, 'Sorry, I'm being so stupid crying over something I can't do anything about.'

'What happened?' he asked gently.

'I didn't tell my teacher how much pain I was in. I didn't want to miss out on the showcase, so I dosed up on painkillers and carried on.' She sighed. 'Turns out that was a huge mistake. By the time of the showcase, I could barely walk. I had a minor fracture in my kneecap and damaged the ligaments. So no showcase and no dancing career.'

'I'm sorry,' Shepherd said, recognising the genuine sadness behind Julietta's blasé description.

She shrugged. 'Can't be helped now,' she said. 'But I never wanted that to happen to Nat, so I made sure she looked after herself. That's why I used to give her lifts to and from college, take her to competitions and stuff like that. I wanted her to have a dancing career; she'd earned it by working hard.'

'You took good care of her,' Burton said, speaking so suddenly that Shepherd and Julietta both jumped. Her voice was slightly muffled as she squatted down to look at the bottom shelf of the bookcase.

Julietta nodded and wiped her face again. 'It wasn't enough though, was it? I should have been there.' She banged a fist against her thigh to emphasise the word. 'What was she doing in the park?'

'She was going to meet someone,' Shepherd said.

'Who?' Julietta demanded. 'Was it Dominic?'

Shepherd raised an eyebrow. 'You said she wasn't seeing him anymore.'

'She wasn't as far as I knew,' Julietta said, 'but who else would she be meeting? I mean—' She stopped speaking and looked down at her

127

feet.

Shepherd continued to look at her, but she avoided his eyes. He turned back and leaned into the cupboard to switch off the light. He moved across to the chest of drawers. Bottles and tubes of make-up and every size of brush imaginable covered the surface.

'Wow,' he said with a laugh, peering at it. 'I thought my wife had a lot of this stuff, but she wasn't in the same league.'

Julietta appeared beside him and picked up one tube. She pulled off the lid and twisted it to reveal a bright-red lipstick. 'Nat always had her face on before she went out,' she said.

'Ready to take on the world?' Shepherd asked.

Julietta shrugged.

'I think we've seen everything we need at the moment,' Burton said. She held up the diary. 'We'll take this with us, and we'll need Natasha's laptop as well.'

'OK.' Julietta opened another drawer in the desk and pulled out a slim MacBook. She took out a charging cable as well and handed them over.

'Thanks,' Shepherd said. 'Do you know if she had a password?'

Julietta nodded. 'It's capital D then a-r-c-e-y-capital B and two-zero-zero-seven,' she recited.

Shepherd raised an eyebrow.

'The year of Darcey Bussell's retirement performance,' Julietta said. 'I tried to get us tickets, but it sold out really quickly.'

Shepherd nodded and then noticed Burton had scribbled it down. He led the way towards the door and down the stairs.

When they all returned to the living room, Mrs Kent looked up at them.

'Did you get everything you needed?' she asked.

Shepherd nodded and held up Natasha's laptop. 'I'll need to give you a receipt for these and we'll get them back to you as soon as we can,' he said.

Burton reached into her handbag and pulled out a notebook. She carefully noted the items Shepherd was holding and then dated and signed it. When she handed the note to Mrs Kent, the other woman looked at her with eyes brimming with tears.

'Please find out what happened to my girl,' she said, holding out a hand to Burton.

'That's exactly what I intend to do,' Burton replied, shaking it firmly.

***

'That was illuminating,' Burton said as they got into the car. She looked down at the silver laptop that was balanced on her lap. 'I think this is the only thing in that room that wasn't pink.'

Shepherd laughed as he started the car. 'It was giving me a headache.' He frowned. 'Is it not strange for an eighteen-year-old woman to have a bedroom like a little girl?'

Burton nodded grimly. 'What's interesting is that the sister did it for her without asking.' She looked out of the window. 'Like she's trying to keep her as a little girl.'

'What are you thinking?' Shepherd asked, putting on the indicator and pulling out of the parking space.

'It seems to be an odd relationship. She claims to know everything about Natasha's life, drives her around everywhere, but we know Natasha was lying to her. She told Julietta that she was at a rehearsal when she was teaching those little kids. Why?'

Shepherd frowned as he braked at a red traffic light. 'It's strange that Julietta thinks she knew everything about Natasha's life, but maybe it was only what Natasha let her see. I mean, secret wardrobes, hidden keys and the ballet dress—'

'Tutu,' Burton interrupted.

'What?'

'It's called a tutu.'

Shepherd grinned as the light turned green and he pulled away. 'Sorry I'm not up on the terminology.'

'What about the dress?'

'Julietta was so surprised by it. Why had Natasha hidden it?' He slowed to allow a car to cut in front of him. 'She also knew Natasha's laptop password off by heart. My sister would never have given me something like that.'

Burton sighed as Shepherd slowed the car at a roundabout.

'Did you find anything?' Shepherd asked, negotiating the roundabout.

Burton frowned. 'Natasha was definitely up to something. There were a load of kids' books, you know the type, *Ballet Shoes* by Noel Streatfeild and the *Bad News Ballet* series. Then, hidden behind that front row, was a book about starting your own business and another on child psychology.'

Shepherd turned his head slightly towards her without his eyes leaving the road. He was slowing for the turn into the police station car park. 'Interesting reading material for someone headed for a career in dance. Mother and sister seem to think that's what was in the offing. No mention of any other plans.'

Burton nodded. 'I don't think they know,' she said. 'She's hidden the books well. You'd only find them if you were looking.' Burton frowned. 'So the question is, why would Natasha be hiding that from her family?'

'Do you think she was actually planning to leave with Travers McGovern?' Shepherd asked, driving around the car park to find a space. He was silent as he concentrated on reversing into a space between a BMW and a Volkswagen Golf.

Burton considered for a moment. 'It might have been in her plan at some point, but when she spoke to us she didn't seem all that bothered that he wasn't telling his wife about them.' She looked out of the window and then asked, 'I wonder what Julietta would do if she thought Natasha was planning to ditch ballet for a teaching job and Travers McGovern?'

Chapter 29

'I really don't think you should go into work,' Dan said as he and Emma met at the bottom of the hill on the walk to the office on Monday morning. 'You look like you've not slept.'

Emma glared at him. 'You know how to kick a girl when she's down, don't you?'

'I'm trying to help,' Dan said, adjusting his messenger bag on his shoulder to detangle it from his jacket collar. 'You had a massive shock on Saturday. You should be resting.'

'I rested all day yesterday,' she said sharply.

Dan snorted. 'Pacing the floor and calling the police's message service every five minutes for updates does not mean resting,' he said. 'Plus, you're not on this story anymore.'

'What?' Emma snapped, suddenly stopping and turning on him. 'Of course I am.'

Dan shook his head. 'Daisy called me last night. She said you couldn't work on the story when you found the body and it's someone you knew. She's asked me to do it.'

'We'll see about that.' Emma marched off up the hill, leaving Dan to catch up.

When they arrived in the office, she found Dan to be right.

'What are you doing here?' Daisy demanded, standing by Emma's desk with her arms folded.

'I have copy to write,' Emma said, sitting down at her computer and switching it on.

Daisy glared, and her response was characteristically blunt. 'Emma, the copy is about you finding a friend dead. Dan is taking the reins on this one. You're not capable.'

'I am perfectly capable,' Emma shouted, standing up so suddenly that both Dan and Daisy took a step backwards. All heads in the office swivelled to look at her. 'Someone murdered a woman who ... they stabbed ... They—' But tears were blurring her vision and Emma sat back down at her computer to hide it.

'All right, back to work,' she heard Daisy shout at the rest of the office, and a hum of conversation started up again.

Daisy took a deep breath and squatted down beside Emma. 'You see what I mean?' she said. 'You need to take a break.'

'What am I supposed to do? Just sit around thinking about it?'

Daisy rested a hand on Emma's arm. 'Go home and get some sleep,' she said, gently. 'You look like you need it.'

'I'm fine,' Emma said, but she knew that the wobble in her voice wasn't convincing anyone, even herself, if she was honest. She knew from Daisy's face that excuses were not swaying her. With a deep sigh, she picked up her notebook and pen and slammed them back in her handbag.

'OK. I'll go home. But you call me the minute you get an update,' she said, pointing at Dan.

He took a slight step back to avoid the jabbing finger and saluted. 'Yes, boss,' he said.

Emma turned and walked out of the office. She needed to find out who could have done it and she knew exactly where to start.

Chapter 30

Burton and Shepherd faced Eleanor Brody across the body of Natasha Kent on the post-mortem table. The Y-shaped incision into her torso was now sewn up and covered modestly by a sheet, which left just her face on show. The overhead lights shone against her skin and her vibrant springy curls made her look as if she might get up at any moment and dance across a stage.

Shepherd was looking down at the body. 'It's always strange to look at someone like this when you spoke to them so recently,' he said.

Burton nodded, but before she could reply Brody tapped her clipboard, calling them to order.

'Do you want to know what I found?' she asked.

Burton and Shepherd nodded and waited for her to begin.

Brody took a deep breath. 'Very healthy body, if not a little underweight, but you expect that from a dancer. The bit that's in the worst condition is these,' she said, pulling back the sheet to uncover Natasha's feet. Burton and Shepherd both wrinkled their noses.

'Ugh,' said Shepherd. Blisters stood out across the toes, which were swollen and red, and calluses had formed on the soles of both feet.

'Ballerina's feet,' Brody remarked, and Burton nodded. 'But what's not characteristic of a ballerina's feet, is these,' Brody said, pointing to thin red lines criss-crossing the tops of Natasha's feet.

'Evening shoes,' Burton said.

Shepherd raised an eyebrow. 'How do you know that?' he asked.

133

'I've had those myself so many times after a night out,' Burton said, pointing down at her own feet. 'Plus, didn't Emma Fletcher tell us that Natasha was doing something different, some ballroom *Moulin Rouge*-style number?' She pointed at the feet. 'She wouldn't have been using ballet shoes for that,' she said. Then she looked at Brody. 'But you don't just want to tell us about her feet, do you?'

Brody shook her head. 'Everything is standard for a dancer in terms of muscle tone, body weight, etcetera. But what isn't typical—' She paused and looked down at the body, resting a hand on Natasha's shoulder. 'Poor Natasha here is two months pregnant.'

Burton and Shepherd stared at her in stunned silence and then the former slapped her hand to her forehead.

'I should have known,' she said.

'How?' asked Shepherd, staring at her.

'When we interviewed her at the college, she couldn't stand the coffee cups being near her. Maybe they were making her feel sick. I had something similar when I was carrying my eldest.'

Shepherd nodded. 'That would also explain why she wasn't dancing very well.'

Burton sighed. 'Poor kid. Pregnant by your teacher who's a married man.'

'Who keeps saying he's going to leave his wife for you, but then never does?' Shepherd put in.

'Or worse, you're trying to break up with him, but now you can't because it's his baby.'

'We can't rule out that it's someone else,' Shepherd said. 'What about Dominic Randall?'

'Her mum said they broke up six or seven months ago and Natasha is only two months pregnant, so it can't be him.'

'Mrs Kent said she thought they'd got back together recently,' Shepherd said, 'but maybe she actually overheard Natasha talking to Travers.'

Burton frowned. 'We need to speak to Mrs Kent again in the light of this.' Shepherd pulled out his notebook and jotted it down.

'I've sent off a DNA sample to test against Travers McGovern's, so I'll be able to give you an answer on that,' Brody said.

'What else have you got?' Burton asked Brody.

The pathologist consulted her clipboard again.

'Time of death was not long before your witness found the body. Three blows to the stomach, delivered with force and with a short, serrated blade,' Brody said, pointing to Natasha's midriff.

'The killer was making sure,' Burton said.

'They're very deliberate thrusts,' Brody continued. 'She would have bled out within minutes.'

'Do you think the killer knew she was pregnant?' Shepherd asked.

Burton was silent for a moment. 'And that's why he or she aimed for her stomach?' she asked.

Shepherd shrugged. 'Could be.'

'But why would someone kill her for being pregnant?' Burton asked. 'If we're right and Travers was the father, why would someone else stab her?' But even as she thought out loud, a shadow passed over her face.

'Sarah McGovern,' Shepherd said, interpreting Burton's look. 'She's got no alibi for her husband's death. I wonder where she was at the time of Natasha's.'

'And she'd have reason to be angry if she found out her husband fathered a child with someone else,' Burton said.

'Well, the killer was certainly angry,' Brody broke in, 'but it was deliberate, not frenzied. She would likely have gone into shock and died after the first blow. The other two were just for the sake of it,' Brody said, looking down at Natasha sadly.

'So she was dead but still bleeding?' Burton asked.

Brody nodded.

'Emma Fletcher must have arrived at the scene almost immediately,' Shepherd said, looking at Burton. 'Reckon she might have seen the killer?'

Burton pursed her lips. 'She heard a rustling in the bushes but didn't see anyone. What worries me more is that the killer probably saw her.'

Chapter 31

Shepherd had to drive up and down the Kents' street three times to find a parking space.

'It's a nightmare down here,' he said, as he parallel parked neatly between an Audi and a Renault Clio. Burton said nothing in reply, and he looked over at her.

'I'm not looking forward to this,' she said as they unfastened their seatbelts.

Shepherd looked across the road at the house. 'Do you think the family already knows she was pregnant?'

Burton exhaled heavily. 'We'll soon find out.'

'Do you want me to lead?' Shepherd asked as he locked the car door with the remote control.

Burton paused at the side of the road to allow a car to pass. 'If you would,' she said. 'I want to watch them and see the reaction to the pregnancy news.'

Mrs Kent answered their knock on the door. Dark circles ringed her eyes and she smiled tiredly as she let them into the house.

'I was wondering when you'd be back,' she said, leading the way into the sitting room. It was empty and she waved a hand to invite them to sit down. 'You've got news?'

Burton nodded as she and Shepherd took seats. 'We've got an update. Is Julietta here?' Burton asked.

Mrs Kent shook her head and sat down. 'Jules went out for a walk.

I can break the news after you've gone.'

Burton looked at Shepherd and nodded for him to begin.

'Our post-mortem confirmed Natasha died from three stab wounds to the abdomen,' he said as gently as possible.

Mrs Kent made a choking noise in her throat and pulled a tissue from her sleeve. 'Would she ... would she have suffered?' she asked.

Shepherd shook his head. He knew stab wounds usually bled out very quickly and he hoped Brody was right and that Natasha had died almost instantly. He wanted to give Mrs Kent some comfort.

Before he could say anything further, they heard a key in the front door and a voice called, 'I'm home.' Julietta appeared in the doorway. Her eyes still looked a little red, but she seemed calm. She stopped dead when she saw Burton and Shepherd, and her eyes travelled to her mother.

'What's going on?' she demanded, marching across to the sofa to join her mother. She gripped her mother's hand so hard the older woman winced.

'Ouch, Jules, not so tight,' she said. But Julietta didn't seem to hear, and her knuckles whitened.

'Have you found something else out?' she asked, looking from Burton to Shepherd and back again.

Shepherd explained and then added, 'But there's more.'

Both women looked braced, so he continued. 'Our pathologist also found that Natasha was two months pregnant,' he said.

Tears ran down Mrs Kent's face again. Shepherd leaned forward, pulled a tissue from the box on the table and silently handed it to her. Julietta sat stiff as a board, still clutching her mother's hand.

'Pregnant?' she asked.

Burton nodded. 'She hadn't told either of you?'

Mrs Kent took a deep breath. 'I suspected something,' she said.

Julietta's head snapped round to look at her. 'You knew?' she whispered, and her mother nodded.

'But she didn't tell you?' Burton asked, looking at Mrs Kent.

Mrs Kent shook her head. 'No, but I was tidying up in the bathroom and noticed that she hadn't used her tampons for a couple of months. Usually she asks me to add them to the shopping list when she needs them.' She took a shuddering breath. 'I assumed she would tell me when she was ready.'

'Do you think someone killed her because she was pregnant?' Julietta asked in a whisper. 'That the father killed her?'

Burton frowned. 'We're keeping an open mind, but yes, that could be one line of enquiry.'

'You need to speak to Dominic,' Julietta said, leaning forward and taking a tissue from the box, but twisting it in her hands rather than using it.

'You think he could be the father?' Burton asked, and Julietta nodded.

'Who else could it be?' she demanded.

When Burton and Shepherd said nothing, Mrs Kent fired up.

'What? You think my daughter was sleeping with more than one person?' she demanded, sitting forward suddenly onto the edge of the sofa cushion.

Shepherd shook his head. 'No, but we have been told that Natasha was having an affair with a teacher at the school, Travers McGovern.'

Mrs Kent and Julietta stared at him in silence. The former recovered first.

'With a teacher?' she demanded. 'No, that's not possible,' she continued, shaking her head and dabbing at the tears starting in her eyes. Then she frowned. 'Isn't that the guy who died last week?'

Shepherd nodded. 'What we need to know is whether you can think of anyone who might have wanted to hurt Natasha?'

Mrs Kent wiped her eyes and shook her head tiredly. 'I said before that I can't think of anyone. Natasha was a good person—'

But Julietta interrupted. 'It was someone else at the dance school. It must have been. They were all jealous of Nat because she was better than them. She worked so hard, she practised more than anyone else.' Her voice was becoming almost manic. 'I made sure she was better than all of them. I—' She stopped speaking abruptly. Then she looked around the room and saw the three faces looking up at her. 'Have you spoken to Dominic?' she demanded.

Burton shook her head. 'Not regarding Natasha.'

'Then you should. He was always really jealous of Nat. He was—'

She broke off. Tears filled her eyes and she ran out of the room. They heard footsteps thunder up the stairs and a door slam.

Mrs Kent sighed and shook her head. 'I'm sorry,' she said to Burton and Shepherd. 'She's very upset, as you can imagine.'

'It's understandable,' Shepherd said. 'They were very close.'

Mrs Kent nodded. 'Not so much when they were younger, because there's such a big age gap. But after Jules stopped dancing, she spent a lot of time supporting Natasha, driving her to competitions and encouraging her to practise. I think Nat sometimes felt a bit overwhelmed, but she was kind enough to never refuse Jules' help.'

Shepherd looked at Mrs Kent. 'You said earlier that you had a feeling that Natasha was pregnant, but she hadn't told you for sure.'

Mrs Kent smiled and nodded, tears starting in her eyes. 'A girl's mother always knows these things.'

'Did you have an idea whose it was?' Burton asked.

Mrs Kent's mouth turned down at the corners. 'I suspected it was Dominic's. They'd been speaking recently. It had been radio silence after they split up, but I heard them on the phone a few times and it seemed quite friendly. I didn't know about this teacher.' She said the last word with disdain.

'What were Natasha and Dominic talking about?' Burton asked.

'I could only hear Nat's side and she was talking very quietly, but I think they were talking about Dominic leaving home.'

Burton raised her eyebrows. 'About him leaving home?'

Mrs Kent nodded.

'What was Natasha saying?' Shepherd asked, scribbling in his notebook.

'It was something about needing time to get the money together, finding somewhere that he liked, not too far away. Maybe she just didn't want him to leave when they've become friends again.'

'Did she say anything else?' Burton asked.

'She said something about needing to get away and be somewhere safe.' She shrugged. 'I'm surprised because he gets on so well with his mum. Plus, he doesn't have a job, so how would he support himself?'

***

'What a mess,' Burton said as the door closed behind them and they walked to the car. She sighed. 'Right, let's get back to the office.' She saw the frown on Shepherd's face.

'What?'

'It's odd that they both assumed the baby was Dominic's even though they broke up months ago.'

'They didn't know about Travers,' Burton pointed out. 'Well, Mrs Kent didn't know about Travers, at least.'

'You think Julietta might have known?'

Burton chewed the inside of her cheek for a moment. 'She seems so into every area of Natasha's life, always buzzing around, picking her up from college. She might have seen them together.'

'Would she really kill her sister, though?' Burton asked. 'I could see her going after Travers if she thought he was going to take Natasha away, but once he was out of the picture?'

'What if Natasha was going to keep the baby? She's only got to get through another couple of weeks at the college, get through this showcase they're doing and she's free to do what she wants. That might explain the teaching books.'

'You think Julietta found out about that and lost control?' Burton said.

Shepherd shrugged. 'I don't know,' he said. 'There's so much emotion at the moment, it's hard to sort out.' He pursed his lips. 'What's also interesting is the conversation about Dominic leaving home.'

'You don't buy it?'

Shepherd shook his head. 'Would the lad who was rushing home to make his mum's dinner really be trying to leave home?'

'Maybe he didn't enjoy having to rush home to make dinner?' Burton asked.

Shepherd rubbed his forehead. 'But he seemed so willing to do it. Something isn't sitting right here, but I can't put my finger on it.'

'I'll give the family liaison officer a call when we get back and get his input. He's been around them all the time, so he might have some

140

insight.'

***

Gary Topping was immersed in a pile of witness statements when they got back to the office. Shepherd called his name and he looked up, bleary-eyed. He was offered a coffee and accepted with alacrity. Shepherd returned with a full mug and two sugar sachets, which Topping immediately opened and added to the coffee.

'Anything?' Shepherd asked, sitting down and pulling one statement towards him.

'I almost wish we hadn't been so thorough,' he said, patting the pile of statements. 'We covered most of the surrounding area and spoke to all the businesses that were open last night,' he said, rubbing his eyes and taking a sip of coffee. 'The uniforms have gone back out today to chase up the ones that were closed.' He sighed. 'Not sure what good it'll do, but I didn't want to dent the enthusiasm of two youngsters.'

Shepherd smiled. 'If they weren't open last night, they probably saw nothing useful.'

Topping nodded. He put his mug down and stretched his arms over his head. 'No one seems to have heard or seen anything. One woman said she thought she heard a scream, but couldn't be sure whether she did or what time it was.'

Shepherd sighed. 'Too much to hope that our killer went out of the front gate covered in blood carrying the murder weapon,' he said.

Topping puffed out his cheeks. 'Did the pathologist say if the killer would be covered in blood, because that could be something,' he said, 'although if they were wearing black, that would have camouflaged it.'

'Wow, you really are in Eeyore mode today, aren't you?' Shepherd remarked.

Topping sipped his coffee. 'I just feel like we're not getting anywhere fast. Seeing a lovely young lass like that, life ahead of her, dead ... It's a tough one to swallow. And her being pregnant too. Do you think the killer knew she was pregnant?'

'And that's why he went for her stomach?'

Topping nodded.

'Well,' Shepherd said, 'when we find him, we can ask him.'

Chapter 32

Emma was waiting in the reception area at the police station when Shepherd entered. She was sitting fiddling with a tassel on her handbag, and a foot jiggled non-stop. She leapt to her feet when he approached.

'I know you wanted to interview me again, so I came in,' she said, rather breathless.

Shepherd smiled at her. 'We were going to come to you,' he said. He glanced at his watch. 'I thought you'd be at work.'

'Daisy won't let me stay; she's put Dan on the story for now.' Emma knew she was gabbling, but after sitting in silence for so long, the words were just pouring out of her. 'But I couldn't just sit at home. Not when Natasha's killer is still out there.'

Shepherd nodded to the officer behind the reception desk, opened the door into the station and led the way. 'Let's get a cuppa and have a chat, eh?' he said. Turning back to the officer, he asked her to call Burton to join them.

As soon as they sat down in an interview room, Emma asked 'So how far have you got? Have you got anything you can tell us? Her family must be devastated.'

Shepherd nodded, but before he could speak, Burton elbowed the door open, three mugs balanced in her hands. She set them down on the table and returned to close the door. She sat down and pushed one of them towards Emma.

'How are you feeling? Did you manage any sleep last night?' she asked, peering into Emma's face.

Emma shook her head. 'Not really. I just kept seeing Natasha's face.' Her lip wobbled and her eyes filled with tears. She looked up to see the detectives regarding her sympathetically.

'It's a horrible shock,' Burton said.

Shepherd pulled out his notebook. 'Are you up to answering more questions?' he asked.

Emma nodded. 'Anything I can do to help, really. I mean, I want to do this for Nat's family. They need to know who did this and—'

She knew she was gabbling and broke off when Shepherd held up a hand. 'Hey, steady on,' he said. 'Take a deep breath.'

Emma tried, but she could feel her chest tightening. She tried to ignore it and braced herself for questions. She needed to get a grip. Her heart was racing.

'Now,' Burton said, 'Natasha left you a voicemail saying she knew who had killed Travers McGovern and asking you to meet her in the park.'

Emma nodded. 'I tried to call as soon as I heard her message, but it went to voicemail. I texted back and she answered straight away saying to go to the park.' Tears trembled on her eyelashes. 'But I had to go the long way round because one street was blocked. Maybe if I'd got there sooner, I could have—'

Shepherd immediately shook his head. 'You've no idea if you'd have got there in time, so don't beat yourself up.' He sipped at his tea. 'Now, you said you only know Natasha through your dance classes?' he asked.

Emma nodded. 'I've been doing them for about a year now. We've talked after class a few times, gone for coffee and had a bit of a heart-to-heart at the class Christmas party but—' She stopped.

'What?' Burton asked.

'Well, I got the impression that she wasn't telling me everything. In fact, I don't think she tells anyone everything.'

'She didn't mention Travers McGovern?' Shepherd asked, making notes.

Emma shook her head. 'Not by name. She said she was seeing some-

144

one and that was causing trouble with an ex. He didn't like the new guy.'

'But she didn't name names?' Burton asked.

Emma shook her head. 'No, like I said, she was discreet, but—' She stopped. 'Do you know who it is? Did he do it? Did he kill her?'

Burton raised a hand, palm outwards. 'I can't tell you,' she said, 'you know that. When you went to the park, did you hear or see anyone around?'

Emma shook her head, feeling a tightness in her chest. 'I walked up to the bench but I couldn't see Natasha. I tried ringing her, but it went straight to her voicemail and then I heard something in the bushes and I—' She broke off and stared at Burton, eyes widening. 'Do you think ... Do you think the killer saw me?'

'Now wait, we're not saying that...' Burton began.

Emma's hand flew to her throat. She could feel a familiar tightening in her chest and realised she was also feeling light-headed.

'Are you OK?' Burton asked, peering at her. 'You've gone really pale.'

'I'm fine,' Emma said, but she knew she wasn't. The room was going fuzzy and sweat was prickling all over her head and neck. The last thing she heard was Shepherd say, 'Grab her,' and saw the floor coming up to meet her.

***

'That's one way to get out of a police interview,' Dan said, gripping Emma's arm as he helped her from the car. He'd parked as close as he legally could to her cottage and was now steering her by the elbow towards the door.

'I can walk, thank you,' she snapped, shaking off his hand before wobbling and almost falling over. Face flushing, she jammed her key into the lock, turned it and opened the door. She stepped into the hall and Dan followed, closing the door behind him. Emma padded to the sofa in her slippers and sat down. 'I'm fine,' she snapped.

Dan stood in the doorway from the hall. 'That's the biggest lie I've ever heard you tell, Em,' he said, shaking his head. 'You're not fine. There's no way you could be.'

Emma looked up at him. 'It was hot in there and I think I forgot breakfast.'

Dan raised his eyebrows. 'You're telling me that was caused by blood sugar?' He snorted and walked across to the kitchen. 'I'd better get you something to eat then, hadn't I?'

'Tea and twenty-five biscuits should do it,' Emma called after him. She heard him filling the kettle and opening and shutting a cupboard.

She lay back against the sofa cushions and tried to relax, but she could feel her heart racing again. She closed her eyes, but then opened them again quickly. All she saw was Natasha sprawled in the dirt, blood soaking her clothes. And she might have been able to save her if only she hadn't taken so long to get there. An elastic band seemed to tighten around her chest and she knew she needed to calm down. She sat up and leaned forward to put her head between her knees.

'Em, are you OK?' Dan strode across the room, putting a packet of biscuits down on the table. She could hear the kettle still boiling. 'What are you doing?'

She sat back on the sofa, fingers scrabbling at her throat. 'I can't breathe,' she said, panting. 'I can't breathe.'

Dan's arms encircled her and he squeezed her gently.

'It's OK,' he murmured in her ear. 'You're OK. I've got you.'

She leaned into him and the sobs began again. He continued to hold her, rocking her slightly until she stopped crying. Once he was sure she could breathe normally, Dan went to the kitchen and returned with a handful of paper kitchen towels and two mugs of tea. He put the tea down on the table on coasters and handed her the paper towels. Then he sat down again. She scrubbed at her face with the tissue.

'I can't stop crying,' she said. 'I went all manic while I was with Burton and Shepherd, babbling like an idiot, and God knows what I said to them.'

Dan shifted to sit on the coffee table so he could look at her face-to-face, almost sitting on the biscuits.

Emma grabbed the packet and ripped it open. She took two and stuffed one into her mouth straight away.

Dan took both her hands in his and continued to watch her. 'Look, you need to take your foot off the gas. You had probably the worst shock you can ever have last night. You've barely slept, you've not eaten and then you tried to go to work this morning.'

Emma swallowed the biscuit and put her face back in her hands. 'And then I thought I could see Burton and find out what they knew.'

'You're going onto autopilot and it's not good for you,' Dan said, getting hold of her hands.

'But Dan, she died because I didn't get to her quickly enough,' Emma said, leaning towards him. 'If only I'd ... I should have...' Her voice died away as she heard an echo of those words from the past.

'Don't torture yourself like that,' Dan pleaded. 'Even if you had got there sooner, there's no knowing if you'd have been able to do anything.' He shuddered. 'You might be dead too.'

Emma took a deep breath. 'Burton thinks the killer was still there,' she said.

Dan sat up straight. 'What do you mean?' he demanded.

'Just before I passed out, she asked if I'd seen or heard anyone. I said I'd heard something in the bushes and that's how I'd found Natasha.' She looked up to see a horrified expression on Dan's face.

'They think the killer was still there?' He paused. 'Emma, do they think the killer saw you?'

Emma shook her head, tears starting again. 'I don't know. I passed out before we got any further.'

Dan took a deep breath and puffed out his cheeks. 'Well, that's it. You're not going out on your own until the police sort this out.'

'What?' Emma demanded. 'You can't lock me up.'

'I will if I have to. Stay away from this. If the killer saw you, then they might think you saw them. Be sensible.'

'What am I supposed to do, then?'

'You need to get some sleep. You look like you're on your last legs.' He glanced at his watch. 'Look, I've got to get back to the office. Promise me you're going to stay here and rest.'

Emma flopped back against the cushions. She was too tired to argue. The panic attack had taken more out of her than she'd remembered it doing before.

'OK, I'll stay here,' she said.

'Lie down there,' Dan said, rearranging the cushions on the sofa. 'I'll come back after work and make sure you're all right.' Emma swung her legs around and lay down. She felt her eyes closing and was soon fast asleep.

Dan smiled down at her for a moment and then covered her with a throw from the armchair. Then he tiptoed out, closing and locking the door behind him with the spare key.

Chapter 33

Sarah McGovern looked unsure whether she was pleased to see Burton and Shepherd or not.

'You don't need to tell me the news,' she said, opening the door and stepping back to let them in. 'Angela has already done that.' She led the way into the kitchen where the family liaison officer was sitting at the table with Tony Standing. The latter leapt to his feet, clearly spoiling for a fight.

'What are you doing here?' he demanded. 'Sarah has already answered all of your questions. She—'

'We have some new ones, in the light of recent events,' Burton said sweetly and Shepherd winced. When the boss was being nice, it didn't bode well for the suspect.

Sarah flapped a hand at her brother. 'Oh Tony, shush.' He stepped back in surprise and sat down with a thump.

She joined the group at the table and Burton sat down, too. Shepherd leaned against the kitchen counter and pulled out his notebook and pen.

'Angela informed you about the discovery of a woman's body in the park yesterday. It was Natasha Kent, the woman Travers was having an affair with,' Burton said.

Sarah's mouth fell open, but no sound came out.

Tony Standing snorted. 'Woman? She was a child,' he snapped.

Burton glared at him. 'Be that as it may,' she continued, 'we also found at the post-mortem that Miss Kent was pregnant.'

Sarah slammed away from the table with a small cry of pain, making everyone jump. She marched to the end of the room and began sobbing, her hands flying to cover her face. Shepherd got to his feet and crossed the room to hand her a handkerchief.

'Don't worry, it's clean,' he said quietly. She took it and with a deep, shuddering breath got her emotion under control.

'Thank you,' she said. Shepherd patted her arm and led her back to the table. He stayed behind her as she returned to her seat.

'I'm sorry,' she said, wiping her face with the handkerchief, 'it's just a shock. As I said before, I suspected he was seeing someone, but I never dreamed...' She trailed away and tears threatened, but she held them back. 'I've always wanted children, but Travers always had an excuse: he needed a better job; we needed a bigger house. Once we got this place...' she gestured around '...I realised he had no intention of having children.'

'How did that make you feel?' Shepherd asked, sitting down next to her.

Sarah looked at him, almost gratefully. 'Devastated, of course. At my age, I'll probably never have children.'

'You feel you've wasted time?' Shepherd asked. The group had fallen silent, as if unable to break their conversation.

Sarah sniffed and shrugged. 'I don't think I'd go that far.'

'Would you have left the marriage?' Shepherd asked. 'Knowing that he didn't want children after all?'

Sarah shrugged again. 'I hadn't decided what I was going to do.'

Burton felt Tony Standing stiffen in his chair and gave him a look that made him decide against interjecting.

Sarah paused and looked at Burton. 'Did he know? Did Travers know she was pregnant?'

Burton nodded. 'We believe he did,' she said.

'Was he going to leave me?' Sarah asked in a small voice.

Burton looked helplessly at Shepherd, desperate not to inflict any more pain.

'We don't know,' Shepherd said. 'We've found no evidence that was the case.' Sarah's shoulders relaxed. She was drawing comfort from his very presence. 'But we have to ask where you were between six o'clock and six thirty yesterday evening,' he said.

Sarah stared at him. 'You're asking me for— You're asking me for an alibi?' she gasped.

Shepherd nodded. 'I'm sure you can understand why we do that,' he said, gently. He could feel Tony Standing glaring at him, desperate to interrupt, and he returned his own 'you're next' look.

Sarah sat back in her chair. 'I was in the car going to my friend's house. I got there at about ten past six and I was there all evening. We drank too much and I stayed over. I called Angela to tell her.' She looked at the FLO, who nodded.

Shepherd looked up from his notebook and smiled. 'A bit of de-compression goes a long way,' he said.

'And you, Mr Standing,' Burton asked, turning suddenly to Sarah's brother, 'where were you?'

Standing looked startled as the focus suddenly shifted to him. He started blustering.

'Why do you want to know that?' he demanded.

'We now have two murdered people, both of whom were hurting your sister, and you had motive for both,' Burton said. Sarah gave a small gasp, but Shepherd held up a hand to stop her from speaking. Tony opened his mouth and closed it again.

Burton sighed. 'I'll ask you again: where were you yesterday evening between six and six thirty?'

Tony stared for a moment and said, 'I was at the social club playing darts. I got there at six and left at eight.' He sat back in his chair and folded his arms as if that concluded the conversation.

'We can check, y'know,' Burton said. Tony only stared back at her as if he'd said his last words. 'OK,' Burton said, 'we'll take down your alibi details and get back to you.' She got to her feet and beckoned Angela into the hall as Shepherd scribbled down details.

'How much do you believe their stories?' she asked Angela.

The other woman frowned. 'Sarah's is pretty accurate. She left here about six o'clock and rang me at nine to say she was going to stay over. Him, I don't like.'

'Why?'

151

'He's always nagging her about something. He mentioned life insurance and said she should claim as soon as possible.'

'Life insurance? On Travers McGovern?' Burton asked.

Angela nodded. 'I've been trying to talk to her privately about it, but he's around a lot.'

'Can you ask her about that ASAP?' Burton asked.

Angela nodded. She looked back towards the kitchen. 'I feel sorry for her. Between a feckless husband and a controlling brother, she doesn't have much luck with men.'

Burton sighed. 'Well, I don't like him either. He's up to his ears with motive. If he's had the opportunity as well, then I'll nail him.'

***

'Good work with Sarah,' Burton said as Shepherd steered the car back towards the police station.

He sighed. 'Her reaction suggests she didn't know about the pregnancy, but what if Travers told her? She could have killed him for wasting her life pretending he wanted children with her when he didn't. Then he has an affair with someone else and gets her pregnant.'

'But why kill Natasha once Travers was gone?' Burton asked, staring out of the window. 'Jealousy? He got Natasha pregnant when he wouldn't do that for her?'

Shepherd slowed for a junction and flicked on the indicator.

'I dunno, boss. I really don't want it to be her.'

'If she didn't know about the affair or the pregnancy, she's got no motive to kill either. Travers sounds like he wasn't a great husband, but on its own doesn't give enough motive.' Burton frowned. 'Right, let's check her alibi, but my money is on the brother.'

Shepherd nodded. 'He seems like he has a temper and knew about the affair, which he clearly hadn't mentioned to Sarah.'

'If he knew Natasha was pregnant as well, that gives him motive to attack her, even if he didn't mean to kill her.'

'And stabbing someone who's pregnant in the stomach certainly sends a message,' Shepherd said. 'Maybe he was aiming for the baby, rather than her, if that makes sense.'

Burton nodded, as the car turned into the station car park.

'Either way, I want his alibi checked as thoroughly as we can. That social club isn't far from the park and I want to know exactly what time he got there, or whether he had time for a little detour.'

Chapter 34

Burton's phone was ringing when they returned to the office and, as she dashed to answer it, Shepherd delegated tasks to the rest of the team.

Her heart sank when she heard her boss's voice on the other end demanding an update.

'Yes, sir,' she said. 'We've got a few leads to follow up. We're checking the alibis of Travers' wife and her brother. She claims not to know about the affair and her reaction seemed genuine. He knew about it and he admits to speaking to Travers on the day he died, so we're looking closely at him. We've got a business owner saying she might have heard a scream in the park near Natasha Kent's crime scene, but isn't sure if she did or what time. She could have heard the woman who found the body.' She listened again. 'Yes, sir, we're going to make an appeal through the media and on social media.' She listened for another couple of minutes, thanked her senior officer and hung up.

She puffed out her cheeks and exhaled heavily. This investigation was not going as quickly as 'upstairs' was hoping for. Looking up, she found Shepherd in the doorway. She waved a hand for him to come in, which he did, followed by another man in a short khaki jacket and jeans, the overhead lights making his bald head glow. The man looked familiar, but she couldn't place him.

'Sir, this is Police Constable Marcus Weston,' Shepherd said, 'the Kents' FLO.'

'Of course.' She got to her feet and offered a hand, which the man shook.

'I just wanted to pop in because, well, I think there's something strange going on,' he said.

'How do you mean?' Burton asked, returning to her seat and waving them both to chairs opposite her desk.

'Well, it's the sister, Jules.'

'How do you mean?' Burton asked.

'I can't quite put my finger on it,' Weston said, settling himself in the chair. 'When you asked her earlier about Natasha being pregnant, she said she didn't already know, didn't she?'

Burton nodded and looked at Shepherd, whose eyes were fixed on Marcus.

'She knew, and about Travers McGovern as well. I heard her talking to someone about it on the phone. She and Natasha had a massive row about it, apparently.'

Shepherd exhaled heavily. 'She follows Natasha around like a shadow, so it's no surprise she picked up on something.'

Burton leaned an elbow on the arm of her chair and rested her chin on her hand. 'You think she killed Travers McGovern to get him away from Natasha?'

Marcus nodded. 'She's very intense about Natasha, and from talking to her mother, it seems she wanted to know where Natasha was all the time.'

Shepherd frowned. 'It surprised her that Natasha hadn't told her where she was going, but then Emma Fletcher said she thought Natasha was good at keeping secrets.'

'She was hiding stuff from her sister?' Weston asked.

Burton shrugged. 'If I was an eighteen-year-old woman with my life to lead, I don't think I'd take too kindly to being stage-managed like that.'

Marcus sat forward in his chair. 'Her mum said she seemed to tolerate Julietta rather than like her attention,' he put in. 'Mrs Kent also said something odd. I asked her about Dominic and how he and Natasha split up.'

'What did she say?'

'She said it was Natasha's decision to split up after Julietta said she'd seen Dominic out with another woman.'

'What's odd about that?'

'It was the way she said it. "I'm almost sure it was her decision" was what she said.'

'Almost sure? What are you thinking?'

Marcus paused a moment. 'I got the feeling she meant it was Julietta who decided.'

Shepherd frowned. 'Do you think Julietta made up seeing him with someone else so Natasha would dump him?' he asked.

Marcus nodded.

Burton sat up straight. 'Natasha told us Travers said he was going to leave his wife for her, that they would be together.'

'But she didn't sound overly happy about it,' Shepherd added.

'What if Julietta found out about it?'

'And killed him to keep Natasha focused on her dancing?' Weston asked.

Burton nodded. 'Or Natasha had tried to give Travers the old heave-ho and he was refusing to let it go,' she said, 'so Julietta stepped in to make sure he did.'

Shepherd puffed out his cheeks. 'I can think of someone who might know,' he said.

Chapter 35

Emma woke as a key turned in the front door. She was lying along the sofa, covered with a blanket and, for a moment, couldn't work out where she was. She tried to sit up, not sure who it was, but her head spun, so she lay back down. Dan appeared in the doorway.

'Hey, how are you feeling?' he asked, putting his bag and a supermarket carrier on the floor. He crossed the room and sat on the coffee table, peering at her. 'You look a bit better.'

'I feel like death,' Emma replied, trying and failing to sit up.

'Stay where you are for a minute while I put the shopping away and then we can talk.'

He went into the kitchen and Emma heard him pottering around, the fridge opening and closing, cupboard doors banging. Then he returned, putting a large glass of water on the table and helping her to sit up.

'Here, drink some of this,' he said, handing her the glass. Emma took a couple of sips and sat back on the sofa. Dan took a deep breath. 'We need to talk about this. You're not fine and I want to help.'

Emma sighed. 'I don't know how I went to sleep,' she said. 'Every time I close my eyes, I just see Natasha lying there.'

'You were exhausted,' Dan said, moving to sit beside her on the sofa. 'You've had a massive shock, so it's not really a surprise that you're freaking out, is it?'

Emma shook her head.

'You know you have to step back from this,' Dan said.

'I need to know who did it. Someone stabbed her in the stomach because she knew who killed Travers and I need to make them pay.' She could feel tears starting again.

'We will find them, but you need to rest. Leave it to me. I'll gather the info and then we'll work out what to do. In the meantime, we need to—'

The doorbell interrupted him.

Dan got to his feet and crossed the room. 'Are you at home?' he asked. Emma nodded. She heard him open the front door.

'Oh, it's you,' he said.

'I've had warmer welcomes,' Shepherd said, following him into the room. He smiled at Emma. 'You're looking a little better than when I saw you earlier. Not much, but a bit.'

Emma smiled tiredly and pulled herself into a more comfortable position on the sofa.

'Do you want a cuppa?' Dan asked, hovering. Shepherd declined his offer and sat down on the sofa.

'This is a semi-social call,' Shepherd said, 'to make sure you were all right, but I also have a couple of questions.'

Emma nodded. 'No problem. Fire away.'

'You knew Natasha was having an affair with Travers McGovern,' Shepherd said.

'Only after he was killed,' Emma said. 'Previously, she'd only told me she was seeing someone, a married man, but she never named him.'

'You've met her sister, haven't you?' When Emma nodded, he continued, 'Do you think she knew about Travers? About the affair?'

Emma thought for a moment. 'I've only met her briefly a few times, but never really spoken to her. She's quite stand-offish.'

'Did you get the impression from Natasha that anyone else knew about the affair?'

'She said there'd been gossip around the school, but nothing else.'

'Someone definitely knew,' Dan put in, sitting down beside Emma.

Shepherd raised his eyebrows. 'How do you mean?'

'Tell him about the sex tape,' Dan said to Emma.

Shepherd's eyes widened. 'Sex tape?'

Emma sighed. 'Travers recorded him and Natasha having sex without her permission. She went mental at him when she found out and made him delete the footage. Then she got an email from someone with the video attached, telling her she was going to pay for what she'd done. That they were going to ruin her life and her future career.'

'A sex tape would certainly do that,' Shepherd said, pulling out his notebook and scribbling in it. 'Did she know who sent it?'

Emma shook her head. 'They were threatening to release it on social media. It happened just before Travers died, so she thought it was him, but—'

'Him? Why would he do that? It would affect him too,' Shepherd said, looking up quickly.

'Her exact words were, "He'd have lost his job and probably his marriage, but men can ride that kind of thing out, can't they?"'

'What did they mean by what she'd done?' Shepherd asked, pen flying across the page.

Emma shook her head. 'Natasha didn't know, or at least didn't tell me. But it can't have been Travers who was blackmailing her because she got another email after he died saying the video would still be released if she didn't admit it.'

'Do you have a copy of the video?' Shepherd asked, and then laughed at Emma's horrified expression. 'Sorry, not that I think you'd share that kind of thing.'

'It's on Nat's phone,' Emma said, blushing. 'She got it by email, so it might be on her laptop as well.'

Shepherd nodded. 'We can easily check that.' He clicked away the point of his pen and pushed it and his notebook back in his pocket. 'You need to make a formal statement,' he said.

Emma nodded. 'I can come to the station tomorrow,' she said. 'I can,' she insisted, glaring at Dan when he made an impatient noise.

'You need to rest,' he said.

'I need to do this for Nat,' she snapped.

Dan shrugged. 'OK, if you're doing that, I'll come with you.'

'Does ten o'clock work for you?' Shepherd asked, standing up.

Emma nodded and tried to stand up, but Shepherd waved her back. 'Don't worry, I can see myself out.' He disappeared down the hall and they heard the door shut behind him.

Emma looked at Dan and exhaled heavily. 'Did you think it sounds like they suspect her sister?' she asked.

Dan frowned. 'Do you reckon she could have done it?'

'I don't know. I've only met her a few times and for a few minutes. She seems very protective of Nat, but enough to kill someone for her?'

'Could it be about the sex tape? I wouldn't like someone releasing that with my sister in it.'

'Nat thought Travers was behind it, maybe Julietta did too, and killed him to stop anyone else from seeing it,' Emma said, leaning back on the sofa cushions.

'But then to kill Natasha? Why would she do that?'

Emma rubbed her forehead. 'My brain feels like such a jumble. I can't even think straight.'

'That's definitely a sign that you need to eat something.' He got to his feet. 'Get ready for my new speciality.' Emma groaned. 'Don't worry,' he said, 'even I can manage not to ruin a microwave curry.' He disappeared into the kitchen, chuckling.

Chapter 36

When Emma and Dan followed Shepherd into the police interview room the following morning, Burton was already at the table. She looked surprised.

'We get the entire team today?' she asked.

Emma nodded as she and Dan sat down opposite.

'I asked Dan to come along because he's been involved in this too.'

Burton looked from Dan to Emma, frowning. 'Involved in what exactly?'

'Let's start from what you told me last night,' Shepherd said. He sat down and pulled some sheets of paper from the cardboard folder he was carrying. He took a pen from his pocket.

Emma recounted her story about Natasha, Travers and the sex tape. When she'd finished, Burton sat back in her chair and puffed out her cheeks.

'Poor girl,' she said. 'If she wasn't already dead, I'd definitely be looking at her for Travers McGovern's murder.'

Emma nodded sadly. 'I asked her that myself.'

Burton stared at her. 'You actually asked your friend if she killed her lover?' she asked, disbelieving.

Emma looked down at the table. 'I felt awful, but once you told me about the peanut oil, I asked her if she knew about his peanut allergy—'

'But apparently everyone knew about that,' Dan interrupted.

161

'Yes, but how many people knew he had a bottle of vodka in his drawer and used to drink it after work?' Emma asked him.

'Natasha knew and she was angry with him about the sex tape,' he replied.

Emma looked from Burton to Shepherd. 'Do you think the same person killed Natasha and Travers?'

Burton nodded. 'I think it's a fair assumption, given their connection. There's something else,' she said soberly. 'The post-mortem showed Natasha was two months pregnant.'

Emma gasped and her hand flew to her mouth. 'What?'

Burton nodded. 'Did she mention it to you?'

Emma shook her head. 'No, she never said a word about it, although she mentioned feeling sick. Was it Travers' baby?'

Shepherd looked up from his notes. 'We're still waiting on DNA confirmation. Her ex-boyfriend was back on the scene apparently, but we don't know whether they were just friends.'

Emma sighed. 'No wonder her dancing was all over the place. Imagine being pregnant on top of everything else. She must have been so confused.'

'Do you think she'd have kept it?' Burton asked.

Emma shrugged. 'I've no idea. But she seemed quite certain that nothing was going to derail her dancing. She didn't even see Travers every day because she had rehearsals and stuff.'

'She seems to have been quite single-minded,' Burton said, fiddling with her watch strap. 'Is there anything else you need to tell us?'

Emma was about to shake her head when Dan elbowed her in the ribs.

'Tell them about Neville Shuster,' he hissed.

Burton and Shepherd exchanged a look and then turned to Dan and Emma.

'Who's Neville Shuster?' Shepherd asked.

Emma took a deep breath and recounted how they'd found Travers' rival and been to interview him.

'You should have told us sooner,' Burton said sternly.

'I was going to call you on Saturday when we'd spoken to him, but then I got Natasha's message and ... Well, you know the rest.'

Burton leaned back in her chair. 'So we've got someone else with a good reason to be angry with Travers.'

'And was in his office the evening that he died,' Dan put in, tapping a forefinger on the table surface.

'What interests me is the text message Travers got and then rushed off. Any idea who sent that?' Shepherd said, looking at Emma and Dan.

They shrugged in unison. 'Neville didn't know,' Dan said, 'but he said it really rattled Travers.'

'Have you got Travers' phone?' Emma demanded. 'It'll be on there.'

'Our tech team is on it. Does this Neville have a reason to kill Natasha?' Burton asked.

Emma shook her head. 'No, I don't think so. It was Travers he wanted to get revenge on. He said he had nothing against Natasha, but if she saw him spiking Travers' vodka, he'd have a reason.' She sighed. 'When Neville said that Travers looked frightened of the text message, I thought maybe it had been Natasha. He knew how angry she was.'

The room was silent, the scratching of Shepherd's pen being the only sound.

'Do you have any other suspects?' Burton asked Emma and Dan.

They both considered.

'Travers McGovern's wife?' Dan suggested. 'Although, that would work better if Natasha had died first.'

'The ex-boyfriend might be interesting,' Emma said. 'What if he kills Travers so he can get Nat back? Then she turns him down, anyway?'

'What we're overlooking, though,' Dan said, turning to face her, 'is why someone killed them. We assume Travers died because he had a fling with the wrong person, but why kill Natasha?'

Emma was frowning. She opened her mouth to speak, but Burton cut in.

'Much as I'm enjoying the brainstorming session,' she said with a half-smile, 'I think it's best you leave this to us. Whoever did this took massive risks, killing both people somewhere they could be caught. In fact, you nearly did catch them—' She pointed at Emma.

Emma looked down at the table, feeling her hands shake a little.

'Stay away from this,' Burton said kindly. 'It's the only way we can keep you safe.'

***

When they got outside the police station, Dan turned to Emma.

'We hit the nail on the head in there,' Dan said, pointing back at the building.

'How do you mean?' Emma asked, heading towards the pedestrian crossing, which had just started to show the little green man.

'We've been so fixated on who could have done it, we've not stopped to really look at why. Why did someone kill Travers?'

'And who would also want to kill Natasha?' Emma asked, taking his hand.

'Exactly. We've been assuming that someone killed Travers because he was having a fling with Natasha, but once he's dead, why go after her?'

'She said in her message that she knew who the killer was and that's why the killer went after her.'

'How did the killer know, though?' Dan asked. 'She wouldn't be stupid enough to tell them, surely.'

Emma walked on silently and then put a hand to her forehead.

'Are you OK?' Dan asked, gripping her hand and peering into her face.

'I just feel a bit light-headed.'

'That's it. I'm going to walk you home, get you settled with a cuppa and then I'll head back to the office. No buts,' he said when Emma tried to argue. 'I've got to interview the Kent family later, so I'll update you tonight.'

'I'll cook,' Emma said, but Dan was already shaking his head.

'Nope, I'm treating you to a takeaway. Doctor Dan's orders.'

She laughed and allowed him to lead her along by the hand.

Chapter 37

Dan did his best sympathetic smile as the Kents' front door opened. A young, brown-skinned woman appeared, and he recognised her as the woman in Natasha's pouty photo.

'Are you from the newspaper?' she asked, blocking the doorway.

'Yes, Dan Sullivan, I was told you were expecting me,' Dan said, trying to peer past her into the hall. She moved to block his view.

'This isn't a good idea,' she said, 'so you can leave.'

Before Dan could move, a hand reached around the door and opened it wider.

'Manners, Jules,' said an older woman with a matronly figure and hair pulled back into tight cornrows. She smiled at Dan with tired eyes. 'Thank you for coming,' she said, gently edging Jules out of the way and opening the door so Dan could step inside.

She waved a hand and Dan followed it into a large sitting room. Mrs Kent directed him to an armchair and then sat opposite him on a squishy sofa. Jules hovered by the living room door, twisting her fingers together nervously.

'My older daughter, Julietta,' Mrs Kent said, holding out a hand to the younger woman. Julietta crossed the room and sat down, taking her mother's hand and squeezing tightly. 'Would you like a cup of tea?' Mrs Kent asked.

Dan shook his head. 'Thanks, I just had one at the office.'

Mrs Kent took a deep breath. 'Sorry, I'm not sure how this works.

The police said you want to do a tribute piece?'

Dan nodded. 'We do that for families of people who've died if they want to do it. It's nice to honour that person, particularly someone like Natasha, who was so popular.' He wasn't sure whether he was laying it on a bit thick, but both women smiled, so he felt he was on the right track.

'She was,' said Mrs Kent. 'Everyone liked her.'

Clearly someone didn't, Dan thought to himself. They talked through Natasha's early life, picking up dancing at a young age and how that had progressed.

'And she was doing well at school?' Dan asked.

Julietta nodded. 'She was one of the best in her year. In fact, she was the best. No one could match her.'

'My girlfriend said she was excellent,' Dan said. 'She really enjoyed her classes.'

Mrs Kent looked surprised. 'Your girlfriend went to school with Natasha? She must be very young,' she said, eyeing Dan suspiciously.

He caught her look and laughed. 'No, Emma wasn't in a class with Natasha,' he said, waving his pen. 'Natasha was teaching her in an adult beginners' class.' There was a brief silence and he found himself looking at two puzzled faces. He'd obviously just told them something they didn't know.

'Natasha taught her?' Julietta asked, sitting forward in her chair. 'What do you mean?'

This surprised Dan. 'My girlfriend went to her dancing classes at the college on a Tuesday night. I wondered where she'd been going. She didn't tell me until recently, after Natasha—'

'Natasha didn't teach classes,' Julietta interrupted. 'She focused on her own dancing and rehearsals.'

Dan frowned. 'It was definitely Natasha. That's what Emma said.'

Julietta opened her mouth to argue, but Mrs Kent raised a hand.

'I think Jules is trying to say that we didn't know she'd been teaching.' She smiled indulgently. 'But I'm not surprised. She was always interested in others.'

'She should have been focusing on her dancing, not messing about with other people,' Julietta snapped. 'I'd told her that. I—' She halted, as if fearing she'd said too much.

Dan cleared his throat, suddenly feeling awkward. 'Was Natasha training for anything specific?' he asked Julietta, keen to get her back onside.

'The end-of-year showcase is in a couple of weeks,' Julietta said, 'and Natasha had two leading two roles.' She spoke proudly, clearly keen to show off her sister's abilities.

'Oh, what parts was she playing?' Dan asked.

Mrs Kent smiled. 'You're not a dance show go-er, are you?' she asked.

Dan grinned. 'Am I not using the right terminology?' he asked.

'It's not quite the same as being in a play. She was in three different numbers, a solo piece from Swan Lake, as well as a *pas de deux* with her partner Dominic, and then a ballroom medley.'

'Two distinct styles from the sounds of it?' Dan asked.

Mrs Kent nodded. She opened her mouth to speak, but Julietta interrupted.

'That just shows you how talented she was, that she could do two different styles and be chosen for both in the showcase,' she said quickly. 'You should write that in the article.' She pointed to Dan's notebook and he dutifully scribbled it down.

'How are students chosen for the showcase? Is it like an audition?' he asked.

Julietta shook her head. 'The school staff choose, based on who had the best performances in the previous year. That's how Natasha was chosen.'

'Would Travers McGovern have been one of those with a vote?' Dan asked, worrying that he was on dodgy territory.

Julietta's face darkened. 'Why do you ask about him?'

'I'd heard they were friends and I assumed he supported her dancing,' he said, aiming for a light tone.

'I don't think you need to write about him,' Julietta said, 'although clearly you know about his connection to Natasha.'

Dan nodded. 'She talked to Emma about it. I'm sorry, this won't go in the article,' he promised. 'I want to focus on Natasha as a person and as a dancer.'

Mrs Kent relaxed. 'You'll probably still want to speak to her dancing partner, Dominic. He's a lovely boy, came round with those flowers yesterday.' She pointed to an arrangement of pink and yellow flowers in a vase on the mantelpiece. 'The colours don't really go together, but it's the thought that counts,' she said with an indulgent smile.

'Had they been dancing together for long?' Dan asked, still scribbling.

'About eight years,' Mrs Kent said, frowning. 'Yes, I think that's about right.'

'But you don't need to talk about him, do you?' Julietta interrupted. 'You're just focusing on her?'

Dan shifted in his seat. 'Well, if they were dancing partners, then I'll have to mention him.'

Julietta looked disappointed.

Mrs Kent eyed her elder daughter and then turned back to Dan. 'Is there anything else you need?'

Dan was scanning back over his notes. 'No, I think I've got everything, so I can leave you in peace.' He pushed his notebook and pen into his bag and got to his feet. Mrs Kent stood up and nudged Julietta to get up as well. They followed him to the door. As he put out a hand to open the door, Dan turned back.

'I know this isn't really my place,' he said, 'but I assume the police are keeping you informed about the investigation?'

Mrs Kent nodded. 'They have. A nice young man has been sitting with us to keep us updated. You've just missed him. He's gone to get us some more tea and biscuits. It seems to be all I've had in the last couple of days.'

'Emma is so upset that someone wanted to hurt Natasha,' Dan said. 'She seems to have been so popular. Can you think of anyone who might have had a grudge or fallen out with her?'

Mrs Kent shook her head and her eyes filled with tears. She dug a tissue from her sleeve and wiped her eyes. 'I can't understand it. Natasha didn't have an enemy in the world. It's just so senseless.'

Dan nodded, feeling bad that he'd caused her pain. He looked at Julietta.

'Would you be able to send me some photographs of Natasha that

I can use in the article? I'm sure you've got some great ones.' He held out his business card.

She took it with a smile. 'I've got loads on my phone. I'll send some this afternoon.' She paused and then sighed. 'I've got to clear out Nat's locker at school tomorrow morning.'

Dan thanked them, pulled open the door and set off back to his car. He frowned as he opened the door and got inside. There was something odd about Julietta Kent that he couldn't quite put his finger on.

***

'It was a slightly odd interview,' Dan said. He was leaning in the doorway of Emma's kitchen, watching her bustle around, making tea.

She turned to look at him. 'How do you mean?'

'Well, the sister is really intense. She tried to turn me away at first, even though they'd agreed to speak to me. She didn't want any mention of Travers; she didn't even want a mention of Natasha's dancing partner.'

Emma stood with the tea caddy in one hand and a tea bag in the other. 'I can understand not wanting to mention the connection between Natasha and Travers, but why not the partner?'

Dan frowned. 'What she said was, "You don't need to talk about him ... You're just focusing on her."'

'The focus will be on her,' Emma said, 'but she must know we talk to other people as well.'

Dan shrugged. 'I got the impression that Natasha is always her focus. She seems a bit ... I don't know ... pushy. Is that the right word?' He stood up straight and ruffled his hair. 'What was interesting was that she was upset she didn't know about Natasha teaching classes.'

Emma finished pouring water from the kettle into mugs and turned around.

'They didn't know?'

'And she did *not* like that.'

169

Emma stared into space, frowning. 'It's funny that you mention it, because now I think back to when she came to pick Natasha up after class, she asked Nat how rehearsals had gone.'

'Rehearsals?'

'It surprised me, actually. Clearly Nat was lying to her sister, but why?'

'The mother didn't seem to know either.'

Emma scrubbed her face with both hands. 'I don't understand. Why would Natasha not tell them?'

'The sister went to great pains to tell me Natasha was the best dancer in the year. Maybe Natasha didn't want to tell her she was moonlighting rather than practising? Is this why she was screwing up everything else?'

'I don't think so. She's been teaching for ages. Travers and the sex tape were a more recent issue, as was the pregnancy.'

'Do you think the sister knows about the sex tape?'

Emma shuddered. 'I doubt Natasha would have told her that.'

'And there's no way she found it?' Dan asked.

'I dunno. Maybe if she had Natasha's laptop password or access to her phone. The blackmailer sent it to Nat by email.'

'What if Julietta saw the video? She'd be livid that he'd done that and that he was taking Natasha away from dancing. Especially if she thought it was affecting Nat's performance.'

'I think that's probably an understatement,' Emma said, returning to fish the tea bags out of the mugs. 'Sorry, I think that might be a bit stewed,' she said.

'I'll drink it however it comes,' Dan said with a smile. 'You know that.'

'What I wonder,' Emma continued, taking milk from the fridge, 'is whether Julietta saw that email and assumed it was from Travers? If she thought he was trying to ruin Nat, I could see her going nuclear and shutting him up.'

Dan nodded. 'That gives her a reason to kill him, but why Natasha?'

'She found out that Nat was pregnant?' Emma suggested, returning the milk to the fridge and stirring the mugs. 'Not much call for a pregnant ballerina.'

Dan took a deep breath and puffed out his cheeks. 'It seems an extreme reaction. Would she not just make Natasha get rid of it?'

'Could she force her into that?'

'Depends how much influence she has.'

Emma thought for a moment. 'She was around Natasha a lot, picking her up after classes and stuff, but Nat got away a few times to meet me, so she wasn't under constant surveillance.'

'But when could she get away?' Dan asked.

'Mostly during the day when Julietta was at work.'

'So, only when Big Sister isn't around,' Dan said. 'Did Natasha always go back to college after you'd met up?'

Emma frowned. 'Now you mention it, yes she did. You think she was trying to make it look like she'd never left?'

Dan nodded. 'I think Julietta had a bit of a complex about Natasha and needing to know where she was. Picking her up from college is one way of controlling her. Nat would have to make sure she was at the right place at the right time for Julietta to pick her up.'

Emma handed him the hot mug and he winced.

'You think she was coercive?' she asked.

'She was trying to control what I could and couldn't put in the story,' Dan said. 'What would she be like with Nat, who she's grown up with? How much influence does she have there?'

'And were there consequences for Nat if she stepped out of line?' Emma asked, sipping at her own mug and wincing at the taste.

'Exactly. We need another chat with Julietta.'

'How are you going to do that?'

Dan sipped at his mug and thought for a moment.

'She's going to college tomorrow morning to collect Natasha's stuff from her locker. I'll hang around for a bit and see if I can catch her.'

'And turn on your charm?'

Dan laughed. 'Of course, you know all women are powerless to resist me.'

Emma groaned and pulled a face. 'Big head.'

Dan put his mug down and pulled her into a hug. 'Don't worry,' he said. 'We'll find out what happened to Natasha. Whatever we have to do.'

Chapter 38

The next morning, Burton was sitting in her office tapping rapidly on the desk with a pen. Then she got to her feet and strode into the main office.

'What have we got?' she barked at the room at large.

'Not much more, sir,' Shepherd said. 'I've chased up the tech team and they're still working on Travers' phone.'

Burton growled in the back of her throat. 'For God's sake, how long does it take to work out a four-digit passcode? Can't they override it or something?'

Shepherd winced. 'I think it's a bit more complicated than that.'

'I wish we'd known sooner about the text message Travers got the night he died,' Burton said. She marched to the murder board and stared at it as if answers might just pop out. Then she looked back at Shepherd. 'Have they got anywhere with Natasha's laptop? We gave them the bloody password.'

Shepherd perched on the end of the desk and shook his head.

Burton rounded on him. 'What are you telling me?' she demanded.

'The password didn't work.' When Burton glared at him, he raised two hands in surrender. 'That's all I was told. Someone changed the password four days ago and it isn't what Julietta gave us.'

Burton put her head in her hands. 'So Julietta's deliberately given us the wrong password. What the hell is she playing at? What's she hiding?'

172

Shepherd shrugged. 'I don't know.'

Burton clenched her fists and then released them again.

'Right, we're going back and she's going to explain why that password doesn't work and give us the right one.'

She turned and strode away, leaving Shepherd to grab his jacket and car keys and hurry after her.

Before they got to the door, a voice called, 'Sir!'

Burton and Shepherd turned and saw Gary Topping jogging across the office.

'I've chased up the alibis for Sarah McGovern and her brother. She was where she said she was. The friend confirmed it, as well as a neighbour saw Sarah arriving and said hi. She knows Sarah because she's seen her around.'

'There's one off the list,' Burton said. 'What about the brother?'

'That's where it gets interesting,' Topping said. 'He says that he got there at six o'clock and the darts team captain backs him up. But...' he paused for dramatic effect, 'the landlord swears it was closer to six forty and Mr Standing was a bit flustered. He told the landlord he'd been with his sister and then stopped for petrol.'

Burton pulled on the end of her ponytail. 'OK, get onto him, Gaz, and find out where he went for petrol. It's easy to check the garage's CCTV or a receipt.'

Topping nodded and turned away.

Burton scowled, hands on hips. 'So we've got Sarah and possibly her brother alibied. Julietta Kent says she was home with Mum—'

'And Mum didn't disagree, so does that cover both of them?' Shepherd asked.

Burton exhaled heavily. 'Normally I'd have agreed, but Miss Julietta is lying about something. Why give us the wrong password? Surely she must have known we'd be able to crack it.'

'Maybe she thought it would hold us up,' Shepherd said, waving at Burton to go ahead. 'Either way, let's find out.'

'And she'd better have a bloody good reason,' Burton said, striding off along the office.

Chapter 39

Dan felt conspicuous as he loitered around outside the gates of the dance and drama school. He pretended to thumb through his phone, as were many of the students, but he knew it was only a matter of time before someone spotted him. Then someone appeared in his peripheral vision and a wave of cigarette smoke blew into his face. He found a young woman with excellent posture eyeing him suspiciously, while puffing at a cigarette she didn't look old enough to buy.

'I've been watching you for the last ten minutes,' she said. 'You're not a student, so what are you doing?'

Dan switched on his most charming smile and pulled out a business card.

'I'm with the *Allensbury Post*,' he said, offering it to the woman. 'Dan Sullivan.'

She took it and read the details carefully. 'I'm Sadie. What are you doing here? Although I'm pretty sure I can guess.'

'I'm writing a tribute piece about Natasha Kent,' Dan said. 'We do that when someone dies who's well known.'

The woman snorted. 'Not sure how "well known" Natasha was outside school, but she was certainly notorious inside.'

Dan raised an eyebrow. 'How do you mean?' he asked.

'She was sleeping with a teacher, Travers McGovern,' she said bluntly. 'He died earlier in the week, too. There were rumours that Natasha had done it.' She took a drag on the cigarette, but blew the smoke away from Dan.

Glancing down at his phone, Dan touched the voice recorder app and switched it on.

'You knew about that?' he said, hiding the phone in his hand and hoping the microphone would pick up her voice.

Sadie laughed. 'It was the worst-kept secret in the world. They thought they were being so careful, but this is a small community,' she said, gesturing back towards the building with her cigarette. 'Everyone knows everyone's business.'

'Would anyone have a problem with her sleeping with Travers?'

Sadie shrugged. 'I could name some names.'

Dan knew he had to play his cards right here.

'Go on then,' he said. 'If you really know names.'

Sadie stood up straight. 'I do know names,' she snapped, firing up as Dan had known she would. 'You could try Tara Wallis and Dominic Randall for a start. They were both on Natasha's case.'

'Dominic's her dancing partner, isn't he?' Dan asked. He prayed the app was getting everything, because he wasn't sure how she would react to his notebook.

The woman stubbed out her cigarette into the receptacle on the wall and started counting on her fingers.

'Sally-Anne was pretty pissed off with Travers, but I'm not sure how she felt about Natasha.'

Dan raised his eyebrows. 'The principal knew about them? Did she not try to stop it?'

The dancer looked scornful. 'Of course she knew; I said it's a small community, didn't I? Whether she did anything about it, I don't know. I assume not because they were still together.'

'Do you know that for a fact?'

The woman shrugged. 'There weren't any rumours that they weren't.'

'Why would Natasha's dance partner be pissed off at her for seeing Travers?' Dan asked.

'They were sleeping together earlier this year as well.'

'At the same time as Travers?'

Sadie shook her head. 'Despite what some people are saying, she

175

wasn't like that. They were properly seeing each other and then they had a massive blowout because he cheated on her.' She pulled a packet of cigarettes and a lighter from her pocket. She offered one to Dan, who declined, and then lit up. 'I got the impression at first that Natasha didn't really believe he was seeing someone else.'

'So why break up with him?'

'Saving face? Not wanting to forgive someone who might be a cheater? Who knows? They've been at each other's throats recently, because she's been screwing up so much.'

'And Tara Wallis?'

The woman snorted and blew out a plume of smoke. 'She's a mediocre dancer who thinks she's better than she is, and she hates Natasha.' Glancing over each shoulder as if looking for eavesdroppers, she leaned in to Dan. He could smell a mixture of super-sweet perfume and cigarettes. 'She said something weird to me the day before Natasha died. We were talking about the showcase, and Tara said, "I'm going to tell Dom I'll do the lead in the tango number." I looked at her and said, "Natasha's doing that," and she replied, "She won't be around for long."'

Dan stared at her. 'You think she was going to do something to Natasha?'

The woman shrugged. 'Tara can be pretty nasty. She wants Dominic, but he still only has eyes for Natasha, so she's been trying to push her out.'

'What about the principal? Would she have killed Travers and Natasha for having an affair?'

The woman waved her cigarette. 'She can be emotional sometimes, but not that emotional.' She stubbed out the cigarette and checked her watch. 'Well, I've gotta go.'

'If you think of anything else, call me,' Dan said, pointing to his business card.

She grinned. 'I just might.' She pulled out a pen and grabbed his free hand. She scribbled a mobile number on the back of his hand and gave him a flirty wink before turning away. Dan quickly stopped the recording app and pushed his phone into his pocket. The woman had barely gone a step when the screaming started.

***

Dan whipped round towards the entrance of the college. Two women were shrieking at each other, fingers pointing. He couldn't understand a word they were saying, but he recognised one as Julietta Kent. He ran over and pushed his way through the crowd that was gathering.

'How dare you talk about my sister like that,' she was yelling at a short blonde woman.

The latter had her hands on her hips. 'I'm only telling the truth, saying what everyone already knows. She was a slag and she'd sleep with anyone if she thought it would help her career.'

Julietta took a step towards her. 'You take that back.'

'If the shoe fits, darling,' Tara drawled. 'It's either that or she got parts because she was black and everyone is trying to be soooo diverse.' There was a collective gasp from the students who'd gathered to see what was going on. One stepped forward and grabbed the blonde's arm.

'Tara, that's enough.'

But Tara shook him off. 'Overlooking other better dancers for her—' she continued, but Julietta cut her off.

'Do you mean you? You're nothing compared to her. Nothing!'

But Tara wasn't backing down. 'She was a crap dancer. Couldn't even bloody stay on her feet recently. She was going to ruin it for everyone else. She was stupid enough to get herself pregnant, so why should she get to dance the lead?'

Julietta recoiled. 'How did you know that?' she demanded.

'Everybody knew,' Tara replied, taunting her. 'What? Didn't you? Your own sister?'

Dan looked at Sadie, who stood beside him with her mouth open.

'*Did* everyone know?' he asked, and the woman shook her head.

Julietta seemed unable to speak, so Tara continued her tirade.

'She was stupid, getting herself pregnant, and not even knowing who the father was,' she said with venom.

Julietta glared at her. 'What?' she demanded.

'You heard me. She was such a slut, she didn't even know who the father was.'

With a roar, Julietta dropped the empty tote bag hanging from her shoulder and launched herself at Tara. She landed a good punch to the face before Dan could dive forward. He grabbed her around the waist and tried to pull her away.

'Jules, it's not worth it,' he gasped, wrestling with her. She was a lot stronger than he'd expected. Somewhere in the background, he heard a car screech to a halt, a door slam and running footsteps. Julietta chose that moment to swing an elbow at him. He only just ducked in time to avoid a blow to the head and lost his hold on her. She flew at Tara again, grabbing a handful of hair and delivering several more slaps and punches before Shepherd appeared and grabbed her more firmly. He dragged her away from Tara, arms and legs flailing, and outside the group of people who had stopped to watch the fight. Wailing loudly, Tara was curled in a foetal position on the concrete flagstones, blood streaming from her nose, and bruises popping around her eye and jaw. Another student knelt beside her, trying to dab at her face with some tissues.

Dan ran a hand over his face and tried to calm his breathing. He turned to see Julietta spitting and swearing and trying to escape from Shepherd's grip.

'Stop struggling,' he heard the detective say calmly. 'Stop struggling or I will put you on the floor.' But Julietta was too far gone in rage to hear what he said. Looking reluctant, Shepherd swiftly, but gently, swiped Julietta's feet from under her. With the help of Burton, he grappled her to the ground and into handcuffs. Several women screamed at his perceived brutality, but Julietta was soon under control when pinned by the two detectives.

Shepherd and Burton knelt beside her, the former speaking quietly to her to calm her. His words worked and she nodded at him. He rolled her onto her side and into a sitting position. Dan could hear him saying the familiar words as he pulled her to her feet, cautioning her she was being arrested on suspicion of assault. She was now weeping, whether in sadness or anger Dan couldn't work out. He suddenly felt exhausted now the adrenaline had gone and his arms were aching.

Seeing Julietta safe with Shepherd, Burton walked across to him.

'Are you OK?' she asked, seeing his shaking hands.

'I think so,' he said, running a hand through his hair. 'More than I can say for her.' He pointed to Tara, still sitting on the floor, now also crying to add to the mess of blood on her face.

'It was unprovoked,' she was wailing to the student tending to her wounds. 'She just came at me. She's mad.'

Dan snorted. 'Hardly unprovoked,' he said. Burton looked at him and he explained what had happened.

She puffed out her cheeks. 'I wouldn't want to hear that about my sister,' she said.

'What on earth is going on?' demanded a voice. Dan and Burton looked up to see David Dickens striding towards the melee. He took in the scene of Tara lying on the ground and Julietta being led away in handcuffs.

Burton stepped forward. 'I'm about to ask the same thing.'

All the watching students began speaking at the same time. Burton raised a hand and they fell silent. A marked police car pulled up and two officers got out. One walked across to Shepherd and exchanged a few words. Shepherd transferred Julietta into her care and followed the other officer to join Burton.

'Right,' Burton said. 'You...' she pointed to Tara, who was still whimpering and dabbing at her face with a tissue '...sit down over there.' She pointed to a wooden bench. 'This officer will come and speak to you once he's got details from the rest of you.' She waved at the assembled crowd. They all nodded and began forming a gaggle around the officer. 'Once you're done, you disperse immediately,' Burton added.

David Dickens started herding the students into a line, demanding that they be patient and wait their turn, but he kept his eyes fixed on Burton and Dan.

'You,' Burton now pointed at Dan, 'need to make a statement as well. Come up to the police station later today and do it then.'

Dan nodded. 'Will do.'

'You don't have any footage of that, do you?' she asked.

Dan was rubbing his arm ruefully. 'For once, no. I was too busy trying to break it up,' he said. 'Nearly got elbowed in the head for my trouble.' He looked at the marked car, which was performing a neat three-point turn. 'How bad is this going to be for her?'

Burton frowned. 'Depends whether the other lass presses charges.'

'She's grieving,' Dan said, 'and it definitely was not unprovoked. But she'd have torn Tara in two if I'd not grabbed her.'

'Couldn't hold on to her though, could you? She's only small,' Burton said, giving him a sly smile.

'She's a lot stronger than she looks,' Dan protested.

Burton was frowning as she stared at the marked car as it pulled out of the car park.

Dan looked at her. 'Why were you here?' he asked. 'You didn't come to break up the fight.'

'Nice try,' Burton said. 'I'm not giving anything away that easily.' She smiled and turned away to walk over to Shepherd.

Dan watched her go, his breathing finally returning to normal. Then he pulled out his phone and started scrolling through his saved numbers.

Emma answered on the first ring.

'You will not believe what's just happened,' Dan said.

***

Watching Dan already tapping at his mobile phone, Burton sighed. The story would be on the *Allensbury Post* website before they had even interviewed Julietta.

She watched for a moment, making sure the students were all under control. A first aider had been called to examine Tara and was gently cleaning blood from around the dancer's nose. She was still whimpering and flinching every time the man touched her. Burton suspected she had a broken nose.

Shepherd appeared at her shoulder, brown eyes worried.

Burton raised an eyebrow. 'Julietta packs quite a punch.'

Shepherd nodded. 'She's a lot stronger than she looks.'

Burton smiled. 'Dan Sullivan said the same,' she said, pointing in the direction Dan had gone. Then her face darkened.

'We need that CCTV,' Burton said, pointing to the camera high on a lamp post that covered the outside area.

Shepherd nodded and turned to go. Burton followed him into the building.

Chapter 40

'Well, that was quite a scene,' a voice called.

Burton turned to see David Dickens scurrying after them. 'What can I do to help?' the teacher asked as he arrived in front of her.

But Shepherd was already at the reception desk and deep in conversation with the security guard to access CCTV. The man nodded and sat down at his computer screen. He was soon handing Shepherd a memory stick.

'Thanks,' Shepherd said. 'Sorry, I didn't catch your name?'

'Hitesh,' the man replied, 'Hitesh Salana.'

'Were you here the night Travers McGovern was killed?' Shepherd asked, twirling the memory stick in his fingers.

Hitesh nodded. 'I told your officers in my statement. I was here, but I didn't see nothing.'

David Dickens appeared at Shepherd's shoulder. 'What's going on, Hitesh?' He pointed at the memory stick in Shepherd's hand. 'What's that?'

'CCTV of that fight,' Hitesh replied, shifting in his chair.

'Do you really need to take CCTV footage?' David Dickens asked, hands on hips.

'We need evidence of what happened out there,' Burton said. 'If Miss Wallis wants to press charges, we need something to prove her story.'

'It won't get in the papers, will it?' Dickens asked, rubbing at his immaculately shaved chin.

'Not from us,' Burton said, 'but unfortunately, a journalist from the local paper just witnessed all that.' She jerked a thumb towards the college doors.

The man groaned. 'That's all we need,' he said. 'Who was that woman and what was she doing on campus attacking one of our students?'

'She's Natasha Kent's sister, Julietta,' Shepherd put in, 'and she'd come to collect Natasha's belongings from her locker.'

Mr Dickens frowned. 'Clearly she shares her sister's temper.'

Burton raised an eyebrow. 'Meaning?'

'Well, just a couple of weeks ago, Natasha and Tara,' he gestured towards the quadrangle, 'had a bust up during one of my lessons. They've never really got on, but this was on another level. We're studying *Romeo and Juliet* and I'd asked Natasha to read the part of Juliet in a scene. Tara made some quite appalling comments about—' he broke off, looking around to see if there was anyone listening, 'about a black actress being cast as Juliet.' He nodded at Burton and Shepherd's shocked expression. 'I was about to take Tara to task when Natasha leapt up and hurled her copy of *Romeo and Juliet*. It hit Tara in the face.'

'Was she badly hurt?' Burton asked.

Mr Dickens shook his head. 'She had a bruise across her cheekbone, but nothing serious. I was so shocked that I didn't know what to do at first. There's never been an incident like that in my class. I sent Tara out of the room and reported it to the principal. She suspended Tara for two weeks.'

'What happened to Natasha?' Shepherd asked.

Mr Dickens puffed out his cheeks. 'I had to punish her, too. I could understand her reaction, but we have a zero-tolerance policy on violence, so Sally-Anne suspended her as well.' He shook his head. 'Such an unpleasant incident.'

'How did the rest of the class react?' Burton asked.

David Dickens shook his head. 'No one really knew what to do. I made them do quiet reading and answer some written questions for the rest of the lesson, but I doubt anyone really got anything done.'

'Useful to know they have a history,' Burton said.

'Was Tara telling the truth that it was unprovoked?' Dickens asked, nodding towards the door.

Burton shook her head. 'Witnesses said Tara was calling Natasha names and throwing around racial abuse again.'

He winced. 'No wonder Julietta was upset.'

'David, what's going on?' called a voice. 'Someone said there'd been a fight outside.'

Sally-Anne Faber appeared, looking surprised when she saw Burton and Shepherd. 'Did you get called because of the fight?' she asked.

Burton shook her head. 'Pure coincidence. We were actually looking for Julietta. Her mum told us she was coming to empty Natasha's locker. Clearly she didn't get that far.'

Sally-Anne winced. 'I'll arrange for Natasha's stuff to be sent to the family. It's probably best if she doesn't come back.' She sighed.

'As we're here, we have some more questions,' Burton said.

Sally-Anne nodded. 'Follow me. We can find somewhere quiet to talk.' She led the way towards a classroom, when Burton noticed David Dickens following.

Seeing her questioning look, he said, 'I think I should be here too, Sally-Anne. I witnessed some of the fight. I could—'

But the principal shook her head. 'Thanks, David, but I think we're OK.'

Burton followed the principal but looked back at Mr Dickens. He was back at the security desk and speaking urgently to Hitesh Salana. When he saw her looking, he held her gaze for a few moments, then turned away and disappeared toward the staff room. Burton turned back to follow Sally-Anne. Clearly, Mr Dickens wasn't happy about being excluded.

Sally-Anne held open the door to the classroom and ushered Burton and Shepherd inside. 'I'm sorry about David. He's very protective of the students. He can be a bit intrusive, but if you could cut him some slack at the moment, it would be great.'

'Why?' asked Burton.

'He lost his daughter three weeks ago,' Sally-Anne said, with a sigh. 'I told him he came back too soon, but he's adamant it's better for him to be here.'

'We'll bear that in mind,' Shepherd said.

'No doubt you've already heard Natasha was stabbed to death in the park.'

Sally-Anne nodded. 'Her mum called me. That poor girl,' she said, tears starting in her eyes. She dashed them away with the back of her hand.

'Can you think of anyone who might have wanted to hurt Natasha?' Burton asked.

Sally-Anne shook her head. 'She wasn't always popular.' When Burton raised an eyebrow, Sally-Anne smiled. 'She was the one everyone wanted to beat, but she was just out of this world as a dancer. Such a talent and such a hard worker.'

'Pushed by her sister,' Burton remarked.

Sally-Anne nodded. 'I think Julietta was projecting onto Nat a bit. She lost her dancing career and she wanted to make sure Natasha didn't do the same.'

'We've heard that Natasha had a history with Tara Wallis,' Shepherd said. 'That there was an altercation during a lesson that involved Natasha throwing a book in Tara's face.'

'Racist abuse being used by Tara,' Burton added.

Sally-Anne winced. 'We've had nothing like that before,' she said. 'Well, not something that's happened so publicly. I had to punish them both. This is supposed to be a safe space for everyone.'

'Has there always been something between them?' Shepherd asked.

'They've always been competitive, but it's escalated in the last few months. I don't know what had got into them.'

Burton regarded Sally-Anne quietly and the principal looked down at her hands, picking at a cuticle.

'Would Tara want to hurt Natasha? Take her out of the running for the showcase?' she asked.

Sally-Anne looked up quickly. 'What? No, I'm sure she wouldn't.'

'Is there anyone who might want to hurt both Natasha and Travers? Someone who knew about their relationship, for example?' Shepherd asked pointedly.

Sally-Anne frowned. 'I don't think that anyone—' She broke off as

185

the implication of Shepherd's words dawned on her. 'You think I killed them?'

Shepherd cocked his head to the right. 'Why not? Travers was abusing one of your students, threatening the reputation of the school.'

Sally-Anne gasped. 'I wouldn't kill him over that. I'd have sacked him.'

'But you didn't.' When the principal didn't speak, Shepherd continued, 'Was there anyone else who didn't like the fact that Travers was abusing a student?'

Sally-Anne winced, as did Burton. 'I don't think anyone else knew about it,' she said.

'It's strange that you should say that,' Shepherd said, leaning towards Sally-Anne, 'because their relationship seems to have been common knowledge on campus. Rumours circulating among the students. Surely the staff will have known something. No one else mentioned it to you?'

Sally-Anne shook her head, but she didn't meet his eye.

Burton held up a hand to break into the conversation. 'Have there been any other altercations recently? Any arguments involving Natasha or Travers? People fighting with them or about them?'

Sally-Anne seemed relieved to have Shepherd's questioning aborted. 'Now you mention it, I saw Julietta Kent having a shouting match with Travers. It was sometime last week.'

Burton raised an eyebrow and Shepherd pulled out his notebook and pen. 'Do you know what about?' Burton asked.

Sally-Anne frowned. 'At first I thought it was Natasha doing the shouting because they look quite similar, but then I got a proper look and realised it was Julietta. She shouted, "You bloody well leave her alone. I know what you're doing and it's sick. I'm going to make sure you can't hurt her anymore; she doesn't need this now."'

'You took the "she" to mean Natasha?'

Sally-Anne shrugged. 'It's the only person I know that they have in common.'

'Did you hear what Travers said back?' Shepherd asked.

'No, he whispered something so I couldn't hear. She didn't like it because she stabbed at his face with her car keys. He only just ducked out of the way. He would have lost an eye if she'd actually made contact.'

'Did no one see that happening? Any other witnesses?' Shepherd asked.

Sally-Anne shook her head. 'No, they were in a quiet part of college.'

'You didn't think to mention this to us earlier?' Shepherd demanded, 'when Travers was first killed and we asked if he'd rowed with anyone?'

The principal seemed taken aback. 'I've only just remembered now. Julietta's always been feisty, but I don't think she would kill anyone.'

'You knew she attacked Travers and, based on her performance outside just now, I don't think you can say that with any certainty,' Shepherd said, glaring at Sally-Anne.

'But this altercation suggests that she also knew about her sister and Travers McGovern,' Burton interrupted, hoping to calm Shepherd. 'It would have been really helpful to have known that already. Do you know if there was anyone else involved with Natasha romantically?'

Sally-Anne sighed. 'Natasha and Dominic Randall were an item about six months ago. They broke up and there was the usual amount of heartbreak and angst that goes on among young people. They found a way to work together and everything seemed to have settled down but—'

'But now she's messing up her dance routines and rowing with everyone and throwing books at people,' Burton said.

Sally-Anne winced. 'Things have deteriorated in the last couple of months. I spoke to Natasha and I asked if everything was OK. She said it was fine, but I could tell something wasn't right.'

'She was pregnant,' Burton said.

Sally-Anne's hand flew to her mouth. 'What?' she gasped. 'Was it ... was it Travers'?'

'We believe so,' Burton said, 'so there's a bit of an explanation about why she was acting out.'

Sally-Anne put her head in her hands. 'That poor girl,' she said again. 'Why didn't she come to me?' She started crying. 'If only I'd tried harder to help her, they might both still be alive. I should have done more to protect her.'

She pulled a tissue from her sleeve, dabbed at her face and took several shaky breaths to get herself under control. 'So, what happens next?' she asked.

'We're going to speak to Julietta, but we'll also need to interview Dominic Randall and Tara Wallis.'

Sally-Anne nodded. 'OK, I can help you find them if you need me to.' She got to her feet and led the way back into the atrium.

As they followed Sally-Anne, Shepherd muttered, 'So, Julietta Kent definitely knew about her sister and Travers.'

Burton nodded grimly. 'She's got some explaining to do.'

Chapter 41

'I've never seen anything like it,' Dan said to Emma as they stood in the car park behind the *Allensbury Post* building.

'You didn't enjoy the cat fight?' Emma asked with a wink.

Dan shook his head, rubbing his shoulder. 'It was more like a kick-boxing match. She nearly pulled my arms out of the sockets.'

'I can't believe Tara said all that,' Emma said, digging her hands into her jeans pockets. 'Do you think it's true?'

Dan shrugged. 'Sadie, the other woman I was speaking to, said that Natasha was sleeping with Dominic Randall earlier this year, but she didn't say when exactly. Maybe there was some crossover between him and Travers McGovern and she really didn't know.'

Emma looked around the car park. 'But how did Tara know Natasha was pregnant? I can't imagine that Natasha told her.'

'Maybe Natasha told someone else and they told Tara,' Dan said, fiddling with the strap of his satchel.

'Like who?'

'Travers. He's the obvious person.'

'And you think he told Tara? Why?'

Dan shrugged. 'There's only one way to find out.'

'You're just going to ask her? How?'

'Hey, I just saved her from potentially being hospitalised. She at least owes me a conversation.'

Emma grinned. 'I can't believe Julietta got away from you.'

Dan glowered. 'Only because I tried to avoid an elbow to the head. She's vicious when she's angry.' He paused and looked down at his feet.

'Are you thinking that if she lost it she could have stabbed Natasha?' Emma asked, watching him.

Dan nodded. 'It would have taken some loss of temper, but maybe they had a row and...' He trailed off.

'In her message, Natasha said she thought she knew who killed Travers. Do you think Julietta could have overheard and followed her to the park?' Emma asked, putting a hand to her chest where a tight feeling had begun.

Dan ran a hand through his hair. 'I don't know, Em, genuinely I don't. Killing Natasha could be a crime of passion, but Travers Mc-Govern's murder definitely wasn't. Someone poisoned him and took away his medication. That's cold and deliberate.'

Emma scratched her head. 'What are you going to do?'

'I'm going to head off to the cop shop and give my statement about this afternoon. Then I'm going to wait for Julietta to come out and see if I can get her to talk to me. What about you?'

'I've just been to see Daisy and she doesn't want me back 'til next week, so I'll head home. You come straight back and tell me everything later,' she said, pointing a warning finger at Dan.

He laughed, raising his hands in surrender. 'Of course.' He leaned in and gave her a kiss on the lips. 'Be safe.'

'You too.'

With a wave, he headed out of the car park and up the hill towards the police station.

Chapter 42

Shepherd's desk phone was ringing when they returned to the office. He dashed across the room and grabbed it. Burton headed into her office to put away her handbag and, as she returned, he was hanging up the phone.

He rubbed his nose. 'That was tech. They're still working on Natasha's laptop.'

Burton groaned. 'How hard can it be to crack a password?' she asked.

Shepherd laughed. 'Harder than you think, from what I hear,' he said. 'But they did say they'll do all the dirty work for us, pulling all the files and emails together.'

Burton harrumphed. 'Can you not work your manly wiles on who-ever's got it? I'm sure that Carol would be more than happy to help you.'

Shepherd gave a wry smile. 'That's a sexist remark,' he said. 'Besides, I don't think she's speaking to me.'

Burton, who was staring at an email that had popped up on her phone, looked up sharply and raised her eyebrows.

'We went out a few times,' Shepherd said, sitting back in his chair and fiddling with a pen on his desk. 'It didn't work out, though.'

'I'm sorry, Mark,' said Burton, really meaning it. She sat on the chair of the adjoining desk.

Shepherd shrugged. 'You win some, you lose some,' he said.

There was a short silence and then Burton cleared her throat.

'Is that the notebook you found in Natasha's room?' she asked, pointing to the book on Shepherd's desk.

Shepherd nodded and handed over the book. 'Only it's not a notebook. It's her diary.'

'The secret life of a teenage dancer?' Burton asked, flipping open the cover.

Shepherd shook his head and settled himself in the chair opposite her. 'It's not that kind of diary,' he said, pointing a finger.

Burton turned a few pages and raised her eyebrows. 'It's just a record of up-coming appointments. I didn't think teenagers used paper diaries anymore.'

'There's more to Natasha than meets the eye, isn't there? What's interesting,' Shepherd said, 'is that she has an appointment with an "MW and AVAW" every Tuesday afternoon at four thirty.'

'AVAW? What the hell is that?' Burton flipped to the current date and then back a few weeks. 'There're times for auditions and rehearsals as well,' she said. 'She's got very neat handwriting, hasn't she? Very girly.' She flipped the book closed and held it up. 'Do you think anyone else ever saw this?'

Shepherd shrugged. 'I don't know. On the receipt I gave to her mum for the stuff we took, I just said it was a notebook.'

'Is there anything else in it?' Burton asked, handing it back.

'There are no phone numbers, so tracking down MW is going to be a challenge.'

Burton frowned. 'Is it not strange that she uses this and not the calendar on her phone?' she asked.

'She might use both,' Shepherd said slowly. 'After all, Julietta has access to the one on her phone.'

Burton pursed her lips. 'That's a very fair point. Maybe this...' she held up the diary '...is for stuff she doesn't want Julietta to know about. That's assuming Julietta doesn't go through Natasha's stuff. Let's check the phone calendar against it when it comes back from tech. I assume they got it at the crime scene?'

Shepherd stared at her, tilting his head to one side. 'Now you mention it, I don't remember seeing a mobile phone on the crime scene inventory,' he said slowly.

Burton snorted. 'A teenager who doesn't have a mobile phone?' she asked. 'Surely that's not possible. She's all over social media, so she must have a way to do that.'

'I'll check in with CSI and see whether they've got it.' Shepherd turned and disappeared out of the room.

Burton watched him lean back over his desk and pick up the phone receiver. He pressed a button that she knew was the speed-dial to the CSI team headquarters. He spoke into the phone for a few moments. Then he frowned. He thanked the person on the other end and hung up. Burton walked across to his desk.

'Well? Have they got it?' she asked.

Shepherd shook his head. 'No mobile phone at the crime scene,' he said.

Burton frowned. 'What? Did she lose it? Drop it somewhere?'

'Or the killer took it,' Shepherd said.

Burton nodded. 'Either way, we need to find that phone.' She glanced at her watch. 'Right, Miss Kent has had time to consider the error of her ways. Let's see what she's got to say for herself.'

***

Julietta Kent had been crying when Burton and Shepherd entered the interview room. A uniformed officer was standing silently in the corner watching her. He nodded to them and went out into the corridor.

Burton sat down opposite Julietta and pushed a plastic cup of water towards her. Julietta looked up and took the cup. She took a few sips and then put it down. Her face crumpled again and tears leaked down her face. She wiped them away with her sleeve.

'So,' Burton started, 'what was that we just witnessed?'

Julietta hung her head, still dabbing at her eyes.

'That bloody woman,' she said. 'She's never liked Natasha, always getting on at her, bullying her, racist shit, y'know. Nat always said she could handle it, but it's disgusting. Now she's talking trash about her when Nat's not there to defend herself.'

'She said that Natasha didn't know who the father of her baby was,' Shepherd said. 'Was that true?'

Julietta's shoulders slumped. 'I don't know,' she mumbled. 'I didn't even know she was pregnant until you told us.'

'Your mum thought it was Dominic's,' Shepherd said.

Julietta snorted derisively. 'He was old news. She'd never have been with him. I saw to—' She broke off again, chewing her lip as if she'd said too much.

Burton raised an eyebrow. 'Ah yes, he told us she'd dumped him because someone had told her he was cheating on her. That was you?'

Julietta looked down at the table without speaking.

'I'll take that as a yes,' Burton said, leaning forward and clasping her hands on the table. 'So, why did you lie to her? I assume it was a lie?'

Julietta nodded. 'The relationship was distracting her; she needed to focus on dancing.'

'And it was up to you to decide that, was it?' Burton demanded.

When Julietta said nothing, Shepherd stepped in.

'When did you realise it was Travers McGovern's baby?' he asked.

Julietta opened her mouth to deny everything, but the look on Shepherd's face made her close it again. She looked defiant. Shepherd slapped his hand on the table.

'Come on, Miss Kent. You keep lying to us and it doesn't look good. See, we've found out from another source that you knew all about Travers and your sister before we told you anything, that you even had a public row with him about it.'

'Who told you that—' Julietta began before stopping herself.

'It doesn't matter who,' Shepherd said. 'All it tells us is that you were lying again, and it makes me wonder what else we shouldn't believe.'

Julietta looked sullen.

'Why did you lie to us about Natasha's laptop password?' he demanded.

Julietta looked at him, surprised. 'What?'

'The laptop password you gave us. It doesn't work.'

Julietta frowned. 'No, that's the password.'

Burton smiled grimly. 'No, it isn't.'

Julietta looked from one detective to the other. 'But it was ... when I looked on—' She broke off, looking down at the table.

Burton leaned forward, resting her forearms on the table. 'Do you know what I think? Natasha knew you looked at her computer without permission, I assume. But there's something on there she wanted to keep private, so she changed the password. I wonder what she was hiding from you. What do think we'll find on there?'

'I ... I don't know,' Julietta replied, looking from one detective to the other.

Burton held up a hand as if stopping traffic. 'Let me get this straight: you lied to your sister to make her dump her boyfriend and when you found out she was in a relationship with someone else, you tried again. But this time, instead of going for her, you threatened him and said that you were going to make sure he couldn't hurt her again. Oh, and you nearly stabbed him in the eye with your car keys. Is that right?'

Julietta looked down at the table, refusing to make eye contact.

'Hey, look at me,' Burton demanded, tapping on the table. Julietta looked up and met her eye. 'Did you kill Travers McGovern to make sure he didn't distract your sister from dancing?'

Julietta leaned forward on the table. 'What? No, I didn't,' she said.

'What did you mean when you told him you'd make sure he couldn't hurt her again?'

'I was going to report him to Sally-Anne,' Julietta said, sitting back in her chair. 'That's all.'

Shepherd clasped his hands on the table like a newsreader. 'She already knew,' he said.

Julietta stared at him. 'What?' she demanded.

'Sally-Anne already knew about him and Natasha,' Shepherd said. 'Someone else had reported it to her and she'd spoken to him. He denied it and she didn't take it any further.'

'Well, she probably couldn't if he was denying it,' Julietta blustered. 'There's no way Sally-Anne would have abandoned Nat if she could have helped her.'

'And yet she did,' Shepherd continued.

Julietta glared at him.

'Where were you on the evening Travers McGovern died?' Burton asked.

Julietta looked taken aback. 'What? I've already told you—'

But Burton interrupted. 'No, you've told us where you were on the night Natasha was killed, and we're still trying to contact your friend to verify your story, but not where you were when Travers died. So, where were you?'

Julietta looked like she was going to refuse to answer, but Burton's steely glare wore her down.

'I finished work late, at about five thirty, instead of five usually,' she said. 'I went straight to the college to pick Nat up.'

'You were on campus that night,' Burton stated.

'Well, yes, but I was with Natasha so I couldn't have been killing him.'

'So you say.'

'Look, anyone could have put peanut oil in his vodka anytime. I only ever come to campus to collect Natasha. I never went near his office.'

'You knew he had vodka in his office, then?' Shepherd put in.

Julietta chewed the inside of her cheek. 'OK, yes, I knew about it.'

'How did you know?'

'Natasha must have told me.'

Burton was looking at Julietta as if she was a specimen in a petri dish. 'Why would Natasha have told you about the vodka if she was hiding their relationship from you?' She paused. 'I don't think she told you anything. I think you've been in his office before, on one of your many trips to campus. Am I right?'

Julietta stared at the table and said nothing.

Burton continued. 'I think Natasha was keeping their relationship a secret because she knew you lied about Dominic. She didn't want you trying to split her and Travers up.'

Julietta said nothing, but glared at Burton.

'I suppose Dominic got off lightly,' Burton said, looking at Shepherd. 'He just got dumped, not murdered. I mean—'

Julietta leapt to her feet, overturning her chair with a crash. 'No, I didn't! I didn't do anything to Travers. I knew about the relationship because...' She trailed off.

'Sit down, Miss Kent,' Burton said sternly. Julietta stood her chair back on its feet and sat. 'You knew about the relationship because...?'

'I made her give me her phone passcode and saw the messages between them,' Julietta said quietly.

Shepherd raised an eyebrow. 'You made her give you the code?'

Julietta nodded. 'Yes, but it was for her own good. I knew something was going on and I needed to stop it.'

'Is that why you have her laptop password as well?' Shepherd asked. 'So you could breach her privacy?'

'It wasn't like that. She needed me; I had to protect her from them.'

'Did Natasha feel like that?' Burton asked. 'She's eighteen, after all. An adult, free to make her own decisions.'

Julietta looked down at the table and said nothing.

'Well, our tech team has the laptop and they'll soon be able to give us access to everything on there. So, if there's something you've not told us, then now is the time to speak,' Burton said.

Julietta shook her head, tears starting in her eyes.

'Right,' Burton said, leaning forward on the table, 'we have the CCTV of the incident earlier and I'm prepared to bail you while we investigate further. But I'll be asking for conditions that you can't go to the dance school or have any contact at all with Tara Wallis. If you break that, we'll arrest you and take you to court. Do you understand?'

Julietta nodded and Burton got to her feet. Shepherd followed, as did Julietta.

'I'm sure we'll be speaking again soon,' Burton said. 'Try not to attack anyone else in the intervening period.'

She swept from the room, leaving Shepherd to escort Julietta out through the reception area.

Chapter 43

Dan was sitting on the low wall outside the reception area of the police station when the front doors swished open. Julietta Kent appeared, red-eyed and pale-faced. She stared at him for a moment, then she approached. He got to his feet.

'Hi,' he said, pushing his phone into his trouser pocket.

'Hi,' she said back, awkwardly. 'You were at the school, weren't you?'

Dan nodded.

'You tried to stop me from...' She trailed off as if considering what had happened for the first time.

'Yup,' Dan said, 'and you tried to elbow me in the head for my trouble.'

Julietta looked down at her feet and blushed. 'I don't know what came over me. I just...'

'I overheard what she said to you,' Dan said. 'I'd probably have reacted in the same way, if it was my sister.'

Tears started in Julietta's eyes and she dashed them away with the back of her hand.

'Nat's not a slag, she's not a...' The tears continued to fall, and Dan led her to sit down on the wall.

Julietta sniffed twice and then wiped her eyes on her sleeve.

'Thank you for the tribute piece,' she said. 'It was really nice.'

Dan nodded his thanks. 'It was an easy one to write. So many people said nice things about her.'

Julietta humphed. 'Apart from Tara this afternoon,' she said.

'Ah well, I don't ask people like that for comments,' Dan said, giving her a bit of a grin and a nudge with his elbow.

She smiled. 'Just as well. People would get the totally wrong impression of Nat.'

'It makes you wonder, doesn't it?' Dan said. 'Why would someone kill her when she was so well-liked?'

Julietta sighed heavily. 'I keep asking myself the same question.'

Dan shifted on the wall. 'Emma, my girlfriend, she thinks Natasha saw something the night Travers McGovern was murdered.'

Julietta looked up sharply. 'What?'

Dan nodded. 'She left a message for Emma on her voicemail saying she knew who the killer was and that she had evidence.'

'She didn't tell her who it was?' Julietta asked, turning on the wall so they were face-to-face.

Dan shook his head. 'No, she said she couldn't talk where she was and she'd tell Emma when she saw her. But, well, you know what happened.' When Julietta was silent, picking at a fingernail, Dan added, 'Emma's really gutted. She's blaming herself.'

Julietta looked up, surprised. 'Why is she blaming herself?'

'For not getting there quicker. They'd agreed to meet at the benches in the park, but Emma got held up on the way and by the time she got there...' Dan trailed off and sighed. 'She thinks if she'd got there sooner, she might have been able to save her.'

'Do you think she's right?' Julietta asked. 'Could she have done something?'

Dan shook his head. 'The police say no, but I can't convince her otherwise. That's why we have to find out who killed Natasha. I think that'll put Emma's mind at rest.' He paused. 'Would you mind if I asked you a few more questions?'

Julietta looked like she was going to say no, but then nodded.

'I need to get back. Mum will be worried.'

'I can give you a lift, if you want,' Dan said, standing up and pulling out his car keys. 'My car's only round the corner. We can chat while I'm driving?'

Julietta nodded and got to her feet. Dan turned and led the way towards the car park.

***

Once they were both settled in the car with seat belts fastened, Dan asked, 'What did the police say? How much trouble are you in?'

Julietta sighed. 'I'm on bail for the assault and I can't go near the school again or Tara.'

Dan glanced at her as he started the car. 'I think that's probably for the best. Do you think she'll press charges?'

Julietta stared out of the window. 'I don't know, but I wish I'd hit her harder.' Then she puffed out her cheeks. 'They were also asking me questions about Travers' murder – did I know Nat was seeing him, had I killed him to get him away from Nat, did I know she was pregnant?'

'And did you? Know they were seeing each other?' Dan asked.

Julietta frowned but said nothing.

'Sorry,' Dan said, as he turned out onto the main road. 'Had Natasha told you she was pregnant?'

Julietta sniffed. 'Yes, well, no. I worked it out for myself. I caught her throwing up on a few mornings. It was a bit of a giveaway, but I asked her about it.'

'Did she give in under interrogation?' Dan asked with a smile.

'I didn't shine a light in her eyes,' Julietta snapped, 'I just asked her, and she admitted it.'

'How did she feel about it?'

Julietta shrugged. 'A bit scared, I think. She wasn't sure what to do. It wasn't in the plan, you see.'

Dan slowed for a T-junction. 'Plan?'

'Her career plan. She was going to ace the showcase and then get a place with a ballet company after that.'

Dan raised his eyebrows. 'She's a lot better at career planning than I've ever been.'

Julietta shrugged. 'Yes, well, we've put a lot into her career. You've got to have ambition,' she said.

Dan filed away the 'we' in Julietta's sentence.

'How's your mum holding up?' he asked, looking over his shoulder before changing lanes as they approached a set of traffic lights. 'It's an awful time.'

'As you'd expect, I suppose,' Julietta said, glancing over her shoulder as well. 'She's up and down. One moment she's OK, the next she's crying and I can't comfort her.'

Dan nodded, watching for the lights to change. 'It's hard when you're grieving as well. You know how you're responding, but not how the other person is feeling or what to say.' He had no personal experience, but the story he'd done with the local grief counselling service was really paying off.

Julietta sighed. 'That's so true. I think it's worse when the person dies really suddenly. I mean, when someone is ill or something like that, you can sort of make sense of it. But when the person is just suddenly gone, it's hard to get your head around.'

'I imagine Dominic has been some support to your mum,' Dan said, shifting the car into gear and pulling away. Even with his eyes fixed on the road, he could feel Julietta tense in her seat.

'What do you mean?' she snapped.

'Well...' Dan sneaked a glance at her '...I just meant that he'd been round to see her, took flowers; he must be really upset as well.'

Julietta shrugged and stared out of the car window.

'You don't think he's upset?' Dan asked, trying to decipher her reaction. When Julietta was silent, he took a punt. 'You think he did it? That he killed Natasha?'

Julietta paused and then said, 'Oh, I don't know. I don't want to think of it, but it's just, well, I saw him when Nat dumped him. He was so angry and he threatened her. Said he'd make her sorry for what she'd done.'

Dan indicated a left turn. 'But that was six months ago, wasn't it? Why would he have waited this long?'

'Maybe he'd just found out about her and Travers. She must have got together with Travers almost straight after him. I know that would piss me off.'

'You think he killed Travers as well?'

Julietta shrugged. 'Why not?' she asked, staring out of the car window.

Dan was struggling to keep his eyes on the road and slowed carefully for a roundabout.

'In other words, you think he found out about Nat and Travers and killed him to get Nat back. Then killed her when she rejected him again?'

Julietta puffed out her cheeks. 'I don't want to think it, I really don't. But, y'know, I've seen Dominic when he loses it. I doubt he'd have even known what he was doing.'

'Have you told the police all this?'

'I've told them to look at him, that he had an axe to grind, but I don't think they're listening.'

'Who do you think their money is on?' Dan asked.

Julietta looked at him sideways. 'They haven't told us anything. Have they said anything to you?' The tone was light, but Dan felt a change in the atmosphere.

'Emma and me wondered at first whether Natasha had killed Travers. I mean, once we knew about the sex tape and—' Dan stopped suddenly, realising he might have said too much.

'Sex tape?' Julietta demanded. 'What sex tape?'

Dan was silent for a moment, pretending he needed all his concentration for dealing with a difficult roundabout. But she continued to stare at him, so he felt like he had to answer.

'Natasha told Emma that Travers recorded them having sex.'

Julietta groaned. 'I feel like I didn't know her at all anymore. The Natasha I know wouldn't have made a sex tape.'

'She didn't, not willingly. He recorded it without telling her. Apparently she went mental with him and made him delete it.'

Julietta put her face in her hands. 'Why didn't she tell me? I could have helped her. We could have sorted it out between us.'

'Sorted out what?' Dan asked, but Julietta ignored him.

'Who else have you suggested to the police?' she asked.

'We've not suggested anyone, well, apart from a guy who was in a theatre company with Travers. Apparently Travers ruined his reputation and got him fired, but he wouldn't have a motive to kill Natasha.'

'Do you think they'll have spoken to Travers' wife about Natasha?'

Dan glanced at her. 'I'm sure they have. Why?'

'Well, maybe she killed Travers, and Nat saw her do it. So she had to kill Nat to get her out of the way,' Julietta said, speaking really quickly. 'It would be just like Nat to have seen something and not realise how serious it was.'

'Was she usually like that?'

'She's my sister and I love her, but she could be a bit scatty,' Julietta said.

Dan frowned, mentally storing that fact to share with Emma.

'But Natasha said she wasn't on campus when Travers died,' he said, 'so she couldn't have seen anything.' He glanced at Julietta and saw a look flit across her face that he couldn't quite describe.

'What do you mean?'

'She told Emma that you picked her up at five thirty. Travers died after that. What time did you get to college?'

Julietta wiped at an eye, but he wasn't sure he could see any tears.

'I ... I don't know. She was out the front of the building when I got there, so it must have been that time.'

Dan turned the car into the Kents' street and slowed down to look for a parking space.

'Just stop here and I'll jump out,' Julietta said. Dan stopped, put on the handbrake and slipped the car into neutral. He turned to face Julietta.

'Look, we're going to find out who killed Natasha, whatever we have to do,' he said earnestly.

She nodded sadly. 'I'm sure the police can get Dominic to admit what he did.'

Dan frowned. 'Do you think Dominic will speak to me?'

Julietta thought for a moment. 'He might, but you'll need to be careful. He can be violent, you know.'

'That's OK, I can handle him. Is he worse than you?' He laughed.

But Julietta was serious. 'Be careful, he's very strong. I certainly wouldn't want to be on the wrong end of him.'

'OK, what's his address, and I'll go to see him?'

She recited it, and Dan tapped it into his phone. Then she pulled the handle and opened the door.

'Just watch him,' she said as she climbed out of the car. 'We know what he's capable of.'

Chapter 44

When Dan knocked on Emma's front door, she answered, looking puzzled.

'It's you,' she said, stepping back to let him in.

'Who were you expecting?' he asked, hanging his coat up in the hall and taking off his shoes.

'Well, you have a key. Why didn't you just let yourself in?'

'I left it here,' Dan said, following her into the living room. He shoved his hands into his trouser pockets. 'I only took it because you were out of it and I wanted to get back in. Now you're OK, I didn't think it was right to keep it without permission.'

Emma stood by the sofa, looking at him. 'Oh, I see,' she said. They stared at each other for a moment and then he broke the silence, clearing his throat.

'What's that you're working on?' he asked, pointing at her notebook on the table.

She looked surprised at the change of conversation, but recovered quickly. 'I've been making a timeline of where everyone was and when.' She sat down and looked up at him. 'How did it go with Julietta?'

'It was interesting,' Dan said, sitting down on the sofa beside her. 'I caught her as she left the cop shop and I gave her a lift home.'

'Nice tactic,' Emma said with a smile.

Dan laughed. 'I felt it was the safest thing to do. Rather than risk her breaking her bail by going back to the school for round two with Tara Wallis.'

'What did you learn?'

'Well, she's fixated on Dominic Randall. Says she doesn't want to think he would do it, but he's got a temper and threatened Natasha when they broke up.'

Emma winced. 'That doesn't sound good. There are countless stories of people being killed by an ex-partner.'

'But they split up months ago. Why would he suddenly do it now?'

'Maybe he just found out about Travers?'

Dan scratched his head. 'You think he killed Travers, so he'd have another chance with Natasha, with no indication she'd go out with him again? Then she rejects him and he kills her?'

'I suppose it's possible,' Emma replied. 'Maybe they were getting friendly again and he wanted more.'

Dan looked down at the notebook. 'How are you getting on here?'

Emma pointed to the pile of screwed-up pages on the floor beside her, and he laughed.

'It's harder than you think, doing this from memory,' she said.

'This is the time Travers was last seen?' Dan asked, pointing to the top of the page. Then he winced. 'Wow, that's a lot of people who were on campus.'

Emma nodded. 'Dominic, Tara potentially, Neville Shuster, Natasha and Julietta.'

'You've got both Natasha and Julietta down there?'

'I had to. I remembered what Nat said when I asked her about where she was. She said she finished rehearsals at five thirty and then Julietta came to pick her up.' She pointed at the page with her pen. 'But she didn't say when Julietta actually arrived.'

'So it could have been five thirty on the dot or any time after?'

Emma nodded. 'Nat didn't say exactly where they met, either. I assumed out the front of the building because that's usually what Julietta does. Nat has to be there waiting when she turns up.'

'You know that for certain?'

'Yup. One time, Nat was a couple of minutes late after our class, and Julietta came in to fetch her.'

Dan frowned. 'Where were you at the time?'

'Just leaving one of the dance studios. She came marching across the atrium, and Natasha looked terrified.'

'Terrified? Of her own sister?'

'That's the only way I can describe it.'

'You don't think,' Dan began slowly, 'Julietta killed Travers, and Natasha helped her cover it up, or vice versa.'

Emma sat back on the sofa. 'No. My inclination would be that Julietta did it, Nat found out afterward and tried to get her to turn herself in.'

'And Julietta killed her to shut her up?'

Emma rubbed her hand over her face. 'I don't want to think it. Julietta loved Natasha, that much was clear, but a lot of coercive controllers claim to love the person they're abusing.'

'God, Em, that's a big accusation,' Dan said, turning to stare at her. 'You got to that just because Julietta was angry Natasha kept her waiting? Maybe she had somewhere she needed to be and was going to be late.'

'Maybe I am overreacting, but if someone was blackmailing you with a sex tape, would you not turn to the one person who has your best interests at heart?'

Dan frowned. 'Maybe Nat didn't want Julietta to know about it. She was probably ashamed of it.'

'Nat had tried to keep the whole Travers relationship quiet from everyone, Julietta included.' She looked at Dan. 'What are you thinking?'

'When we were talking, Julietta said, "We've put a lot into her career," like it was a joint enterprise. Imagine what would happen if Natasha told her she was pregnant. As we said before, there goes the career, everything they've worked for.'

Emma rubbed her face with both hands. 'Who else could be involved? It would have to be someone close to Travers or Natasha.'

'His wife?' Dan asked.

Emma's shoulders slumped. 'I thought that too, but it's the wrong way round. If Nat had died first, I'd think of her, but why would she kill Travers and then Natasha?'

'Fair point.' Dan rubbed his chin. 'Could the principal be involved?'

'Sally-Anne Faber?' Emma asked. 'Why would you think that?'

'Travers was sleeping with a student ... If that got out, the college's reputation would be shot to pieces. She would probably have been sacked by the school governors and could face criminal charges for not intervening. She would have been on campus when he was killed and might have known about the vodka.'

Emma picked up her pen and poised over the list of people on campus when Travers died. 'Motive for killing Natasha?'

Dan thought for a moment. 'We know Nat was on campus and it's likely that she saw something because she said she knew who the killer was. Maybe she told Sally-Anne that she was going to tell the police. Sally-Anne couldn't have that, so she killed her.'

Emma nodded. 'It's a good theory,' and she added Sally-Anne's name to the list. 'Anyone else?'

'You've put Tara on that list as a possibility. Do we know if she was there?'

'There were rehearsals going on, although I don't know which ones. She might have been there.'

Dan nodded. 'There's one way to find out.' Emma looked up at him. 'We speak to her. Well, I'll speak to her,' he added.

'You're just going to walk in there and ask her?'

Dan gave her a gentle nudge on the arm. 'No, of course not. Like I said before, I'm going in as the person who saved her from a proper kicking and wants to see how she is. If I happen to bump into Dominic as well, so much the better.'

'No, Dan, not Dominic. We need to work out a way to get at him without making him angry. Maybe I should do that?'

Dan snorted. 'What? You think I'm letting you do that one alone? Not a chance.'

Emma frowned. 'OK, but don't see him on your own. I'll have a think of how we can tackle him.'

Dan rubbed his hands together. 'So, we have a plan. I'll go back to the school tomorrow and see if I can track down Tara.' Then he rubbed his stomach. 'But now I'm hungry. Are you rifling the cupboards or are we ordering takeaway?'

'Takeaway,' Emma said, picking up her phone and finding the delivery app. 'I've not been to the supermarket.' She handed Dan the phone and watched as he scrolled through the choices.

Maybe, she thought, it would be more likely that there would be food in the house if there were two people to remember to shop.

Dan looked up and saw her staring at him. 'What?' he asked, reaching over to pat her knee. 'What's the matter?'

Emma shook her head. 'It's nothing. It can wait.'

As Dan turned back to the app, she frowned. They'd been together a while now and they'd never even been on holiday together. She'd not really thought about it before, and what did that say about their relationship? Before she got any further, Dan shoved her phone back in her hand.

'It was a tough decision, but is Chinese OK?' he asked.

Emma looked down at the screen and nodded. But she struggled to focus. Was this relationship what she wanted? She shook herself. Let's not get into that now, she thought, tapping the screen. It was one for another day.

Chapter 45

Burton was sitting at her desk scanning a page of the *Allensbury Post* when Shepherd appeared in her office doorway.

'He's done a good job,' she said, holding up Dan's tribute piece to Natasha. She scanned the page again. 'It's hard to imagine that anyone would want to kill her.'

Shepherd crossed the room and took the newspaper from her hands. 'Lovely comments from everyone,' he said.

Burton sighed. 'I bet he didn't ask Tara Wallis?' she said.

'Did you see who picked Julietta up outside here yesterday?' Shepherd asked, pointing to Dan's by-line.

Burton nodded. 'I don't know whether that was pre-arranged or a chance meeting. Either way, I wonder whether he'll have got anything useful out of her.'

'More useful than us?' Shepherd asked, sitting down opposite her.

Burton leaned her elbows on the desk and cradled her chin in her hands. 'There's something not right here. When we first asked about Travers and the pregnancy, she tells us she knows nothing. Then she admits that not only did she know about both, she also knew he had vodka in his office.'

'And claims she's never been to his office,' Shepherd said.

Burton rolled her eyes. 'I'm sure that's a lie, too.'

'What I can't get my head around is her making Natasha hand over her phone and laptop passwords. I mean, you just wouldn't, would

210

you?' Shepherd asked.

Burton rubbed her forehead. 'Agreed. You wouldn't give someone that much access to your private life.'

'Maybe it was gratitude for what Julietta's done for her, or fear of reprisals?' Shepherd asked.

'What sort of reprisals? What can Julietta do to her? She won't want to stop Natasha from going to college or doing dancing stuff that Natasha obviously loved doing.'

Before Shepherd could answer, Gary Topping appeared in Burton's office doorway. He held up a brown A4-sized envelope.

'You playing postman, Topper?' Shepherd asked. The man grinned.

'Contents of Natasha Kent's laptop,' he said, waving the envelope. Burton held out a hand, and he presented it to her like a crown on a silk cushion.

'Thanks, Gaz,' she said. Topping turned and left the room. Burton weighed the envelope in her hands. 'Wow, there's a lot in here.' She got up and walked to the round table in the corner of her office and began spreading the pages out on its surface. 'Right, let's see what we've got,' she said.

For the next twenty minutes, Burton and Shepherd barely spoke as they trawled through all the documents. Suddenly, Shepherd gave a sharp intake of breath.

Burton looked at him. 'What have you got?'

'I'm into her email inbox and there's an interesting one here. Start at the bottom.' He held out the page.

Burton took it, scanning the contents. Her hand flew to her mouth, and she stared at him, wide eyed. 'Good God, what would Julietta have done when she found out about that?'

Shepherd's face was stony. 'I think we already have an answer for that, don't we?'

'Right,' Burton said, 'you get over to the Kents' house and pick up Miss Julietta. Oh, and see if the mother knows where Natasha's phone is.'

'On it,' said Shepherd, getting to his feet.

When Shepherd knocked at the Kents' door, it was Mrs Kent who answered it.

'Do come in,' she said, drying her hands on an apron tied around her waist. 'Sorry, I'm all in a mess. I was doing some drying up.' She paused and then registered his facial expression. 'Why are you here? Is there an update?'

Shepherd shook his head. 'There's nothing new to tell you at the moment,' he said. 'We're following up some new leads, but I can't share any of that yet.' That one of them is your other daughter is something we'll save for later, he thought to himself.

'So, how can I help you? It's not about Jules, is it? She told me what happened yesterday.'

'I need to speak to her again,' Shepherd said. 'Do you know where she is?'

'She just popped to the shop for me. She shouldn't be long.'

Shepherd nodded. 'In the meantime, I was wondering whether you've seen Natasha's phone.'

Mrs Kent looked puzzled. 'Was it not in her handbag when you ... when you found her? She was almost surgically attached to it.'

Shepherd shook his head. 'No, we've not been able to find it and I wondered whether she might have left it here.'

Mrs Kent frowned. 'I've not seen it, but if it's anywhere, it would be in her room. She wasn't one for leaving her things lying around.' She got to her feet and led the way to the top floor of the house. 'I've not touched anything since you were here last,' she said. 'Although Jules has been in and out a bit.' She pushed open the door and then stood back to let Shepherd go ahead.

'They were close, weren't they?' he asked, heading straight for Natasha's desk.

Mrs Kent nodded. 'Yes, particularly once Jules stopped dancing,' she said. 'She seems to have lived out her potential career through Nat.'

'She was good, then? Julietta?' Shepherd asked, looking over at Mrs Kent.

She nodded. 'Not as good as Natasha, but certainly good enough to have made a career out of it.'

'It must have been hard for her to watch Natasha doing so well,' Shepherd said.

Mrs Kent shrugged. 'If it has been, she's never shown it. She's always looked after Natasha and encouraged her so much.'

Shepherd smiled. 'Exactly how an older sister should be,' he said. He looked under the desk, spotting a mobile phone charger plugged into a plug socket.

'She doesn't take her charger with her?' he asked.

Mrs Kent shook her head. 'She has one of those portable battery things. She always says it's easier than trying to find a plug socket, particularly if you're at competitions. There's never that kind of thing around.'

Shepherd nodded and started rifling through the desk drawers. Mrs Kent sucked a breath in through her teeth, causing Shepherd to look around in surprise.

'Sorry,' she said. 'Natasha would have hated having someone looking through her things. She was such a private person.'

Shepherd nodded. 'It's my least favourite bit of the job,' he lied, 'but it's not idle curiosity, I promise. It might help us find a clue about what happened to her.'

'Did you not already look through those?'

'Just checking to make sure there's nothing we missed.'

He searched the drawers and some shoe boxes in the bottom of the wardrobe, but yielded nothing new, apart from a pair of ballet shoes still in their tissue paper wrapping.

Mrs Kent took them and cradled them in her hands, her mouth turning down at the corners. 'Never worn,' she said. 'I suppose we'll have to give them away.' She sighed. 'We've no use for them now, but they might help someone else down at the school.' She handed them to Shepherd, who carefully packed them back into their box. He got to his feet and looked around the room.

'Is there anywhere else she might have put the phone? Somewhere safe she used?'

Mrs Kent frowned and then shook her head.

Shepherd nodded. 'Thanks for letting me look around.'

As he headed out of the bedroom door, Shepherd turned and asked, 'Natasha had an appointment in her diary every Thursday with an MW. Do you know who that might be?'

Mrs Kent shook her head, but couldn't quite meet his eye.

There was a crash downstairs as the front door opened and closed heavily.

'Mum, I'm back,' Julietta's voice called. When she saw Shepherd following her mother down the stairs, her jaw tightened.

'Jules, you've not seen Nat's phone anywhere, have you?' Mrs Kent asked, giving her daughter a quick hug.

Julietta frowned. 'No. I thought you would have it,' she said, eyeing Shepherd.

He shook his head. 'Your sister didn't have it with her.'

Julietta shrugged. 'I've no idea where it would be,' she said. 'Is that all you came for?' she demanded of Shepherd, looking past him to the front door as if hinting he should leave.

'Sadly, no, I've come for you,' he said. 'We've got your sister's laptop back and we need to have another chat.'

Chapter 46

'We've found more lies, Miss Kent,' Burton began, once they were all seated in the interview room. Julietta glared at her, face flushed and arms folded, but said nothing.

'You told us that the first you knew of Natasha's pregnancy was when we told you,' Burton continued.

'I didn't know she—' Julietta began, but Burton interrupted.

'Don't lie to me,' she snapped. She slid a piece of paper across the table to Julietta and tapped it with her forefinger. 'Can you clarify what this is?'

Julietta looked at the piece of paper and her flushed cheeks paled.

Burton continued to stare at her. 'In case you can't see it from there, it's an email trail in which you tell your sister that you've booked her an appointment for a termination. That's the confirmation email from the clinic that you forwarded on to her.' Burton turned the sheet of paper over. 'Here's where Natasha emails the clinic ten days ago, saying she wants to cancel the appointment.'

'Unfortunately,' Shepherd put in, 'when confirming the cancellation, they've copied you in as the original contact point.'

Julietta said nothing, but her eyes were wary.

'So,' Burton said, leaning forward on the table, 'how did it feel when you found out your little sister, who you were trying to help, was going against your orders?'

'What? No, I didn't order, I was—' Julietta began, but Burton waved a hand.

'No, see, what I think happened was that you found out Natasha was pregnant, and you were forcing her to have a termination. After all, a baby didn't fit in with your career plan, did it?'

'She didn't want the baby. I was helping her,' Julietta said, tears starting in her eyes.

'Oh, really? Even though she was in a relationship with the father, that she was happy about it?' Burton asked.

'She didn't know what she was doing,' Julietta snapped. 'She'd only just found out she was pregnant. I told her there was still time to deal with it, to—'

'Deal with it?' Shepherd interrupted, incredulous. 'That's how you describe making your sister abort her pregnancy?'

Tears were sliding quietly down Julietta's cheeks.

'What did you do when you found out she was pregnant?' Shepherd asked.

'I yelled at her. She was so stupid, to be throwing away an amazing career, something we've worked for so long and we—' She broke off.

'We? As in, you and her?' Burton asked. 'I thought she was the one doing the dancing.'

Julietta said nothing.

'Did you consider her career to be yours? Is that why you pushed her, trained her, and drove her everywhere so she could have the career that you lost?' Burton asked. She felt Shepherd wince, but she wanted an answer.

'Is that so bad?' Julietta asked. 'I gave everything to support her; I did everything I could for her and that's how she repaid me? Getting knocked up?'

Shepherd leaned his forearms on the table. 'Who else knew about the pregnancy?' he asked.

Julietta stared at him. 'Just me and Nat,' she said. 'We didn't tell anyone else.'

'There you go with the "we" again,' Burton said. 'Like you got to decide for her. Well, Natasha told someone; how else did Tara Wallis know? That's what she was yelling at you yesterday, wasn't it, that Natasha was pregnant and didn't know who the father was?'

Julietta was silent, the realisation crossing her face like a slow wave.

'Natasha wouldn't be cowed any more, would she?' Burton demanded. 'She had another life to look after now and I bet she was prepared to do anything to protect it. She started saying no to you.'

'No, I—' Julietta began, but Burton cut across her.

'You thought the father was Travers McGovern. When you found out about their relationship, you yelled at him as well and told him to leave her alone. But he wouldn't, would he? Did he say it was his responsibility? That they wanted to be together?'

Julietta's jaw tightened, but she said nothing.

'He was going to leave his wife for her, leave his philandering ways for her and they were going away, weren't they?' Burton continued, leaning forward across the table. 'But you couldn't have that, so you killed him, thinking she'd give in and get rid of the baby once he wasn't around.'

'No!' Julietta shouted. 'I didn't do anything to Travers. I threatened him, told him to leave her alone, but I didn't kill him.'

Burton sat back, glaring at Julietta. 'So who did? If it wasn't you, who else had a motive?'

'Dominic,' Julietta said immediately. 'He was angry because Nat finished with him. He could have killed Travers to get Natasha back.'

'You seem a bit too keen to point the finger at Dominic,' Shepherd said. 'After all, it was you he should have been angry with, given that the end of their relationship was your fault.' He thought for a moment. 'I bet Natasha didn't want to dump him, did she? Did she believe you when you told her you'd seen him with someone else?'

Julietta shook her head. 'No, but I insisted. I told her repeatedly that she had to end it, that he was bad for her and—'

'In other words, you coerced her,' Burton said, glaring. Julietta seemed about to respond, but then thought better of it.

'There's something wrong in a relationship where you force someone to give you their laptop and phone password,' Shepherd said. 'It's a total invasion of privacy, but that didn't bother you, did it? You thought you were entitled to be in her life, to control everything, didn't you?'

Julietta began weeping.

Burton placed both of her hands on the table. Then there was a knock on the door. 'Come in,' Burton called. Gary Topping appeared with a note, which he handed to Burton. She read it and her brow furrowed.

'Wait here, Miss Kent. We're not finished.'

She got to her feet and swept from the room, followed by Topping, leaving Shepherd to sort out Julietta and hurry after her.

Chapter 47

'OK,' Burton said when they got back to the CID office, 'this had better be good.'

Topping gestured for them to follow him to his desk. He sat in his chair and spun round to face his keyboard. 'I've checked the college CCTV from the night that Travers died,' he said, 'and look what I found.' He moved the mouse and set the video running.

Burton leaned on the desk, peering at the screen. Shepherd stood at Topping's other shoulder.

'What am I looking at?' she said.

'It's what you're not seeing that's important,' Topping said. 'Look at the time stamp.'

Burton and Shepherd looked, and the latter shook his head. 'Sorry, Topper,' he said, 'am I being thick? I don't follow.'

Topping gave him a look that suggested he was indeed being thick. 'Julietta Kent said that she came to pick Natasha up at five thirty, didn't she?'

Burton nodded and then said slowly, 'Oh, I see what you mean.'

'Well, I'm glad someone does,' Shepherd said, still baffled.

Burton pointed a manicured finger. 'If she had come at five thirty, she would be here, waiting for Natasha.'

'She could have parked somewhere else,' Shepherd said.

Topping shook his head. He ran the video forward and pointed as a Renault Clio pulled into the car park and stopped outside the front of the building. 'There she is, with a time code of six o'clock.'

'Meaning Natasha was also on campus after that,' Burton said.

'How long does Julietta wait there?' Shepherd asked.

Topping consulted his notes. 'Natasha finally comes out of the building at about six thirty-five.'

'I bet Julietta didn't like that. I'm surprised she hasn't gone in to find her,' Burton said, with a laugh.

Shepherd exhaled heavily. 'We know Travers died sometime between six thirty and ten thirty, based on the post-mortem, but the vodka had to be spiked earlier that day. So, none of this really matters,' he said. 'Really, what we need is someone who was on campus earlier in the day, but that could be anyone on the list so far, even Natasha. Someone could have seen her spike the vodka earlier in the day, realised later what she'd done and killed her for it.'

'Or Natasha saw who spiked the vodka and got killed for it,' Topping put in.

Burton scrubbed at her face. 'Either of those is possible, but I'm leaning towards yours,' she said, pointing at Topping. 'After all, Natasha told Emma Fletcher that she knew who'd killed Travers.'

'We don't know where she was when she made that call, but she didn't want to be overheard, so presumably somewhere that the killer could have overheard her,' Shepherd said.

Burton sighed heavily and walked across to the murder board. The two men followed her.

She pointed to the timeline. 'So, we have Travers going to his office at five thirty. Then, according to Emma Fletcher, Neville Shuster visits and gets kicked out of Travers' office at about six o'clock. He sees Dominic Randall in the vicinity after he leaves, but we don't know if Dominic goes into the office or not.' She sighed. 'We're missing something. I think we need another chat with Dominic.' She stared into space again, then clapped her hands. 'Right, Gaz, can you go back through the statements and see whether anyone saw him after that? I have a feeling that there was someone, but I can't remember who.' Topping nodded. 'We also need to interview Neville Shuster to back up Emma's story.'

'It has to have been someone on campus who could move around easily with no one noticing they were there,' Shepherd said.

Burton groaned. 'I feel like we're just walking into brick walls everywhere we turn,' she said. Then she pointed at Shepherd. 'Mark, tell Miss Kent she can skedaddle for now, but she's still on bail for the assault. When you come back, take over from Gaz checking out the CCTV for the rest of the evening, inside the building and out. See who else on our list was on campus and when. Sorry,' she added, seeing Shepherd's pained expression. 'I need to give Gaz's eyes a rest.' Shepherd slapped Topping on the back, nodded and strode away down the office. 'Gaz, can you find someone to help Mark, going back through the day and see who went up the stairs near Travers' office while he potentially wasn't in it. His class schedule is in the computer file. Apparently, he could be careless about locking his door.'

Topping nodded. 'No probs, boss,' he said, returning to his desk and picking up his mug. 'More coffee required, I think.' Burton patted him on the shoulder. 'Where are you going next?' he asked as she headed into her office and returned with her handbag.

'I've got to update the boss and tell him we're no further forward.' She groaned. 'That'll be a fun conversation.'

Chapter 48

Burton and Shepherd called on Dominic Randall early to catch him before he headed off to the school.

'Only a couple of streets from the Kents,' Shepherd commented as he turned the car out onto the main road. 'That must have made it easy meeting up for lessons and stuff.'

'Do you reckon Julietta gave him lifts to and from college as well?' Burton asked with a sly grin as she looked out of the window at the passing buildings.

Shepherd laughed. 'I doubt it.'

He parked in the street and approached Dominic's house. Shepherd pounded on the door.

Burton laughed. 'This isn't a dawn raid on a drug den. You'll frighten the lad half to death.'

Shepherd looked shamefaced. 'Early starts bring that out in me,' he said, looking down at his feet.

After about half a minute, Dominic Randall opened the front door. He wore a T-shirt and tracksuit bottoms and carried a slice of toast.

'Oh, it's you,' he said, cheeks flushing. 'I'm just having breakfast. Do you want to come in?'

They followed him into the house and down a corridor into the kitchen. Breakfast things were set out on a scrubbed wooden table in the middle of the room.

'Do you want a coffee?' Dominic asked, pointing to a filter machine.

'I've made too much, as always.' Both detectives accepted a cup.

'We need to talk to you about Natasha,' Shepherd began. When he saw Dominic's eyes fill with tears, he added, 'We're sorry for your loss. I know you and Natasha were close.'

Dominic sniffed and turned away. 'We weren't close,' he said, his voice muffled as he wiped a sleeve across his face. 'Well, we were, then we weren't, and now...' He trailed away as he turned back.

'You were getting close again?' Shepherd asked.

Dominic said nothing, but his bottom lip wobbled dangerously.

'Why didn't you tell us you'd been in a relationship with Natasha?' Burton asked.

'I didn't think it was relevant,' Dominic said. 'We'd split up months ago.'

'We heard you cheated on her,' Burton said.

Dominic fired up. 'That was a lie; I told her it was, and she believed me. But then her bloody sister stuck her oar in. She never liked me.'

'I suspect Julietta wouldn't like anyone that Natasha wanted to go out with,' Shepherd remarked, 'including Travers McGovern.'

Dominic sighed. 'I warned her about him as soon as I found out she was seeing him. Going out with him was such a mistake.'

'Was that because you wanted her back?'

'No, well, yes, no ... Sorry, what I mean is, yes. I wanted her back, but that's not why I was trying to get her away from Travers.'

'Why were you?'

Dominic stared. 'Why wouldn't I? He was disgusting. Letching over all the girls, sleeping with half of them. Nat didn't deserve to be treated like that.'

'Is that why you told him to leave her alone and that you'd finish him?' Shepherd asked.

Dominic put his head in his hands. 'Yes. He was distracting her; she was messing all the routines up and her career was going to be over before it had begun. I told him all that and he just laughed and told me to sod off.'

'What did you mean by finish him?' Burton asked.

Dominic sighed. 'I didn't mean I was going to kill him,' he said. 'I was going to report him to the principal.'

223

'And did you?' Burton asked.

'Well, I sent her some pictures anonymously. I got a few that showed exactly what they were up to.'

'Did she do anything?'

Dominic shrugged. 'Not that I know of. Maybe she spoke to Travers because Nat knew about the photos. She didn't know it was me, though.'

'Did you know Natasha was pregnant?' Burton's delivery was blunt but didn't get the reaction she was expecting. 'You already knew.'

Dominic nodded. 'I kept asking why she was screwing up the routines and eventually she told me.' He shrugged. 'One of our routines has a lot of lifts in it and she wanted to be safe.'

'Was it yours?'

'No, well, I suppose it could have been. We had a one-night stand a couple of months ago. We'd been texting, and I'd apologised for our break-up. She said she knew what Jules had done and she was sorry.'

'Then what happened?' Burton asked.

'We met up a few times outside of school. It was tricky because Jules always picks her up and drives her everywhere. She's always been a bit obsessive and if Nat's not where she says she'll be, Jules gets really arsey.' He stopped. 'Recently, I'd seen bruises on Nat.'

'Julietta was physically abusing her own sister?'

Dominic looked down at the table. 'I think so. It's usually just following her around, always wanting to know where she is. She's probably got a tracker app on Nat's phone.'

Burton and Shepherd exchanged a look. They needed to find Natasha's phone.

'Were you and Natasha getting back together?'

Dominic shrugged. 'I don't know. Like I said, we'd been talking more; we had the one-night thing, but while Travers was on the scene...'

'Did you remove him from the scene?' Burton asked bluntly.

Dominic shook his head tiredly. 'No, I didn't. Nat said she was handling it.'

'What did she mean by that?'

'Presumably that she was going to dump him.'

'A witness saw you having an argument with her on the mezzanine floor at the school on the night Travers died,' Shepherd said.

Dominic pulled a face. 'God, there's always someone spying on you, isn't there? It wasn't an argument, as such. I was saying she needed to get away from him immediately. She'd had another crap day of rehearsals, she'd rowed with me, and then Tara Wallis had stuck her oar in, as always. He was going to ruin her if she didn't get away.'

'You told us you saw her, but you didn't mention the argument. Why?'

'I didn't think it was relevant,' Dominic said lamely.

Burton glared at him, so Shepherd interrupted.

'And she told you she was going to sort it? Did you grab her arm?'

'Only so she couldn't walk away without explaining what she meant. As it was, she told me not to worry, it was all in hand and she'd be free soon. Then she kissed me on the cheek and left.'

'What did you do?'

Dominic sighed. 'I told you I got a text from my mum about dinner, and I went back down the stairs and out of the building to the car park.'

'Did you see anyone else near Travers' office as you were leaving?'

Dominic thought for a moment. 'Actually, now you mention it, a guy barged past me going down the stairs as I was coming up.'

'Can you describe him?'

'Erm, about the same height as me, solid build, dark hair and wearing a blue coat, I think.'

'Thanks, that's helpful,' Burton said, as Shepherd scribbled down the description. 'We have to ask, where were you on Saturday night between six and six thirty?'

Dominic's shoulders slumped. 'I can't believe you're asking me for an alibi, but I was out with some mates in Tildon all night. They'll vouch for me.'

'I'll need names and numbers,' Shepherd said, offering a clean page of his notebook, 'and if you can remember any bars you went to and when, that would be great.' He exchanged a look with Burton as Dominic scrolled through his phone and wrote out a list of names and numbers.

She got to her feet and thanked Dominic for his time.

'We don't want you to be late for school,' she said as she left the room.

At the front door, Shepherd paused and handed Dominic a business card. 'If you think of anything else, call me.'

Chapter 49

When Dan got to campus, he strolled through the entrance atrium, engrossed in his phone, hoping to avoid questions. He'd been home to change into tracksuit bottoms, trainers and a T-shirt, hoping to fit in with the other students, and it seemed to work. So long as no one dragged him on to a stage and asked him to dance. Then it would not be pretty.

Fortunately, Tara Wallis was easier to find than he thought. The dancer was sitting in an armchair in the café with a mug on the low table in front of her. Her hair hung loose around her face, but still didn't camouflage the black-and-blue bruises on her face or the slightly swollen lip. Dan would have expected a faceful of make-up to cover her war wounds, but clearly she was wearing them with pride, or more likely, for sympathy. She was so absorbed in the screen of her phone that she didn't notice Dan until he sat down in the chair opposite her. She stared at him for a moment, looking puzzled.

'You don't mind if I sit down, do you?' Dan asked.

'I don't seem to have a choice,' she replied, looking irritated at the interruption. Then she frowned. 'You were here yesterday, weren't you? When that stupid bitch tried to kill me?'

Dan nodded. 'I tried to stop her.'

'Well, you didn't do a very good job,' she said, pointing to her face.

Dan gave her a sceptical look. 'To be honest, with what you were shouting, I should have just let her have free rein,' he said. 'Racist abuse is the lowest of the low. As it is, I saved you from a more serious beating, so I reckon you owe me.'

Tara leaned forward and picked up the mug in front of her. It smelled horribly herbal to Dan's nose. She took a sip, regarding Dan over the lip of the mug.

'I've seen you around a bit recently, but you're not a student, are you? Are you a friend of hers? Come to ask me to drop the charges?' she asked, clearly thinking she had the upper hand.

Dan shrugged. 'She's no friend of mine,' he said, and Tara's face fell slightly.

'Then why are you here?'

'I'm a reporter from the *Allensbury Post*. My girlfriend was friends with Natasha, and we're trying to find out what happened to her.'

Tara tried for an unconcerned shrug but didn't quite manage it. She sipped from her mug again and put it back on the table.

'I don't care what happened to her.'

Dan raised his eyebrows. 'A teacher and then a fellow student get murdered and you don't care?' he asked. 'God, I would if it was me.'

'What do you mean?' Tara asked.

'Well, we've been asking questions everywhere and we can't find anyone who would want to hurt Natasha or Travers,' Dan lied. 'Emma, that's my girlfriend, thinks that anyone who was on campus the night Travers died might be at risk. After all, Natasha was here and...' Dan let his sentence trail away.

Tara fell straight into his trap.

'I was on campus that day, but I don't know anything,' she said. 'Would someone come after me?'

Dan glanced over each shoulder as if checking for eavesdroppers and leaned forward. Tara leaned forward too.

'I don't agree with Emma. I think they did something bad and that's why someone killed them. But until we know for sure, I think everyone who was here should be very careful,' he whispered.

Tara looked worried. Dan moved to sit in the chair next to her and kept his voice low.

'How well did you know Travers?' he asked.

'I didn't.'

Dan frowned. 'You don't know him at all?' he asked. 'You must do. From what I've heard, he was quite a big name on campus.'

Tara sighed heavily, but said nothing.

'Come on, Tara, you need to help us. Don't you want to know who's targeting people from the school?' He paused. 'This Travers guy, do you know if him and Natasha knew each other?'

Tara's face darkened. 'If you call sleeping together a connection, then yes, they knew each other.'

Dan tried to look shocked. 'They were sleeping together?' he asked, voice low. 'A teacher and a student?'

Tara shrugged. 'She wasn't the first and she wouldn't have been the last if someone hadn't put a stop to it.' She looked at Dan and took another sip from her mug. 'You said you can't find anyone who'd want to do it?'

'We're a bit stumped at the moment because I don't think we're looking at the full picture.'

'How do you mean?' Tara asked, angling her body so she was facing him.

'I hoped you might know if there was someone else we should look at.'

Tara paused and picked at a cuticle on her fingernail. 'Like who?'

Dan took a deep breath, hoping he wasn't about to burn the bridge he'd so carefully built.

'I heard that you and Travers had a row a couple of days ago and that you shouted that you'd make him regret what he'd done.'

Tara's bottom lip wobbled. Dan waited in silence, falling back on the technique of forcing the other person to speak.

'He was sleeping with me too,' Tara said. 'He said he loved me and he was going to leave his wife for me.' Tears started rolling down her face.

Dan's eyes widened and he felt his breath catch in his chest. A chilly feeling spread over him and he suddenly felt queasy. Another victim of Travers McGovern. Just how many students had he been sleeping with? He quickly found a clean tissue in his pocket and handed it to her.

'He sounds like a total bastard,' he said.

229

She nodded. 'Then I found out that he was sleeping with Natasha as well. When I asked him about it, he told me she was pregnant and he was going to leave his wife. They were going away straight after the showcase so he didn't want me anymore.' Dan couldn't help himself and put an arm around her. She continued to sniff, trying to hold back sobs.

'You see, she wasn't the only one who got pregnant,' Tara said, raising watery eyes to Dan's, 'except he made me get rid of it.' Dan's stomach clenched. 'He said he didn't want a child; he only wanted me.' Tears began falling and Dan put his other arm around her and held her as she sobbed. He felt his heart beating faster. Travers was a complete bastard, that was true, but he was now hugging someone with a huge motive to kill both Travers and Natasha.

***

'Is there someone you can talk to about all this?' Dan asked when Tara returned to the table. She'd been to the ladies to splash water on her face and now had on what she called her 'face' of make-up. She still looked a little red-eyed and puffy, but it was an improvement on how she'd looked moments before.

Tara shook her head. 'You're the first person I've told.'

Dan's heart sank. 'You need to talk to someone, a counsellor. Here.' He dug in his pocket for his wallet and looked inside. In a moment of luck, he found a card for a local counselling service in his pocket and was glad he'd taken it when he did a story about it. He handed the card to Tara. 'Call these guys. I've heard they're really good.' Dan glanced at his watch. 'I'm sorry, I've got to go. Will you be all right?'

Tara nodded, took a deep breath and shook herself. 'Yes, I'll be fine. Thanks for listening to me.' Clearly, she did not know that she'd just talked her way onto the suspect list.

She picked up a bright pink sports bag from under the table and Dan stood up, too. She led the way out of the café, and as they entered the corridor, Dan noticed a display of flowers with two photographs, one of which was Natasha.

'That's nice,' he said, stepping towards it.

Tara shrugged. 'It's the only way we can honour them, really. Well, that and the showcase.'

Dan looked more closely at the second photo. 'Who's that?'

'Bella Dickens,' Tara replied.

'When did she die?'

'Three weeks ago. She had a car crash in December and she'd been in a coma since.' Tara gazed at the picture. 'So sad. She was lovely.'

'She didn't have anything to do with Travers McGovern, did she?' Dan asked, hoping for a negative.

Tara shrugged. 'I don't know.' She paused. 'But if you want to know about her, her dad works here and—' She stopped suddenly as if feeling she'd said too much.

'What?'

'Well, I heard him arguing with Travers last week.'

'What were they saying?' Dan asked, his stomach starting to flicker.

'I couldn't really hear, but they were right in each other's faces. It was like they would have been yelling if they thought there was no one around.'

Dan's chest clenched again, but before he could ask anything more, Tara's phone buzzed. 'Sorry, I've got to go,' she said. 'Thanks again,' and walked away quickly.

Dan looked at the photo of Bella Dickens. It was a pretty face with lovely, long, curly red hair that reminded him of Emma. Now he had to find out what had happened to Bella. In his head, he paraphrased an Oscar Wilde quote: 'To lose one student may be regarded as a misfortune, to lose two looks like carelessness'.

Chapter 50

Emma was halfway down a pint of pale ale when Dan arrived, panting slightly. He flopped into a chair and grabbed the other pint on the table, taking a big gulp.

'I needed that,' he said.

Emma peered at him as he took another gulp, half the pint gone. 'Are you OK?'

Dan recounted Tara's story and Emma took a gulp of her pint, too.

'Oh my God, that poor girl,' she said, staring at Dan in horror. 'That makes what I found out even worse.'

Dan took a deep breath. 'OK, I'm braced. Tell me.'

'After I got your message, I popped up to the office. Daisy tried to kick me straight back out, but I said I just needed to go to the archive.'

'Did she demand an explanation from you about what you were doing?' Dan asked, mimicking Daisy's voice when she was being strict.

Emma laughed. 'No, but she had her hands on her hips, so I got what I wanted and got out of there quickly.'

'Why did you need the archive?'

'I couldn't find what I was looking for online, so I went straight to the source.' She paused for a sip of her drink and pulled out her notebook. 'You were right though, the name Bella Dickens was familiar. She was involved in a car accident six months ago and she'd been in a coma since then.'

Dan paused with his glass halfway to his lips. 'And then died three weeks ago without regaining consciousness. How awful,' he said. 'What happened in the accident?'

'She was driving and went off the road, smashed head on into a tree,' Emma said, looking down at her notebook. 'We covered it at the time, but there wasn't much to report. But, I got the distinct impression from the roads policing unit at the time that they didn't think it was an accident.'

Dan stared at her and put his glass down without drinking. 'They think someone forced her off the road?'

Emma shook her head. 'Worse, they thought she did it on purpose.' Dan gasped, but she raised a hand to stop him from interrupting. 'We didn't put that in the paper, but I remember they showed me pictures they'd taken of the crime scene, and there were no skid marks. She hadn't tried to brake.'

Dan sat back in his chair and ran a hand through his hair. 'Shit, she was trying to kill herself?'

Emma's eyes filled with tears. 'That's what the police thought. They asked me not to include that, and we ended up doing an appeal for witnesses and nothing more. We didn't do a tribute piece because she wasn't dead. I'd asked if the family would do the appeal for witnesses, but apparently because of the circumstances, the police wouldn't let me near them.' She shook her head. 'If she did it deliberately, I can't even imagine what was going through her head. I'm not sure I even wanted to talk to the family. I mean, how do you speak to someone when their daughter killed herself, and in that way?'

Dan puffed out his cheeks. 'Well...' he raised his glass '...to Bella, rest in peace.' Emma raised her glass and clinked it against his. They finished their drinks in silence and then Dan asked, 'How does this link to Tara's story?'

'We're going to need another drink for that.'

Dan winced and got to his feet. He headed to the bar and came back with two more pints of pale ale. Placing one in front of Emma, he settled back in his chair. He took a swig and then he leaned his forearms on the table. 'So? What did you find?'

'Well, I had a bit of a dig around on social media,' she said. 'Bella was on various photo and video-related social media sites, similar to

Natasha. Her accounts are all still active, in that the family hasn't closed them down. The first two were mostly dancing videos or photos of dancers and costumes, that kind of thing. But I found this.' She fiddled with her phone and then turned the screen to show Dan a photograph of Bella and Natasha, grinning into the camera, arms around each other.

He raised his eyebrows. 'They were mates?' he asked. 'Natasha didn't mention that.'

Emma shrugged. 'I never asked her about Bella; there was no reason for her to say anything. There's also this.' She scrolled a little further up the account and showed Dan a picture of Bella and Travers, clearly in the middle of acting out a scene in rehearsal.

'She was in Travers' class,' Dan said. 'So she had a connection with him and Natasha.'

Emma nodded. 'It's an acting class so you can't tell how much is made up, but they look pretty comfortable standing so close together.'

Dan was sipping his pint and choked. 'You think he was seeing her as well?'

'I wouldn't put it past him.'

Dan ran a hand through his hair again. 'If she was seeing him and he broke it off, in the same way he did with Tara, would that be enough to make you try to kill yourself?'

'Pregnant and alone, unable to tell your family or ask for help?' Emma asked. 'I can see someone thinking it's the only way out.'

'Well, we have an opportunity to find out,' Dan said.

'How do you mean?'

'Tara said her dad works at the school,' Dan said.

'Wait a minute,' Emma said, staring at him and holding up a hand to interrupt. 'I've bloody met him. Mr Dickens. He's the one who shooed me away from Natasha on the day Travers died.' She frowned. 'Do you think he knew what Travers was up to, what he'd done to his daughter, and he didn't tell anyone?'

Dan shrugged. 'I assume he didn't, because surely there would be one hell of a furore going on if he had.'

'But why didn't he report it, either to the college or the police?'

'Saving his daughter's reputation?'

Emma sighed. 'But he's a teacher; he's responsible for these young people. Wouldn't you want to protect them?'

'Maybe he did,' Dan said, taking a sip and eyeing Emma over the rim of his glass.

She stared back. 'You mean stop him permanently, as in kill him?'

Dan shrugged. 'Why not? I mean, I feel like killing Travers myself and I have no genuine connection to any of them. Plus, Tara heard them arguing.'

Emma pointed to her phone screen with the picture of Bella and Natasha on it. 'I think it's time to ask if the Dickens family wants to do a tribute piece and then slide this into the conversation off-the-record.'

'It's worth a try.' Dan paused and sipped his drink. 'What do you think I should do about Tara?'

'How do you mean?'

'Normally I'd be all guns blazing, telling Burton that there's a new suspect on the block, but, well, she's really vulnerable and I feel bad about dropping her in it.'

Emma frowned. 'But Dan, she has a huge motive to want both of them dead. Imagine getting dumped when you've just had a termination, which he made you have. Then add in finding that he's been seeing someone else, got her pregnant and is keeping her baby.' She growled. 'God, that man really is a bastard. If he wasn't dead already, I'd bloody kill him myself.'

'But what if Burton is really horrible to her? I mean, she's—'

'Dan,' Emma interrupted, 'Burton won't be horrible to her. They have specially trained officers for interviewing people who've been abused.'

'So you think I should tell them?'

'Yes, and sooner rather than later. Better you tell her now than have her find out later that you knew and said nothing.'

**

'I don't normally do house calls for media updates,' Burton said, as

235

Dan held open the door to his flat. 'But as I was passing when I got your message, I thought I'd drop in.'

'Thanks,' Dan said, leading her into the living room, wiping his hands on the sides of his jeans. 'It's not really an update I'm after.'

'Are you all right?' Burton asked, eyeing him. 'You seem really on edge.'

'I need to tell you something. Have a seat,' Dan said, gesturing to the sofa.

'Do you want a cuppa?' Emma asked, appearing, kettle in hand.

'I might have known that you would be involved in this,' Burton said with a smile. 'None for me, thanks; my dinner will be on the table soon.'

Emma disappeared and returned empty-handed.

Dan sat on the armchair opposite Burton while Emma perched on a dining room chair.

'OK, out with it,' Burton said. 'The suspense is killing me.'

'I think I've found another suspect,' Dan said, 'for both murders.' He recounted his interview with Tara.

Burton stared at him, open-mouthed. 'Jesus Christ,' she gasped. 'That poor kid.'

'But you see,' Dan said, 'she's got reason to kill both of them.'

'Did she say where she was on the night of the murders?' Burton asked.

Dan shook his head. 'I didn't ask. The whole termination thing freaked me out so much. I made her cry.'

'I think it was the story rather than you,' Emma remarked.

'I feel awful,' Dan said, looking at her and then at Burton.

'You're not the one who should feel awful,' Burton said, face colouring angrily. 'The people who knew he was abusing students and did nothing are the ones that should feel it, and they will, believe me.'

Dan and Emma looked at each other.

'Someone knew?' Dan asked.

Burton seemed about to say something, but then changed her mind. Instead, she said, 'You leave that with me.'

'What are you going to do?' Dan asked.

'We'll speak to Tara,' Burton said, 'but don't worry, we'll go gently.

Your name won't come up. She and Natasha didn't get on, to say the least, so that's our angle with her.'

'What does that mean?' Emma asked.

'There was a book-throwing incident, which left Tara with a nasty cut to her face.'

Dan winced. 'Facial injuries from both of the Kent sisters. She doesn't have much luck, does she?'

'She could try not racially abusing people,' Emma snapped. 'It makes them less likely to whack you.'

'Another reason to see her, to discuss the assault charges against Julietta Kent,' Burton said.

'Do you think she'll press charges?' Dan asked. 'I mean, Julietta is grieving, and Tara started it.'

Burton got to her feet. 'We'll see. Julietta won't be able to duck it, given how many witnesses there were—' She pointed to Dan. 'It may have to come down to the mitigation, but we'll see how that goes.' She picked up her handbag. 'If there's nothing else, I'll be away.'

Dan shook his head and led the way to the front door.

'It goes without saying, if you come across any other information, you bring it straight to me,' Burton said. 'We don't want the killer going after you two as well.'

After he'd shown Burton out of the flat, Dan returned to the living room, rubbing the back of his neck.

'What?' Emma asked, recognising the action as uncertainty.

'She said someone knew Travers was abusing students. I wonder who that was.'

Emma frowned. 'You think it was Mr Dickens? That Tara overheard him confronting Travers over what he'd been doing?'

'If it was him, then he has a reason, protecting his daughter. But there is someone else as well. Someone with a lot to lose if the school's reputation gets damaged.'

'Sally-Anne Faber, you mean?'

'Exactly, but I've no idea how we find out.'

'I think I should pop round and see Mr Dickens and offer my condolences,' Emma said, 'and see if I can find out what he knows.'

Chapter 51

Shepherd was sitting at his computer typing up notes with two fingers when Gary Topping swept into the office.

'How was Neville Shuster?' Shepherd said, saving his file and then turning to his colleague. Topping flopped down into the chair at the desk behind him.

'He's a very angry man,' Topping said, logging onto the computer. 'The irony is that Travers McGovern got Shuster into trouble for messing around with a young actress.'

'Actor,' Shepherd corrected automatically.

'What?' Topping asked, not looking up from his screen.

'You don't say actress anymore. They're all actors now.'

Topping gave a sort of nod, as if acknowledging the point without really getting it.

'And had he?' Shepherd asked.

'Had who done what?' Topping asked, eyes fixed on the screen and fingers tapping urgently at the keys.

Shepherd sighed. 'Will you look at me? Had Shuster been messing with a young woman?'

Topping spun his chair around and shook his head. 'He says no and that she would stand by it. Says there's no truth and they've never even been alone together.'

'Do you believe him?'

Topping grinned. 'Never take anything at face value,' he said. 'He gave me her number and I spoke to her. She swears blind that nothing happened. In fact, her exact words were, "If he'd tried anything on, I'd have broken his fucking nose." Actually, she's more embarrassed to be caught up in it.'

Shepherd winced and Topping laughed.

'I quite liked her,' he said, 'if only she wasn't about twenty years younger than me.'

Shepherd laughed. 'What do you think of Shuster?'

'He seems like a genuine guy,' Topping said, turning back to his computer. A few clicks and a video started playing on his screen. 'Aha, yes!' he said, leaning forward to peer at the screen.

Shepherd scooted his chair over. 'What have you got?'

Topping pointed at the screen. 'Shuster said it was closer to five forty-five when he arrived at Travers McGovern's office. Now, there he is coming down the stairs—'

'Almost knocking over Dominic Randall going up the stairs,' Shepherd said, sitting forward in his chair. 'There's Natasha Kent on the mezzanine, and she walks away in the opposite direction to Dominic.'

'Exactly. But then,' Topping tracked the video forward, 'there's McGovern alive and well about five minutes later, leaving his office. He looks a little stressed and hustles off across the mezzanine.' He looked at Shepherd, who was frowning at the screen. 'What's the matter, Sarge?'

'First off, where's McGovern going?' Shepherd said. 'Did Dominic leave campus straight after that, and where did Natasha go? Was it her that sent the text, and Travers was going to meet her?'

Topping shook his head. 'No idea.' Then he leaned forward towards the screen, rewound the video and ran it. 'Hel-lo,' he said slowly. 'Who's that?'

A short blonde woman with her hair scraped back into a bun was standing in the corridor, watching Travers scuttle away. She waited a minute and then followed him.

'I know exactly who that is,' Shepherd said, 'and helpfully, she's next on our interview list.' He stood up. 'Keep watching that CCTV. I want to know when you see Dominic Randall and Natasha Kent on the mezzanine and when they leave.'

Chapter 52

'Are you going to arrest me?' Tara Wallis asked in a small, shaky voice.

Burton and Shepherd watched on the video on Saturday morning as the specialist officer shook her head. They were both feeling slightly sick, having listened to Tara detail her relationship with Travers Mc-Govern and its outcome. But this was no interrogation room; instead, it had comfortable sofas and armchairs, and a tell-tale box of tissues. Tara clutched a tissue in her hand, and she was wiping at her eyes.

'Not at the moment,' she said. 'You've been very brave telling me all this.'

Tara gave a tight smile.

'It didn't seem like I had much of a choice,' she said.

The officer smiled. 'It's important that we learn everything we can about Travers McGovern and what happened in the days before his death.' She looked up at the one-way glass that concealed Burton and Shepherd. 'Now, there are two other detectives who need to ask you more questions about Travers McGovern and Natasha Kent's deaths. Do you feel up to that?'

Tara looked down at the floor and nodded slowly. The officer squeezed her hand and beckoned to Burton and Shepherd. When they entered the room, the officer moved to sit next to Tara.

'You know why we want to speak to you,' Shepherd said gently. 'You knew both Travers and Natasha and you had a reason to want both of them dead.'

Tara shrugged and said nothing.

'Come on, Tara. You have more reason than most to want to kill Travers. We've heard your opinions about black people and what you thought of Natasha. She embarrassed you in class, didn't she? Humiliated you by throwing that book?'

The officer gave Shepherd a look that told him she felt he was pushing too hard.

'Is racist abuse really your thing,' he asked, 'or were you just trying to wind Natasha up? Push the buttons you know she'd react to?'

Tears started leaking down Tara's face. 'I was jealous, OK,' she snapped. 'She got all the best roles, all the ... all the...'

'She got Travers McGovern?' Shepherd asked quietly, leaning forward on the table as if taking Tara into his confidence.

Tara nodded and wiped her eyes on her jumper sleeve. 'Oh crap,' she said as make-up smeared across the fabric.

Burton dug in her handbag and came up with a packet of baby wipes. Tara looked surprised as she held them out. 'The benefits of being a mum,' Burton said.

Tara gave a small smile and wiped her face. Shepherd fetched the bin from the corner of the room, and she dropped the used wipes into it.

He sat down again. 'You've just told the officer here that you knew about Natasha and Travers' relationship,' Shepherd said.

Tara wiped her face again and nodded. 'He told me. He was bragging about it.'

'And he told you she was pregnant and they were going to be together. You must have been angry.'

Tara shrugged, but tears were starting again. 'We were together for a few months,' she said. 'He told me he loved me and that he was going to leave his wife. Then, when he dropped me, I found out he was seeing Natasha as well.'

'That must have hurt you, him moving on to someone you hated,' Shepherd said quietly. 'You blamed Natasha for Travers finishing things with you?'

Tara nodded, sniffing. 'If she'd just left him alone, she could have anyone she wanted. I just wanted him,' she wailed, breaking into sobs.

Burton and Shepherd exchanged a look. The officer was now on the edge of her seat, glaring at them both.

'Look, Tara,' Burton said, leaning forward and resting her elbows on her knees, 'he wasn't a good man. He was abusing you, abusing Natasha. As your teacher, he was supposed to look after you, not treat you like that.'

Tara took a few gulps of air and it seemed to calm her.

'You knew about his peanut allergy,' Shepherd said.

Tara nodded. 'Everyone knew about that.'

'Where were you on the day he died?' Shepherd asked.

Tara stared at him. 'What?'

'It's a simple question,' Burton remarked. 'Where were you?'

Tara blinked and looked at the officer, who nodded. 'Well, I was at college,' she said, 'but I didn't see Travers.'

'Didn't see him at all?'

'Well, I saw him in the hallway. We'd just finished a rehearsal in the theatre and as we were coming from the backstage area, I saw him leaving through the auditorium exit.'

'He'd been watching your rehearsal?' Burton asked.

Tara shrugged. 'I'm guessing he was there to watch Natasha and she was putting in an awful performance. Kept falling over.'

'What about earlier in the day?' Burton asked. 'Where were you?'

'I had two hours of ballet in the morning and then rehearsal started at about eleven o'clock. Then I had lunch in the café with a couple of friends. I don't think I was on my own at all.' She pulled out another baby wipe and rubbed her face again. Without the make-up, she looked even younger and more vulnerable.

'Where were you in the afternoon?' Burton asked.

Tara looked surprised. 'I left campus at about three o'clock and went home,' she said, refusing to meet Burton's eye.

Burton sighed. 'I prefer it when suspects don't lie to me,' she said.

Tara's head snapped up and she stared at Burton. 'What do you mean?'

'We have you on CCTV outside Travers' office at about six o'clock?'

Tara stared at the photograph but said nothing.

'Moments after this,' Burton said, tapping the photograph, 'Travers left his office after getting a text message that worried him, and you followed him.'

'Did you send him the text, asking him to meet you?' Shepherd asked.

Tara shook her head. 'No, I never texted him. You can check my phone.' She pulled a smartphone from her pocket, opened the messaging app and handed the phone to Shepherd. He scanned the messages and found a conversation with Travers. He held it up.

'Open it,' Tara said. 'It's from last week after we'd rowed.'

Shepherd checked the date and time on the message and nodded to Burton.

'Where did he go when you followed him from his office?' she asked.

'I lost him in the corridor,' Tara said. 'He was in a hurry and I didn't want him to see me following. I turned the corner and he'd gone. I've no idea where.'

'What did you do then?'

'I went back to the changing rooms, grabbed my stuff and went home. I said bye to Mr Dickens as I was leaving, so he'll be able to confirm the time.'

'What about when Natasha was killed?' Burton asked.

Tara thought for a moment. 'That was my cousin's daughter's birthday. We went bowling.' She winced.

'Not the trendiest of activities,' Shepherd said with a smile.

She smiled back. 'I only watched. I didn't want to risk a pulled muscle or something before the showcase.'

'You didn't leave the bowling alley at all?' Burton asked.

Tara shook her head. 'No, my cousin's daughter kept squabbling with her brother, so I had to be there to referee. They'd have noticed if I left at all.'

'OK, thanks,' Shepherd said.

Tara's shoulders sagged with relief. 'I can go?' she said.

Shepherd nodded. 'Yes, I think that's all. We'll be in touch if we need anything else.'

The officer got to her feet, switched off the video camera in the corner. She pulled out a memory card and held it up.

'I'll send the footage as soon as I get back to the office,' she said to Burton and Shepherd. Then she turned to Tara. 'I'll show you out. Is

243

someone coming to meet you?' The door closed behind them before Burton and Shepherd heard the response.

Burton groaned and flopped back on the sofa she was sitting on, stretching her arms over her head.

'Another one bites the dust,' she said. 'We've got alibis left, right and centre.'

Shepherd frowned. 'Well, she said something interesting. What was Mr David Dickens doing on campus at six o'clock when he was supposed to be at home? He didn't mention that earlier, did he?'

'Right,' Burton said, standing up so forcibly that the sofa squeaked on the wooden floor, 'let's get back to the office and regroup. We need to think about how we tackle him.'

But before she could take another step, the door opened again and a uniformed officer appeared.

'Hi Jack,' Shepherd said, 'what brings you here?'

Jack looked serious. 'You'll never believe what's happened now,' he said.

Chapter 53

When Emma knocked on the Dickens' front door on Saturday morning, a little boy of about five opened it.

'Hello,' she said, bending down to his level. 'Is your daddy around?'

The boy nodded. 'But he won't talk to you because we're going out to my dancing class soon.'

'Oh, I see,' Emma said. 'What kind of dancing?'

But before she could find out, David Dickens appeared, ushering the boy back inside.

'Get your shoes on,' he said over his shoulder, and then faced Emma.

'Mr Dickens, I'm Emma Fletcher from the *Allensbury Post*,' she began, but Dickens' face had already darkened.

'I recognise you,' he said. 'I saw you with Natasha after Travers McGovern died, but I already knew who you are.'

Emma's instincts told her this conversation would not go well.

'I'm sorry to call on you like this at home,' she said, 'but I heard about Bella, and I just wanted to offer my condolences.'

But Dickens was not softening. 'Oh, so you're interested in her now? Now that she's dead? You weren't interested when we wanted her accident investigating, when we were desperate to know what had happened to her.'

Emma winced. 'I wanted to talk to you, but the police said you didn't want to speak to the media.'

Dickens looked a bit mollified. 'Well, what do you want now?'

'To offer my condolences and to see whether you'd like to do a tribute piece now? I'm sure there are a lot of people who'd like to talk about her. I know we found that with Natasha, that—' But she realised immediately that she'd said the wrong thing.

Dickens' face reddened and he seemed to swell to fill the doorway. 'That girl,' he almost spat. 'Everyone acting as if she was wonderful, a saint, when she was *not*. I assume you know what she was up to?'

'I know she and Bella were friends, that—'

'Friends?' This time Dickens did spit, and some landed on Emma. She resisted the urge to wipe it away. 'She was no friend to my Bella with what she did ... with what they did...' He trailed off and tears filled his eyes. He dashed them away with the back of his hand and took a step towards Emma. She took half a step backwards, ready to run if necessary.

'You get off my doorstep,' he yelled. 'We want nothing from you. If I see you again, then you'll regret it.' He slammed the door so hard it reverberated in the frame.

Emma turned away, heart beating like she'd run a one-hundred-metre sprint. In among that rant, she thought she'd learned something new, but she just couldn't put her finger on it.

Chapter 54

Dan's mobile rang in the office as he was eating a sandwich with one hand and typing with the other. He quickly wiped his fingers and looked at the screen. It wasn't a number he recognised.

'Hello?' he asked cautiously.

'Is that Dan?' a young-sounding female voice asked.

'Yes. Who's that?'

'It's Sadie.'

Dan frowned, wracking his brains for a clue as to who that was.

'Sadie, from the dance school,' the voice repeated, slightly exasperated.

'Oh, yes, sorry, I was in the middle of something,' Dan said, looking down at his BLT. 'I didn't recognise your voice. What can I do for you?'

'It's more what I can do for you,' Sadie said.

Dan waited.

'You'll never guess what's happened?'

'Probably not, so you might as well tell me,' Dan said.

'Someone broke into Natasha Kent's locker,' Sadie said, sounding gleeful.

Dan sat up straight in his chair, sandwich forgotten. 'What?' he asked. 'What do you mean, broke into?'

'Someone forced the door open and took all of her stuff.'

'Her mum was supposed to be collecting it. Are you sure she didn't come for it?'

'I don't think so because the police are here and it looks like they're testing for fingerprints.'

Dan thought quickly. 'Do you know if the college has been in touch with Natasha's family about it?'

'No idea. Well, they'd not tell me, would they?' Sadie said. 'Anyway, I just thought you'd want to know.'

'No, wait, hang on a minute,' Dan said, thinking quickly. 'Did you say they've taken everything from the locker?'

'As far as I know,' Sadie said.

'Do you think you could sneak in and have a look?'

'There's still crime scene tape, but I'm sure I can find a way around it.' She paused. 'Do you think they've missed something?'

'I don't know,' Dan said, 'but it's worth checking to be sure. Are you on campus now?'

'I'm here for the next two hours,' came the reply.

Dan thought for a moment. 'Right, can you have a poke around now? I'll head down to the college and see you outside in about twenty minutes. Does that sound OK?'

'No problems.' Sadie sounded cheerful. 'See you then.'

Dan finished his sandwich in three bites, almost choking on the last one.

The deputy news editor looked over at him. 'You'll give yourself indigestion eating like that,' he said. 'What's the hurry?'

'I've got to pop out,' Dan said, getting to his feet and wiping his fingers on his trousers. He grabbed his bag and was heading out of the door before questions were asked.

What on earth was going on at the school?

***

When Dan arrived, Sadie was waiting outside, shifting excitedly from one foot to the other.

'You've been ages,' she said accusingly.

Dan glanced at his watch. 'It's been fifteen minutes,' he said, holding it up for her to see.

'Well, it felt like ages.' She paused. 'I didn't know you worked on Saturday.'

'All hours. Did you get a look in the locker?'

Sadie grinned. 'I snuck in and then dropped my purse. The change went everywhere, and I had to scrabble around on the floor for a while. I poked around inside the locker, and I thought it was completely empty.'

'But it wasn't?' Dan asked, feeling his pulse quicken.

'Right at the back, stuck in the corner, was this,' Sadie said, pulling a small piece of card out of her pocket with a flourish. She handed it to Dan, and he looked down at it, feeling slightly disappointed.

'Oh, it's a coffee shop loyalty card,' he said. 'You collect stamps and get a free coffee.'

'Do you think it's important?' Sadie asked, taking a step closer so she could look at it, too.

Dan shrugged. 'No idea.' He turned the card over in his hands and then shoved it into his pocket. 'Thanks for getting it, though,' he said hastily, not wanting Sadie to think her work hadn't been worth it. 'Have the police said anything about the break-in?'

She shook her head. 'I've not heard anything, but everyone's a bit freaked out that someone stole Natasha's stuff right after she died. Apparently, her mum is devastated. She came down earlier today to collect it and that's when they found it had gone. She cried.'

Dan puffed out his cheeks. 'I'm not surprised. Adding insult to injury, I suppose.' He frowned. 'Was that the first time someone noticed the break-in?'

Sadie shook her head. 'One of my friends said she'd been in there and seen the door open and the locker empty and assumed the stuff had already been collected.'

Dan nodded, his brain racing. Why would someone steal Natasha's stuff? What had she kept in her locker that was so important?

Chapter 55

'And now someone has broken into her bloody locker,' Burton snapped at Shepherd as they stood in the changing room, watching the locker being dusted for fingerprints. She'd been glowering for the whole journey from the police station to the college. 'Anything?' she demanded of the man with the fingerprint powder and brush.

He glanced at her over his shoulder and shook his head. 'The perp must have worn gloves,' he said, braced for Burton's reaction.

She growled, turned away and stamped out of the room. The man looked at Shepherd and winced.

'You're in for a good day,' he said, packing up his equipment.

Shepherd nodded. 'It's this case. Everywhere we turn, there's a brick wall. Natasha's mum was supposed to come and collect the stuff so we could check through it.'

'Ah,' the man said, getting to his feet. 'I see.'

Shepherd smiled, said goodbye and turned to follow Burton. Then he turned back.

'Hang on, did you say there are no fingerprints at all?'

The man nodded.

Shepherd went out into the corridor and found Burton pacing.

'Mark, what the hell is going on? What was in that bloody locker that someone would risk breaking into? Anyone could have disturbed them.'

'There aren't any fingerprints on the locker,' Shepherd said.

Burton stared at him. 'Hang on a second. Not even Natasha's?'

Shepherd shook his head. 'Someone must have wiped it down after they stole the stuff. Judging from the people Jack spoke to earlier, no one remembers it being broken yesterday, but those who were first in today said they saw the door open.'

'And they didn't think to report it?' Burton demanded, hands on hips.

Shepherd shook his head. 'They thought her mum had already cleared it out and that's why it was open.'

'And what does the security guard have to say for himself? Hitesh, isn't it?'

Shepherd shook his head. 'A different guy. He's had a look at the CCTV and there's no one on it.'

Burton was chewing on her lip, clearly trying to control her temper. 'Right, as planned, back to the nick and try to work out what the bloody hell we need to do next.' She turned and marched away with Shepherd hurrying to catch up.

But before they'd taken more than a few steps, David Dickens appeared to block their way.

'What is going on, Detective Inspector?' he demanded. 'Two people are dead, and now Natasha's belongings have been stolen. What are you doing about it?'

'Isn't it funny, Mr Dickens, how you turn up every time there's trouble?' Burton snapped.

Mr Dickens stepped back as if she'd slapped him. 'Well ... I ... erm,' he began.

'Why are you here on a Saturday, sir?' Shepherd asked, hoping to diffuse the tension.

'My son has a ballet class,' he said, eyeing Burton as if she were about to bite him.

'I wanted to check something in your statement from the night Travers McGovern was murdered,' Shepherd said, pulling out his notebook.

Mr Dickens looked completely blindsided. 'I can't remember where I—'

'You told us,' Shepherd continued as if Dickens hadn't spoken, 'that

251

you left school at about three o'clock to pick your kids up from school. Is that right?'

'Yes, I did. I like to be home for tea and bath time.'

Burton's shoulders relaxed as she realised where Shepherd was going.

'Did you come back to campus at all later in the day?'

'No, I was at home with my children. My wife has her book club that night.'

'So, why do we have a witness who says she saw you in school at about six o'clock? The witness said she waved to you and said good night.'

Mr Dickens stared at him and said nothing.

'Did you come back to see Travers McGovern?' Shepherd asked. 'You'd worked out that he was arguing with Dominic Randall about Natasha Kent, hadn't you?'

Mr Dickens' hands trembled. 'I know nothing about anything like that,' he said. Then he took a deep breath. 'I remember now. I came back to get some papers, essays I needed to mark. My wife stayed with the children and she was a bit late going out.'

'I thought you came into school early in the day to do that,' Burton said, looking at him sharply.

'Well, I decided to, erm, do it that night as my wife would be out.'

'What time does your wife go out?'

'Usually about seven o'clock. Then she's back around ten o'clock.'

'What about the night Natasha was killed? Where were you then?'

'I was at home with my family,' Mr Dickens snapped. 'Now, is there anything else?'

Shepherd shook his head. 'That's all for now.'

Mr Dickens marched away across the atrium and Shepherd slid his notebook into his pocket with a satisfied smile.

'You believe he was at home?' Burton asked.

Shepherd shook his head. 'Nope and I'd like to speak to his wife to find out.'

Burton turned back and looked at the police tape covering the changing room door. 'I just don't get what his motive would be,' she said. 'If he found out Travers was sleeping with students, why not

252

report him to the principal or to the board of governors? Why kill him?'

Shepherd looked towards the front doors of the college and frowned. 'No idea, but I want to look more into this guy. Like you said, he seems to turn up whenever there's trouble.'

***

After giving instructions to the uniformed officers to keep them updated, Burton and Shepherd also headed towards the front door. Outside they found Mr Dickens shading his eyes and staring across the quadrangle at a couple having an intense conversation.

'Who is that man?' he demanded. 'I know him from somewhere.'

Shepherd looked in that direction and just stopped his eyes from rolling as he saw Dan talking to a young woman.

'A journalist on the local paper,' he said. 'He was here when Julietta Kent and Tara Wallis had their fight, trying to break it up. It's no surprise that the local paper is interested in two deaths on campus.'

Mr Dickens harrumphed. 'Well, I wish you'd get them away from campus. They shouldn't be harassing students.'

They watched as the young woman smiled up at Dan and handed him a piece of card, which he turned over in his hands.

'What's that she's given him?' Burton asked.

Shepherd squinted in the sunlight. 'I can't see from here,' he said, 'but it doesn't look like she's being harassed.'

They watched as Dan and the young woman spoke for another minute or two, then he patted her on the arm, turned and walked away.

'Isn't there a way to keep them off campus?' Mr Dickens asked.

Burton frowned. 'We'll have a word with him, but if the students invite him in, there is nothing we can do.'

Mr Dickens scowled. 'I have to protect the students,' he said. 'If I see any of the journalists around again, I'll throw them out myself.'

'Them?' Shepherd asked, even though he suspected he knew who it was.

Mr Dickens swallowed hard. 'I had the crime reporter, Emma something, on my doorstep this morning. It's all too much. If I see them again, they'll regret it.'

'We'll ask them to stay away, but we can't physically stop them,' he said. 'If you receive any complaints from staff or students, let us know.'

Mr Dickens didn't respond immediately. He was watching Dan walk away and staring at the young woman he'd been talking to. She seemed to become aware she was being watched, glanced at the trio and walked towards them.

'Sadie, who was that you were talking to?'

The woman shrugged. 'He's a friend of Natasha Kent,' she said. 'He was just asking about her locker being broken into.'

'How did he know about that?' Burton asked.

'Sorry, who are you?' Sadie asked.

Burton and Shepherd presented their warrant cards and Sadie looked taken aback.

'Oh, I see,' she said. 'I don't know how he found out, but I think he knows her family.' She fidgeted from one foot to the other under the watchful eyes of Burton and Shepherd. She pulled out her phone and checked the screen. 'I'm sorry,' she said, shifting her bag onto the other shoulder, 'I have to get to a rehearsal.' She walked round the group and through the front door of the building. Mr Dickens turned and watched as she walked away. He turned back to Burton and Shepherd.

'I need to get back to my son.'

Burton shook her head. 'If you think of anything else, please get in touch. You have my card.'

Mr Dickens nodded and turned to walk back into the college.

'I wonder what our journalist friend was up to,' Burton said, as they walked back to their car.

'She was lying about how he found out.'

'You think she told him?'

Shepherd nodded.

Burton chewed her lip. 'I'd love to know what she gave him.' She paused and frowned. 'Maybe we need to have a little chat with Mr Sullivan.'

'What interests me more,' Shepherd said as they walked towards their car, 'is why Emma Fletcher was on Dickens' doorstep this morning.'

Chapter 56

Dan was halfway up the hill to the High Street when his mobile phone rang.

'Where are you?' Emma's voice demanded. 'I left you a message ages ago about when we're meeting up.'

'I went to see that woman, Sadie, at the dance school,' Dan said. 'Someone broke into Natasha's locker.'

'What?' Emma gasped. 'Why would someone do that?'

'Obviously, they thought she'd hidden something in there.'

'What could that possibly be? What would be important enough for someone to risk breaking into her locker in a busy school?'

Dan took a deep breath. 'I think she had something that identifies the killer. They couldn't find it on her body, so they went to see if it's in the locker.'

'So the killer is someone from the school?' Emma said, slowly.

'It's the only way they have got into Travers McGovern's office and broken into that locker without anyone seeing them,' Dan said. 'It's someone who's there every day, so their presence isn't noticed.'

'It doesn't even narrow our suspect pool,' Emma said. 'Unless we count Julietta Kent.'

'How do you mean?' Dan asked.

'Well, she's probably not known to most of the students. They'd have noticed her. Plus, we agreed she had a motive to kill Travers McGovern, though not Natasha.' Emma sighed. 'Anyway, where are you? Are you going back to the office?'

'No, I'm off to an internet café on Gloucester Street.'

Emma snorted. 'You're so nineties,' she said.

Dan laughed. 'It's called retro.'

'Is there something wrong with your phone that you can't use the internet on that?'

'I asked Sadie to have a poke about in Natasha's locker and see if there's anything that they missed.'

'And?'

'She found a loyalty card for the internet café,' Dan said, pulling it out of his pocket and looking at it. 'It's almost full of coffee stamps, so Natasha must've been going there a lot. There's a series of numbers on it as well, but the writing is really scrappy, so I can't read them.'

'You're hoping that someone in the café will recognise Natasha?'

'If she goes there often enough, someone will have seen her.' He turned into Gloucester Street as he was speaking and looked at the front of the shop. It was dingy, with windows so dirty you could barely see in. The front section of the shop sold new-age style clothing and jewellery. The smell of incense was strong enough to make him feel sick even out in the street.

'Looking at the state of this shop, Natasha would have stuck out like a sore thumb.'

'But why would she need to use an internet café, when they presumably have Wi-Fi at home and at school and she has a mobile with data on it?'

'That is an excellent question,' Dan said. 'Presumably she had something she wanted to keep secret.'

'So secret she couldn't do it on her own laptop?' Emma asked.

'That's exactly what I was thinking.' Dan glanced at his watch. 'Look, I'm going to have to get this done so I can get back to the office. I'll let you know how I get on.'

Emma said goodbye and he hung up the phone.

Dan made his way to the computer section at the back of the shop. He approached the counter, which was set up as a coffee stand, as well as the place you could book a computer.

A woman with dark purple hair, heavy black eye make-up and

chunky silver rings on every finger, and a thinner one through her nose, smiled at him.

'Can I help?' she asked.

Dan asked if she could book a computer and order a coffee.

'That's yes to both,' the woman said cheerfully. She looked down at a clipboard on the counter in front of her. 'Number twenty is free.' She pointed to the computer in the corner. 'It's three pounds per hour for the internet, and two pounds for the coffee.' Dan handed over the five pounds and the woman smiled again.

'Do you have a loyalty card?' she asked. Dan handed over Natasha's card and the woman picked up the stamp. Then she looked at it, front and back, and stared at Dan.

'Where did you get this?' she demanded in a low voice. 'Who are you?'

'My name's Dan and I'm a friend of Natasha Kent,' he said, surprised by the reaction.

The woman frowned.

'I'm trying to find out what happened to her,' Dan continued. 'Do you know something?'

'Not here,' the woman whispered. 'Go to the computer and I'll bring your coffee over.'

Dan went to number twenty and sat down. He logged in and kept an eye over his shoulder for the coffee woman. She eventually arrived and sat down in the chair at the next computer and pulled it closer to him. She placed the coffee on the desk and leaned in. A wave of heavy perfume filled his nostrils, something that contained patchouli, and bells tinkled on the hem of her velvet top.

'It was horrible what happened to Natasha,' she said, eyes welling with tears. 'I couldn't believe it.'

Dan looked at her. 'How did you know her?' He wasn't sure how clean-cut Natasha had crossed paths with someone who dressed like this.

The woman smiled. 'We went to primary school together,' she said. 'We'd lost touch when Nat went off to dance school, but then we bumped into each other a couple of months ago. She came in here to rent a computer.' She gestured around her.

Dan frowned. 'Why? She had a laptop at home.'

The woman shrugged. 'She said she wanted somewhere that she could work privately. She said she was always being watched at home. I got the impression that time to herself was in short supply.'

'How did you know it was her card?' Dan asked, holding it up.

The woman took it and pointed to the string of numbers in the top corner of the card. 'That's my mobile number,' she said. 'Last time Nat was here, about a week ago, she was really on edge, scared almost.'

'Why?' Dan asked.

The woman shrugged. 'She wouldn't say, but I told her to call me if she needed help.' Her mouth turned down at the corners. 'She never called and the next thing I knew, she was dead.'

'What was she doing here that she couldn't do at home?' Dan asked, glancing around.

The woman frowned. 'I'm not sure, but she didn't seem to be just checking emails or surfing like most people,' she said. 'She'd fiddle around nonstop, eyes glued to the screen for the full hour and then save something on a memory stick.'

Dan leaned forward, feeling the tell-tale flickering in his stomach. 'What did she do with it?' he asked.

The woman pulled a USB stick from her pocket. 'She left it with me and asked me to keep it safe,' she said. She handed it to Dan. 'I checked it when I heard that she'd died and it didn't seem all that relevant. It was just personal papers, so I was going to take it to her family.'

'I've met them before. Would you like me to take it and give it to her mum?'

The woman nodded. 'Would you? Just in case it's useful for them.'

Dan thanked the woman, who wandered back to her coffee counter. He logged off the computer and shoved the memory stick into his pocket. The secret life of Natasha Kent might be about to come out into the open.

***

The USB stick was burning a hole in Dan's pocket all afternoon. He had to go back to the office to file some copy, and it took four attempts before the news editor was happy with his story.

'For God's sake, Dan, what's the matter with you this afternoon?' she shouted across the office. 'We're on a deadline here.'

Dan rubbed his forehead. 'Sorry, I must be hungry or something.'

He jumped as his mobile rang on the desk.

'Mate,' Ed's voice asked. 'Where are you?'

'I wish people would stop asking me that today. My girlfriend's already stalking me.'

Ed laughed. 'She called me too, said you're onto something.'

Dan brought him up to speed on Sadie and the USB stick.

Ed gave a low whistle. 'I'm guessing you're not giving that to the Kents straight away.'

'Hell no. As soon as I'm done in the office, I'm heading home to check it out. You want in?'

'Yes, sir. What time are you back?'

Dan risked a glance over his shoulder at the news editor. 'Maybe an hour? I think we're almost done here.'

'OK, cool. Tell Em to get over to our place and I'll supply the pizza and beer.'

'The way we've solved all our previous cases, you mean?' Dan asked, grinning.

Ed laughed. 'Why mess with perfection?' he asked.

'Great, I'll give Em a shout and get her there in an hour. Let's hope it's worth the excitement.'

Chapter 57

When Emma arrived, Dan had the USB stick plugged into his laptop and Ed had the food delivery app standing by. She quickly gave her order and then accepted a bottle of beer from Ed.

'Just like old times,' she said, clinking her bottle against his.

Ed chuckled. 'That's exactly what I said earlier. Three heads are better than two, so they say.'

Emma walked over to Dan and gave him a quick kiss on the lips.

'It sounds like you've had a busy day,' she said, ruffling his hair.

He grinned and took a sip from the bottle of beer placed at a safe distance from his laptop. 'I'm hoping this USB stick will be a breakthrough we're looking for.'

Emma pulled up a wooden-backed chair and sat beside him at the dining table. 'I can't believe you started without me,' she said.

Ed laughed. 'Don't worry, we waited. It's more than our lives would be worth.'

Emma grinned. 'Too right.' She took another swig from her bottle and placed it on the table on a coaster. 'You may now begin.'

Dan double-clicked on an icon and a box opened on the screen. In it were several folders labelled 'flat', 'bank' and 'other stuff'.

'At least she was organised,' he said, choosing the file named 'flat'.

He double clicked on a PDF document and gave a sharp intake of breath when it opened.

'It's a tenancy agreement,' he said. 'She signed it two days before she

261

died.'

Emma was staring at the screen, mouth open. 'She was moving out? She never mentioned that to me.'

'It was after the last time you spoke to her,' Ed pointed out, 'apart from ... well ... you know...' He trailed off as Emma's eyes filled up, and he reached over to squeeze her hand.

Dan was staring at the computer screen. 'She wasn't just leaving home, she was leaving town.' He frowned at the screen and then turned to Emma. 'The flat is in Tildon.'

'And it looks like she was keeping it a secret,' Emma said.

Dan nodded. 'Wouldn't you if you had a sister like Julietta? Imagine what she would do if she found out Natasha was leaving.'

'You think she was moving away because of her sister?' Ed asked.

'Julietta seems to think of Natasha's life as an extension of her own,' Dan said. 'She couldn't stage-manage Natasha from a distance.'

'Tildon isn't far away, so I'm guessing she wanted to stay close to her mum,' Ed said.

'Especially given that she was pregnant,' Dan said. 'She would need her mum to help with the baby.'

Emma was frowning. 'What if Julietta found out Natasha was planning to leave?' he asked. 'What if she found out that Travers McGovern was involved?'

'Natasha signed the lease after Travers died, so she was still planning to go,' Dan said, reading through the document. 'Do you think Julietta killed Travers, thinking Natasha would stay if he wasn't there?'

'And when she found out Nat was going anyway, she...' Emma trailed off, a sick feeling in her stomach. She swigged a beer, hoping to make it go away.

'But how would Julietta find out about the plan to leave? Natasha hid the documents, and the café woman hadn't shown it to anyone,' Ed put in.

Dan nodded. 'I bet these documents aren't anywhere else than on here.' He pointed to the USB stick plugged into his laptop.

'But how was Natasha going to afford rent, bills etcetera on a...' Ed peered at the screen '...one-bedroom flat in Tildon? That won't come cheap.'

'Nat was teaching your ballet class, wasn't she?' Dan asked.

Emma nodded. 'And at least one other kids' class at school that I know about, but I can't imagine that would be enough to cover rent and bills, let alone leave anything to live on.'

'Well, let's see, shall we?' Dan double-clicked on the folder labelled 'bank', and a series of PDF documents appeared on the screen.

'Bank statements,' he said, double-clicking on the first document. It opened on the screen and he took a sharp intake of breath. 'Blimey,' he said.

Emma peered at the amount of money in the bank account and give a low whistle. 'She's definitely got some income,' she said.

Dan was staring at the screen. 'There's over five grand in here. Clearly she doesn't just get paid for dancing classes.'

Ed leaned in over his shoulder. 'These look like the payments from the school for the dancing lessons,' he said, pointing to a BACS transfer of two hundred pounds that repeated regularly. 'But that on its own wouldn't get her a flat in Tildon.'

'But there is a nice little cash payment of two grand here,' Emma said, pointing at the screen. 'There's the flat deposit and one month's rent, with some change left in her pocket if she was careful.'

'But who would that have come from?' Ed asked, sitting back in his chair.

'Bank of Mum?' Emma asked.

Dan was clicking through the other saved statements. 'She's been stockpiling for over six months,' he said.

'But a flat in Tildon would be nearly eight hundred pounds a month, judging by the property ads in the paper,' Emma said. 'That money would disappear in no time. She'd never make rent payments on the money she's got coming in.'

'Maybe she's getting a loan?' Ed asked.

Emma shook her head. 'No one would lend to her with such low income.'

'So what was she going to do?' Ed asked. 'She must have been desperate to leave home if she's going without enough money in place.'

Dan sighed. 'I just keep coming back to the fact she was pregnant. She couldn't support herself, let alone a baby.'

'There would be no dancing jobs if she was pregnant,' Ed put in. 'Did she say if she had something lined up when she left college?'

Emma shook her head. 'I don't know. She didn't mention anything to me.' She looked at Dan. 'You've got that look on your face.'

'I can think of two options here. Either she was planning to get rid of the baby or she was leaving dancing.'

'But she's worked her whole life to be a dancer,' Emma said. 'Why would she want to give it up?'

'Maybe she wanted the baby more,' Dan said, 'but what would she do instead? Maybe she only planned to have a quick break from dancing while she had the baby and then was going to go back.'

Emma rubbed her face with both hands. 'None of this makes any sense,' she said. 'She would need help with the baby. Why move away from her family and set up by herself when it'll put her in financial hardship?'

'Hang on,' Ed said, standing up and walking a few steps across the room. 'We're assuming that the baby was Travers', but what if it wasn't. What if she was sleeping with someone else as well?'

Dan puffed out his cheeks. 'That's one theory,' he said. He looked at Emma. 'Do you think that's likely?'

Emma shrugged. 'I don't know. You said that this Dominic Randall, the dance partner, is on the scene and that they used to go out. What if they got back together?'

'Before or after Travers died?' Dan asked.

Emma put her head in her hands. 'No wonder Nat was distracted from dancing,' she said. 'Imagine having to manage all of this and not being able to tell anyone?'

At that moment, the doorbell rang.

'Oh, thank God,' Ed said, heading into the hall. 'I'm starving.'

Dan removed the USB from his laptop and shut it down.

'There's my first job tomorrow,' he said, looking at Emma. 'I need to talk to Dominic Randall.'

Chapter 58

When Dan raised a hand to knock on Dominic Randall's front door, he had to admire the well-cared-for frontage of the grand pre-war terraced house. There was the sound of a hoover going inside the house, but it stopped after his knock. He hoped he was not about to come face-to-face with a parent. Fortunately, a burly young man opened the door. He peered suspiciously at Dan and looked like he might slam the door when Dan explained who he was.

'I want to talk to you about Natasha,' Dan explained, preparing to stick out a foot if necessary.

'Why?' Dominic demanded, drawing himself up to his full height. Quite intimidating, Dan thought. 'Haven't you used her enough for column inches?'

Dan shook his head. 'My girlfriend found Natasha's body. They were friends and she wants to find the killer.'

This took the wind out of Dominic's indignant sails. His shoulders sagged. 'Well, I suppose you should come in.' He stepped back and held the door open. Dan stepped inside and immediately almost fell over the hoover positioned in the middle of the hall floor.

'Oh, sorry,' Dominic said, squeezing past him and clearing a path towards the kitchen. 'It's my turn for chores this week.' He led the way down the hall into the kitchen and indicated for Dan to sit down at the scrubbed pine table. 'Coffee?' he asked and, when Dan nodded, he busied himself with putting on the kettle. He turned and leaned against the work surface. 'What do you want to know?'

Dan took a deep breath. 'We found a USB stick that Natasha had hidden with a friend.'

Dominic sighed. 'How did you find that?' he asked.

Dan stared at him. 'You know about it?'

The other man nodded. 'It was my suggestion.'

'You know what was on it?'

Dominic nodded. 'Yes, I told her to keep that sort of stuff somewhere other than her laptop.'

'Why?'

'Why do you think? Julietta.'

Dan frowned. 'She was snooping on Nat's laptop?'

Dominic nodded. He turned as the kettle boiled and made two cups of instant coffee. He added milk and then came to sit down opposite Dan at the table.

'She insisted on having Nat's laptop password and the passcode to her phone,' he said. 'She was really obsessed, reading her texts and her emails.'

'Why did Natasha let her do that?'

Dominic looked down at his hands clasped around the mug. 'It was easier that way,' he said.

'How do you mean?'

Dominic was silent for a moment and then sighed. 'Jules can get nasty if she doesn't get her own way. When Nat and I were going out, I saw bruises on her.' When Dan's eyes widened, Dominic nodded. 'Grab marks on the arms, but never where you could see them.'

Dan rubbed his hand across his chin. 'She was abusing Nat?'

Dominic nodded again. 'It got worse when Nat and I started seeing each other. She's always been a bit full-on, pushing Nat to train, taking her to competitions and stuff. When Nat and I started dancing together, she was against that.'

'Why? Is that not a good thing to be partnered up?'

Dominic nodded. 'Prima ballerinas have to dance with a partner, as well as solo, so I couldn't understand why Jules was like that. Maybe she just didn't like me, but I didn't see her coming up with any other men for Nat to train with.'

Dan sipped his coffee. 'What did she do when you guys started seeing each other?'

Dominic sighed. 'As soon as she found out, she went mental at Nat. All the crap about it distracting her, ruining her career, etcetera, etcetera. She made it really difficult for us to see each other, always giving Nat lifts everywhere, insisting on meeting her straight from college. She told Nat she should dump me.'

'How did you get around that?'

Dominic laughed. 'We used to sneak back to my place in the afternoons. Jules was at work so she knew nothing about it. Then we'd get back to college in time so that Nat would be waiting when Jules turned up.'

'Meeting at weekends must have been tricky,' Dan said.

Dominic nodded. 'It's amazing how creative you can be when you have to sneak around.' He sighed. 'Although Jules caught us once. Would you believe her boyfriend Evan saw us out one Saturday afternoon and went to her work to tell her?'

Dan stopped, coffee cup halfway to his mouth. 'What?'

Dominic nodded. 'Exactly. He's such a snitch. Totally under Julietta's thumb. I wouldn't be surprised if she was controlling him as well. Anyway, we were in the park and she came and found us on her lunch break.'

'How did she know where you were?' Dan asked.

'That's when we found she had one of those find-my-family apps on her phone that showed her where Nat was.'

'Woah, that's a bit—'

'Insane?' Dominic asked. 'Yes, very.'

'What did she do when she found you?'

'We were sitting on the grass and she grabbed Nat by the arm and dragged her away to her car. I tried to intervene, but she started shouting at me that I was ruining Nat's life and I was a waste of space.'

'What did Nat do?'

'What could she do? She had to let Jules drag her away. She mouthed she was sorry and she'd call me. We met up the next day and she told me she couldn't see me anymore because I'd been cheating on her.'

'Was that true?' Dan asked.

Dominic snorted. 'No, it wasn't. It was one of Julietta's lies. I tried to argue Nat out of it, but she showed me the bruises on her arms. She had to wear long sleeves for a week after that.'

'What did you do?'

Dominic looked down into his half-full coffee mug. 'I didn't handle it very well. I yelled at her, told her she was weak and I didn't want a girlfriend like that anyway.' He paused. 'She started crying and I felt so horrible. I didn't mean any of it.'

Dan was silent as Dominic wiped a finger under his eyes.

'I was angry with Julietta,' Dominic continued, 'but there was nothing I could do. I was so frightened that if I did anything, tackled her, that she'd hurt Nat even worse.'

'And now the irony is that Nat has been seeing Travers and it seems Julietta knew nothing about him,' Dan said.

Dominic nodded. 'Until recently.'

'When do you think she actually found out about him?' Dan asked.

Dominic shrugged. 'I don't know. She had Nat's laptop password and phone code, but Nat wasn't stupid enough to keep anything on there. She had a second phone. A pay-as-you-go, so she at least had some privacy.'

Dan stared at him. 'A second phone?'

Dominic nodded. 'She'd been texting me from it, so I assume she used it for him as well. The police probably have it.'

Dan mentally stored that as a question for Burton and Shepherd. 'So Nat also had the USB stick to hide those documents?' he asked.

Dominic nodded. 'She had to keep the tenancy agreement and the money hidden from Jules.'

'She would have found out when Natasha and Travers left together after the showcase, wouldn't she?'

Dominic looked down at the table. 'She wasn't going away with him.'

Dan stared. 'So who was she going away with?' he asked.

'She was going on her own to get away from Jules. She was dumping him, but then the sex tape appeared.' He noticed Dan's lack of reaction and said, 'You obviously know about that already.'

Dan nodded. 'Natasha told Emma. Em was going to help her find out who had sent it to her.'

'Nat thought at first that it was Travers. As far as she knew, he was the only one who had it, although she thought he'd deleted it. But then after he got killed, another email popped up, so obviously it wasn't him.'

Dan swirled the cold coffee in the bottom of his mug. 'If she wasn't going away with Travers, where did the two grand in her account come from?' he asked. 'We'd assumed it came from him.'

Dominic looked up at him. 'It was me. I had some money from an inheritance after my gran died. Nat and I had a one-night stand a couple of months ago and I thought the baby might have been mine. I couldn't let her cope with all of that on her own.'

'Were you going to live with her?' Dan asked, inspiration striking.

Dominic shrugged. 'We hadn't really decided. I helped her find the flat, but she was more concerned about keeping it away from Jules than anything else.'

'Do you think Jules found out and killed her to stop her from leaving?'

Dominic stared down at the table and when he looked up again, there were tears in his eyes.

'I don't want to think it,' he said, 'but she's got such a temper, I wouldn't be shocked if she had. She could have killed Travers to get him away from Nat.'

'And then found out that Nat was going, anyway.'

Dominic nodded, swiping away a tear before it could trickle down his cheek. 'It would have been easy for her to find out where Nat was that night through her phone.'

Dan stared into space, thinking quickly. Julietta Kent could have known exactly where Natasha was without having overheard the message she left for Emma. Equally, she would know where Natasha was before she went to the park. But did she know about the second phone, and where was it now?

Chapter 59

Emma sat at her dining table with her laptop in front of her, elbows propped on the table and her chin resting in one hand.

While she was waiting for Dan to come back, she'd done yet another trawl of Natasha's social media, trying desperately to find something she'd missed. But there was nothing. She sighed heavily and flopped back in her chair.

The bank statements were puzzling her too. Natasha was regularly making a couple of hundred pounds a week. That must have been dancing classes like hers. But as far as she knew, Nat was only teaching one or two. It seemed like too much. Was Nat teaching elsewhere? Or did she have another job?

She looked back at the laptop screen and scrolled through Natasha's page again. Nothing. Then she had a flash of inspiration.

She's only tapped a couple of keys when the doorbell sounded, and Emma debated pretending that she was out. The only problem was that the caller could see that the lights were on. She hurried to the door and opened it. Dan stood on the doorstep, grinning.

'I thought you were going to pretend you weren't here,' he said, following her into the living room after removing his shoes.

Emma looked round at him. 'I don't do that,' she said.

Dan laughed. 'You did it last week to those charity collectors.'

Emma waved a hand, desperate to get back to what she was doing. 'Never mind that now,' she said, sitting back down in front of her laptop.

Dan leaned against the back of the sofa behind her chair. 'What are you doing?' he asked, peering at the screen. 'You've scanned her social media so many times you probably have it memorised.'

'I had a flash of inspiration,' Emma said, pointing to the search function. 'Instead of just her, I've searched for "ballet" as well. You never know, it might do something.'

Dan nodded. 'Worth a shot. Want a glass of wine?'

Emma nodded without turning round, and, smiling and shaking his head, Dan padded across to the kitchen.

She scrolled through the multitude of options available. This was going to take forever. But as Dan arrived back, a glass in each hand, she suddenly said, 'Eureka.'

'What have you found?' he asked, perching again and handing over one glass. She quickly clinked her glass against his and took a swig. Then she put it down and pointed to her screen.

He looked at it. 'That's a kid's birthday party,' he said.

Emma clicked on the page to open it up. 'And look who's there,' she said, clicking on a picture.

Dan squinted at the screen. Then his eyes widened. 'That's Natasha,' he said. Then he laughed. 'What's she come as? A piece of bubble gum?'

Emma gave him a look. 'She's the Sugar Plum Fairy,' she said, as if that was totally obvious.

'Oh, I see,' said Dan, taking a sip of wine and clearly none the wiser. 'Could this be her other job? Doing kids' parties?'

Emma was flicking through more photographs on the Facebook page.

'Look,' she said, pointing, 'she's not in costume in this one, just her regular training gear.'

'There's a little kid in the photo with her. Aww, she's cute. She's trying to copy Natasha.' Dan laughed. 'Does this mean she's running her own ballet classes outside college? Has she started her own business?'

Emma pursed her lips. 'There's one way to answer that,' she said, leaning in to stare at the screen. She pointed at another photo of Natasha posed with a woman who had her arm around Natasha's waist. 'I think this woman might know.'

'But we don't know who she is,' Dan said.

Emma pointed to the photo caption. 'We do,' she said. 'We just have to find a contact number for Melinda Waters and hopefully she'll be able to help us.'

Chapter 60

A pained groan reminded Shepherd of Gary Topping's presence. He looked across the top of his monitor to where the detective constable was rubbing his eyes.

'You got the CCTV job again?' he asked, and Topping groaned again.

'The boss knows how much I love to watch a bit of telly,' he said, widening his eyes as if that would wake them up a bit. 'I'd rather it was the football, though.'

Shepherd laughed. 'I've got screen time too,' he said, pointing to the sugar-pink laptop on the desk in front of him.

'Ugh, that colour would give me a headache,' Topping said with a grin. 'Did that lass own anything that wasn't pink?' he asked.

Shepherd nodded. 'By and large, her clothes are normal colours.' He frowned. 'You should have seen her bedroom, but then I got the feeling that the pink was her sister's idea, not hers.'

'Trying to keep her like a little girl?' Topping asked.

Shepherd slapped a hand on the desk. 'Exactly,' he said, pointing at Topping. 'That's been bothering me for days and you've hit the nail on the head. Keeping Natasha young means she has better control of her.'

'Control? That's a bit sinister,' Topping said.

Shepherd nodded. 'Possessive is the word I would use. The sort of relationship where someone wants you all to themselves.'

273

Topping puffed out his cheeks. 'A dangerous type of relationship,' he said, 'particularly if the victim tries to fight it.' He rubbed his eyes again and turned back to the screen. 'Only ten more hours of this,' he said, sighing.

Shepherd stared off into the distance. Something was hiding in the back of his head, another feeling, but he just couldn't make it surface.

He turned back to Natasha's laptop and opened her emails again. They must be missing something, but the answer seemed further and further out of reach.

Natasha's inbox suggested that she never deleted anything. But, hidden among the usual newsletters for make-up, dance company touring schedules and fitness videos, Shepherd spotted something that made him sit up straight. When he clicked on the email, he took a deep breath. At last, another lead.

He looked up and spotted Burton heading back down the office, balancing three mugs of coffee. He waved and she headed over, stopping briefly to drop off one cup with Topping. She laughed as he gasped and grabbed the mug as if it was a lifeline.

'What have you got?' she asked Shepherd, putting the cup down at a safe distance from the computer.

'Where's Natasha's diary?' he asked.

'Gone into evidence, but there are a few pages printed out there.' She pointed to the whiteboard where notes about the case were being kept. Shepherd leapt to his feet, almost spilling her coffee, and strode across to the board. He peered at the photocopied diary pages and gave a 'yes' of satisfaction. He turned and pointed at the diary note which said, 'MW and AVAW'.

Burton raised an eyebrow as he returned to his desk and pointed to an email.

'It's not AVAW,' he said. 'It's Ava W.' He sat down and opened the attachment on the email. A bespectacled little girl in a pink ballet tutu and leggings stood somewhat clumsily in the first position, arms stretched out at her sides.

'She's cute,' Burton said, sipping her coffee. 'What's the connection?'

'Judging by the email conversations, Natasha has been tutoring Ava in ballet.'

Burton smiled. 'Lucky Ava.'

Shepherd grinned. 'That's not all,' he said.

'Go ahead,' said Burton, sipping her coffee.

Shepherd pointed to the name signing off. 'I've found MW from Natasha's diary,' he said. 'It's Melinda Waters, Ava's mum.'

***

Melinda Waters' hands gripped her coffee mug as she stared at Burton and Shepherd.

'I can't believe someone murdered Natasha,' she said in a hushed voice, as if afraid to be overheard. 'Why would anyone want to hurt her?'

Shepherd smiled sadly. 'Had you known Natasha for long?' he asked.

'About six months,' Melinda Waters said. 'We saw her perform in a show at the theatre in Tildon. My husband got tickets for me and Ava.' She gestured towards the conservatory, whose doors opened out onto a small patio and a green lawn. Ava pranced and curtsied across the smooth green grass. 'She's been going to ballet classes for over a year now. She's not a natural and she gets frustrated. Natasha enthralled her, so I spoke to Natasha afterwards and asked if she gave lessons.'

Shepherd was scribbling in his notebook. 'What did she say?' he asked.

Melinda sipped at her mug again. 'She said she'd started doing Tumble Tots at the college when their teacher went off sick. Ava is too old for that now, so I asked if she was doing any other classes. She wasn't, so I asked if she'd do one-to-one sessions,' she said.

Burton frowned. 'And she went for that?'

Melinda nodded. 'She said it would have to be at the college and before five o'clock, but that was fine for us because I finish work at three so I can get Ava from school. Natasha was a natural at teaching and I told her so. Ava is clumsy and Natasha really seemed to understand what it was like.' She looked out of the window just in time to see the child tumble to the ground while attempting a pirouette. She grimaced. 'I hoped that some of Natasha's grace would rub off on her.' Burton and Shepherd both smiled as they watched Ava scramble to her feet. Melinda put down her mug and swept both palms over her face as if she were smoothing on face cream.

Shepherd looked at her. 'Were you paying Natasha?'

Melinda nodded. 'Oh yes, we'd never have expected her to do it for free.' Then she looked worried.

'What's the matter?' asked Shepherd.

'Well, it was only a hundred quid for a couple of sessions a month, but we paid cash-in-hand. Was that wrong?' she asked.

Shepherd shook his head. 'I don't think it'll be a problem. Do you know if she was teaching anyone else?' he asked.

Melinda Waters shrugged. 'I'd recommended her to a few other mums, but I don't think she'd really got started yet,' she said.

'What do you mean?' Burton asked.

'Well, she was due to leave college soon and I asked what she was going to do. She seemed a bit awkward, but then she said she was thinking of starting up some group lessons for little kids.'

Shepherd stiffened and exchanged a look with Burton.

'There are loads of kids Ava's age who want to do lessons, but there's a shortage of classes,' Melinda continued. 'She would have been very popular. I told her she should go for it and I'd recommend her to other people.'

'She was talking about setting up her own business, then?' Shepherd asked.

Melinda nodded. 'I set up my catering company and she was asking about how I did that, how much money she would need, etcetera.'

'Is there a lot of money in teaching dancing?' Shepherd asked.

Melinda nodded. 'Well, if you do it right, you can create a good business. We sat and did a bit of maths on it, looking at venue hire for classes, any equipment, how much she could charge and so on. The one thing I warned her about is the set-up cost.'

'Did that bother her?'

'That was the bit that was her sticking point. She said she didn't have much income and she asked about a bank loan. I said to stay away from that. Without proof of income, they wouldn't touch her. She'd need some funding behind her.'

'So she could have made a business from dancing classes?' Burton asked.

'She had a few other ideas,' Melinda said. 'Last month she came to Ava's birthday party dressed as the Sugar Plum Fairy, with a pink sparkly tutu and a wand and everything.'

Shepherd pulled out his phone and flicked through to the picture he'd taken in Natasha's wardrobe. 'Is this it?' he asked.

Melinda peered at the screen and nodded. Shepherd showed the picture to Burton and then slipped the phone back into his pocket.

'It took days afterwards to get rid of the glitter from the carpet,' Melinda said with a smile. 'But it was worth it to see the little girls' faces. It was as if a real Disney princess had arrived.'

'Did she stay for the entire party?' Burton asked.

Melinda nodded. 'Yes, she spent the time teaching them a dance routine,' she said. 'One of her ideas was whether she could include kids' parties in her business plan. We paid her about a hundred and twenty quid for the afternoon, so there was scope for that. I suggested she went away and made some notes, brainstorm some ideas and I'd help her work on them.'

'It sounds like she was really thinking about it,' Burton said.

Melinda smiled. 'She was really fired up. I think it was the first time she'd thought about anything other than dancing.' Her mouth turned down at the corners. 'It's so sad that she'll never get the chance to do it. She was such a lovely girl. We saw in the paper that she had died, but I've not told Ava yet. I don't know how she'll take it.' She looked out of the window again to watch her tiptoe across the garden, her arms raised in a circle over her head. The little girl turned and saw her mother watching. She made a deep curtsy, which resulted in another tumble on the lawn. Melinda smiled wryly.

Burton smiled back. 'A bit of work to do, maybe,' she said.

Melinda sighed. 'A lot of work to do,' she said. Then she looked from Burton to Shepherd and back again. 'I'm afraid I don't really know anything else.'

Shepherd smiled. 'When you last talked to Natasha, how did she seem?'

Melinda frowned. 'I don't understand.'

'Was she happy, sad, anxious?' Shepherd asked.

Melinda frowned. 'She was a bit, well, not quite herself. She was upset about her teacher dying, but she also said her plans were coming together.'

'What did you think she meant?'

'I thought she meant her business plan, because we'd been talking about that previously. I asked if she'd found some funding and she said she thought she'd found a way.'

'What did you understand by that?'

Melinda shook her head. 'I didn't ask, I'm afraid. I wish I had,' she said sadly.

'You think the need for money got her into trouble?' Burton asked.

Melinda shrugged. 'It seems like suspicious timing, doesn't it?'

Burton glanced at Shepherd, and he clicked away his pen. He put it and his notebook in his pocket.

'Have I been helpful?' Melinda asked.

'Yes, you've certainly helped us answer a few questions,' Burton said, giving the woman a smile.

'Oh good,' Melinda said, her shoulders relaxing. 'I'm glad I could help. Hopefully, I did the same for her friend who called earlier.'

Burton and Shepherd looked at each other. 'A friend?' Burton asked.

Melinda nodded. 'Yes, her friend Emma. She said she was worried about what happened to Natasha and asked a lot of the same stuff as you did about how Natasha seemed and whether we were paying her.'

Burton's face hardened. 'Where did the friend get your contact details?'

'She'd seen some pictures of Ava's birthday party on Facebook and found us through directory enquiries,' Melinda said. 'I was just happy to help her get a bit of closure,' she added with a smile.

Burton thanked Melinda for her time and then followed Shepherd out of the front door and to the car.

'So, the Disney princess has a few secrets,' Shepherd said, unlocking the doors, 'and we have an explanation for the books in her room.'

Burton nodded. 'Yes, and now I want a word with our nosy local reporters who haven't taken the hint to stay out of the investigation.'

Chapter 61

Emma was flicking through her social media account. It was a displacement activity while her brain whirred with what Melinda Waters had told her. She blinked as a notification popped up that Julietta Kent wanted to send her a message. Emma accepted immediately and a chat box popped up.

Hi, I think you were a friend of my sister, Natasha, and you work with Dan at the Allensbury Post, it said. *I know Dan has been looking into what happened to Nat and I think he said you're the one who found Nat's body. I was wondering whether you'd meet me so I can thank you for trying to get some answers about Nat. Would you be free for coffee tomorrow?*

Emma responded that she'd love to meet up and suggested the Italian café on the High Street the following morning. An answer appeared, confirming the time and place.

Emma leaned forward and put the laptop on the coffee table and stared at it. Why was Julietta Kent approaching her, and not Dan? And how had she known that Emma would be online now?

***

When Dan rang the doorbell at Emma's cottage, he had Burton and

Shepherd in tow.

'Look who I found on the doorstep,' he said in a fake cheerful tone, his eyes telling Emma they were in trouble. Burton looked very grim.

'Do you want a cuppa?' Emma asked, as she waved for them to sit on the sofa.

'No,' Burton said sharply as she sat down. Shepherd sat beside her, and Dan and Emma perched on the edge of the other sofa. 'So,' Burton continued, 'when I told you to stay out of the investigation, that it was the only way to keep you safe, what did you actually hear? Keep sticking your nose in?'

'Well, we—' Emma began, but Burton raised a hand.

'You had no right to contact Melinda Waters. She could have been involved and you'd have put her on her guard. It could have derailed our investigation.'

This time, it was Emma who held up a hand. 'Judging by the pictures on the Facebook page, there was no way Melinda Waters would have hurt Natasha. It's clear they were friends, so I took a chance.'

'A chance is right,' Burton snapped. 'Why did you contact her?'

'Well,' Dan began, 'it comes back to the USB stick.'

Burton and Shepherd looked at each other and then back at Dan.

'What USB stick?' Shepherd asked.

Dan dug a hand into his bag and pulled it out. He held it out to Shepherd, who took it and looked at it, eyebrows raised.

'Is that what the kid at the dancing school gave you?' he asked.

Dan's eyes widened. 'How did you know about that?'

'We saw you with her outside.'

'Ah, I see,' Dan said. 'Well, no, that's not what she gave me.' He explained about the coffee shop card and his conversation with the woman there.

'That's a lot of effort to just hide a memory stick,' Burton said.

'There's a good reason for that,' Dan said, explaining the contents.

Burton's eyebrows shot up. 'She was moving out? Leaving home?' she asked.

Emma nodded. 'Leaving town. We were wondering how she was planning on paying for everything. Someone had put two grand in there, which we assumed was to cover the deposit and first month's rent. But her money wouldn't have lasted much longer.'

'As you've done so much work on this,' Burton said, 'any idea where the two grand came from?'

'At first, we thought it was Travers McGovern,' Emma said. 'He and Nat were supposedly going away, and the baby was probably his.'

'Who is it really?' Shepherd asked.

'Dominic Randall,' Dan said.

'What?' Burton and Shepherd said together.

'Where did he get two grand?' Shepherd demanded.

'Part of a legacy from his gran, apparently,' Dan said. 'He said Natasha was dumping Travers and leaving on her own. It sounded like she was actually escaping from Julietta.'

'But why was he paying her?' Burton said.

'I think she was desperate and he wanted to help. They're friends, plus he said he wasn't sure if the baby was his and he didn't want her to struggle on her own.'

'That's certainly not on her laptop,' Shepherd said to Burton in a low voice, gesturing with the USB stick. 'Probably because Julietta knew the password.'

'But Natasha had changed the password, remember,' Burton said, equally quietly. 'The password Julietta had didn't work.' She looked up to see Dan and Emma looking at them expectantly.

'Did Julietta know Natasha was preparing to leave?' she asked.

Emma shook her head. 'We don't know. From what Dominic said, she didn't. Plus, it looks like everything Nat needed was on there, safely hidden.'

'I think Julietta was another reason for Dominic to help,' Dan interrupted. 'He said she physically abused Nat as well. She has a tracker app on Nat's phone to keep tabs on her all the time.'

Burton was silent for a moment and looked at Shepherd. She wasn't sure what to say or do next.

'Have you got Nat's phones?' Dan asked.

Burton stared at him. 'Phones? Plural?'

Dan nodded. 'Dominic told me she has two. One that Julietta can access and has a tracker on. There's also a separate pay-as-you-go that she uses for other stuff.'

'Like Travers,' Emma said.

'And probably you as well,' Dan said, 'keeping her teaching jobs away from Julietta as well.'

Burton sighed heavily. 'So now we have two phones to find and no idea why the killer would take either of them.'

They all looked at each other in silence. Then Burton got to her feet.

'We're taking that with us,' she said, pointing to the USB in Shepherd's hand.

Emma opened her mouth to argue, but Dan elbowed her and she closed it again.

'OK, no problem,' he said.

He ushered Burton and Shepherd out of the door and returned to the living room.

'Why did you let them take it?' Emma demanded.

'Because I've already copied it all to my laptop,' Dan said, as if Emma was missing something. 'I'm not daft enough to just hand it all over.'

Emma laughed. 'I've always said you weren't just a pretty face,' she said. Then she squealed as he grabbed her and started tickling her. She fought him off and collapsed onto the sofa, giggling.

'So what's the next step?' he asked, sitting down and putting an arm around her.

'Do we think Julietta really didn't know about this?' Emma asked.

'Nat's moving plan, you mean?'

Emma nodded. 'I could just ask her,' she said. She told him about the message from Julietta Kent.

Dan shook his head. 'I dunno, Em, if she knew, then what would she have done to stop Nat from leaving? We need to be cautious. Maybe chat about other stuff and see if you can get a sense of what she knows, but be careful.'

'I always am,' Emma said with a grin.

Chapter 62

Julietta Kent was twenty minutes late. Emma had finished her cappuccino and was preparing to leave when she hurried in the door.

'Sorry, I couldn't get away,' she said, sounding out of breath. She pointed to Emma's cup. 'Can I get you another?'

Emma nodded and watched the other woman weave through tables to the counter. She resembled Natasha and moved with a similar elegance. After a couple of minutes, she returned with Emma's coffee and a black Americano for herself.

'Why did you want to meet?' Emma asked, when Julietta settled in the chair opposite her.

'I had a couple of reasons,' Julietta said, beginning to stir her coffee for no apparent reason. 'I wanted to thank you for trying to help Natasha.'

Emma looked down into her cup, feeling her bottom lip wobble a bit. 'I didn't really do much,' she said, 'at least not when it mattered.'

Julietta shook her head. 'You couldn't have known what would happen,' she said, putting down her spoon. She paused and then asked, 'Do you think Nat knew who killed Travers?'

Emma frowned. 'That's what her message said. Why she chose to meet in the park or didn't go straight to the police, I'll never know.'

Julietta took a sip of her coffee and began stirring it again. 'She must have wanted your advice about what to do next.'

'If only I'd got to the park sooner,' Emma said. 'If I'd got there, I might have—'

But Julietta shook her head. 'You did everything you could.' She stirred her coffee casually, but Emma could see her shoulders tense up. 'Do you know if the police have her phone?'

Emma frowned at the slight change of subject. 'They said she didn't have it with her, which is weird because she called me on it.'

'They searched her room and took her laptop, but there was no phone.'

Emma frowned. So, if Burton and Shepherd didn't have it, and the family didn't have it, then the killer had taken it. But why?

'I just wish the police would tell us more,' Julietta continued. 'We have this bloke hanging about, a liaison who's supposed to keep us updated, but I'm sure there's more than they're letting on.' She looked down at her cup but peeped up at Emma through thick eyelashes. 'I don't suppose they've told Dan any more, have they? He said he was keeping an eye on things.'

Emma shook her head. 'They're pretty tight-lipped, but it's always the way with an investigation like this,' she said. 'They keep details back, stuff that only the killer would know, so they know when they're onto a genuine lead.'

Julietta nodded and shifted in her seat. 'I've been wracking my brains, but I still can't think who would do this to Nat,' she said. Tears suddenly filled her eyes and she grabbed a napkin out of the dispenser to dab her face.

'Or who would hurt Travers McGovern?' Emma asked.

Julietta snorted. 'I reckon there were quite a few people who would have cheerfully hurt him,' she said.

'Because he was abusing students?' Emma asked.

Julietta flinched at the word. 'Abusing?'

Emma shrugged. 'He's in a position of power as a teacher, so he shouldn't be allowing a relationship to happen, even though Nat was eighteen and technically an adult.' She stirred her coffee. 'I can't believe no one at the school knew about it.'

Julietta raised her eyebrows. 'If I were you, I'd speak to Sally-Anne. She's very protective of the school and its reputation. What would she do if she thought he put that at risk?'

Emma stirred her own coffee for a moment, brain whirring. Sally-Anne was on their list. Maybe she'd acted to protect the school by killing Travers and then killed Natasha because she'd witnessed something.

She looked up to see Julietta looking at her.

'Do you know Bella Dickens?' Emma asked.

Julietta looked surprised. 'Who?'

'She was a student at the college and she had a car accident and ended up in a coma,' Emma said, but Julietta looked none the wiser. 'She died three weeks ago, and I found some pictures of her and Natasha on Nat's social media. It looked like they were good friends.'

Julietta was frowning, then her brow cleared. 'Ah yes, I know who you mean. She was a bit of an oddball, very over-emotional.'

'How do you mean?'

'Well, she lost out on a few parts to Nat and she always acted like it was the end of the world. Nat couldn't help that she was better. She worked hard for it.'

Emma looked at her cup and then back at Julietta. 'They fell out because Natasha got a part that Bella wanted?' she asked. 'That seems extreme.'

Julietta shrugged. 'I think so.'

'When was that?'

'About six months ago, something like that,' Julietta said. 'I remember Nat said that Bella had just started blanking her, but wouldn't explain what was going on at first. Then they had a massive row, her screaming at Nat in the middle of the atrium at school.'

'Saying what?'

'Nat wouldn't talk about it. But it upset her for a while because Bella had her accident before they could make up. I don't think Nat really knew what had happened.'

Suddenly, a bell rang in Emma's head. The blackmail email. It told Natasha to admit what she'd done. Was this it? Natasha had done something to Bella?

She suddenly realised Julietta had asked her a question.

'What?'

'You look miles away,' Julietta said, peering at her. 'Do you know something?'

Emma shook her head. 'Sorry, I was just thinking.' She didn't want Natasha to be responsible for Bella's death, but clearly someone thought she was, and Travers as well. The person was using the sex tape as a hold over them both, but who could have got their hands on it?

Emma felt the familiar tightening in her chest and tried to concentrate on breathing.

Julietta glanced at her watch and downed the last of her coffee.

'I'm really sorry, but my lunch break is almost over, so I'll have to get back.'

Emma nodded. 'Thanks for speaking to me, and for the coffee.'

'No worries,' she said, getting to her feet and picking up her handbag. 'Look, if you hear anything from the police, you'll tell me, won't you?'

'Of course, but I doubt they'll tell us anything that they don't tell you.'

'Thanks. See you later.'

With a quick wave, she crossed the café and the bell over the door jangled as she left.

Emma sat back in her chair. Something wasn't right here. She grabbed her phone and dialled Dan's number.

'How did it go?' he asked, without even saying hello.

'It's weird. She was trying to find out what the police have told us. Clearly they're keeping stuff from the family.'

'You think the police suspect her of being involved?' Dan asked.

'It would make sense. She was asking about Nat's phone, so clearly the family hasn't got it, and neither do the police.'

'Her actual phone or the burner phone?' Dan asked.

Emma froze. 'What?'

'Remember, Dominic said Natasha had a second phone. The one she used to call and text him and Travers on.'

'And both phones appear to be missing.'

'Exactly,' Dan said. 'We can assume the killer took the phone that Nat had with her, presumably the evidence she had was on there.' He paused. 'Or they thought it was.'

'You think it wasn't?'

Dan sighed heavily. 'I'm trying to decide whether I'd carry blackmail evidence with me for safekeeping or hide it where no one would find it.'

'She also suggested Sally-Anne as a potential suspect.'

'Sally-Anne? Why would she want to kill Travers and Natasha?' Dan asked, then answered his own question. 'The school's reputation.'

Emma nodded. 'Yup, I think we need to have a word with her. Shall we reconvene after work and make a plan?'

'Yeah, come to mine. I'll cook you something nice.'

'Fingers crossed,' Emma said, laughing at Dan's protestations, before saying goodbye and hanging up.

Chapter 63

Mrs Kent's hand trembled slightly as she filled the mugs on the kitchen counter with boiling water from the kettle. It may only have been instant coffee, but Burton and Shepherd's noses twitched at the scent. They'd bypassed the office, and their usual caffeine hit, to head straight round to see the Kents. Mrs Kent brought the mugs to the table where they were sitting, along with a matching milk jug and sugar bowl. Once the drinks were made to their satisfaction, Mrs Kent joined them, clasping her hands around her own mug.

'What can I do for you?' she asked.

Burton extracted a copy of Natasha's bank statement from her handbag and passed it across the table. 'Were you aware of this?' she asked.

Mrs Kent took it and looked down at the page. She nodded. 'I helped her set it up because she wasn't quite eighteen when she did it. It was our secret. Jules didn't know about it.'

'She's putting a lot of money in there,' Burton said, indicating the deposits column, 'but not taking anything out.'

Mrs Kent shook her head. Then she got to her feet and fetched the purse from her handbag that sat on the kitchen work surface. She sat back down and opened the card holder section. She pulled out a red-and-white bank card and handed it to Burton, who looked down at the name 'Miss N Kent' on it.

'This was her card?' Burton asked, holding it up.

Mrs Kent nodded. 'Yes, she asked me to keep it for her. I think she didn't want to be tempted to spend any of it.'

Shepherd looked up from his notes. 'You knew she was saving up for something?' he asked.

Mrs Kent looked into her coffee cup as if searching for the answer. 'Yes, but she didn't tell me what it was.'

'Did you not wonder where the money was coming from?'

Mrs Kent sighed and looked up at them. 'I knew she had a teaching job at the school, but that was all.'

'Did Julietta know about the teaching?'

Mrs Kent shook her head. 'Nat wanted to keep it a secret. It wouldn't have gone down very well,' she said.

Burton raised her eyebrows. 'Julietta wouldn't like Natasha saving money for the future?' she asked.

Mrs Kent picked up a teaspoon and stirred her coffee. 'Natasha thought it would be easier that way.' She put her spoon down on the table and looked up at Burton and Shepherd. 'Jules invested a lot of time and energy in Natasha's career.'

'More so than Natasha?' Burton asked.

Mrs Kent shook her head. 'No, you don't get as good as she was without putting in the hours. But Jules could sometimes be over the top.'

'And you didn't stop her?'

'It's difficult when you know it's coming from the right place. Whenever I tried to tackle it, Jules just said she was doing it for Natasha's own good.' She sighed. 'It's hard to argue in the face of that.'

Burton exhaled heavily. 'Did you know about this?' She produced a printout of the tenancy agreement.

A tear started down Mrs Kent's cheek.

'You don't seem surprised,' Shepherd said gently, aware that Burton was getting irritated.

Mrs Kent wiped away the tear with the back of her hand. 'Not entirely. Things were very intense at the moment. Jules was pushing Nat harder and harder with dancing because it's so close to the showcase.'

'And Natasha wasn't happy about it?'

'There was something else going on; she was distracted, irritable.'

She shrugged. 'Presumably it was the pregnancy. They had a massive shouting match at one point and I had to get between them.'

Shepherd stared. 'They had a physical fight?' he asked.

'Almost,' Mrs Kent said. 'Don't get me wrong, Nat has a temper. They both do, but I've never seen her go for Jules like that before. Anyway,' she tapped a finger on the tenancy agreement, 'this makes sense of the conversation she had on the phone. She was the one moving, not Dominic.'

Mrs Kent put her cup down and buried her face in her hands. Shepherd gave Burton a look that said, 'Gently does it.'

'How would Julietta have reacted if she found out about it?' he asked.

A tear-stained face looked up at the detectives. 'I don't know,' came the reply, almost in a whisper. 'I thought I was helping Nat by setting up a bank account for her. When she wanted to go out without Jules knowing, I covered for her.'

'Were you not worried about how Julietta was behaving? That Natasha seemed so scared of her?' Burton asked, incredulous. 'We've been told that Natasha sometimes had bruises after she did something Julietta "didn't like". Did you not notice that?'

'She never told me,' Mrs Kent said miserably.

'Did you know Julietta was trying to make Natasha have an abortion?' Shepherd asked. 'She'd even booked the appointment, but Natasha later cancelled.'

Mrs Kent started crying. 'I had no idea,' she said, pulling a tissue from her sleeve but finding it too shredded to be of any use. Burton got to her feet and fetched a few sheets of kitchen roll. She rested a hand on Mrs Kent's shoulder as she handed them over. There was no point in torturing this woman any further.

She sat back down, and Shepherd took over the questioning.

'Not wishing to make this any worse, Mrs Kent—' he began.

'Can this get any worse?' Mrs Kent interrupted through the piece of kitchen roll.

Shepherd winced. 'Where was Julietta when Natasha was killed?' Shepherd asked.

Mrs Kent sniffed and looked up at him with bloodshot eyes. 'She

291

was here with me, but then—'

'Then?' Shepherd asked.

'I'd forgotten. She got a message at about half past five and said she had to go out.'

'Did she say where she was going?'

'Just that a friend of hers, Dougie Lennon, his car broken down and he needed help.'

'What time did she come back?'

Mrs Kent frowned. 'About six thirty. She said they'd had to drive to a petrol station to buy fuel and then go back to his car.'

'Where was Natasha then? Do you know?'

Mrs Kent frowned. 'She was at school. She'd said her rehearsal had overrun and Jules said to call when she needed a lift.'

'There was no rehearsal,' Burton said. 'Natasha lied to Julietta. We don't know where she was, but she called Emma, one of the *Allensbury Post* reporters, at about five thirty to say she knew who had killed Travers McGovern.'

Mrs Kent stared at her. 'Why did she call a news reporter?'

'They're friends,' Burton said. 'Emma was helping Natasha to find out what happened to Travers.'

'Is that the poor girl who found her?' Mrs Kent asked. When Burton nodded, Mrs Kent added, 'Make sure you take good care of her. Anyone who tried to help my Natasha must be a good person.'

***

When they got back into the car, Burton was fuming.

'You know what this means, don't you?' Shepherd said.

Burton nodded grimly. 'We have Julietta Kent out of the house at the time Natasha died. I'd bet my house that message was a notification on that app telling her Natasha had left college.'

'And it would tell her exactly where Natasha was.'

Shepherd indicated and pulled out of the parking space.

'We need to find Dougie Lennon,' Burton said. 'Let's see what he's got to say for himself.'

Chapter 64

Emma had just arrived at Dan and Ed's flat when her mobile burst into life with its jaunty ring tone. She answered it, spoke for a few minutes and then hung up with a groan.

'What's up?' Dan asked.

'Daisy wants me to come in for a "little chat".' Emma sketched the quote marks in the air.

'What, now? Is she still in the office? I thought she was finishing early today.'

Emma nodded. 'Apparently it's the only time she's got and as I'm not doing anything, I've got to come in now.'

'It's a good job I haven't started dinner,' Dan said with a grin. 'Otherwise it would get ruined.'

'What are you making?' Emma asked.

'I was going for chicken chasseur with mashed potatoes and carrots,' Dan said, smugly.

Emma raised an eyebrow. 'Supermarket's finest? Peel the lid, and twenty minutes in the oven?'

For once, Dan glared. 'I was going to make it from scratch,' he said. 'Mum gave me the recipe. I thought I'd do something nice for you for a change.'

Seeing the crestfallen look on his face, Emma stepped forward and planted a kiss on his lips. 'Sounds lovely,' she said. 'You get cracking and I'll hurry back.'

Watching her leave, Dan headed into the kitchen. He peeled, diced and got the chicken and sauce into the oven. It was ambitious for him, but he wanted to make something special.

He returned to the living room and walked across to the dining table where his laptop lay. There was a note from Ed stuck to the lid.

Thanks for the use of your laptop. I had another look at the files from that USB stick and found that there was one that was hidden, so we didn't see it the first time, it said.

'What?' Dan said out loud to himself.

The note continued: *Anyway, I un-hid it, but I didn't look because I thought you'd want to see it first.*

'Too right,' Dan said.

Ed's tight crabby handwriting added, *I'm out 'til about six o'clock, but you can fill me in on everything when I get back. I expect dinner on the table.* Ed had ended the note with a smiley face, and Dan laughed. Ed knew that dinner would never be on the table with Dan in charge.

He opened the laptop and logged in. Clicking through to the hidden folder, he opened it and waited as a series of video files appeared on the screen. There were a couple of picture files and he opened one. The photograph of Natasha and Bella Dickens hugging each other filled the screen. Dan felt a pricking behind his eyes. Here were two young women with their whole lives ahead of them, both now dead because they'd had the misfortune to cross paths with Travers McGovern.

He moved on to the video files and, clicking on one, found himself looking at the sex tape of Natasha and Travers. He closed it down quickly, feeling queasy. Then he clicked on another video and froze. Where had Natasha got this one?

On the screen, a man was walking across Travers' office. A motion sensor must operate the camera. Dan's heart beat faster as the man opened Travers' desk drawer and took out the bottle of vodka. The figure on the screen unscrewed the lid and poured something into it from a smaller bottle. Then he replaced the lid and put the bottle back in the drawer. He opened another desk drawer, removing what Dan knew were EpiPens. Then he checked the pockets of the coat hanging on a peg by the door. More pens taken. The man stopped and looked at a scarf hanging beside the coat and Dan saw his body stiffen. Then he glanced around the room again and left.

Dan had recognised the figure at once. The man clearly didn't know he was on camera. But Dan knew exactly who he was.

There were a few saved emails. The first was the email from Natasha's blackmailer threatening to release the video.

The next was much more interesting.

You think you can blackmail me, but I've got worse, Natasha had written. *Meet me at school. We need to talk.*

Another email from Natasha, dated the day she died, said: *You can't hurt me now. I've got the video and I recorded you when you admitted it. I'm going to the police and you can't stop me.*

Dan winced. The blackmailer had certainly made sure Natasha stopped.

If Natasha had recorded a confession, then where was it? Then he remembered how he had recorded his first chat with Sadie and then the locker break-in.

Slamming the laptop lid, he grabbed his car keys. He needed Natasha's phone, and he now knew exactly where to find it.

Chapter 65

'So?' Burton demanded when Gary Topping entered the office, tie flapping.

'Dougie Lennon confirms Julietta Kent's alibi. She was with him from five thirty to about six fifteen.' He grinned. 'He seemed a bit unsettled about having to call Julietta for help.'

'Couldn't he call roadside recovery?' Shepherd asked.

Topping shook his head. 'Apparently, he doesn't have it and he was very grateful that she'd come out. But he admitted his first call the next morning had been to a roadside recovery service to sign up. He said she'd made a big deal of him owing her, and I don't think he liked that.'

Burton groaned. 'But that takes Julietta out of the frame, given that she has an alibi and the notification wasn't from a tracker app.'

Topping opened his mouth to speak but, before he could utter a word, Shepherd's desk phone rang. He turned on his chair and picked up the receiver. After listening for a minute, he thanked the caller and hung up, turning back to Burton and Topping.

'That was the tech guys,' he said. 'They've been doing more work on Travers McGovern's laptop and they've found a shortcut to a cloud storage account that they hadn't seen before.'

'I thought they said they'd done a full sweep,' Burton asked, looking irritated.

'They thought they had, but I asked them to take another look. They're emailing me the contents,' Shepherd said.

'Well, I hope they hurry,' Burton said.

Before she'd finished speaking, there was a ping from Shepherd's computer. He grinned and turned back to the screen. He clicked his mouse button a few times and then a video opened on the computer screen. His eyes widened as he realised that with it was another of Travers' home-made sex tapes.

'Woah,' Topping said, stepping forward and staring at the screen. 'What the hell?'

Burton scooted her chair forward and peered over Shepherd's shoulder.

'That's not Natasha Kent,' she said.

Shepherd nodded. 'I think that's Tara Wallis,' he said. 'So it seems Natasha definitely isn't the only star of the show.'

Burton looked disgusted. 'My guess is that he kept the videos to stop the women from reporting him.'

'That's certainly one way of doing it,' Topping said.

Shepherd clicked his mouse button again and the video disappeared. He moved the mouse along the line of video files on the screen.

'I'm betting that these are all different women,' he said. 'That's ten in total.'

'That's a lot of people with a reason to kill him,' Burton said. 'We're going to have to watch all of them and see if we can identify the women.'

Shepherd turned to look at her. 'Not really a job I fancy,' he said.

'Emma Fletcher told us that Natasha didn't know he'd recorded the video and when she found out, she made him delete it. But he didn't delete it from here,' Burton said.

'But how did he make the video without her knowing?' Topping asked.

Burton slapped her hand to her forehead. She marched across to the whiteboard and studied the picture of Travers McGovern's office. Then she jabbed at it with her finger. 'That, there.' She turned back to see two puzzled faces. 'Think about the angle of the camera, nicely facing the sofa. I bet it's in one of those bloody books. Obviously the video automatically saves into here.' She tapped a finger against the screen. 'We're going to have to watch these. It's adding to our suspect list.'

Shepherd turned back to his screen and clicked on the next video file.

The next video was very much the same as the previous one, but the woman was different.

Topping stepped forward again and leaned down to peer at the picture. 'You can't quite see her face,' he said, 'but he's looking directly at the camera.'

Suddenly Shepherd gasped. 'Christ, I think I know who that is.'

Burton and Topping looked at each other and stared at Shepherd as he rifled quickly through the pile of folders on his desk.

'Brody didn't do the initial autopsy,' he said, pulling out a sheaf of papers and flipping through so hard that he tore one page from the staple that held them together. Then he turned to Topping and Burton and held out a photograph. The woman was still and pale, the photograph was taken post-mortem. 'There, look, on her shoulder.'

'What am I looking at?' Burton asked.

'It's a tattoo,' Topping said. Then he frowned. 'Whose autopsy is it?'

Shepherd pointed to the name and Burton's eyes widened.

'Oh my God,' she said, almost in a whisper.

'And there's a big motive for murder,' Shepherd said.

Chapter 66

It was almost six o'clock when Emma escaped from Daisy and got to Dan and Ed's flat. She was just pressing the buzzer on the outside door when Ed appeared behind her, making her jump.

'Danny boy not with you?' he asked, pulling out his keys.

Emma shook her head. 'I left him up there about an hour ago, making chicken chasseur.'

Ed stared at her. 'Really?'

'And not from a packet.'

'Wow, it must be a special night,' Ed replied. 'I can make myself scarce if you like.'

Emma laughed. 'No idea what he's up to,' she said, as they climbed the stairs, 'but I'm surprised he isn't answering the door.'

Ed turned his key into the lock and stepped through the door.

'Hi, honey, I'm—' But the words died on Ed's lips. Acrid smoke hung in the air in the hall, and the smoke alarm was shrieking. 'Oh, for the love of God, what's he done now?' Ed yelled, sprinting down the hall towards the kitchen.

Emma followed, coughing and fanning the air with her hand. She watched as Ed yanked open the oven, leaping back as a plume of smoke burst out. He flung open the kitchen window and then dashed to the balcony doors and yanked them open.

'Oh God,' he said, wiping his eyes, which were smarting. The smoke alarm was still shrieking, so Ed climbed onto a chair to press the reset button. The room fell silent, but the beeping still resonated in their ears.

Emma ventured into the kitchen and pulling on oven gloves, took a blackened tureen out of the oven. She placed it on top of the hob and looked at Ed.

He shook his head in disbelief. 'This is a new low, even for him. Forgetting that he's put the dinner on.' He turned on the expel air above the oven.

Emma coughed several times and then frowned. 'So where is he?' she asked. 'He wouldn't have gone out and left the dinner cooking, would he?'

Ed shrugged and went back into the living room. He pointed to the laptop.

'He's been on there because I left the lid closed and it's now open,' Ed said. 'This note was stuck on top.' He pointed at the sticky label now attached to the surface of the table.

Emma picked up the note and read it. 'A hidden file?' she said.

Ed nodded. 'No idea what was in it, but maybe Dan's had a look.'

Emma frowned. 'So if he was looking at the hidden file, where's he gone? Why didn't he wait for us?'

'Call him and see where he is,' Ed said. 'I'll see if there's anything else to eat apart from what used to be chicken chasseur.'

As Emma pulled out her phone, it beeped. A text message appeared on the screen.

'It's from Dan,' she called to Ed. She opened the message and stared at it.

'What the hell?' she said, staring at the screen.

Ed came back into the room holding a packet of tea bags. 'What's the matter? What does it say?'

'"I'm at home and I'm just going to stay in,"' Emma read aloud. '"I need a bit of a break tonight, so please don't come round. I'll talk to you later."'

Ed's eyes widened. 'What's he playing at?' he asked. 'Why the hell did he text you that?'

Emma was rereading the text message as if it was a secret code. 'I've no idea.' She looked around the room. 'He must have left a clue about where he was going.'

She walked across to the laptop and pressed the enter key. The screen lit up, asking for Dan's password.

Ed followed her and sat down in the chair by the laptop. He tapped at the keys.

'You know his password?' Emma asked.

Ed nodded. 'It's for emergencies only,' he said, 'and I think this counts as one of those.'

The password was accepted and Dan's desktop appeared in front of them.

'He's been going through the hidden folder I found from the USB stick,' Ed said, clicking his mouse to open the folder. They both scanned the contents of the folder.

Emma pointed to the screen. 'He's got one of those emails open,' she said. Ed clicked the mouse and the email opened in front of them. They scanned the contents and Emma gasped.

'Natasha had a recording of them, confessing. She must have hidden it before she came to see me.'

'But where would she have hidden that?' Ed asked.

Emma frowned. 'She seems to have hidden anything important on the USB stick, but that confession doesn't seem to be on here.'

She looked around the room as if the answer would miraculously appear. Then she slapped a hand to her forehead.

'What's the matter?' Ed asked.

Emma was already grabbing her bag and heading for the door of the living room. 'I know where Natasha's hidden the recording and I think Dan's gone to get it.' She was already in the hallway when Ed caught up with her.

'Unfortunately,' Emma said, waving her phone, 'I think the killer might have had the same idea.' She yanked open the front door and headed for the stairs at a run. 'And I know who it is.'

Chapter 67

Dan was glad to find that the college was still open. A security guard sat at the reception desk and nodded to Dan as he passed. Trainers squeaking against the floor, Dan headed for the changing room where Natasha's locker was. He didn't see the man reach for the phone on his desk.

He slipped inside and looked at the bank of lockers in front of him. There were about fifty and he wished he'd asked Sadie which one was Natasha's. Systematically, he began checking each one. Fifteen minutes later, he was on his hands and knees, poking inside a locker on the lowest level, when he felt the back panel give a little under his fingers. He almost had to lie on the floor to reach inside and use his door key to loosen the screws that Natasha had not re-tightened properly when she replaced the panel. He'd realised that was why the coffee card Sadie found had been stuck in the very corner. The thief who'd emptied the locker had looked at the belongings, not at the surroundings, and missed it.

He sighed in satisfaction when the panel came away and he could get his fingers inside and pull out a smartphone. He sat back and lit up the screen. It showed a picture of a ballerina *en pointe* as a screensaver and requested a password. But that didn't matter; the phone was going straight to Burton and Shepherd.

Then the door creaked open, and a voice said, 'I hoped this was why you came here.'

Dan tried to stand up, but the man waved him back, a sharp-bladed knife in his hand. 'Not so fast.'

'Hello, Mr Dickens,' Dan said.

Chapter 68

Burton was waiting, foot tapping, while Shepherd knocked on the door of David Dickens' house. They were waiting about a minute before a woman pulled open the door. Warmth and the sound of children playing drifted out from behind her.

'Yes?' she asked.

Burton and Shepherd held out warrant cards. 'We need to see your husband,' Burton demanded.

The woman looked surprised. 'You've just missed him.'

'What?' Burton asked.

'He just got a call, some problem at the school, and he dashed off. I just hope he doesn't come back with his shoes covered in mud like last time.' She tutted as if he were a naughty child.

'When was that?' Shepherd asked, quickly.

The woman thought for a moment. 'Last Saturday, I think. He'd gone out to get us a takeaway, but had to stop off at school. I don't know why they always ring him. Probably because we live so close but—'

Burton and Shepherd were already running to the car, leaving her open-mouthed.

Burton's mobile started ringing. She pulled it out of her pocket, looked at the screen and groaned.

'Emma Fletcher. That's all we need.' She swiped at the screen. 'Emma, I've told you before to call—'

But Emma interrupted. 'No, listen.' Burton could hear the car revving in the background. 'I think Dan has found Natasha's phone. He's gone to the school to get it. But I think the killer knows as well.'

'We're on our way,' Burton said, before Emma could get any further.

Chapter 69

Dan tried again to get to his feet, but Mr Dickens waved him back. Dan's hand went to his pocket and he pulled out his phone, thinking he could call for help. But Mr Dickens stepped forward and snatched it from him.

'Open it,' he commanded. With the knife waving in his face, Dan had no choice but to apply his thumb print to unlock the phone. Mr Dickens stood for a minute tapping at the screen.

'My girlfriend knows where I am,' Dan lied. 'She'll come looking for me.'

But Mr Dickens gave an icy laugh and held up the phone. 'No, she thinks you're at home and don't want to see her this evening. That should buy us enough time.' He dropped Dan's phone on the floor and stamped on it. Dan winced as it broke apart and pieces spread across the floor.

'Now,' Mr Dickens continued, stepping towards Dan, 'you're going to give me that phone as well.'

Dan tried to get to his feet, but his shoes slipped on the floor and all he could manage was an undignified scrabbling movement. But it had created a bit of space between him and the knife in the man's hand.

'No,' he said, 'at least not until you've explained it to me. I know Bella had an affair with Travers, but was that really enough of a reason to kill him?'

Dickens snarled. 'He was put down like the animal he was. My poor girl, she was—'

'He dumped her, didn't he? Did you know she'd been seeing him?'

Mr Dickens shook his head. 'It was only after she tried to ... tried to ... kill herself that—' He broke off, wiping a hand across his eyes. 'I'd already threatened Travers that I would go to the governors because I knew what he was doing with female students. I'd seen him with Natasha Kent and I told him it had to stop. And do you know what?' Mr Dickens' voice cracked. 'He laughed. Told me he'd had my daughter too, that it had just been a bit of fun. My little girl...' Dickens jabbed a finger towards his chest '...my gorgeous little girl was just a bit of fun to him.' He spat out the words. 'I didn't believe him. I told him that, and he said he had the video to prove it.'

'And you still didn't report him?'

'Not long after that conversation, I found Bella's diary in her room. She'd just died and I was tidying up some stuff. When I read it, I was—' He took a deep shuddering breath. 'It sickened me, what he'd done, by what—'

'And you realised he was the reason she'd tried to kill herself,' Dan said quietly.

Mr Dickens' eyes filled with tears. 'So much heartbreak caused by that man.' He almost spat. 'Do you know what he did to her?'

'I can hazard a guess from speaking to other students at the college,' Dan said.

Mr Dickens glared at him. 'Yes, you've been quite the busy bee, haven't you? Sticking your nose in where it wasn't wanted.'

'What did you do when you found out?' Dan asked, trying to keep Mr Dickens talking while he came up with a plan.

'I told him I'd report him, but he said he would ruin Bella by publishing the video.'

'Someone threatened to do that to Natasha as well and—' Dan broke off. 'That was you, wasn't it?'

Dickens gave a sickening grin. 'I thought two can play at that game. She was as guilty as him about Bella. She was her friend.'

'Where did you get the video from?' Dan asked.

Mr Dickens shrugged. 'I think I'll keep that as my little secret.'

'So finding Bella's diary triggered this whole thing?' Dan asked.

'Yes. I told him he had to stop this thing with Natasha, to break up with her, but he said he wouldn't. He loved her and they were like Romeo and Juliet.' He finished the sentence in a whingy, mock-romantic voice. 'Romeo and bloody Juliet? He could never understand that. But if he wanted to be Romeo and Juliet, I could help him to do that.'

A penny dropped. 'That's why you poisoned him,' Dan said, 'and made sure he didn't have any EpiPens.'

Mr Dickens nodded.

'But why did you go after Natasha if it was Travers you wanted stopped?'

Mr Dickens was fiddling with the knife, turning it over in his fingers. 'She tried to blackmail me. Somehow she had a video of me doctoring the vodka.'

'There's a hidden camera in Travers' office,' Dan said. 'That's how he made the videos of the women he had sex with.'

Mr Dickens bared his teeth. 'You see,' he said, pointing at Dan with the knife, 'you see what he was like? Why I had to stop him?'

Dan was inching across the floor, trying to work out how to get to his feet to make a run for it. Mr Dickens was between him and the door, but he was hoping there might be an opportunity.

'I saw Natasha's email,' he said, hoping he could keep Mr Dickens talking while he came up with a plan. If Emma was still with Daisy, she'd see that text and think it was from him. He was on his own. 'She was blackmailing you.'

Mr Dickens nodded. 'She came to me and said she had this video of me and that she knew what I'd done.'

'She got you to admit to killing Travers and recorded the conversation on here?' Dan asked, holding up the phone.

'Yes, and she said she was going to the police. But you see,' Dickens said, stepping forward and waving the knife, 'that wasn't what we'd agreed when we had that conversation.'

'So you had to stop her?'

'I needed to find the phone. I overheard her arranging to meet someone in the park and I knew I had to stop her before she told them. But I needed the phone as well.'

'You took it when you stabbed her,' Dan said. 'You must have been gutted when you realised it was the wrong phone,' he added, finding that he'd slid across to the wall. He used it to lever himself into a standing position, but his legs burst into pins and needles and he leaned against the wall, clenching his teeth.

'She was screaming at me, said the recording was safe and I'd never find it. I had to shut her up.'

'You stabbed her three times,' Dan said. His brain was rattling, trying to work out how he was going to get out of this. Mr Dickens was blocking his exit.

'I didn't want to,' Mr Dickens said. 'She and Bella used to be friends, but Natasha just dropped her when she took up with Travers. If she hadn't done that, Bella wouldn't have—' He broke off, jaw clenching. 'Now you're going to give me that phone and I'm going to finish you off as well.'

He advanced but, with a yell, Dan hurled the phone at him. His aim was excellent and it smashed into Mr Dickens' face, knocking his glasses askew. The other man roared as Dan threw himself forward, knocking Mr Dickens off his feet. Scooping up the phone, he shoved it into his pocket but, as he turned to run, Mr Dickens threw out a foot and tripped him up. Dan fell to the floor. Winded, he turned onto his back just in time for Mr Dickens to fall on him, pinning him to the floor.

He cried out in pain as the knife stabbed once, twice, three times into his side. Dimly, he saw Mr Dickens leap to his feet and dash for the locker room door. Dan clasped his hands over the wound, but blood was spurting. He heard shouting in the corridor, and the door flew open again. A voice was screaming his name and Emma appeared. Then she was shoved aside by Burton, who ripped off her jacket and pressed it hard against Dan's stomach.

'Sorry,' she said as he whimpered, 'but it's the only way to stop the bleeding.'

He heard Burton yelling into her phone and demanding an ambulance, and Emma sobbing before everything went black.

Chapter 70

The first thing Burton and Shepherd saw as they hurried down the hospital corridor was Emma's tear-stained face and Ed's shaking hands. They glanced at each other, fearing the worst.

'How is he?' Burton asked, as soon as they were within earshot.

Emma wiped a tissue under her eyes and took a deep breath. 'They've taken him into surgery to repair the stab wounds, but they won't tell me anything else.'

Burton didn't know what to say. She'd seen enough stab wounds to know this one was serious and Dan had lost a lot of blood.

Shepherd handed Emma a fresh tissue. 'They'll do everything they can,' he said, patting her arm and knowing his words would be little comfort.

Ed snorted. 'What does that even mean?' he snapped. 'What if everything isn't enough?' His voice cracked and he turned away, wiping his eyes on his sleeve.

Burton could see that Emma and Ed were barely holding it together and she did not know what to say. Dan had frequently been a thorn in her side, but right now she was happy for that to continue.

Shepherd took Emma's arm and led her back to a chair, sitting her down on it.

'We will be speaking to David Dickens soon,' he said gently, 'and then we'll get some answers.'

Emma sniffled and wiped her nose on the tissue. 'It's all about his daughter,' she said. 'Bella was the start of all of this.'

Before she got any further, a woman's voice called, 'Emma!'

Emma looked up to see a slim woman in her sixties hurrying down the corridor towards her. 'Dan's mum,' she said to Shepherd, stepping forward to meet the woman who threw her arms around Emma.

'How is he?' the woman asked, holding Emma at arm's-length and looking into her face.

'He's in surgery,' Emma said, wiping at her face. 'They haven't told us any more yet. It's been hours.'

Mrs Sullivan pulled Emma back to the chairs and sat down. 'He's tough, you know that.' But her hands were shaking and tears stained her face too.

'I know, but the blood—' Emma's voice cracked, and she started sobbing.

Mrs Sullivan put an arm around her and reached out a hand to Ed, who gripped it.

'Now, you two have been sitting here for hours,' Mrs Sullivan said. 'Why don't you get a coffee? You can come straight back,' she said, holding up a hand as Emma began protesting, 'but you need a break. I'll be here if there's any news.'

Mrs Sullivan watched Ed put an arm around Emma's shoulder as they walked away down the corridor, and then turned to Burton and Shepherd.

'Are you the police?' she asked. Burton and Shepherd introduced themselves.

'I'm sure I'll hear an incredibly heroic tale from Daniel later,' she said, clearly trying to sound more confident than she was, 'but can you tell me what happened?'

'We're not sure yet,' Burton said. 'We're still waiting to speak to our suspect and we'll need to take a statement from Dan once he's awake.'

Mrs Sullivan pulled a tissue from her pocket and dabbed at her face. 'I don't know what he was playing at,' she said.

She got no further because a doctor appeared and said, 'Are you Dan's next of kin?'

Mrs Sullivan whipped around to face him. 'Yes, that's me. What's happening?'

'Why don't you come with me, and I can explain?'

The doctor led her a short distance away, speaking urgently in a low voice. Burton and Shepherd watched in horror as Mrs Sullivan's legs gave way. She crumpled into a chair and sobbed.

Chapter 71

Six weeks later

Emma watched the pallbearers lower the coffin into the ground and felt a tear slide down her face. She clutched tightly at the bouquet of roses she held, barely noticing when a thorn poked her finger.

She felt a hand take hers and squeeze. She looked up to see Ed watching her.

'If only I'd got there sooner,' she said in a low voice.

Ed shook his head. 'You know there was nothing else you could have done, that anyone else could have done.'

Emma shrugged. 'It doesn't make any difference to how I feel,' she said. 'It's my fault.'

But Ed shook her arm. 'Hey, no, it's not your fault. What is it they say on the telly? It's the fault of the person who killed them?'

Emma sighed and looked down at the coffin, feeling tears beginning to fall. Ed put an arm around her and squeezed.

The priest intoned the final blessing ending the funeral service and the mourners turned away.

'Nice day for it,' a voice said, and Emma and Ed turned to see Burton and Shepherd standing behind them.

'As much as the day of a funeral can be,' Emma replied with a pale smile.

'David Dickens was up in court for committal yesterday,' Ed said. 'Still insisting he's not responsible.'

Burton rolled her eyes. 'Going for a plea that he wasn't in his right mind. That his mind was unbalanced through grief over his daughter.'

'The magistrates didn't seem all that impressed with him,' Ed said. 'It was hard to not jump up and shout at him across the court.'

'I can imagine,' Shepherd said. 'You looked like you were thinking about it.'

'The evidence is pretty overwhelming though, isn't it?' Emma said. 'I mean, they've got him on video. How does he think he'll get away with it?'

Burton puffed out her cheeks. 'It gets worse. We checked more footage from the camera in Travers' office and it captured the moment he died,' she said. 'Not easy to watch I can tell you, but it also shows Mr Dickens looking through the glass plate in the door and watching.'

Ed's mouth fell open. 'He actually watched Travers die?' he gasped.

Burton nodded. 'So, we've charged him with murder, but I think his legal team will try to get the charge dropped to manslaughter.'

'That's where the "deranged by grief" comes in?' Ed asked, and Burton nodded.

'He's got a lot of material in mitigation for Travers McGovern, but not for Natasha,' she said. 'She was as much a victim of Travers as Bella, or any of the other girls.'

'Travers was disgusting,' Emma said, wrinkling her nose. 'Once I found what he'd done, I would have killed him myself if he hadn't already been dead.'

'Why didn't Mr Dickens just come to you when he found out about the abuse?' Emma said.

'That's what he told Travers he was going to do, but he was worried about the video of Bella. Then Travers describing himself and Natasha as Romeo and Juliet seems to have tipped him over the edge,' Burton said.

'That's why he poisoned one of them and stabbed the other,' Emma said.

Burton nodded. 'And then Natasha tried to blackmail her blackmailer. He might have been able to let her go if she hadn't started that,' Shepherd said.

'What does he get for what he did to Dan?' Emma asked.

'Attempted murder,' Burton said, turning to look at Dan sitting on a bench at the edge of the churchyard, his face tilted to the sun. But he was sitting stiffly, as if he was trying to protect the wounded area on the right side of his abdomen.

Emma followed Burton's gaze and grinned. 'You're pleased to see him, aren't you?' she said with a wink.

Burton laughed. 'Definitely. Although whether I'll still be saying that once he's back from sick leave, I don't know.'

Ed and Emma said goodbye to Burton and Shepherd and went to collect Dan. He winced as he got to his feet and she took his arm.

'Have you done your physio exercises today?' she asked.

He shook his head. 'They were really painful when I tried.' He puffed out his cheeks. 'This recovery business is harder than I thought.'

Ed's mobile rang and he stopped to answer it, motioning for them to continue.

'You need someone to keep an eye on you and make sure you do them,' Emma said with a grin. 'Clearly Ed isn't doing the job properly.'

'Are you volunteering?' Dan asked.

Emma took a deep breath. 'Well, someone has to,' she said, 'but it would be much easier to do that if we lived in the same place.'

Dan grinned down at her. 'Well now, that's an idea.'

'Was that what you wanted to talk about before all this started?'

Dan nodded. 'It had been on my mind. Shall we think about it?'

Emma grinned. 'Yes, let's think about it.'

'I'm glad we've sorted that out,' Dan said, grinning down at her. 'Now I'm starving.'

'You're not going to try to cook again?' Ed asked, appearing on Dan's other side. 'The flat still hasn't recovered from the chicken chasseur incident.'

'Maybe I should just admit that I'm not a natural chef,' Dan said. 'I think we'd better eat out.'

Ed and Emma laughed.

'Well, since we saved your life recently, I think lunch is on you,' Ed said.

'Definitely,' Dan said, laughing.

Chapter 72

PEANUT OIL KILLER CONVICTED

By Ed Walker, court reporter

A teacher was today convicted of the murders of a fellow teacher and a student at Allensbury Dance and Drama School.

David Dickens, 50, of Allensbury, was unanimously convicted by a jury at Tildon Crown Court after they heard he killed colleague Travers McGovern in cold blood.

Dickens doctored a bottle of vodka in Mr McGovern's office with peanut oil, knowing this would trigger anaphylactic shock due a severe allergy. He also removed the EpiPens that would have provided life-saving treatment.

Less than a week later, he stabbed student Natasha Kent, 18, three times in the stomach after she discovered what he had done and tried to blackmail him.

Assisted by an accomplice who overheard Natasha make a phone call arranging to meet a friend, he followed her to the park and demanded she delete the recording. When she refused, he killed her.

The court heard how Dickens had acted after his daughter, who had been in a relationship with Travers prior to a car crash earlier in the year, died from her injuries.

John Evesham KC, prosecuting, said: 'This was a cold and calculated murder. Video evidence shows that Dickens watched Mr McGovern die, making no move to help him.

'Miss Kent's murder could be described as a crime of passion, committed in the heat of the moment, but, as Dickens went to the scene armed, we can be in no doubt that her death was a deliberate act.'

He added: 'The defence will tell you in mitigation that Dickens planned to expose Mr McGovern over alleged sexual abuse of students, but there were other channels to pursue rather than resorting to murder.'

Mary Cusack KC, mitigating, told the court that discovering the abuse of his daughter after her death was enough to tip Dickens over the edge.

She said: 'This is a father driven mad by the discovery that his daughter was being abused and may have tried to kill herself, as a result. His grief is such that we cannot hold him responsible for his actions.

'He tried to stop Mr McGovern's relationships with students. But when he threatened to go to the police, Mr McGovern produced a video of himself and the defendant's daughter having sex and threatened to publish it. What father would not be deeply distressed by seeing this?

'Mr Dickens alleges that the abuse was known by the college principal, who failed to act, putting the school's reputation ahead of the safety of its students.'

She said the defence intended to launch an appeal based on instability of mind when the crimes were committed.

Dickens was also convicted of attempted manslaughter against *Allensbury Post* reporter Daniel Sullivan.

He was tried alongside accomplice Hitesh Salana, 30, of Allensbury, who was found guilty of assisting an offender. The court heard how father-of-two Salana, who was a security guard at the school, called Dickens to warn him about Natasha's plans to go to the police. He also told him that Mr Sullivan was at the school and likely to find Natasha's hidden mobile phone.

Sentencing for both will take place at Tildon Crown Court in four weeks.

***

SEX ABUSE SCANDAL ROCKS ALLENSBURY SCHOOL
By Emma Fletcher, Crime Reporter

David Dickens' conviction has led to an in-depth police investigation into allegations of sexual abuse of students at Allensbury Dance and Drama School.

Specialist police officers are carrying out interviews with several female students who are believed to have been involved with Travers McGovern.

It is thought that Mr McGovern had relationships with students and secretly videoed them committing sex acts. The videos meant that students could not report him because of the risk to themselves.

The *Allensbury Post* has heard that several students had become pregnant and McGovern forced one to have an abortion.

College authorities claim to have had no knowledge of the abuse, although Principal Sally-Anne Faber was immediately suspended from her post pending the outcome of the enquiry. Photographs of Travers McGovern and Natasha Kent were discovered in her office, clarifying that she knew of their relationship. Police are considering whether she will face criminal charges for failing to act on the abuse claims.

Andy McAllister, head of the school's board of governors, expressed his horror at the news.

'I can't understand how or why this could have happened and that it was not reported to us as governors,' he said. 'I feel sick at the thought of what has been going on here. We will be supporting the police investigation every step of the way to make sure the students affected can get any help they need.

'Specialist counsellors have been brought in and there will be a thorough re-examination of our hiring procedures, which allowed this type of man to become a teacher.'

The news of events unfolding at the college has left students and parents shocked.

One parent, who did not wish to be named, told the Post: 'I sent my daughter to school every day because it was the best place for her to pursue her dancing career. If I'd known that I'd been putting her at risk of being attacked by a sexual predator, I'd have chosen another school. I can only hope she hasn't been left traumatised by these incidents.'

Detective Inspector Jude Burton, from Allensbury CID, is leading the investigation.

She said: 'The fact that Travers McGovern could perpetrate these crimes against so many students is horrific.

'At present we know of three students who have been involved and I'm sure that we will find more as the investigation continues. We will make sure that every student affected receives the support and care they need, that they should have been given by a responsible college leadership.

'Investigations are underway as to whether prosecutions will take place once evidence has been gathered and the full picture emerges.

'We would like to thank parents and students at the school for their patience while we investigate.'

Ms Faber declined the Post's request for a comment.

A message from me...

Thank you for reading A Deadly Portrayal.

I hope you enjoyed reading it as much as I enjoyed writing it. Please do leave a review where you can and spread the word you your friends.

The other books in the Allensbury Mysteries series are:
A Deadly Rejection
A Deadly Truth
A Killer Christmas.

If you want to keep in touch with me and my work, pop along to https://lmmilford.com and sign up for my newsletter.
You can also find me on Twitter or join my author page on Facebook.

Acknowledgements

It's always difficult to write this section, because so many people play a part in getting a book from idea to shelf. There's always a risk of leaving someone out.

I'd like to say thank you to my editor Donna Hillyer for her fantastic advice and guidance, my proofreader and good friend Victoria Goldman for her support and skill, and to Jessica Bell for yet another beautiful cover design.

My writing colleagues continue to provide endless support and entertainment through their own books and also when we meet at events.

And, as always, thanks to my family – for never saying 'you can't do that' when I announced at a young age that I was going to be a writer and for keeping me going when the going gets tough.

About me

LM Milford is a crime fiction author who writes the Allensbury mysteries, covering the exploits of local newspaper reporter Dan Sullivan. A former newspaper journalist, Lynne's experience has influenced her work, although her stories were never as exciting as Dan's.

Lynne was born and brought up in the north-east of England, but now lives in Kent with her husband and far too many books. She loves cooking, baking and holidays in Spain. She's partial to a good red wine and plates of cheese.